RED HOT FURY

A SHADES OF FURY NOVEL

KASEY MACKENZIE

ACE BOOKS, NEW YORK

THE BERKLEY PUBLISHING GROUP
Published by the Penguin Group
Penguin Group (USA) Inc.
375 Hudson Street, New York, New York 10014, USA
Penguin Group (Canada), 90 Eglinton Avenue East, Suite 700, Toronto, Ontario M4P 2Y3, Canada
(a division of Pearson Penguin Canada Inc.)
Penguin Books Ltd., 80 Strand, London WC2R 0RL, England
Penguin Group Ireland, 25 St. Stephen's Green, Dublin 2, Ireland (a division of Penguin Books Ltd.)
Penguin Group (Australia), 250 Camberwell Road, Camberwell, Victoria 3124, Australia
(a division of Pearson Australia Group Pty. Ltd.)
Penguin Books India Pvt. Ltd., 11 Community Centre, Panchsheel Park, New Delhi—110 017, India
Penguin Group (NZ), 67 Apollo Drive, Rosedale, North Shore 0632, New Zealand
(a division of Pearson New Zealand Ltd.)
Penguin Books (South Africa) (Pty.) Ltd., 24 Sturdee Avenue, Rosebank, Johannesburg 2196,
South Africa

Penguin Books Ltd., Registered Offices: 80 Strand, London WC2R 0RL, England

This is a work of fiction. Names, characters, places, and incidents either are the product of the author's imagination or are used fictitiously, and any resemblance to actual persons, living or dead, business establishments, events, or locales is entirely coincidental. The publisher does not have any control over and does not assume any responsibility for author or third-party websites or their content.

RED HOT FURY

An Ace Book / published by arrangement with the author

PRINTING HISTORY
Ace mass-market edition / July 2010

Copyright © 2010 by Heather Faucher.
Cover art by Judy York.
Cover design by Judith Lagerman.
Interior text design by Kristin del Rosario.

ISBN: 978-0-441-01892-5

ACE
Ace Books are published by The Berkley Publishing Group,
a division of Penguin Group (USA) Inc.,
375 Hudson Street, New York, New York 10014.
ACE and the "A" design are trademarks of Penguin Group (USA) Inc.

PRINTED IN THE UNITED STATES OF AMERICA

10   9   8   7   6   5   4   3   2   1

This first one's for my mother, Debbie. While we don't always see eye to eye, we do agree on one thing: how much we love each other. Thank you for teaching me I could be whatever I wanted and encouraging my love for books. Without you, this book would never have been possible. Dedicated also to the memory of William Allen Nipper, my daddy.

CHAPTER ONE

SOMETHING SEEMED FISHY ABOUT THE CORPSE stretched out on the sand, and it wasn't the heavy odor of Boston Harbor hanging in the predawn air. Cupping my hands around an oversized Starbucks container to warm cramped fingers, I tried to figure out what was bugging me—other than the fact that a rare few hours of sleep had been rudely interrupted by a call from Dispatch. Smashing the hell out of the phone had been my initial instinct, but when duty called, a Fury answered. Especially when she also happened to be the city's Chief Magical Investigator.

Yeah, long-ass hours and getting called to crime scenes at five freaking A.M. Lucky me.

Slugging back a gulp of caffeine goodness, I focused on the problem at hand. The very naked, very dead woman kissing the damp sand before me. I shone my flashlight on the tangled black hair shielding most of her back and arms from view. No, black didn't even come close to describing the flecks of vibrant color that sparkled in her hair where flashlight beams hit it. My pulse picked up speed as the inevitable thought occurred to me.

Denial was my first instinct. *No, it can't be. Dispatch would have warned me if . . .*

Then I remembered who had actually been responsible for passing the call on to me. Zalawski. *That asshole.* Probably hadn't bothered to fill Dispatch in on that very crucial, not-so-minor detail.

I steeled my heart for the realization my brain had already reached. Settling onto my haunches, I brushed ebony-dark locks away from the corpse's right arm and cursed up a storm. A brilliant, emerald-hued serpent had been tattooed on her arm, making the ID indisputable. The dead woman wasn't just any arcane being—she was a Fury. Like me, she had been born into an ancient bloodline sworn to protect both mortals and immortals from those who would use magic to harm them. Even if it meant sacrificing her own life. Which it had.

Grief flared and tears threatened to spill, but I wouldn't let them. I had to be strong for my fallen sister and see that justice was done. *Then* I could grieve.

Nothing had clued me in to the fact that the corpse called in that morning would turn out to be a Fury. True, arcane beings of myriad species had been vanishing without a trace at a higher rate than usual lately—two or three every other month or so—but no Furies had been reported among their number.

I scooted closer to the body and ran my gaze along it in a slow, considering line. The nagging sense of wrongness I'd been feeling intensified. Her tattoos looked . . . off.

An overeager uniform stepped up for a closer look, and I bared my teeth. "Back away from the vic. *I'll* let *you* know when I need your help." My Amphisbaena, which appeared as snake tattoos when I was in mortal or partial Fury form, and physically manifested as real serpents when I took on full Fury form—like now—arched hooded heads and hissed at the man who'd upset me. Amphisbaena were spawned from the blood of others who died violently, always in pairs, and acted as if they were two halves of one whole. Part familiars, part companions, they shared an empathic and sometimes telepathic link with Furies that only their deaths could sever.

Furies *could* survive losing their Amphisbaena, although technically those who do are no longer Furies. They're monsters.

"Oh hell," I mumbled under my breath. I caressed the crimson coils of the serpent wound around my left arm before turning my attention to the one on the right. Chaotic emotions swirled through our bond, and I did my best to soothe them. "Calm down, ladies. The man's not a threat. Just an idiot."

"Terrifying the rookies again?" a voice tinged with the Deep South drawled behind me. "That's the fourth you've made piss his pants this month."

My body relaxed at the familiar voice. "Well, if Dispatch would stop sending me pansies with severe fear of snakes, we wouldn't have a problem."

Trinity's generous lips curved. "No pity for the mortals, huh, Riss?"

Shrugging, I turned my attention from the super-tall detective and onto the body that had us here at oh-god-early in the morning, leaning in to study the bright green snake tattoo running from the shoulder to just below the elbow. Then it hit me. "The color's wrong."

Trinity knelt beside me, careful not to piss off my little beauties. "I've seen different colors on Fury tats."

"That's not what's bugging me. Three classes of Furies, three separate colors. Green for Megaera, red for Tisiphone, and blue for Alecto. Four, if you count silver for Elders." I pointed to the bottom of the woman's elbow, where the tattoo ended in a splash of color duller than the rest. "Green means this Fury served as a Megaera, but look here. The color's not consistent throughout the tattoo. It's *way* too patchy."

Trin leaned back on her haunches, dark eyes glinting with interest. "So, what does that tell you about the vic?"

I winced. *Vic* seemed such a cold word to use for one of my sisters, although I'd used it myself. Getting emotional during investigations meant getting sloppy, something I tried to avoid when it came to the job. My love life, on the other hand . . .

"Well, other than the fact that she served the Fury patroness who gives the green-eyed monster its name, I'm not sure."

Clearly, it was time to do something I was dreading. "Did they get all the photos they need?"

It was Trin's job to deal with the mundanes—like the Crime Lab Unit—as much as possible. They got even more nervous around Furies than the uniforms. You'd think we bite.

She nodded. "They're the ones who noticed the tats and insisted you be called."

"Nice to know the Department employs the occasional nonmoron. Too bad Zalawski didn't get the same sensitivity training."

She didn't rise to my bait. "Gonna turn her over?"

"Yeah. Have to ID her."

"Need help?"

We both knew I didn't, but I *did* appreciate the gesture. "No. I'm good."

Electric-blue energy flared when I touched fingers to the woman's back. Directing the flow underneath her body, I motioned my hands from left to right and mentally *pushed*. The corpse flipped from stomach to back in one smooth motion, barely disturbing the sand beneath.

"That is *so* freaky."

Trin said that at least once during every investigation. "No fuss or muss this way."

"Yeah, but it's *still* freaky."

The habitual banter settled my jangled nerves. I glanced down at the woman's face. Midnight-dark hair obscured it, so I reached down and brushed it to each side—and fell flat on my ass.

"Oh hell." I stared down at the face I hadn't seen in three long years. Not since half my family disowned me.

Trinity came up alongside me, concern marring her pretty features. "What's up, Riss?"

I pointed shaking fingers toward the vic, then shuddered. That word seemed even colder now that I realized who the corpse was. The sister Fury I'd nearly given up hope of finding—and the reason I had subconsciously been so reluctant to turn the body over. "I know this woman, Trin. She is—she was—Vanessa Turner. My best friend."

TRINITY PLACED A HAND ON MY SHOULDER and squeezed. "Oh, Riss. I'm so sorry. Fuck." She squeezed again. "I remember that case. Didn't they think the ex-boyfriend was involved?"

My fingers clenched and I gave a jerky nod as I tried to damp down the grief welling in my chest. "He didn't take well to the breakup at *all*. When she started seeing someone new, he flipped out on her. She had to get a restraining order. She disappeared not too long after that, but we could never prove he was involved . . ."

Trinity's lips tightened grimly. An all-too-familiar tale for cops.

I could still remember our last conversation—though *fight* was probably a far more accurate word to use—me bitching that she had accepted her first solo assignment way too soon. It was probably my calling her an overeager virgin itching to pop her cherry that sent her over the edge . . . Okay, so maybe I could use a little sensitivity training of my own.

Vanessa's eyes had narrowed and I recognized her mentally counting to ten before responding. "I am *not* a fragile mortal like David or Cori, Riss." Kind of a low blow for her to drag my brother—her brother-in-law—and our shared niece into the argument. She'd slashed a hand through the air. "And I'm not Aunt Allegra, either."

Okay, correction. Mentioning my dearly departed mother was way worse. So we'd parted in anger. And then she'd disappeared.

I stared down at Nessa's body, eyes drawn once more to the tattoos on each bare arm. Emerald green where mine were ruby red. But something just wasn't right. And then what I'd noticed when first arriving on the scene—but hadn't given a second thought to—sucker punched me in the gut. "Her body . . . this corpse is too fresh. No *way* it's been in the water three years."

"Maybe the killer dumped it recently." Trinity cleared her throat, licking her lips when I arched a brow in her direction. "Ah, Riss, I know you two were close, but is there any chance she . . . ran off?"

My vision grew red and hazy. Gooseflesh broke out along my skin, and magical energy raised every single hair on my body. I fought back the superhuman Rage that was both strength and weakness for a Fury, sending a brief prayer skyward that *this* would not be the time I lost the battle. Bit by bit my vision cleared, and my pulse slowed its thunderous crashing. For now, I got to keep my mind—and soul.

Once I could speak without growling, I tossed a sardonic look Trin's way. "You mean she took off without telling a single person, and then just happened to wash up in Boston Harbor three years after being stalked by an ex-boyfriend?" I shook my head. "No way, Trin. First of all, Nessa would never have done that to her family or friends. Secondly, she *couldn't* have done it to the Elders. Once a Fury binds herself to the Sisterhood, there's no turning back. Not without going Harpy, and we'd be able to tell *that* just by looking at her. Furies who can't control their Rage murder their serpents before going batshit insane, which means no more tattoos."

She patted my shoulder again. "Sorry, Riss, but the question had to be asked."

I blew out a breath and ran fingers through my hair. "You're right. Shit. It's so hard to do this for someone I care about."

Trin tilted her head. "But who else is there?"

Who else indeed? Furies served as the investigators—and often judge and jury—of crimes committed by or against supernatural beings. Kinda hard to drag in most arcanes for trial if they weren't willing to cooperate. We'd acted behind the scenes for millennia, back before the mortals learned that creatures of myth and legend were neither. Since coming out fifty years earlier, we Furies had become the bridge between mundanes and arcanes, thanks to the fact that we started out as mortals before manifesting our magical abilities and pledging ourselves to the Sisterhood of Furies.

Now, many of us juggled our duties for the Sisterhood with the jobs we had taken serving on the mortal police forces. We were spread so thin I'd been pulling fourteen-hour shifts for months. There just wasn't anyone else I could hand this off to. Not unless a Mandate came down from on high.

I hissed in realization. "I should have guessed Nessa was still alive when no Mandate went out."

Trinity tilted her head. "What the hell is a mandate?"

How to explain a Mandate—with a capital *M*—to a mortal? Especially a self-proclaimed atheist? Oh, life's little ironies, that someone who had met several deities face to face worked with someone who steadfastly refused to admit they existed.

"Mandates are basically tasks handed down from . . . er . . . upper management for certain magical crimes. They're fairly rare—I haven't gotten one in a few years—and they generally only go out when a magical-related case has repercussions for either a large segment of humanity or the Gens Arcana. A Fury working under a Mandate is compelled to work that case until the crime is solved."

"And you *don't* feel compelled to solve this crime?"

I rolled my eyes. Mortals had such a gift for understatement. Compelled to solve crime—that was like saying Cats and Hounds didn't get along too well. "Only in the sense that Vanessa was my dearest friend in the world. The fact that I don't feel a Mandate—and no other Fury has shown up at the crime scene—means something is beyond screwed up. They almost *always* go out when a Fury is murdered."

I hunched down next to Vanessa's body. Since there were no visible wounds on the corpse, there had to be enough blood inside for me to work my mojo.

"I'm gonna run a trailer." I motioned to Trin. "Make sure they don't freak out."

I paced around the corpse, tracing a circle in the sand. Not, strictly speaking, necessary for this particular spell, but circles helped focus both the caster's attention and magical power. Something sharp bit into the ball of my foot, and I cursed under my breath. After making sure whatever I'd stepped on wasn't embedded in my trusty leather boots, I closed my eyes and called to the Power resting beneath me. Nemesis and Nike (no, *not* like the shoes) hissed again, this time in pleasure at the magic pounding through all three of us. Electric-blue light danced in the air, increasing in brilliance and size until not even the mundanes could miss it.

I waited for the magic to reach a fever pitch and directed it into Nessa's flesh and bones, willing it to seek out traces of blood. Several moments passed, moments that felt like an eternity, and then magical Hell broke loose.

The full force of magic rebounded from Nessa's body and shrieked inside my own. Agony raced along every magical and physical nerve ending. I screamed in shock, scrambling to ground myself more solidly and funnel skittering energy into the earth. Never, not even as a punk-nosed apprentice, had I experienced anything like this. Magic did *not* rebel against a well-placed spell.

Trinity shouted in the background, ordering the uniforms to stay back and then trying to pierce my veil of pain. It was just the bit of reality I needed to remember what I'd been trying to do. Nemesis and Nike added their strength to my own, and we fought against the magic coursing through our veins, thrusting it along the cord of energy connecting us to the earth. Amphisbaena could amp up a Fury's supernatural abilities and possessed a few of their own. Bit by agonizing bit, the magic obeyed our combined wills, flowing through that channel in a white-hot flood of light and dissipating harmlessly.

I dropped to hands and knees, panting as nerve endings continued to roar in protest. Trinity fell to the ground beside me, hands brushing my hair back and asking urgent questions. It took several more minutes before I could form a response.

"Oh thank the gods, it's not Vanessa. That corpse is made of pure magic. There's not a mortal bone in its body, and there never was." Which meant it couldn't be a Fury, since we start out mortal. I found myself torn between relief that the body wasn't Vanessa's and anger that someone would *dare* impersonate a Fury, even if only in death. "Some son of a bitch altered another person's corpse to look like my best friend's. And I'm going to find out why if it kills me."

And *that's* when the mind-shaking onslaught of full-on Mandate slammed against me with the force of a freight train. Now I would have to keep that oath—even if it *did* kill me.

CHAPTER TWO

IT TOOK SOME WRANGLING, BUT I FINALLY convinced Trinity to escort the body to the morgue while I ran home to regroup. Not to mention take an actual shower, since I hadn't had the time earlier. Trin objected to my heading off alone so soon—strongly—but finally relented when I reminded her, "Hey, super-healing immortal badass here, remember?" Good thing she couldn't read my mind or she never woulda cut the apron strings.

Truth was, I hurt like hell. Physically, magically, and most definitely emotionally. Even supernatural powers of healing can't fully erase pain, especially not from magical backlash. Probably one of the ways the Powers That Be kept Furies (somewhat) humble.

My hands shook so much it took me three tries to get the key inserted in the lock of my Cambridge town house. "Shit!" I muttered under my breath, tempted to just shift to

Fury form and rip the gods-bedamned door off its hinges. But then I'd just have to pay for a new one later, and three front doors in one year was plenty, thanks.

I made a beeline for the liquor cabinet and my soon-to-be-best-friend, Jack. The cure for what ailed me. In light of the alcoholic gene running rampant through my mortal father's family tree, damned good thing it was so hard to get a Fury drunk. Copious amounts of whiskey just barely took the edge off when I needed it most.

After my father learned I would be following in my mother's arcane footsteps, he drank himself into an early grave. I still remembered running up the stairs to his office to tell him it had finally happened. I was sixteen and my Fury powers had stuttered into wakefulness just hours earlier. Granted, they'd almost pushed me into cold-cocking a smartass into the hereafter during final period (earning me a week of detention), but who the heck cared now that I had Fledged?

Apparently, Daddy Dearest did. He was waiting for me in the wingback chair behind his massive desk, the obligatory Scotch on the rocks resting in the spot where the ugly coffee mug my mother made him during her short ceramics phase had once sat. For years, since my mother had disappeared in the line of duty, he'd been an emotionless shell. But that day he'd finally let his anger, his rage and grief, loose. When I told him proudly that I'd already pledged myself by blood and magic to the Sisterhood, he'd told me to leave and never come back.

I fled before I could do or say anything I would regret, though regret I did. That was the last time I ever spoke to my father. My brother, David, had found him, sprawled barely breathing in front of the fireplace, the next morning. Alcohol finally gave him the peace he sought so long—in the form of a coma that lasted for weeks until he slipped away forever . . .

So no big surprise that the alcoholic's daughter sought it out now to soothe her once again bruised heart. But not Scotch—*never* Scotch, and never on the rocks. The sound of ice clinking on glass could dredge up memories best left hidden, or at least ignored. Like now.

I returned the mostly full bottle to the liquor cabinet and dragged myself upstairs to the shower. Just shy of eleven A.M. Barely enough time to dress and grab a sack-o'-heart-attack on the way to fill out the paperwork on that morning's gruesome discovery. Just another day in paradise.

I STARED INTO THE SMUG EYES OF BOSTON PD's biggest asshole and tried to make sense of the words he'd just spit out in near-orgasmic pleasure. The four walls of his dingy hidey-hole challenged my tolerance for closed-in spaces, but damned if I would let him see that. His beady little eyes actually glowed as he watched my reaction to his pronouncement. I'd expected a commendation for the discovery I'd made. Not this BS.

"What the hell do you mean, I'm suspended? I should get an award for breaking through that frigging spell, not suspended." My voice rose an octave every other syllable. What in blazes was going on here?

"*Without* pay." Lieutenant Detective Tony Zalawski drawled the words so gleefully I almost offered him a cigarette. When his nasty, chapped lips peeled back to reveal even nastier yellow teeth, I decided the last thing he needed was another smoke.

Nausea settled in my stomach. Shit. Being suspended without pay was *not* a good thing. It would definitely go on my PD record, even if I was later exonerated. For what? That was the worst part; I had not a clue. Years had passed since I'd done anything that could even come close to warranting suspension. Mentally disemboweling Zalawski repeatedly didn't count. "You can't possibly be serious. Cappy would never authorize this."

Zalawski's grin widened even more. Too bad I couldn't just wipe the expression off his ugly face. The last time I'd given in to that urge nearly got me transferred to West Podunk, Massachusetts—yeah, the incident that almost got me suspended. The bastard knew he was safe from retribution as he sat there behind his crappy little desk in his crappy little office, which just made things even worse.

"You *really* pissed someone off this time, Holloway. Charges of misconduct have been brought against your sorry ass, so you better not show your face while the investigation is pending. Now, hand over your badge and sidearm."

"But for what?" I tried to keep Rage out of my voice.

"It's not *my* job to tell you that. Hand 'em over."

I slammed my badge and Sig Sauer (my last line of defense rather than first) onto his desk, my mind still not comprehending what was going on. How *could* it make sense of the fact that, after several years of serving as arcane liaison with the Boston PD, and another five as Chief Magical Investigator, I was being mysteriously suspended—*without* pay—for making what could be the most crucial discovery in a baffling, three-year-old case? Or brand-new, to be more accurate. I didn't believe for a second the body I'd examined earlier that day belonged to Vanessa.

Did someone higher up the food chain not appreciate the fact that I'd seen through the magical disguise? I shifted uncomfortably at that thought, since it suggested the attempted ruse might be an inside job. *No way,* I thought, gritting my teeth. Zalawski I'd believe it of. Cappy or his superiors? *No effing way.*

Zalawski continued smirking as I stalked out of his hellhole of an office. I was surprised he hadn't taken the opportunity for public humiliation by escorting me out of the building himself. That thought had a snarl exploding from my lips. Mortals took one look and scurried off in the opposite direction, civilian and cop alike. My fists clenched as I stomped down the crowded hallway and tried to bottle the Rage bubbling all too close to the surface.

Stupid jackass. I can't believe he *was the one to suspend me.*

When Cappy—Captain—Peterson realized just how poorly the two of us got along, he'd taken to assigning Trin to my cases as often as possible. It stung that he'd assigned the asshole to suspend me now. Especially since, if I were a full-blooded mortal, I would outrank Zalawski's sorry ass. Why the hell hadn't Cappy had the balls to do it himself, or at least hand off the task to Trin?

As if the thought summoned her, she materialized at my side. "Sorry, Riss. I just heard. Cappy's battling it out with the feds, trying to get your suspension overturned."

My footsteps faltered. "Feds? What do *they* have to do with this?"

"Bizarre, right? No one seems to know what's up, but can't miss the men in black no matter how secretive they try to be."

I frowned while we trotted down the stairs. Feds, as a general rule, got involved only in magical crimes that crossed state lines, or high-profile cases that risked destroying the Peace Accord that ended the Time of Troubles. Or, as Vanessa had preferred to call it, *the* War.

Admittedly, it had been a full-on war in all but name. Fifty years ago, arcanes had begun emigrating to the mortal realm en masse. Not that the arcanes really had a choice, seeing how most of the Otherrealms were dying, and nobody, not even the wisest of Oracles or the Fury Elders, could figure out why, or how to stop the spreading plague.

Once the arcanes began to arrive in very large numbers, the mortals stood up and took notice. And when the Sidhe continued to treat humanity like the uncivilized pets they'd always considered them to be, things went to hell—and war—fast. Only the mundanes' sheer numbers and technological might had prevented them from being completely wiped out by the Gens Arcana.

It had been the Sisterhood of Furies, who straddled the fence separating mortal from immortal and were committed to fostering peace between both groups, that had finally brokered the agreement ending the violence. One reason we were stretched nearly to the breaking point. We'd lost too many sisters forging that blood-soaked truce, the Accord.

"If the feds are involved, it must be something to do with the Accord," I mused out loud.

At the bottom of the stairs, Trin leaned against the heavy banister and pursed her lips. She ignored the blaring rise and fall of voices, curses, and all-out cacophony cutting through the lobby around us. "Hmm. Wonder how the body of one arcane disguised as another could upset the Accord?"

"Good question. Why *would* the mortals care if someone tried to pass one arcane off as another? Just opens up a Migration spot they can sell to the highest bidder. What I'd *really* like to know, though, is why an arcane would bother." My mouth and eyes widened as I remembered just how screwy the Fury tattoo had been. Surely any arcane who could disguise a corpse magically would be smart enough to get that major detail correct. A mortal, on the other hand . . . To them, color variations on a tattoo would seem perfectly normal. "Unless it wasn't an arcane who altered the corpse after all."

Trin's eyebrows rose. "You said it yourself: The body's made of pure magic. Plastic surgery didn't alter that corpse."

I waved off that little detail, suddenly sure the flash of insight had been right on the money. "Trust me, Trin, when it comes to magic, *much* stranger shit has happened. I could list at least a half dozen ways mortals could pull something like that off, and those are just the methods I'm familiar with. There are darker ways to manage it. Like blood sacrifice to seal a deal with demons."

"Demons? That's crazy." She fanned flushed cheeks with both hands. "You're shitting me, right?"

I took off toward the main entrance, walking backward to address her questions. "It's not as crazy as you think. Lucky for the world, few arcanes—and even fewer mundanes—have the ability to summon demons. And would I shit you about something so impor—"

Thunder struck. Lightning arced into my back, lanced through my chest, and passed mere inches from my heart. I crumpled to the ground amid a sea of pain. Civilians screamed and dove to the floor while officers pulled weapons, herded people behind furniture, and struggled to figure out what was going on. Trinity shielded my body with her own, sidearm aimed toward the door. Toward the now-shattered glass of the empty door frame, to be more precise. And that's when shock gave way to realization.

"Holy shit. Some jackass *shot* me."

Trin shifted in order to provide my body more cover. "Stay down, Riss. Paramedics are on the way."

I tried to tell her not to bother, but Nemesis and Nike recovered enough from their shock to get busy doing what they did best—adding their catalytic properties to my own magical abilities. In this case, superhuman healing.

That healing came with a hefty price. The agony dancing through my body doubled, then tripled, as magic pushed the foreign lump of metal out, then started knitting flesh and blood vessels back together. We got damned lucky that nothing major was damaged (my superhuman healing has its limits), but I couldn't bite back a scream. Trin shouted for someone to hurry the *fuck* up. Agony increased ever-so-slightly, but I managed to keep silent, thanks in large part to the gods-blessed serpents working their mojo. Finally, both pain and magic faded to bearable levels. I pushed myself to a sitting position, and Trin whirled from scanning the empty doorway, eyes widening as she took in the ragged hole in my leather vest created by the exit wound—and the perfectly knit flesh beneath.

"Jesus." She let out a shaky breath. "I knew you guys healed quickly, but that's . . ."

"Freaky?" I offered with a small smile. "Yeah, you've mentioned my status as freak of nature before. Can't say I mind so much at the moment."

She nudged me backward, angling for a battered desk that would shield us from the empty doorway. "No shit. Riss, you should *so* be dead right—"

Renewed gunfire punctuated her words in sharp staccato. This time *she* dropped to the ground, blood darkening the sleeve of her crisp white blouse. Surprise flickered across her face. My superhuman reflexes snapped into gear before the third gunshot echoed. I grabbed her by the uninjured arm and thrust her behind the desk.

"Officer down!" I ripped the clean sleeve from her blouse and pressed it tightly against her wounded shoulder. Her typically dark brown skin paled as her breathing became ragged.

Shock faded enough that she knocked my hands away and replaced them with one of her own. "I'm fine. Go. Get that jackass."

I hesitated. She'd become the closest thing I had to a best friend in the years since Vanessa disappeared, and the thought of abandoning her didn't sit too well in my stomach. Yet the adrenaline pumping through my body demanded I take down the psycho who had shot us both.

"Riss, it *has* to be you. You have superhuman healing, for God's sake. *I'm* sure as hell not going."

Biting my lip, I squeezed her thigh with a nod. "The bleeding seems to be slowing. You"—my voice grew husky—"you be careful."

She met my eyes unflinchingly. "No, darlin', *you* be careful. Someone's obviously got a hard-on for you. And not the good kind."

My lips stretched in a faint facsimile of humor. I shifted to mortal form and back again, washing away the vestiges of pain and restoring my dark red uniform to its former leather glory. This time, I shifted into *full* Fury form. My mortal honey-blond hair shaded to deepest charcoal; deep-blue eyes became faceted emerald; brilliantly drawn tattoos burst into real-life serpents. And, of course, the bloodred leather vest, pants, and boots that signaled my status as magical badass to other arcanes materialized.

"Time to hunt," I whispered to Nemesis and Nike, then leapt into action.

Magic responded to my call in an instant. I gathered arcane energy and thrust it inside my body, grunting as threads of magic temporarily reknit the fabric of my being. Although I couldn't manage true invisibility, this particular spell allowed me to redirect my normal shape-shifting abilities into a hyped-up form of camouflage. I dashed along the nearest wall, blending in with the natural play of light and shadow. Adrenaline flashed through my body, and I allowed it to amplify, dancing along the edge of full-blown Rage. And then I surrendered, allowing my mortal psyche to be subsumed by Fury.

Late-afternoon shadows aided my attempt to pass unseen through the empty doorway. I ran my gaze along the roofs of the buildings across the street. They ran the gamut from modern steel and glass to faded red bricks and mortar. At first, nothing seemed out of the ordinary. But then a glint of sunlight striking metal caught my attention, and I took off. Literally.

Wings nearly as wide as I was tall spread to each side, catching the magical breeze I summoned and pumping in staccato rhythm. For a moment, nothing happened, but then magic and physics worked in tandem and I rose straight into the air.

I zeroed in on the building where the flash of light had caught my eye. The closer to direct sunlight I drew, however, the less effective my camouflage became. Just before passing completely out of shadow, I traded magically enhanced stealth for superspeed, clearing the nearest edge of the several-story building in less than a second. One thing immediately struck my attention. The guy who'd shot me was mortal—completely mortal. My wing feathers stiffened at the insult. Then the black-clad man noticed me.

"What the—" As I landed on the roof he raised his weapon in slow motion—well, slow to me—but I jerked it from his hands and bent it into a useless lump of metal, tossing it fifty feet away in one brief motion. His eyes widened, and then he did something unexpected. He jumped, but not toward me. Off the building.

My eyes widened, and thought slowed to a crawl. By the time I realized I wasn't hallucinating and leapt into the air, it was too late. The man's body hit pavement seconds later, crumpling with the force of impact.

Nemesis and Nike hissed in displeasure. I hovered for a moment, staring down at my attempted assassin's body. From this distance it looked like a child's broken doll—until you factored in the glistening pool of blood spreading in all directions. I shook my head and let out a hiss of my own. Who sent a single mortal after a full-grown Fury, and how the hell had they talked the man into committing suicide rather than being captured?

The only obvious answer to the first question was other

mortals. Ones who either couldn't, or didn't dare, risk hiring immortal thugs to handle their dirty work. Which meant my earlier suspicion had been right on the money. This *had* to have something to do with the Accord. And someone would do anything, kill or be killed, to try and keep their dirty little secrets.

CHAPTER THREE

ONCE DISBELIEF GAVE WAY TO A FURY'S IN-
nate sense of self-preservation while fulfilling a Mandate,
I got the hell out of Dodge. Exhaustion echoed through my
body from the strain of using too much magic in too short
a time. The strange jittery tingle of an unfulfilled Mandate
buzzed at the back of my brain. That buzzing would turn to
outright pain the longer it took to fulfill my task. I hovered
over the Boston skyline and tried to catch my breath. *Calm
down, Riss, and think.*

Okay. Step one: Call in the location of the body. Check.
(Thank the gods for cell phones.) Step two: Lead any other
potential assassins *away* from Trin and company. Easy
enough. But Step three—head home for a quiet night with
Jack—didn't seem like the brightest thing to do. Ranked
right up there with crawling back to my ex-boyfriend,
something I'd never yet resorted to.

The stink of blood and sweat assaulted my nose, and I scowled. *Gods, I need a shower.* But where could I go while I tried to figure out who wanted me dead? *Not* home. Staking out the PD while neglecting my home would be plain stupid, and of all the things I could call the many people who'd tried to kill me over the years, that wasn't one of them.

Speaking of staking out the PD, my earlier suspicion that this might be an inside job came back with a vengeance. What were the odds that the three shittiest things to happen to me since Nessa's disappearance and my explosive breakup with the aforementioned ex—all on the same day, no less—were all mere coincidence? Yeah, even more minuscule than Zalawski's . . . intellect.

If things weren't on the up-and-up with my mundane employers, it was time to bring in the big guns: the Conclave of Fury Elders. If you're picturing something like the kindly, batty fairy godmothers from Disney's *Sleeping Beauty*—get that image right out of your mind. Substitute it with ageless badasses more like Maleficent, the wicked witch of that particular tale, and you get a little closer to the truth. It took a lot of strength—mental *and* magical—to head up the arcane equivalent of mortal law enforcement, and the Elders had both in spades.

Unfortunately, reaching the Palladium, the Fury version of the Batcave, was not as simple as clicking one's heels three times. Nah, that would be *entirely* too easy. I gritted my teeth and prepared to do one of the things Furies did best (other than maiming and killing). Fading into the background.

After landing in an alley several blocks from the police station, I channeled Fury magic, shifting red leather clothes and boots into more practical T-shirt, jeans, and sneakers. My own face wavered and was soon replaced by a pale, mousy face that few would notice. That theory was proven by the half dozen people who nearly mowed me down on the ten-minute walk to the nearest T (what most Bostonians called our subway system) stop that suited my needs. The walking assholes in people's clothing were lucky I was in incognito mode, because by the time I finally stumbled through the subway turnstile I was ready to murder someone. Or at the very least horribly disfigure them.

Nobody claimed Furies were cute and cuddly. Least of all me.

Some jackoff actually tossed his discarded cigarette at me, and I nearly leapt on him then and there. But the walls began vibrating with the low-key buzz signaling an incoming train, and I was in a hurry, so I dodged the flying cancer stick and pelted toward the end of the platform. In an eye blink I went from mousy woman blending in with passersby to winged Fury blending in with the background more effectively than a life-sized chameleon. The magical camo was damned handy but also took way more energy than it was usually worth and was hard to maintain in direct sunlight—thus the plain-Jane disguise being my usual preferred method of dodging attention.

The train's doors slid shut, and it began pulling away from the platform. I edged backward until the gum-covered wall touched my butt, then took a running leap forward, flapping both wings rapidly, gaining just the right amount of altitude before my body slammed down on the top of the rearmost car of the train. Hard.

I winced, hands scrabbling to slow down my motion, my emerging talons digging in to find purchase. My breath whooshed out in relief when my body slid to a stop, boot heels dangling over the edge but not—quite—banging into the rear door. Missing hurt like a son of a bitch. Which I'd found out my first time through, since it'd taken five freaking trains before I finally managed the trick of *not* busting my ass on the tracks.

The train accelerated rapidly when it reached a long straightaway. I stiffened my body and closed my eyes, summoning Nemesis and Nike from the magical limbo they inhabited when in tattoo form. Only those bonded to the Amphisbaena—and traveling faster than a Fury could manage in such a confined space—could cross the threshold I was about to pass. A foolproof magical security system, if ever I'd seen one.

Nemesis and Nike adored zipping through the darkened subway tunnels. Had they been dogs, they would have hung their heads over the side of the car and leaked slobber for a country mile. Since they weren't, they did the next best thing: wound their way along my trembling arms and flicked their forked tongues in what passed for serpentine pleasure.

Magic tingled along my skin, signaling the approach of our stop. Granted, it wasn't listed on the MBTA's maps and wasn't so much a stop as it was a leap of faith. I kept my eyes scrunched closed. Doing what needed doing was bad enough; watching while I did it always made me want to hurl. A bad idea, considering that the force of our passage would push it right back into my face. And yeah, I speak from experience.

The magic built to a fever pitch, and the girls tightened their slender bodies around mine. "Here's where we get off," I muttered, more to hear a reassuring sound than anything, and let go.

The train's solidity vanished as momentum hurled me backward. Magic picked up where steel left off, suspending me in a warm cocoon as it began cataloging my species and checking for the presence of my little beauties. If we didn't pass the arcane test, we'd take the same face-plant I'd taken many times before, only at the speed of a bullet rather than a metallic snail's pace. But of course we checked out—as I inwardly chanted, *There's no place like home*. The magic shot us straight upward in a cyclone of garishly colored light that somehow imprinted itself onto my eyeballs despite screwed-shut eyelids, and the overwhelming light became earsplitting sound as we pierced the veil separating the mundane world from the arcane pocket of the Otherrealms claimed by Furykind. And, as always happened, no matter how I struggled against it, the light and sound sent my senses into overdrive, clubbing them into unwilling submission, and both mind and body gave out. At that point, the unconsciousness sweeping over me felt better than sex . . . well, almost.

ONE MOMENT, BLESSED DARKNESS; THE NEXT, I found myself kneeling on cold marble, shivering. Disorientation flooded all five senses. My mind clawed its way through the confusion, finally catching up with what my body had already processed. I was safe and sound in the heart of the Palladium.

Footsteps sounded on the floor, helping me focus on the here and now rather than the maelstrom I'd just left behind. But the sight of a completely unexpected woman smiling down at me had my brow raising.

"Stacia? Where the hell did *you* come from?" I accepted the hand she offered, letting her bear most of my weight as she jerked me to my feet. My eyes roamed around the small antechamber just outside the imposing hall where the Conclave met. Nope, the usual low-level flunky I'd expected to find was nowhere to be seen. Instead, one of the seniormost Elders had been sent to meet me. I didn't know whether to feel complimented or worried. Then again, at least they'd sent my mentor.

Stacia inclined her head, faceted emerald eyes lighting up with amusement. "You don't seem too happy to see me, Marissa."

"No, no, that's not it at all. I'm just . . . surprised."

She stroked the silver serpent with crimson eyes twined around her right arm, right-side fingers drumming against her thigh. "Ah, yes, the rumors of my retirement were greatly exaggerated, I can assure you."

I ran suddenly sweaty palms along the slick leather of my uniform pants. Crap. The last thing I wanted to get caught up in was Fury politics. They could make mortal politics seem downright friendly. "Ah, well, you haven't exactly been a frequent fixture on the scene around here lately." When her features tightened, I felt honor-bound to defuse the situation. "You never call, you never write. I was beginning to think you'd dumped me."

Annoyance battled amusement on her face, until her sense of humor came out the victor. She placed a hand on my back and urged me toward the massive double doors on the far side of the room. "What, and give up on the best Tisiphone I ever sponsored to the Sisterhood? I don't think so." Her expression sobered once more. "I've had—other matters to tend to. Matters of grave importance. Now then, you didn't suffer through the miserable journey to get here just to chat with an old friend. What news is so important you had to bring it in person?"

We reached the entrance intended to shock and awe all approaching supplicants. And believe me, it worked. The cold, white marble doors towered over even the tallest of supplicants and spread out farther than four Furies with arms spread out could reach. It brought to mind ancient Greek and Roman architecture, and for good reason. This place was as old as—older than—those now-crumbled mortal ruins.

I shot Stacia a sideways glance. "Someone's trying to kill me."

She bared her teeth in a feral grin. "Now then, *there's* a novel concept."

I couldn't help returning her smile. As the arcane community's closest thing to a police force, Furies were no strangers to people wanting to kill them—me especially. I tended to maim first and ask questions later. "Someone mortal."

Her lips tightened into a thin line of disapproval. "Ah. The Accord then."

That's what I loved about Stacia. No bullshit with her; she just cut right to the chase. Mortals trying to kill Furies could only spell trouble for the already-shaky mortal-immortal peace treaty.

"Exactly." I gestured toward the doors. "Is the Conclave in session?" Time flowed differently in this place, dictated by the whims of the Elders who conducted most of their business here rather than in the mundane realm. The only guaranteed method of ensuring complete discretion from both arcane and mundane alike. Spies couldn't make it here—or survive long—if they tried. Few would be stupid enough to risk it.

"The Lesser Consensus is, yes."

I relaxed. Good. The fewer Elders present to bicker with each other, the better. "Shall we, then?"

She sent magic flowing through the doors with a flick of her fingers. They immediately responded, rumbling open as ancient stone doors brushed ever-so-slightly against ancient stone floor. I took a deep breath and stepped forward. Fourteen Elders—five members of each Fury class when Stacia was added to their number—sat around three sides of a solid mahogany table arranged in the center of the room. Fourteen pairs of identical, faceted green eyes watched expressionlessly as I strode across the room, the red, low-heeled boots I never went anywhere without ringing against the tiled floor. Stacia shot me a reassuring look before taking her place near the head of the table. That left me to claim the single chair at the foot of the table, separated from the next closest chairs by a good half dozen feet. The hot seat.

My palms grew even sweatier when I recognized this session's Moerae, a thin-faced Russian named Ekaterina, the youngest Elder by far, seeing as how she'd been born barely a century ago. She took great pride in rubbing her position in the face of other young Furies. I shuddered inwardly. You couldn't *pay* me to be an Elder. Not that this little fact had ever mattered much to Ekaterina. She'd nearly lost her position to my mother—and, now that Mom was gone, had transferred her animosity to me. Joy, joy.

Ah hell, she's gonna make this a lot harder than it needs to be.

Ekaterina waited a half minute longer than courtesy dictated before acknowledging me with a nod. She spoke in barely accented English, the language most arcanes had adopted as a common tongue for conducting official business when Latin crashed and burned a couple centuries earlier. Yeah, so the mundanes had given up on that dying language long before the arcanes, who take that whole beating-a-dead-horse thing way too seriously.

"We trust you have an excellent reason to appear before us, unsummoned and without first petitioning for an audience."

Yeah, she was definitely going to be a pain in my ass. By custom, she should have granted me the courtesy of a title, whether as formal as *Tisiphone* (the class of Furies responsible for solving most homicides) or as simple as *sister*. "A reason of grave importance, Moerae. It touches the Accord itself."

Expression flickered across their faces at last. Elders shifted in their seats, formal robes swishing against chair legs as they exchanged glances, voices muttering softly before the Moerae gestured for silence. "Explain yourself."

So I did, starting with the discovery of the false Fury and ending with the ambush at the precinct. I tried to keep my recitation dry and factual, not wanting the heat of emotion to lessen the impact of my words. Once finished relating the day's events, I fell silent, glancing from Elder to Elder, trying to see which were sympathetic to my news and which were not. Not an easy thing to do; they were true experts at the ice-queen routine.

Ekaterina leveled a blank stare my way. "Have you further testimony to give?"

"No, Moerae."

"Very well, then. You may return to the antechamber until you are sent for."

I blinked, mouth dropping slightly open. Wait. She was dismissing me without the usual Q&A session? "But—"

Her fists clenched on the table before her. "That will be sufficient, Tisiphone. We will send for you if we have any questions."

My gaze flew to Stacia, who gave me a silent look of warning. I fought for composure, pushing back from the table and retracing my steps of moments before. Something was *beyond* rotten in Denmark.

The doors seemed to slam shut more forcefully than usual, though that was probably my imagination. The missing flunky now inhabited a desk across the antechamber, fingers flying over the keys of a laptop computer as she sorted through e-mails from earthbound Furies that would run the gamut from petty complaints about their current posts to noteworthy news gained while performing their various duties. And a pile of petitions from sisters requesting official audiences with the Conclave. Yeah, technically speaking I should have sent advance warning before dropping by for our little chat. But screw formality. *My* news had been too urgent to wait, dammit.

When Rage welled up anew, I summoned Nemesis and

Nike into physical form to help ground myself. I let my gaze roam around the antechamber, settling it on the flunky seated behind the sleek, contemporary cherry desk loaded with office accessories that could have—and probably had—come straight from Staples. The ultramodern laptop looked newer, and more expensive, than the battered model I used at home. As usual, the incongruity of finding the mundane amenities nestled among the ancient architecture had my lips twitching in amusement. And wasn't it ironic as hell that the seniormost Furies, who generally eschewed mixing with mortals more than necessary, didn't hesitate to use the best technology humanity could provide?

This time I really did cool my heels, settling into a cushioned bench, fingers tapping against thighs in random rhythm. Gods, they really needed to pipe in some elevator music or something.

I began to rack my brain, trying to figure out what I could have done differently to get the Elders to recognize the urgency of the day's events. I felt sure that the fake Fury corpse showing up, my suspension, and the attempt on my life were related—and those events were probably only the tip of a sinister gods-bedamned iceberg. The Elders should have shown *some* sort of emotion in response to my testimony, even if only unwillingness to connect the dots I'd painted for them.

Inevitably, my thoughts turned back to Vanessa and that long-ago conversation that had proven to be our last. She'd been so excited as she packed for her first solo mission, but I'd done my best to burst her bubble. As usual.

"Nessa, it's just too soon for this. You've never done a stint this long, or so far away, especially not solo. And after that whole fiasco with Andre Carrington—"

Her eyes took on a brownish tinge. Annoyance. "No fair bringing Dre into this, Riss. We haven't heard from him in over a month, now. The restraining order—"

Frustration had me stalking right up to her and allowing anger to color my own eyes. "Restraining orders don't always protect women from jealous psycho exes, Nessa. I've learned that the hard way working with the PD."

She rolled her eyes. "PD, schmee-dee. You and your obsession with the mortal police."

My frown deepened. "The 'mortal' police, Ness? We were both fully mortal not even a decade past, and you sound like a crotchety Elder already. That attitude is what sparked the Time of Troubles to begin with."

Vanessa's hands jerked as she tried to jam the suitcase lid down on the scraps of fabric poking out. "Don't throw that mortal PR at me, Marissa. Call it what it was—the War."

I waved a hand in the air. "Not the point, Vanessa."

Another eye roll. "No, the point is that you have the mistaken impression you are bigger and badder than everyone else in the world and that we need you to wipe our asses."

My mouth dropped at Vanessa's blatant crudity. Usually, I was the one to engage in that sort of imagery. Nemesis and Nike, twined around my waist because I'd had the mistaken impression Vanessa would listen to me as an older Fury, if not as her friend, sent a blast of amusement through our bond. A succession of images flashed into my mind, indicating Vanessa had learned from my example well. Too well . . .

Renewed humor flowed through our bond in the here and now, echoing that of years before. "Yeah, yeah, yeah, ladies, you tried to warn me how *that* one would go."

Something about the remembered conversation had my eyes narrowing. Back when Nessa disappeared, I'd been *so* sure that her jealous ex had abducted her, corroborating evidence or no corroborating evidence. When his uber-expensive, uber-slimy attorneys managed to thwart my every attempt to get his ass investigated more thoroughly, that'd only made me all the more determined to nail it to the ground someday. But if, like I was beginning to suspect, mortals were involved in the attempt to pass off the fake Fury corpse as Vanessa, things might be way more complicated than I'd ever suspected.

I let my mind chew over things while I waited. And waited some more. My stomach growled long before the wait was over, which meant several hours had gone by. I crossed my arms over my chest and glared at the double doors, willing them to open, then nearly fell off the bench when they actually did.

They opened only far enough to allow Stacia to slip past. Her feet had barely cleared the doorway when it shut with surprising speed. She beckoned me to fall in step, heading for the exit on the other side of Flunky Numero Uno. The fact that I couldn't read her mood disturbed me. She may have possessed the typical Elder poker face, but she'd taught me everything I knew about being a Fury and I could usually read her like a book.

Our boots clicked loudly as we made our way down the Palladium's winding corridor that separated the Conclave behind us from the living quarters of the Elders to the left and the common areas to the right. I opened my mouth to speak three or four different times, then decided to let her break the silence first. She waited until we reached the room housing my ride back home.

Slamming the door behind us, Stacia turned to me with intensity burning in her eyes. Her voice sounded equally urgent when she spoke. "Be careful, Marissa."

I frowned. "What did the Conclave decide, Stacia? Are they sending you back to assist me?"

Her expression grew shadowed. "I'm afraid not. They decided that any action now, barring sufficient proof of some mortal plot, could be seen as our violating the Accord. As such, you are to return to your post and carry on with your normal duties."

My mouth dropped nearly to my chest. "What the hell do you mean, resume my normal duties? Did they hear the part where a mortal tried to kill me and then committed suicide rather than be taken into custody?"

Stacia's left hand stroked the serpent on her right arm while the fingers on that hand tapped against her thigh. "Oh, they heard you, Marissa. They even believe you. They've just chosen to sit on their collective asses for the time being."

"So what, they expect me to go home and wait to be assassinated in my sleep?"

She stepped forward, taking my hands into her own. "Officially, we can give you no other orders. Not officially."

I paused, mulling over her deliberate repetition. Stacia usually spoke with an economy of words, rarely saying anything twice. "And unofficially?"

Her lips twisted into a half smile. "Did you hear the part about 'barring sufficient proof of some mortal plot'?" She squeezed my fingers tightly. "Go find the proof we need, Marissa. It's high time someone put the mundanes back into their proper place."

Hot damn. That was as good as permission to do whatever I needed to get the job done. I didn't pay too much attention to Stacia's comment about putting the mundanes into their "proper place." Elders, especially those who thought in terms of centuries rather than years, tended to conveniently forget the fact that all Furies started out as mortals until their abilities manifested and they were sponsored into the Sisterhood. As Stacia had sponsored me when my mother could not.

I turned toward the vortex of magical energy waiting to return me to the subway tunnel, nerves jangling as I realized just how vulnerable the ride would make me.

Especially if someone had managed to tail me earlier and now lay in wait to ambush me upon my return. Suddenly, getting off in a different area of the subway than I'd gotten on seemed a *very* good idea. I nodded decisively. "You can depend on me, Stacia."

This time her smile lit up her entire face. "That's what I'm counting on."

ONCE BACK ON THE BOSTON STREETS, I tracked down a pay phone and called a reporter acquaintance of mine to check on Trinity. I was relieved to hear that she'd been rushed to the ER but was in stable condition. The reporter tried to grill me on my whereabouts, but I thanked him and hung up.

After taking a deep breath, I blended into the crowds scurrying along, trying to decide on my first course of action. Someone—likely a group of xenophobic mortals—was up to no good and had become desperate enough to kill both mundane and arcane in order to keep their secret from being uncovered. Hell, they'd somehow managed to get me suspended in record time for doing my damned duty. And since the Elders couldn't give me official help until I had more to go on than a hunch, that left only one option. I was on my own.

Still, I couldn't maintain red alert twenty-four/seven. I'd have to sleep sometime. Arcanes might have ridiculously long life spans, but we still had many of the same physical needs as mortals. Which meant I'd also need money to eat and somewhere safe to crash. Couldn't exactly use my own credit cards, now could I? I needed to recruit someone, preferably someone arcane, to serve as backup. And I could think of only one supernatural being still alive I trusted enough to watch my back. My ex, Scott Murphy.

The thought of crawling to him and asking for his help didn't exactly thrill me, but beggars couldn't be choosers.

I thought back to the last morning we'd woken up in bed next to each other. We'd gotten frisky for a few minutes until he decided to rain on my parade. Him, deliciously naked, sitting back and casually mentioning that his father was stepping down from the Shadowhounds—the family's mercenary business—early to become the chief of security for none other than Vanessa's ex, Dre Carrington.

Scott's concern had given way to what *had* to be feigned puzzlement. "Did you hear me, baby?"

My laughter hadn't contained the slightest hint of humor. I'd heard it, but I just couldn't fucking believe it. I'd sworn to bring Carrington down at *any* cost. Even if it meant turning my back on the one and only man who'd ever convinced me he was worth trusting enough to fall head over heels in love with him. I leapt out of bed.

Scott had scrambled after me, nearly sliding off the slick sheets and busting his ass on the hardwood floor. "Riss, wait, you just didn't understand me. It's not like tha—"

The venom in my eyes—the Rage in my voice—had stopped him cold. "Not like what, Murphy? Not like your money-hungry family is betraying the Sisterhood—betraying *me*—by going into business with the rat responsible for killing one of our sisters?" I couldn't help the break in my voice, or the tears pricking my eyes, so I ran from the room without waiting for him to dress. Furies can haul ass with the best of them. I'd made it to the front stoop of Murphy Central before a haphazardly dressed Scott caught up with me.

He'd tried to explain. Told me he couldn't tell me everything but that his dad really needed him.

In that moment, I knew. Knew that, for my Warhound, family would *always* come way above me. He'd never even told me he loved me . . . No way I could live like that, knowing that I would come in last place for yet one more person I loved. For my mother, the Sisterhood came first. For my father, the bottle. For my brother, his wife and daughter. And now Scott—and him I loved more than life itself. Staying with him would eventually destroy my poor, withering heart more surely than death ever could.

So I unleashed the anger raging beneath the heartache and cut him off before he could hurt me anymore than he already had. Said things to him that only the Rage could have given voice to. When I was done, we went our separate ways, and hadn't seen each other since. Except in memory . . .

With a muttered curse, I reminded myself I was here to eat a little crow. Or Hound, as it were. I wound my way toward Boston's magical Underbelly, the part of town where the less savory members of the arcane community tended to congregate, along with the smattering of rough-and-tough mortals deadly enough to get down with them. Scott Murphy was the mongrel son of two such people—his parents were an arcane bitch and the big, bad human mercenary who loved her.

That wasn't an insult. Scott's mom was a literal bitch, member of the Egyptian-based Cabal made up of shape-shifting Warhounds. And, seeing as how arcane genes tend to be dominant in a major way, Scott took after his mother more than his father, inheriting her shape-shifting and martial abilities.

My skin tingled when I crossed the border separating relatively normal Chinatown from the anything-*but*-normal Underbelly. The scents of a dozen different arcane races, all tinged with various flavors of magic, hit my nostrils. A mortal would have compared the smells to mundane spices: the sweetness of cinnamon and sugar warring with the spicy tang of cayenne and cumin. My nose itched with the urge to sneeze, but I fought it back. I reassumed Fury guise, knowing that only one form would gain true respect from *all* members of the Gens Arcana.

There was a very simple reason Furies wore our flashy red uniforms, beyond the fact that the magically treated leather was stain-resistant and provided a rudimentary form of armor. They made us look badass. And when one was responsible for policing a vast array of magical badasses, looking the part was more than half the battle. Plus, let's face it, most Furies have a vain streak wider than the Mississippi. Even if we'd never admit it.

Drab brick buildings of short stature lined the Belly's outskirts, giving way to taller, cleaner-looking glass-and-steel structures the farther I walked. The streets morphed from pockmarked asphalt to unnaturally smooth, magic-worked cobblestones. The illusion of days gone by without their bumpy inconvenience. Businesses took up the bottom floors of the largest buildings, ranging from the seedier establishments on the border to more respectable boutiques and shops farther in. After a brisk, ten-minute walk, I finally reached my destination.

Neither overly glitzy nor disreputable, Hounds of Anubis took up most of the ground floor of a block-long structure crouched at the intersection of the Belly's two largest thoroughfares. Though the building itself was a sturdy-looking brownstone, the shop's storefront was much more gilt than gold. I stared up at the store's crudely carved insignia, tracing the row of fake gold Egyptian letters surrounding an ugly, dog-headed man wearing an ornate headdress. Anubis, patron god of the Cabal. A pretty badass dude himself, and not someone I wanted to meet again anytime soon.

Nemesis and Nike curved their way from lower arms to upper, radiating calm as well as chastisement. I was stalling. They knew it. I knew it. Hell, the entire surrounding two-block radius no doubt knew it. Scott's and my breakup had been very public, conducted on the steps I now scuffed my boot soles along.

"Fuck," I muttered, glaring at the crimson-scaled traitors on my arms. "Yeah, yeah. Let's get this over with."

The store wasn't simply a front for the Murphy mercenary enterprise known as the Shadowhounds. Liana Murphy, former heiress to the Banoub dynasty, operated her own lucrative business selling magical odds and ends along with priceless arcane art and antiques. She may have given up her once-glamorous world of power and privilege to settle down with a "lesser" human and her brood of mutts, but that hadn't made her any less driven to succeed. An ear-piercing chime sounded when I opened the door and crossed the threshold, the tone alerting the store's occupants that a dangerous arcane had entered the building. My lips curved slightly, and the compliment calmed me in a way nothing else could have. I turned my stalk into a strut, radiating as much confidence and danger as I could. Like always called to like in the Belly.

A pleasant, slightly gravelly voice rang out when I approached the front counter. "Can I help you?" A shaggy-haired brunette turned, then bared razor-sharp canines when she recognized me. "What the hell do *you* want?"

"Down, girl." I made the phrase a carefree drawl, trying to ignore the pain from someone who had once been a friend now treating me like an interloper.

Kiara Murphy, Scott's older and very protective sister, slapped both hands down on the counter, spiky tufts of hair bristling. I had once considered her and his oldest sister, Amaya, close friends. "You said all that needed to be said when you chased Scott off like he was some no-good mutt. Just like our mother's oh-so-fine family. Now get the hell out."

I crossed arms over chest like I didn't have a care in the world. She'd be over the counter and at my throat if I showed the slightest shred of weakness. "That's not the way it went down, and you know it. Where's Scott?"

"He's nowhere *you* need be—"

"Kiara!" My voice cracked with every ounce of Rage I'd been suppressing for the past hour. "This is Fury business. Don't make me ask again."

She closed her eyes, hands balling into fists at each side as warring instincts boiled inside, the urge to protect her brother battling with the deeply ingrained belief that Furies must be obeyed at all costs. Not every arcane felt that urge as strongly as others, but Warhounds were fiercely honorable as well as deeply loyal.

Amber-yellow eyes opened, and she nodded. "Fine, then. Show yourself to the back room. But mark me well, Marissa. This had better damned well *be* Fury business, or you'll regret lying to me."

I headed for one of several doors in the rear of the room, unable to resist throwing a "Good girl" over my shoulder.

Her low growl had me grinning until I reached the centermost door. My fingers curled around the doorknob, tingling at the buzz of magic. When the security system recognized me as Fury, the tingle faded and the door responded to my touch. I drew in a deep breath, opened the solid length of steel, and stepped into my ex-lover's domain.

Everything in the Murphys' Command Central looked exactly the same as it had two years earlier. Battered but comfortable chairs circled a beat-up poker table in one corner of the room, with a fully stocked wet bar in the opposite corner. Warhounds could drink just about any other arcane under the table. Except maybe Satyrs and, of course, Furies. The walls were made of dark wood paneling, faded by years of smoke from both cigars and the humongous fireplace crouched in the center of the wall directly opposite the door behind me. Boston winters grew cold indeed, especially for a race bred mainly in the hot desert sun of Egypt. I wrinkled my nose when the musky cigar odor hit. God, I hated that smell.

Three men and one woman sat around the table, cards in hand and cigars beside them. Morgan, Scott's dad, was glaringly absent, no doubt holding the hand of my Public Enemy Number One. That thought had a scowl darkening my face and my fingers clenching. Great. The perfect mood to be in for a good ol' ass-kissing.

Scott's well-muscled back caught my attention immediately. Thick red hair flowed just past his shoulders in gentle waves. I widened my eyes. He used to keep his hair buzzed as short as possible, refusing to offer enemies any advantage in a fight. His deeply bronzed skin and hellaciously sexy body remained the same from what I could see. Secretly I'd hoped to see him gain a hundred pounds in my absence, but it looked like I was SOL.

The woman seated across from him glanced my way, boredom giving way to interest when she recognized me. Her dark black hair and slanted golden eyes gave her away as one of Scott's innumerable cousins, and I placed her name a half second later. Elliana Banoub, so secure in her lofty position in the Cabal that she socialized with the ostracized Murphys with no fear of repercussions. Unlike Kiara and Amaya, she'd disliked me from the moment we'd met, and the feeling was entirely mutual.

I didn't recognize the long, lean redhead to her left, although something about the shape of his eyes seemed strangely familiar, but the guy facing him was Scott's youngest brother, Sean. Seemed bizarre to think he was old enough to join in the family business. Then again, he'd been nineteen the last time I saw him, with a penchant for trailing after me like a little lost puppy. When his glance met mine, he gave me the first welcoming smile I'd seen since strolling into the building.

Elliana murmured something, cattiness (ha) darkening her yellow eyes to pure amber. My fingers itched with the urge to scratch them out. Scott's back stiffened. He threw his cards down, pushed his chair back, and spun. As always, his exotic mix of Egyptian and Irish—the shoulder-length red hair paired with his mother's intense golden eyes and coppery-brown skin—took my breath away. The Cabal's great height meeting his father's brawny muscles. Long, elegant fingers seeming so at odds with the calluses covering them, the latter gained from hours of weaponry practice with his relatives. Once, I'd known no greater pleasure than feeling those rough but gentle hands roam all over my body. Now, they only seemed to mock me as they clenched and he eyed me with cold disdain.

This was going to be even harder than dealing with Ekaterina.

"Well, well, well," Elliana drawled from behind him. "Look what the Cat dragged in."

I straightened, recognizing the insult for what it was. Warhounds absolutely despised their longtime enemies, the Bastai. Otherwise known as Cats. "And if it isn't the Cabal's number one ice princess, slumming it up yet again," I shot back. "Just what *does* your fiancé think of that, Ellie baby?"

The ruff of baby-fine fur along her neck rose. She started around the table, but the unfamiliar man barked one sharp word, and she grew still. Interesting. Once upon a time, she'd never have taken orders from any of the arcanes around her, especially not when someone insulted her as badly as I just had. I knew good and well her fiancé had rejected her over a year ago, once it'd come out that she'd had an affair with an associate of Scott's. My eyes went back to the unfamiliar redhead. Aha, guess *that* little rumor was true after all.

Yeah, yeah. So I'd paid more attention to Scott and his family than I should have. Sue me.

Scott, direct as always, cut to the chase. "Why are you here, Marissa?"

The ice in his voice raised shivers along my spine, though I refused to let anyone else see that. *Marissa*. Once he'd always called me *baby*, or *Riss*.

"I want to hire your services."

His jaw worked with the obvious effort not to curse. Obvious because I'd once known him better than any other man.

Elliana broke in before he could answer. "The whores work five blocks down, Marissa. Perhaps you can find your little lost friend there."

I was halfway across the room before any of them had time to react. Scott and Sean broke into smooth, well-rehearsed motion just in time, Sean gathering Elliana and herding her back a half dozen paces while Scott grabbed my arm and jerked me across the room and into the back office. He slammed the door and pushed me against a wall. Hard.

Despite the anger in his eyes and grip, his sheer physical proximity made a shiver of desire run down my spine. "What the hell kind of game are you playing at, Riss?"

"I need help, Scott. And you're the only one I can trust."

His hands tightened slightly along my upper arms, falling away when Nemesis and Nike worked their way from waist to lower arms. They permitted him certain liberties they accepted from no other, but their tolerance extended only so far. I apologized mentally to them and shifted them back into tattoo form.

He stalked several short paces and settled his well-shaped rump against an ancient wood desk. "*You* need *my* help? Now isn't that just rich. The high and mighty Fury crawling to the no-good, scum-of-the-Belly merc for help."

I tightened my lips, biting back the instinctive insult bubbling just beneath the surface. There was one thing the day's events had helped me see: Maybe the situation with Dre Carrington *wasn't* as black and white as I'd painted it when we broke up. "I know I said some shitty things, Sco—"

His bark of laughter sounded far bitterer than I'd ever heard. I didn't like hearing it from him. Not the larger-than-life, carefree lover I'd once cherished. "Had you been a member of my mother's stuck-up clan, I'd have killed you for the insults you spat at me on my family's own front steps. Give me one reason I should help you."

"Because I'm in deep shit, Scott, and it has to do with Nessa." The stark terror and longing in my voice hadn't been intended, but they affected Scott more strongly than calculated emotion could have. Thank the gods for Warhound loyalty and protectiveness. Instinct kicked into overdrive even when they didn't want it to.

"This is Fury business, then?"

I let out a deep breath. If he was willing to discuss the situation, then he would help me.

"Yes. I need backup in a bad way, Scott. This goes high up the mortal chain of command in the PD."

The beginnings of interest lit in his eyes. He'd always been fascinated by his father's people. "The PD, huh? Still working for them?" As if he didn't know.

"I did until they suspended me a few hours ago."

Smugness flicked through his expression, though I couldn't really blame him. After all, I'd wished to see him fat and miserable.

"What'd you do *this* time?"

"Proved that Nessa's corpse wasn't, in fact, Nessa's corpse."

He arched both brows in an expression I'd tried but could never duplicate. "Okay. You have my attention now. Explain."

I did so quickly, starting with the predawn call from Dispatch and ending with the assassin's nosedive to escape capture. That interested Scott more than anything else.

"Huh. A mortal willing to kill himself rather than risk interrogation. Don't see that every day."

"Yeah. Comes from that whole fear-of-death thing."

He grinned at the sarcasm in my voice, and for a moment I could pretend the past two years had never happened. But then he got back to business.

"You'll pay double the usual consulting fee."

I bristled. "This is official Fury business!"

"Yeah, that's why you're paying double. Hazard pay. Last time we accepted a Fury commission, we nearly lost two of our best mercs. So double or nothing."

My breath whooshed out again, and I wondered which of the region's Furies had hired his family's services without giving me a heads up. A smart one, obviously. I would have bitten her head off otherwise.

"Fine. If this helps track down a Fury's killer, the Elders won't quibble about the price."

His lips settled into a smirk, but he simply nodded.

"I have a condition of my own. I want you, Scott, and only you." His fingers grew white as they pressed into the desk beneath him, so I clarified. "Not your bitchy cousin, or your cute but inexperienced brother, or the guy I don't recognize."

"Elliana's husband," he supplied. "Patrick MacAllister."

Damn. The girl'd worked fast in the months since her fiancé dumped her.

"Whatever. I'm planning to go in fast and hard on this one, and I need someone I've worked with before. Someone who won't slow me down."

Pleasure at my compliment battled with his reluctance to be alone with me any more than necessary. "You'd be safer with more eyes watching for trouble."

I wiggled my arms, flashing my tats. "Have two extra pairs right here. Besides, I meant it. Fast and furious on this one, Scott. Operative word being *furious*."

He finally nodded, pushing away from the desk and moving around to the chair on the opposite side. He sat down and tapped at the ultramodern computer facing him.

"Somebody upgraded." My eyes widened now that they'd been drawn to the piece of technology. "I thought your father *hated* those things."

Humor glinted in his eyes. "He does. Which is one reason I let Mac talk me into buying it. Besides, Da's usually busy . . ."

His voice trailed away, and I forced back a smartass comment. We both knew just what his father was busy doing.

"What are you looking for, anyway?"

He continued tapping away at the keyboard. "Checking for any hits on you."

My mouth worked silently for seconds. "Hits? You think they'd hire arcanes once mortals failed?"

"I think it's a safe enough assumption, and may give us a place to track down some answers."

"Hmm. I just assumed anyone nuts enough to take a face-plant from ten stories up worked for a group just as fanatical."

"You mean one of those 'earth is for mortals' types?"

I nodded.

"Could be, I guess. But even the most fanatical of those groups will slum it up when it comes to taking out someone they see as particularly dangerous." His fingers grew still above the keys and he let out a whistle. "Shit, Riss. You've really done it this time."

My palms grew sweaty and I sucked in a huge breath. "Bad?"

His eyes were concerned when he glanced at me. Further proof that he cared more than his outward show of anger would suggest. "Worse than bad. Harpies."

Shock had my mouth dropping open. "Are you shitting me?"

He shot me one of his *Don't be stupid* looks. "One of the hottest new arcane web forums seems innocent enough at first glance, unless you know what to look for." He tapped a line of text on the monitor. "And this username is a code-word used by a freelance assassin group."

"Let me guess. One staffed by Harpies." Great, just my luck to come across the one group of mortals crazy enough to hop into bed with the craziest monsters in all the arcane realms.

"Give the girl a cigar."

I made a face. "No thanks." Cigars were an absolutely nasty habit as far as I was concerned, and one of the things about him that had always driven me insane.

Scott shoved back his chair and stood. "We're going to need more than just the two of us, Riss." This time his voice brooked no argument.

"Fine, then. But not your brother." I couldn't bear the thought of dragging someone so young and innocent into the shit storm I'd stirred up. "Who else is available?" On the plus side, I was safe from the ice queen. No way in hell *she'd* gone merc.

The smirk spreading over his face was my first warning. "Funny you should ask. The only others available right now are my bitchy cousin and her husband."

Oh hell. Some days it just didn't pay to get out of bed.

CHAPTER FOUR

"EVERYONE IN PLACE?" SCOTT'S VOICE TICK-
led my ear, sounding tinny in the earpiece he'd foisted on
me earlier. He sat, safe and sound with the others, in a van
a block or two away from the branch of the city morgue
that handled arcane stiffs; I, on the other hand, just used
every bit of magical camouflage I could dredge up to sneak
in behind several men delivering a new arrival to the city
morgue. After some discussion at Shadowhounds headquarters, I'd decided that what I really needed was another
look at that corpse, and I knew Scott and his crew could
help me get some face time with her. It was risky, though.
Considering the magical booby traps I'd also had to avoid
or disarm, it was a miracle I'd made it this far.

"Roger that." Sarcasm tinged my tone, but I dialed it
back a notch. "We clear?"

"Aye, lassie." A voice straight from the shores of

Scotland raised shivers along my spine with its smooth-as-molasses vibe. Patrick "Mac" MacAllister, new husband of the ice queen. Elliana was a lucky woman. The bitch.

"Great. Then open sesame."

Mac worked his computer voodoo, and the heavy door separating my quarry from me swung open. A room crafted from cold metal and equally cold air spread out before me. I tiptoed forward with breath held tensely. My body relaxed when no alarms sounded. Now it was time to work my own brand of voodoo.

My steps fell kitten-soft across the antiseptic white-tiled floor, zeroing in on the steel-coated door marked *Turner, Vanessa*. That had me rolling my eyes. Properly, the label should have read *Doe, Juno*, but whoever was behind this cover-up had obviously gone into overdrive. The door handle felt even cooler than the air when I cranked it open and tugged. Metal squeaked, alarmingly loud in the dimness.

"Quiet," Scott's voice warned. "There's a lab tech two rooms over."

"Easy for you to say," I muttered, trying to ease the tray open a few more inches without waking the dead. Ha. The body had been draped in white cloth inscribed with archaic runes. Runes meant to prevent the dead from doing just that. Waking. Arcane corpses had a nasty habit of rising from the dead, and one of the compromises negotiated into the Accord had been teaching humans how to safeguard against Ghouls. I peeled back the cloth, fingers clenching when Nessa's likeness stared up at me.

"Stop daydreaming, Fury. We don't have all night."

I didn't reply to Elliana's venom. Reaching into the messenger bag on my hip, I drew out four brightly colored candles, made of rare wax blessed by Egyptian priestesses and supplied for the spell by Scott's mother. After placing them at each corner of the cooler tray, I summoned a tendril of fire and the wicks burst into flame. I draped a rainbow-striped scrap of fabric across her chest and then called to the Power beneath me.

Magic responded, bubbling up from the ground and pooling into mini reservoirs above the candles, each feeding into the magical nexus hanging above the body's chest. I tapped into the energy, pushing it *down* into the flesh and bones of the freeze-dried corpse.

The corpse's eyes snapped open, and its mouth let out a silent scream. And then the exact thing I'd been hoping for happened. Its spirit shucked off its not-so-mortal body, sat straight up, and stared around in confusion. Just like I'd expected, the spirit that had inhabited the corpse most certainly did *not* resemble Nessa.

I frowned, trying to figure out exactly which arcane creature it *did* resemble. Gorgeous, silvery-white skin, flowing turquoise hair, tilted, metallic blue eyes, and oversized, slanted ears. Something about its ethereal beauty and Technicolor hair tugged at my memory. An unearthly voice began speaking in a fluid language I didn't understand. Feminine eyes turned to regard me unblinkingly. And that's when it hit me.

"Oh holy hell," I breathed. "She's Sidhe."

And that opened up a whole can of worms on its own, seeing as how the Sidhe were freaking extinct.

Elliana sounded even more disgruntled when she bit out, "What the hell does 'She's *she*' mean?"

"Not s-h-e. S-i-d-h-e. One of the Shining Folk." As most mortals called them, elves, or faeries. Bearing about as much resemblance to Santa's helpers or Tinkerbell as the Elders bore to fairy godmothers.

"Did you hit your head on the way down, Fury?"

The woman whose body bore the likeness of my dearest friend held a hand out toward me, cutting off my comeback before I could make it. This time, she spoke in perfect English. "Help me. Oh, please, help us all."

Shivers danced along my skin at the eerie beauty of her voice, not to mention the strong desire to do whatever she wanted me to. The fact that she could affect me so strongly, dead as she was, *should* have disturbed me greatly. But perhaps even more alarmingly, it didn't. I dredged up the willpower to shift more fully. Nemesis and Nike hissed into action, winding their way along my arms and grounding me in a way I could never ground myself. They were none too happy to see the spirit hovering alongside me.

She regarded us solemnly, metallic eyes seeming just a shade too large for her face. It should have detracted from her beauty, but it didn't. "Please, Fury, you are sworn to avenge *all* creatures harmed by magical means, are you not?"

Against my better judgment, I nodded. "That I am, but were you not held captive by mortals?" In my job as Chief Magical Investigator, I solved any murder cases involving immortal victims or criminals. But as a Fury, I was only sworn to investigate and avenge murders that were brought about by magical means.

Her lips curved ever so slightly. "Clever you are, lass. Aye, mortals it was who captured me. Mortals it is who hold my brethren still. But magic it was that slew me."

The formal cadence of her speech reminded me of the oldest Fury Elders. And no wonder. Some of them had Sidhe ancestors as well as mortal. But this strange spirit floating next to me was the first full-blooded Sidhe I'd ever encountered.

"How can there be even one of you still in existence? You were wiped out during the War."

"Ahhh, but the mortals only made it seem that way. They captured a group of us, then convinced our arcane enemies to launch their own slaughter against our race. They did not want to share the prize they had stolen."

"And what prize is that?"

"The secret to our immortality, of course. And the keys to our most powerful magic. The glamourie."

My lips and eyes widened. Glamourie, one of the oldest, most powerful magics. Sidhe half bloods could manage a bastardized version called glamour. But their illusions were just that, illusion. Full-blooded Sidhe, on the other hand, could actually take on the physical shape of those they impersonated. Making them the only shape-shifters who could take on an infinite number of forms besides Furies. In their favor, of course, is the fact that they're not sworn to the gods to use their shape-shifting skills only under certain conditions, unlike *moi*. They can also maintain their assumed forms for longer periods of time and at a lower magical cost to themselves.

If mortals gained mastery of *that* magic—added to their superior technology and numbers—arcanes would *never* get a fair shot under the new world order.

"So *that's* how your body came to resemble my sister Fury."

"Indeed. They forced me to assume her shape just before they executed me."

"Why would they execute you, if you hold the keys to immortality?"

"Because they feared the influence I had over the other captives. Which they were wise to do, since I was the last."

"The last?"

"Aye. The last of the Trueborn Sidhe."

"But you mentioned brethren—"

"Children, more like. Our children. Some bred naturally in captivity. Some unnaturally born, not children in the true sense of the word, but flesh of our flesh and bone of our bone nonetheless. Bred and born of the unMagic our captors have perfected."

Suspicion gnawed at my stomach, a suspicion that made me slightly ill. "You can't possibly mean—"

"Clones," she hissed. "The mortals have succeeded where we could not and cured our flagging fertility. By creating Sidheborn clones."

My pulse skittered. If word of this spilled out among the arcane community, the Accord would be shattered as painfully as it had been forged. And Furies might well be added to the endangered species list. We could *not* withstand another War, not so soon.

"Uh, Riss." Scott's voice buzzed in my ear, but I brushed it off like an annoying insect.

"Where are they being held?"

Her eyes took on a pleased glow and she relaxed her body. "Somewhere to the west."

Damned Sidhe and their thrice-damned riddle-speak. No wonder they'd been able to screw so many mortals over in ill-made bargains over the ages. The gods may have cursed them to always speak the truth, but there are *all kinds* of truth. "We're on the frigging East Coast. That's an awful lot of west."

Her lips curved. "I meant the west of this particular province. What do the mortals call it? Oh yes, the commonwealth."

Well. That helped somewhat. Western Massachusetts was a whole hell of a lot smaller than the west of the entire effing country.

"Who exactly is holding your brethr—"

"Riss, *move.* Someone's coming your way!" Scott's words thudding into my earpiece jerked me into action. "Shit. Sorry. I'll try and contact you later." To that end, I drew out a knife, cutting a lock of hair from the Sidhe's corpse and slicing a small section of skin, careful to make sure drops of blood clung to it as I wrapped the materials in the scarf. I jammed the candles and scarf into my bag, covered the corpse, and shoved the cooler closed. Just in time to hear the room's door begin creaking open.

I wrapped myself in camouflage, partially unfurling my wings and beating them, gaining just enough leverage to launch myself over and behind an examining table shrouded in shadows on the far side of the room. No sooner did I drop into place than several figures stepped through the doorway. I kept my body completely still and peered through the opening in the table's bottom. One thing caught my attention right off the bat. Only one of the figures wore the typical scrubs of the city coroner's office. The other three skulked around in cheap three-piece suits straight from the covers of *Yes-Men-GQ*.

Elliana took exception to my delay. "Move your ass, Fury!"

"One sec." I breathed the words as softly as I could while still being picked up by the microphone. Good thing the room was so damned long. "Feds."

The ME led the other men straight toward the cooler marked *Turner, Vanessa*. My fingers clenched on the steel underside of the exam table. If they turned the body over, they were going to notice the little souvenir I'd taken.

But the feds just gave the body a cursory inspection. They dismissed the ME with pointed looks toward the door, waiting for him to disappear before speaking.

"Looks like she hasn't been here, at least."

"Yes, but the fact that she hasn't yet returned to her home is a problem."

The third suit shook his head. "Merely a complication. She will turn up sooner or later. Furies always do."

I stiffened when I realized they meant me. Sure, I'd suspected that the feds, or at least someone very high up on the food chain, was involved somehow. But this sounded an awful lot like *they'd* been the ones trying to have me killed . . .

"We have several more men seeking her out. And the Harpies may well succeed in flushing the Fury out into the open."

The first man crinkled his nose, flicking at invisible specks of dust on overstarched cuffs. "I detest dealing with such unpredictable elements. We have absolutely *no* control over them."

The patterns of their speech seemed off-kilter to me. More formal than the cops I dealt with. Then again, they *were* feds.

"Which may be what it takes to bring the Fury down." GQ Number Two nodded toward the exit. "Now then, gentlemen, we must be on our way to Salem. Our erstwhile quarry may well be holed up there."

My heart thudded painfully as fingers dug into cold metal. I wanted to leap upon all three men and rip their throats out right then and there, but I didn't. We needed more answers if we were to have any hope of figuring out just who these assholes worked for.

I waited several agonizing minutes after the door slammed shut to begin retracing my path through the complex warren of hallways peppering the morgue. What I *wanted* to do was drop the camo and run like hell, but I didn't dare. "Did you catch that, Scott?"

His voice sounded unusually serious when he responded. "Yeah, Riss. Your brother and his family?"

My eyes snapped shut as I admitted what I would rather have denied. "Still live in Salem."

For once, Elliana's voice didn't burn my ears. "Then get a move on, Fury."

And, as much as I could manage without losing control over the magic, I did.

THE OLD FAMILY HOMESTEAD LOOKED JUST the way I remembered, perched high on a hilltop several hundred feet from the ocean. It towered three stories, its imposing mass overpowering the landscape and driveway surrounding it. The perfect picture of New England architecture, from weathered white clapboard to pseudo-Victorian towers at both ends. I inhaled the tang of salty air, taken by surprise when a pang of homesickness welled up in my throat. I absolutely *loved* living in the heart of Harvard Square in Boston, and had never regretted making the move there during my college years. Still, I couldn't deny the inexorable tug of my childhood home on my heartstrings. Even despite the frustration that my repeated phone calls from the prepaid cell phone Scott gave me had been answered and then abruptly ended when my voice was recognized. Gods-bedamned sister-in-law. I was going to kill her myself if the feds hadn't gotten to her first.

"No place like home, right?" Scott prompted after several silent moments.

I glanced at Scott, forcing myself to release the tension clenching my body in its grasp, and caught him dropping his hand as if he'd been reaching out to touch me. I pretended not to notice, though my pulse picked up speed. "Yeah. The more things change, yada yada yada." I drew in a breath. "Let's get this family reunion over with."

We strode along the driveway, he still in mortal guise while I pulled my Fury form around me like the well-wrought armor it was. I'd need every inch of it to deal with my not-so-charming sister-in-law. Since of *course* Jessica was the one to answer the buzzing doorbell. Her eyes washed over Scott without recognition (probably all that wavy red hair that had once been completely buzzed) but zeroed in on my face in milliseconds flat. She slammed the door shut on it. Or tried to, anyway.

I pounced, shoving her back several steps. Scott slammed the door and twisted the half dozen locking mechanisms into use. Paranoia, thy name is Jessica Holloway.

Her mouth opened and closed, producing no sound until shock faded enough for her brain to kick into gear. "What the hell do you think you're doing? We said all that needed saying when your stupidity got my sister kidnapped. Now, get out!"

She was never going to forgive me for "letting" Vanessa take off on her first and last solo mission. Never mind that I'd cried more tears and spent far more of the intervening years searching for Nessa than she had. Nope, as usual, Jessica's grief took front and center over everything else. Like just because she'd been more mother to Nessa than sister after their mother, Olivia, had died, that made her grief more valid than mine. She'd always been deeply jealous of the fact that I shared something with Nessa she never could—the bonds of Fury sisterhood.

I struggled to sound cool, like her words didn't bother me in the slightest. "No can do, Jess. Sorry."

Her eyes narrowed and she marched toward the impressive stairway leading to the second floor. "We'll see what David has to say about this!"

"Yes, let's do. But make it fast. They'll be here soon."

She faltered, right foot not quite making it to the first step. "They?"

"The group of super-secret agents hoping to use you all—well, most of you—against me, thus luring me into a trap I won't be able to escape, et cetera, et cetera."

"Jesus, Mary, and Joseph. You *do* take pride in bringing danger down on this family."

"That's just my number one goal in life. Jeez, Jessica. Could you stop bitching long enough to take care of what matters? Getting you all to safety."

Her eyes widened and she clenched the railing. "Oh my God. Cori."

My body tensed. "Where is she?"

"Softball practice."

I should have known. My niece practically lived and

breathed softball. "Shit. Scott, you get Jess and David back to your place. I'll grab Cori and meet you there."

He leveled unblinking eyes on me. "I don't think so. Elliana and Mac can handle your brother and sister."

"In-law," Jess and I replied in tandem, then glared at each other.

"Sister-in-law. I'm not leaving you alone until this is over."

"But I'll be faster flying."

"Unless they're already waiting for you there, in which case you could just be deader. Now, could you stop bitching long enough to take care of what matters? Getting your niece to safety."

I hated it when he turned my own logic against me—something he'd always been adept at. The bastard.

The doorbell rang, signaling that Ellie and Mac had been tuned in to our conversation. I left Scott to deal with them, jogging up the stairs, careful not to touch my sister-in-law, heading to the room in the house my brother loved above all others. Our father's onetime study.

My hand clenched on the room's wooden door frame. David reclined in our father's old wingback chair, fiddling with a fancy ballpoint pen as he stared out the window at the waves rolling in the distant seascape. Classical music played softly in the background, a taste inherited from our father during his sober days. Silver touched the hair at each of his temples and faint lines shadowed his eyes. That was something new. He looked so much like Dad I fought back tears. My older, beloved brother. The one who'd abandoned me for his shrew of a wife.

Not fair, Riss, my conscience pointed out. *He never completely cut you off, despite what she wanted. What she ordered. But he had his daughter to think of. And, much as he loves you, you're only his sister. Not his wife.*

Logic did nothing to lessen the hurt. It never did.

I licked my lips. "David?"

He leapt to his feet and hurried across the room. "Riss? Oh my God, it's good to see you. Feels like years!"

I kept my expression bland as he hugged me tightly. It *had* been years.

"You look fantastic. The same beautiful you." He brushed the tips of his hair self-consciously. "While I look positively ancient."

A grin slipped before I could shove it away. "Oh, completely. What are you now? Fifty? Sixty?"

He shot me a mock glare. "Not even a day over forty. Well. Perhaps a few days over."

Several more than that, seeing as how I was in my thirties and he was thirteen years my senior. He'd developed a habit of "losing" time the past few years.

Initial pleasure gave way to practicality. "Wait. Jessie actually let you in? What happened? Oh, God. Cori?"

"Is perfectly safe. And I'm going to make sure she stays that way. But some very nasty people are on the way here, hoping to use my family against me. Friends of mine are going to take you and Jessica to safety."

He wrapped both arms around his chest, lips tightening in the stubborn line I knew all too well. "So I'm supposed to sit back in safety and watch you put your life in danger yet again?"

My breath whooshed out. I'd hoped he wouldn't bring up this tired old argument. Why couldn't he accept the fact that I *had* to fulfill my duties, same as our mother? Furies were meant to protect those unable to protect themselves from the arcane things that went bump in the night. Even at the risk of our own lives. "David, please—"

Stalking to the oversized bay window, he stared out at the waves crashing against the shoreline. Just as our father had done so many times during my childhood, waiting for our mother to return home from whatever mission she'd been sent on, until the night she went out and never returned . . .

"Promise me one thing." His voice sounded as ancient as he'd joked about being just moments before. "Make sure what happened to Vanessa and Mom doesn't happen to Cori."

The fact that Cori could develop Fury abilities later in life—just as I had—was something I knew must weigh on his mind constantly. His request shattered my heart into a hundred more pieces. But I couldn't—wouldn't—let him see that. "She'll be safe. I promise." The words tasted empty. Too much like the vow our mother made our father that final night.

"Go. Just go."

Once again, I fled the room I'd come to hate without saying another word.

CHAPTER FIVE

SCOTT LEFT IT ALONE UNTIL WE REACHED THE local high school. "That went better than I expected."

I focused on the ball field several hundred feet in the distance. "What, because Jessica didn't break out a shotgun?"

This time he didn't resist the impulse to touch me. I nearly closed my eyes and purred when he stroked a hand along my hair. "Riss, you can't take it personally. She's hurting."

"And I'm *not*?" I wanted the words back the instant I said them. "There they are. Let's go."

He made several more attempts to talk, but I ignored each one. What kind of man actually tried to talk about touchy-feely shit when women weren't strong-arming them into it, anyway?

The kind you fell in love with, my conscience whispered.

Who the hell asked you?

We pulled up alongside the field before I could continue the pointless argument with myself. I jogged the last few steps to the dugout ahead of him, trying to pick out the coach from the female bodies zipping this way and that. It wasn't easy. Finally, I approached the sixteen-year-old holding a clipboard, figuring she would know. She squinted cornflower eyes against rays of fading sunlight. "I'm Coach Jennings. Can I help you?" Those eyes widened when she picked out my red leather uniform and low-heeled boots, added them to the snake tats, and came up with the obvious assumption. "Has something happened to one of my girls?" Gods, I was getting old. Apparently she only *looked* sixteen. She had to be in her twenties at least to be coaching high schoolers.

"That's what I'm here to prevent." Normally I would have flashed my badge to speed the process along, but that asshole Zalawski had confiscated it. I nodded toward the field. "Some dangerous people are planning to use my niece, Cori Holloway, against me. Her parents sent me here to get her to safety."

She tapped pen against clipboard, then barked, "Cori! Front and center!"

My heart picked up speed as one of the girls tossed a ball to another and jogged toward us. Gorgeous cheekbones and deeply tanned complexion came from her mother, but the honey-blond hair and brilliant blue eyes were all David's—and mine. I'd only seen her in pictures the past two years and couldn't believe how much she'd grown. She had to be almost sixteen now—the age where she'd start exhibiting a Fury's abilities, if she'd inherited any. I both hoped for and prayed against that. Cori's eyes zeroed in on me immediately, and she let out a squeal. "Aunt Riss! You're back!"

Her body slammed into mine and she nearly cracked my ribs in a bear hug. I breathed in the opposing scents of fruit and sweat, hugging her back more gently. I really *could* crack ribs.

"I knew you weren't dead!"

My hands tightened around her. "Dead?"

"Yeah, Mom said you were as dead to us as . . ." Her voice faltered, but we both knew what she'd been about to say.

Coach Jennings intruded on our reunion. "Well, at least I don't have to worry you're not who you claim."

Cori stepped back, keeping an arm around my waist. "Of course she's who she says she is. My Aunt Riss, the Fury. Chief Magical Investigator of Boston." She rolled her eyes. "I knew Mom was being figurative about the whole death thing. Your picture's plastered across the *Herald* every other month."

Goose bumps prickled as Nemesis and Nike stirred beneath my skin, and I stiffened. Something was wrong. "Scott?"

"They're here," he murmured, body alert but eyes on me.

"Who's here?" Cori peered around us. "Mom and Dad?"

"Cori, sweetie, you're going to have to trust me. Can you do that?"

She shot me a look that was pure teenager, one that clearly suggested I was an idiot.

"Okay, grab my hand and don't let go, no matter what happens. We've got to get away from your teammates right now. Trouble's coming."

Excitement glinted in her eyes. "Got it." She tossed her glove to Coach Jennings, then grabbed my hand with both of her own. "I won't let you down, Aunt Riss."

Gods send I didn't let *her* down in the moments to come. "Ready, Scott?"

He nodded, spun, and took off running at the same time I tapped into the magical energy beneath my feet. I thrust it into Cori's body all at once. No time for finesse.

Her eyes widened. "What *is* that?"

"Just stay with me!"

I burst into speed, jerking Cori along. Thanks to the magic pouring into her, she kept up easily. Fence posts blurred past us as we ran.

"Whoa, look how fast we're—" She cut herself off, hands clutching me more tightly as she noticed the three men facing off against Scott on the far side of the field. "Aunt Riss?"

"Just hold on to me, baby, and don't look at them." I pointed toward Scott's souped-up sports car a hundred feet away. "That's our getaway car. If something bad happens to Scott and me, you get in that car, drive *straight* to the Belly, and call your parents on the way. They'll send someone to meet you."

"But I don't have my license ye—"

"No *buts*. Your parents will need your help if something happens to me."

Her lips tightened mutinously, but she fell silent for the moment. Good enough. It'd have to be. Things weren't going as well for Scott as they should have gone.

I faltered a step when I saw that. Granted, Scott was one against three, but that shouldn't have mattered. Not for a Warhound.

Scott took a bad hit in one leg, but kept on swinging his fists—wait, why was he using his fists when he *never* went anywhere unarmed—oh shit . . . his opponents had actually managed to disarm him, not once but five times, judging by the glints of metal on the ground. He was able to knock one of the men to the ground while the other two converged on him. They moved with inhuman speed, ducking his lightning-quick attempts to hit them with equal swiftness. Something about that just wasn't right. Two more kicks slammed into Scott's abdomen, and his roar of pain echoed across the field. The sound cut to my heart and sent fear skittering through my veins.

"What the hell?" I muttered.

How could three mortals be kicking Scott's ass? They *had* to be mortal. I would have sensed otherwise in the morgue.

"Aunt Riss?"

But they obviously *weren't* mortal, senses be damned. Though nothing a Fury and Warhound combined couldn't handle. I just had to get to them first.

"Cori, get in the car. Now."

"But—"

"Now!" I grabbed her by the waist and tossed her over the chain-link fence separating us from the car, making sure magic cushioned her landing. "Start the car!"

She flailed, caught her balance, and threw a mutinous look over her shoulder, but obeyed, running toward the car as fast as she could. My pulse slowed slightly.

I shifted, beating newly formed wings and using them to half jump, half fly the fifty feet separating me from the fight. The ground rose up more quickly than expected. I lost my footing, stumbling halfway to the earth before regaining my balance. Damned lucky thing, too, because a leg zoomed past where my head had just been.

Growling, I rushed at the man who'd kicked at me, reaching for his leg to snap it. At least, that had been the plan. But neither he nor his leg were where I'd expected.

I gaped, twisting to find he'd somehow managed to get halfway behind me. "What *are* you?" Stupid question— like he was going to tell me. Nemesis and Nike responded to my call, bursting from lifeless tattoos to larger-than-life reality. I grabbed them both and tossed them straight toward my opponent's unprotected neck.

I turned to the man now grappling with Scott hand-to-hand. That just left the one on the groun—

Pain exploded in my knee. I clutched it as I dropped and the world faded to black. I came dangerously close to passing out, but Nemesis and Nike sent tendrils of magic my way, just enough so that I was able to force back the pain and open my eyes.

The third goon, the one I assumed had been out cold, turned his attention to Scott. He brandished a heavy aluminum bat, answering the question of what I'd been socked with. Good gods, that had *hurt*. These sons of bitches were far stronger than they had any right to be. And that just pissed me off. No time to waste for healing. Not if I wanted to keep Scott's mangy butt alive. I sucked in magical energy wildly, using it to cut the rest of my body off from the agony pulsing inside my knee. *Gonna pay for that later*. Gritting my teeth, I leapt on the goon's back.

Rage pounded, and I let it, channeling its all-fired furor and using it to focus. I teetered on the edge of the abyss separating Fury from Harpy, the biggest danger in allowing Rage to flow unchecked. But my current goal was more than enough to keep me on the straight and narrow.

Talons sprouted from my hands to match the half-furled wings along my back. I wrapped powerful legs around the goon's waist, raking claws up and down his arms. He screeched, an inhuman sound in the dying light of day, and then he did just what I wanted him to: focused on me, rather than the still-struggling Scott.

"That's it, asshole. You wanna play? I'm more than willing."

He spoke, the first time one of them had uttered a word during the entire attack. "Let's see just how willing you can become, Fury."

His hands twisted, coming to rest on my wrists and squeezing. At first I thought he meant to break them, but he merely wanted to ensure a solid grip. I snarled, trying to shake him off, but his strength was equal to my own. My heart skittered. I'd never faced another arcane as strong as me. Bad, bad, bad.

It got worse. A warm haze radiated outward from the man's hands, spreading along my arms and tickling my neck. I shivered, at first repulsed, but then the warmth wrapped me from head to toe, and I was lost.

My legs loosened and dropped to the ground. He turned, somehow managing to maintain his grip, and smiled, his entire face lighting up in the most glorious expression I'd ever seen. His face flickered, something that should have seemed odd but barely managed to penetrate my current fog. Great gods, how could I have had the audacity to attack this amazing specimen of arcane perfection? He was gorgeous, he was splendid, he was everything amazing and right in the world and I wanted only to please hi—

What the hell? I've never thought that about anyone. *Not even Scott!*

"You want to please me, don't you?"

His smirk reminded me of Tony Zalawski, and that was just the impetus I needed to regain sanity. I kept my gaze deliberately vacant, smiling like an idiot and purring my reply. "Oh, yes. Just tell me what to do."

He aimed my body in Scott's direction. "Kill your partner and then return to me. That will please me greatly."

Like hell I will. Aloud, I murmured, "As you wish," visions of *The Princess Bride* running through my head. His hands fell away, but the haze continued fluttering over my skin. Fortunately I hadn't succumbed completely, or Scott would be a dead man.

I covered the distance to Scott in ground-eating strides, calling out, "Duck!" at the very last instant. He immediately dropped. I flapped my wings and jumped, floating over his body and smacking straight into his opponent. The man's open-mouthed *O* of surprise was almost enough to make me smile.

No more Ms. Nice Fury. I made my first a killing blow, jabbing talons back and forth with blinding speed, hitting the man's windpipe directly. A sickening crunch hit my ears, but I kept my mind on the task at hand: putting these assholes down for the count.

The goon who'd mesmerized me screamed as his dying comrade fell to the ground, his eyes rolling back in his head and hissing noises emerging from his ruined throat for several seconds, until he fell silent and his limbs stopped thrashing. Scott jumped to his feet, spinning to deal with the screamer, but he'd already taken off across the field. My body tensed with worry until I realized he was heading away from Cori, toward a dark-colored sedan with engine still running.

I was surprised to see him abandoning his comrades, both living and dead, and then realized there was only the dead. Nemesis and Nike radiated smugness when I bent down to retrieve them from the puncture-ridden corpse on the ground. Their venom was fatal to any being, mortal *or* arcane, in large enough doses, and fang marks riddled the man's visible skin like Swiss cheese. My little lovelies didn't mess around.

Scott grunted behind me, and I whirled. He had hands pressed to each side, trying to stanch the blood flowing from open wounds. I shifted to partial Fury form so I could properly support his weight without Nemesis and Nike getting bitchy. Maybe it was my imagination, but he seemed to cling to me more than was strictly necessary. That, or wishful thinking. We hobbled toward the nearest opening in the fence surrounding the softball field and headed toward his car, trailing blood and corpses in our wake.

"That went better than I expected." Scott's voice came out breathy and racked with pain, but the fact that he spared the energy for humor reassured me.

"What, just because they didn't break out shotguns?"

He laughed, then winced and coughed. "Shit, Riss, don't do that."

"You started it," I pointed out, then leaned him against the passenger-side door.

Cori popped out of the backseat, eyes wide and teeth nibbling worry lines in her lower lip. "Oh, God. He's not— not gonna—you know."

She opened the passenger door as she stammered, showing that she was made of sterner stuff than her mother. More like her aunt. Both of us.

Scott managed an eye roll. "No, but *he* could really go for a bottle of whiskey right about now." A Jack D lover after my own heart. Which *almost* made up for the cigar habit.

His bravado reassured her. She helped me ease him into the passenger seat before returning to her own. Once I settled behind the wheel, adrenaline faded. My knee burst into agony once more, an agony that wouldn't be easily healed after what I'd just put it through. I clutched the steering wheel as the entire battle scene flickered through my mind. I processed every image, sound, and sensation, and then tried to make sense of the unfathomable. *Superhuman strength and speed. Check. Archaic patterns of speech. Check. Ability to hypnotize others with a single touch. Check.* My eyes widened.

"Son of a—" I spied Cori hanging on my every word, and swallowed the curse. "Those goons were Sidhe."

Scott paused in the act of bandaging his wounds using the first-aid kit he'd pulled out from under his seat. His body relaxed slightly at my pronouncement. "Oh, thank Anubis. For a second there, I thought I was losing my touch."

As if that will ever happen.

My eyes narrowed in sudden realization. "That Sidhe-born witch."

Scott arched a brow.

"The spirit inhabiting—" I caught sight of Cori in the rearview mirror again. "The spirit in the morgue. The Sidhe. She had to have known the mortals had at least some of her so-called brethren on their side. And she didn't warn us. That could have *so* gotten us killed."

He went back to patching his boo-boos. "Seems another little chat is in order."

"Oh, don't worry," I purred, and caressed the steering wheel as I zipped away from the carnage. "We're gonna chat all right. And she's not gonna like what I have to say, not one little bit."

Because if there's one cardinal rule in the arcane community it's this: Never piss off a Fury unless you kill her first—even if you're dead.

CHAPTER SIX

JESSICA POUNCED THE MOMENT WE STUM-
bled into the back room of Hounds of Anubis. "Oh my
God, there's blood on her. You said you were going to keep
her safe!" She yanked Cori from my side, where she'd been
helping support both Scott and me. We adjusted for her
sudden absence and watched as Jessica examined her now-
flustered daughter from head to toe.

"Mom, stop. I'm fine. Chill." She pushed at Jessica's
hands but didn't have much success. "Jesus, Mom, it's not
my blood!"

"Are you sure?" Jessica couldn't seem to help herself,
poking and prodding a few more spots on her daughter's
chest and abdomen. Once reassured, she narrowed her eyes
and shot Cori one of those mom looks, barking a sharp,
"Language!"

Cori flushed, nodded, and turned to her father. He went

through a similar ritual to assure himself she was all in one piece, although he was way more subtle about it.

Jessica turned on me, eyes flashing and fists clenched. "I want to know what's going on, and I want to know *now*. What evil has your filthy magic brought about *this* time?" Her mouth twisted around the word *magic* as if it pained her.

Scott slipped his hand into mine and his eyes glowed with reassurance, both of which made me feel as if I'd come home. No harm in accepting his strictly platonic support for a minute or two. Or ten. I clutched his hand gratefully and counted to five before responding. "If you will recall, Jessica, I didn't bring about the evil last time. Your sister's ex-boyfriend did." Or at least, that's what we all had assumed back then . . . Cori leaned forward, soaking in my every word. Hell. I wasn't even sure how much of the truth they'd told her. Still, Jessica had opened this can of worms. She could damned well live with the consequences.

"Not to mention, this case is linked to hers. Would you have me ignore the chance to find out what happened to Vanessa? Or would you rather I walk away and forget the whole thing ever happened?"

Emotions warred across her features, ranging from anger and bitterness to hope and then, finally, determination. "Of *course* you can't forget the whole thing happened. No more than I can. This—whatever *this* is—may help you find Nessa?"

I wanted to close my eyes against the hope in her voice. By now, most people would have given up hope of finding Vanessa alive and realized the most likely outcome at this late date was meting out justice. Justice, and maybe a little vengeance. Fury-style.

Then again, Jessica was a skip, one of those members of an arcane-talented family who had no magical abilities herself, and she could never truly understand what being a

Fury was like. David could be considered a skip, as well, because there were no male Furies, but he could certainly pass those traits on—which meant the odds of Cori inheriting a Fury's gifts were about as high as it got without being absolutely certain. *Time enough to face* that *mess in the future.*

"Yes, the case I'm working now—the case some very powerful people are trying to make sure I quit working— may lead us to the answers we need. I can't tell you everything right now, but Nessa's name has come up several times in this investigation." No less than the truth. "Which is only making me more determined to dig up the secrets someone has tried very hard to keep buried. I want to find out what happened to her just as much as you do."

Her face grew haggard, and for once she didn't argue. "I know you do." I nearly fainted, since that was the closest to saying something nice to me she'd gotten in years. "What—what can we do to help you?"

I bit back the sarcastic comment tickling my lips. Old habits die hard. "For now, you can stay here and keep safe. The fewer people they have to use against me, the more likely I can crack this case." Her eyes grew shadowed. Cori's lips tightened again, and even David seemed disappointed. It was obvious they all wanted to do *something.*

I pointed toward the office door. "There's a computer in there. Why don't you dig up any old articles you can find relating to Nessa's disappearance? Also, see if you can round up all the stories on the recent arcane disappearances, or unsolved arcane murders. I'm starting to think we *were* all wrong three years ago."

Jessica tilted her head. "Wrong about what?"

"Maybe Nessa's asshole ex had nothing to do with her disappearance after all. Way too many arcanes have vanished lately to be mere coincidence."

Despite my halfhearted attempts to continue casting

Dre in the role of supervillain, the evidence was pointing elsewhere. Besides the fact that no Mandate had gone out when Vanessa disappeared three years earlier, something else supported my growing suspicions. While Sidhe only had to *see* a picture of someone to cast a glamour, full-on, shape-shifting glamourie was another story entirely. They actually had to *touch* the person they wanted to impersonate while the person still breathed. There was also a time limit on using that person's likeness, unless they personally killed the individual and consumed a portion of that person's life force. I *highly* doubted any Sidhe would be stupid enough to murder a Fury and then beg another for help. We could make even the Afterlife a living hell for those who murdered our sisters. Which meant that the Sidheborn woman whose corpse bore Nessa's likeness had to have come into contact with her at some point. And that meant Nessa had, at least recently, still been alive. Waiting for us to find her.

"GET AWAY FROM ME, YOU HELL-SPAWNED bitch!"

Kiara bared her teeth at me, more in amusement than threat. She rolled her eyes and turned a pointed look on Scott. He bit back a smile, scooting close and pressing me onto the empty bed.

"Hell-spawned *son* of a bitch."

They laughed, but neither backed down. I grunted and finally gave in with ill grace. *Healing myself would be a hell of a lot easier. And less painful.*

But I'd made that impossible by using magic to separate myself from the pain of my injured knee, rather than immediately healing it, or simply fighting through the pain without touching the wound with magic. A Fury's ability to use her Amphisbaena to jack up her own superhuman healing had a very short shelf life. Either she healed the injury right away, or she dealt with the fallout. Not that I could have chosen otherwise and lived with myself. Scott would have died while I took the time to heal my injury, all just to avoid a little—okay, a hell of a lot of—pain and a potential lifelong limp. And that said more about my latent feelings for him than I wanted.

Being here, back in the bedroom where we'd spent so many nights together, had me longing for things I couldn't have. Frustration colored my voice even hotter. "What are you waiting for? Either get me a shot of Jack or get on with it already!"

Kiara muttered under her breath in her mother's tongue, one I could have understood if I'd bothered to expend the magical energy. But since I had a pretty good idea she was cursing both me and my lineage, that would have been a wasted effort.

Her hands were gentle as they touched the black-and-blue mess my knee had become, belying the curses and caustic glances she threw my way. Then again, Kiara had always reminded me more of a kitten than a hound when it came to temperament. Definitely the odd puppy out in her family, and the main reason she helped her mother run the shop rather than taking direct part in the merc business like most of her brothers and sisters. She moved my knee side to side, hands still gentle, but I hissed and tried to rise up off the bed as stars flashed in front of my eyes.

"Sorry." She stopped manhandling my knee, turning to the basket of magical odds and ends at her side. Not exactly a full-fledged magical Healer, like Oracles or Druids, she could still pull off some damned impressive tricks with that magical first-aid kit she'd concocted. I'd seen her save lives that might otherwise have been lost.

The pain faded to a more bearable level, and I relaxed my body. Scott loosened his grip on my shoulders, fingers beginning to knead rather than press downward. "Mac's in the office, getting your family set up. He seemed impressed. And trust me, that's damned hard to do."

I nodded. David and Jess ran their own software empire now. They had started out as programmers themselves, and now they ruled the boards of several companies.

"It seems like they're teaching Cori to follow in their footsteps?" Scott asked, his head inclined.

His soft tone and firm touch helped distract me from the pain of his sister's ministrations. "Yeah, though she's usually much more interested in soft*ball* than soft*ware*. Still, she knows a hell of a lot more about those damned things than I do."

I could hear the grin in his voice. "Careful or you'll sound like my father."

My eyes fluttered closed. Damn, his hands felt like magic. "Didn't use to hate them so much. Stupid police and their even stupider paperwork."

"You've come a long way, baby." Oh gods. He'd called me *baby* again. "From mere arcane liaison to Chief Magical Investigator. Can't you pass off the paperwork to the peons?"

That had me snorting. "What peons? I have a hard enough time getting the mundanes on the force to cooperate during investigations. No way any of them will serve as my secretary."

"No other Furies to help?"

"No go. There are barely enough Furies to handle the region's caseload. Sure can't pull one off cases to act as a glorified typist."

"And what about other arcanes?"

I would have tossed him one of Cori's *Are you stupid?* looks if he could have seen my face. "You kidding? We're lucky we got the mundanes to accept Furies as permanently attached liaisons. Shit, it took forever for me to convince them to let a few of us become full-fledged officers. No way in hell we're getting other arcanes on the force so soon."

His voice grew disgruntled. "That's discrimination." It was something that half mortals like Scott and me struggled with, never quite fitting in fully with either the arcane or mundane worlds. It was a wrong Scott had always been passionate about fighting. In fact, before he'd taken over the family business, I'd thought he might become one of the rare arcanes who actually won over enough mortals to serve in public office. But that'd been before he'd thrown over his high ideals (not to mention me) for his family and the almighty dollar . . .

"*You* know it, *I* know it, *they* know it. But the Time of Troubles—the War—is too fresh in most people's minds. Too many mortals die—"

Blinding hot pain flared in my knee, and then—nothing. Sweet, blissful nothing.

"There." Kiara wiped her hands on an unused bandage and eyed her work with satisfaction. "That should hold you till you can see a real Healer. Just don't overdo the running and fighting thing, okay?"

I touched the soft white cloth wrapped around my knee. A heavenly scent wafted upward, making me sigh with pleasure. "What's in that stuff?"

"A bit of this and that." She pursed her lips. "I mean it about the no running and fighting, Marissa. The spell on those bandages has a limit, and the more you exert your knee, the sooner it will wear off. And then the pain will be back full force, and if I'm not nearby you're shit out of luck."

I waved her warning off. "Yeah, yeah, I get it. No acting like Superfury for a while." Scott's hand was still on my back, lingering when it didn't need to. Suddenly self-conscious, I pushed myself away. My eyes widened when I stood and was rewarded with absolutely zero pain. "Wow, that's some good shit."

Kiara snorted. "Indeed. Now, if you two will excuse me . . ." She disappeared from Scott's bedroom before we could react.

"I can't believe she just left us alone in your bedroom."

"She knows there's nothing to worry about."

The words cut more sharply than I expected. "Yeah, well, this *nothing* had better take herself to bed. Good night."

I stepped toward the door, but his hands moved to my arms and he whirled me roughly. "Dammit, Riss, you know that's not what I—oh, screw it."

His lips crushed down on mine, and fire exploded inside my body. I moaned, arms clutching his to keep from falling. *This is a mistake. We shouldn't—oh, screw it!* His mouth opened slightly, and I took advantage of the opportunity, thrusting my tongue inside and tasting, long and deep. He tasted as good as—better than—ever, a mixture of masculine scents and the slightly feminine berry-flavored candy he sucked on to stave off cigarette cravings. He'd quit that nasty habit for me, and the evidence that he'd kept it up sent pleasure radiating straight to my belly. Then again, that could have been the sheer lust our kiss ignited.

Then, as suddenly as he'd begun it, he ended the kiss with another curse, shoving me away and stalking toward the bedroom's oversized window. At first, I thought he was pissed at me, and that had me shoving my hands on my hips and scowling. After all, *I* hadn't been the one to jam my tongue in his delicious mouth . . . Okay, that wasn't helping settle the desire overloading my system. My eyes narrowed in sudden realization. That desire was an obviously mutual feeling. Which meant he still wanted me. And now we both knew it.

His words echoed my thought perfectly. "Don't ever say you're nothing to me. You should damned well know better."

I considered questioning that statement, seeing as how, after what I'd thought was an amazing eighteen months together, he'd chosen both his family and money over me, but now didn't seem the time to dredge up old grudges. Time enough for that later.

"I—okay. Maybe I'm not exactly nothing to you, but what'd you expect me to think when you said that?"

He ran an impatient hand through his shaggy hair, and then turned to face me. "When I said Kiara knows there's nothing to worry about, I meant because she'd love it if we got back together."

My mouth snapped shut on the comeback I'd managed to cobble together as his words sank in. And the warm fuzzies they generated had my cheeks blooming with color. "Could have fooled me. I thought she hated me."

He rolled his eyes. "Oh yeah, she hates you so much she's nagged me to call you at least once a week since you left."

That had my mouth popping wide open again. "She— did?"

"Yeah. Called me an idiot for letting you go like that."

"Then why . . ." I jerked my mouth shut again. So much for not dredging up old grudges.

"I had my reasons," he said. "I still do, so this is prob-ably a huge mistake." He approached me again. I wasn't sure what to expect, which made it all the more surprising when he caressed my hair in an achingly familiar gesture.

He was right. Things were too unresolved between us. So much time had passed, so many bitter things had been said. I thought I had put it all behind me. Being with him again . . . it was hard to know where we stood, but it was easy to see that nothing had really changed. He was work-ing for the man who I once thought had something to do with Vanessa's disappearance, who could *still* be involved at some level.

But Scott had been showing that he wanted me back in his bed with a dozen little looks and touches since getting over his initial anger. He'd never been afraid to go after what he wanted, one of the things that most attracted me to him, and he didn't hesitate to draw me into his arms once more.

That fact was enough to have me surrender to the desire still thrumming along every nerve ending. Gods, it'd been so long since I'd been touched like this. Years since I'd been intimate with a man—with him. And I found myself throwing caution to the wind. Who cared if we both regretted it later? For now, we wanted each other.

He nudged me toward his bed, and I went gladly. Heat flared between us, a slow, steady burn that flashed into a firestorm as skin touched skin and our breathing grew ragged. His hands slipped beneath my T-shirt and zoomed straight toward my black satin bra. I gasped as he caressed the sensitive skin through the insubstantial fabric, somehow driving me crazier than if he'd been touching bare flesh. When his amazing fingers finally *did* skim beneath the satin, I arched my back and grabbed on to his hair. A dozen sensations danced across my skin, a dozen memories of other times we'd been locked in heated embraces in this very bed flashed through my mind. The man making love to me with his hands always knew how to touch me, both physically and emotionally, never failed to make me feel in a way no other man could.

Oh, shit. I still care about him.

That had me scrambling out from under him and off the bed so fast my head spun. My knee trembled, although Kiara's remedy worked as promised and the pain remained masked. Scott flipped himself over and into a sitting position, face excruciatingly blank.

"What, it wasn't good for you, baby?" The derision in his voice could have made me cry if I let it.

"This *is* a mistake. One we can't repeat."

My hands had the door half open when he got off his parting shot. "Run away, Riss. Just like you always do."

Tension clenched my body, and I considered turning to argue. But that would be pointless. He was right, but I didn't give a damn. Sometimes, running was the only smart thing to do. I wouldn't—I couldn't—let him break my heart again. Being immortal didn't mean being indestructible.

CHAPTER SEVEN

THE DOOR TO MURPHY COMMAND CENTRAL jerked open before my fingers could settle on the knob. My pulse leapt and I assumed an aggressive stance, halfway to shifting when brain caught up to instinct and cataloged the person on the other side of the doorway as friend rather than foe.

Sean Murphy lifted both hands in an *I'm unarmed* gesture. His nostrils flared and his eyes, the color of old whiskey—the darkest of all the Murphys—narrowed in an oddly fierce expression. Before I could ask him what was wrong, though, he leaned against the doorjamb, his stretched tank top outlining the chiseled perfection of well-cut abs and chest in a way that made me uncomfortably aware of just how much Scott's little brother had grown up.

"Where you running off to so fast?"

His words unknowingly echoed the last his brother

had thrown at me. I struggled not to take the sudden flash of Rage out on him. *Innocent bystander, Riss.* "I need to check on something real quick."

He glanced over my shoulder to the hallway leading to the building's residential area, where most of the Murphys made like one big happy family in a warren of cushy apartments. "And big brother isn't shadowing your every move?"

His voice teetered on the edge separating humor from bitterness, catching me off-guard. Two years ago Sean had all but worshipped Scott, no doubt one of the reasons he'd formed a mild crush on me. I'd never embarrassed him enough to call him on that infatuation, but now I couldn't help speculating. Had my breakup with Scott somehow prompted the mix of hope and frustration seething across his features?

I kept my tone light. "Nah, I'm a big girl. I can take a walk by myself if I want."

His lips, narrower than Scott's but no less attractive, curved upward. "I could keep you company, if you like."

"Maybe some other time. I need to do this on my own."

He stepped forward with a suddenly intense expression on his face. One of his hands settled on my shoulder, sending my pulse skittering madly for no reason I could put name to. *When the hell did little Sean get so damned hot, anyway?* Okay, no reason I *wanted* to put name to.

"Riss, I know it's none of my concern, but I'd hate to see you get hurt again. You deserve better, you know?"

I struggled to fight hormones that had no reason to be stirring, trying to convince myself they were all by-products of the heavy petting session I'd just walked away from. No way on earth did I find Scott's *little brother* in the slightest way sexy. "Ah, sorry. Deserve better?"

Brown eyes darkened even further. "Better than *him*. You have to know how I feel about y—"

Oh, hell. This conversation had just bypassed uncomfortable and zoomed straight to creepy. "Ah, sorry, Sean. Really gotta go!" I broke away and scurried toward the door to Hounds of Anubis, ignoring his attempted protest and slamming the door open and shut with dizzying speed. My typical luck—which was to say, crappy—held, and the last person I wanted to see was the first person to catch sight of me as I made my escape. Liana Murphy, Scott's mother. Panic set in fast when her eyes met mine from across the store and she started walking my way. *Shit, she's gonna know we made out!* Of *course* she was going to know. Her son's scent was all over me, and she was a Hound.

She touched her left cheek to my right, then vice versa. "Good to see you, Marissa." My mouth dropped open. "Close your mouth, dear. Wouldn't want the flies to get in."

I obeyed automatically, much as everyone else who came into contact with Liana. "Wha—how—good to see you, too."

She took my arm in hers and led me toward the entrance. "Molly, mind the store. Marissa and I are going for a stroll."

Suspicion immediately dawned. No wonder she was being so nice. She just wanted to get me into a back alley so she could dispose of me without witnesses.

"Worried, dear?" She closed the door behind us with a snap. "You need not be. You may have fooled everyone else, but I'm not so easily snookered."

Snookered? I mouthed the word, having trouble picturing it in the elegant woman's vocabulary. Then again, she *had* been married to Morgan Murphy a damned long time now.

I tried to bluff my way through it. "No idea what you're talking about, Liana."

She tugged me along the cobblestoned walkway, deeper into the Belly. "Of course you do, silly girl. You still care about him. And he still cares about you."

My mouth dropped open so far, every fly for a mile around had the perfect opportunity to make good her earlier admonition. I focused on the dingy bricks at our feet, trying to figure out her angle. She had to have one. Why else would we be strolling along the street, arm in arm, like we were bosom buddies?

I drew to a halt, jerking my arm away from hers, eyes narrowing. "Where are you taking me?"

She faced me, biting her lip nervously. "Andre Carrington wants to see you. Morgan asked me to bring you by."

Rage welled. I had to fight even harder than usual to push it back to a manageable level. "And you were going to lead me there like a lamb to slaughter? Did you think I would just go along meekly?"

Impatience flickered in her eyes. "Now, when would anyone make the mistake of thinking *you* meek? Use your brain, girl."

Unease settled in my stomach. "He threatened you somehow, didn't he? That son of a—"

She gripped my hand in one of her own. "Calm down, Marissa, or neither one of us will survive five minutes inside. And, yes, he strongly *suggested* I bring you there."

"As if I'll just let you drag me there?"

Her hand ground the bones of my knuckles painfully. "Could you fucking shut up and listen for once in your life? Everything's not always about *you*, Marissa. Haven't you noticed that a certain Murphy has been mysteriously absent the past two years?"

Profanity from the supremely elegant Liana Murphy?

Now *that* was a first. I frowned as her question sank in. Suddenly, things clicked into place. "He blackmailed Morgan into taking him on as a client. That's why Scott took over the business instead of—" My eyes widened. "Instead of Amaya." Amaya Murphy, Scott's older sister, the Warhound Morgan had been grooming as his successor until . . . until she apparently vanished two years ago. All of Scott's other close relatives were present and accounted for. Amaya's disappearance was pretty much a news flash to me, since nobody had bothered to share that tidbit. I wondered how the hell they'd managed to keep a lid on that bit of gossip. Surely I would have heard it by now if it had become common knowledge.

Relief that Scott hadn't chosen money over me conflicted with betrayal that he'd never confided in me. How could he *not* have told me about Amaya's being held captive? That would have changed *everything* two years ago. I never would have broken up with him if I'd known that Dre Carrington had blackmailed his family into protecting him from my Rage. "Where is he holding her?"

Liana's hand dropped away, and she aged decades in the space of seconds. "If we knew that, she'd be home and he'd be dead. He has a sorceress on his payroll, concealing Amaya from us entirely."

Guilt clawed at my heart, guilt and Rage. "He wanted you all to protect him because he thought I'd find something. Some sort of proof that he *was* involved in Vanessa's disappearance. And he knew that the only mercs who had even a snowball's chance in hell of staying my hand . . ."

"Were Scott's family." She reached out and took my arm again. This time I didn't pull away. "I'm sorry, Marissa. There's so much I want to say, so much you need to hear, but Dre didn't give us much time to get there. He claims he has something you'll want. Something that can help you."

A bitter laugh exploded from my lips. "Something that

can help *me*, or keep me from killing him?" I zeroed in on her eyes, which were truly the windows to the soul for Warhounds. Few of them could lie outright once you knew them with more than passing familiarity. "Is he the one who's trying to kill me? Can you be sure this isn't some trap? Just tell me—did he take Vanessa?"

Liana hesitated, making me wonder if I was going to have to beat it out of her, but she shook her head. "I don't know. But Morgan and Scott don't believe so. Not directly." I started to rant, but she raised her voice above mine. "They do believe he knows something, which is the reason they have been keeping close watch over him."

I stumbled when she drew me to an abrupt stop several moments later. A monstrosity constructed of steel, glass, and many-layered spells crouched above us, taking up an entire city block. Trust Dre Carrington to choose the most expensive—and gaudy—building in the entire Belly to call home.

"Dre Carrington *owns* the most expensive, gaudy building in the entire Belly."

Liana's dry comment indicated I'd spoken the last thought out loud. Shit. I'd have to watch that bad habit once we were inside. Being flustered was no reason to let down my guard. Especially considering the fact that we were about to walk into a viper's nest.

A snake in sheep's clothing whisked the door open before we reached it, bowing and smiling us inside the grand entranceway. His elegant tuxedo-like uniform and dapper doorman's cap didn't deceive me. He walked with deadly grace. Dre Carrington surrounded himself with trained killers, even those working as doormen.

The concierge at the front desk recognized Liana and buzzed us into a swanky private elevator before she even said anything. Crushed velvet fabric draped the walls, and a cushioned bench took up the entire rear wall of the spacious room. Another elegantly clad employee whose name tag read *Doreen* was all smiles as she urged us to make ourselves comfortable on the bench. Good ol' Doreen didn't fool me. The tingle of a spell swept across my skin, and I stiffened. Her body tensed as well, and sharp eyes zeroed in on my tats.

I let a slightly feral smile touch my lips but kept control of my emotions, remaining in partial Fury form only. The spell had been a simple one checking for weapons. No need to go batshit on anyone.

Not yet.

The sorceress not-quite-disguised as an elevator operator pressed several buttons, the elevator doors swished shut, and we began whisking upward at a dizzying rate of speed. Yet another attempt on Dre Carrington's part to put people off-kilter before they came into his presence. No doubt he believed it gave him an advantage, security-wise. Idiot. If he thought parlor tricks were going to keep me from ripping him limb from limb should I deem it necessary, he was an even bigger fool than I suspected. No matter *how* many thinly veiled bodyguards he had crawling around this place.

Rage stirred inside, a reminder that a very large part of me would just *love* to indulge in that little fantasy. Even if that day's events were suggesting that he might not be the mastermind behind Vanessa's disappearance. He was still an asshole who had kidnapped Scott's sister.

Liana patted my hand, smile fading when I met her glance. She twitched her head slightly in the direction of the doors. Telling me to get myself under control before they opened. Easier said than done, but I made an effort.

A chime tinkled merrily seconds later, and the doors zoomed open. The penthouse suite, of course, made evident by the bank of floor-to-ceiling windows greeting us when we stepped outside the elevator, not to mention several impressive skylights that cut through the ceiling overhead. I whistled softly. Mortals just several city blocks away would *kill* for this amazing view.

I clenched my fists. For all I knew, Dre Carrington *had* killed for it.

Liana clutched my arm. The fact that she knew me well enough to sense my seething frustration both pleased and dismayed me. A short, slender man with dark hair and pale blue eyes stepped forward with an officious expression on his face.

"Mrs. Murphy, Inspector Holloway. Thank you for your promptness." He spoke with a crisp British accent and smiled an achingly polite smile my way. "I'm Alexander Denton, Andre Carrington's *personal* assistant. Mr. Carrington is wrapping up a videoconference now and will be right with you."

Sure enough, a nearby door opened, and out stepped the very rat-bastard we were here to see.

His physical features hadn't changed in the years since I'd seen him last, but that was no surprise. Sun-kissed, perfectly bronzed skin, set off by deep green eyes. Golden blond hair fell past his shoulders in soft waves, styled in a careless rock star 'do he'd no doubt paid hundreds of dollars to obtain. Medium height, medium but muscular build. Gorgeous in the way only an Orpheus could be. The original Orpheus was hailed far and wide in ancient Greece as a divinely gifted poet and musician, and his songs could make immortals weep. He won back his wife from Death himself thanks to those magic hands and voice of his—and lost her again when he became overconfident and ignored the warning not to look back as they fled the underworld. His descendants carried on that family tradition of arrogance.

Dre raised both hands in a gesture of surprised pleasure when he caught sight of us. I barely choked back a snort.

Yeah right. He'd known the exact *second* we'd entered his building.

"Liana, so nice to see you again." He made a kiss-kiss gesture in the air, then turned his killer green eyes on me. His sense of self-preservation kicked in enough that he didn't bother with the kiss-kiss. "Marissa, you look stunning as always. I'm so pleased you could stop by for a visit."

"I would say the same, Dre, but we'd both know I was lying." Liana's fingers dug into my skin. I focused on the pain so as not to beat the living snot out of him. "You look even *more* stunning than usual."

Amusement flicked across the inhumanly perfect lines of his face. He knew what I'd really meant, but as long as I played the game, things would go smoothly. Which was probably a good thing, considering the sheer number of arcane beings I sensed in the rooms around us.

"Please, step this way. Would either of you like a drink?" At our—okay, Liana's—polite refusal (no way I would let my guard down enough to drink in his presence, not even for Jack), he ushered us into a room filled with priceless antiques and musical instruments. The tools of an Orpheus's trade.

"Make yourselves comfortable." More a command than an invitation. His teeth widened in a shark's smile, one I wanted to smash into itty-bitty pieces. "Liana, I think you'll be happy to hear my proposal."

She arched a brow. "Proposal? What could I possibly offer that you want?"

"Not you." He nodded at me. "Marissa is the one I wish to barter with. But the commodity at hand is one very dear to you, Liana darling."

"Amaya," she murmured, as if I hadn't already guessed.

"Yes, the lovely, loyal Amaya. Since time enough has

passed that I believe certain individuals might be more amenable to actually discussing things rather than, shall we say, shooting first, now seems the perfect time to make my proposal."

Liana shot me a stricken look, eyes pleading for me to maintain my cool. Shit, you'd think Furies never served as negotiators in sticky situations the way she kept poking and prodding me.

"Dre, *darling*, I would be happy to hear your proposal. Just vow by all the gods and goddesses that you had absolutely nothing to do with Vanessa's disappearance." Though such a vow didn't hold any magical weight, in a world where gods and goddesses existed—and kept close tabs on their arcane children—few of us were stupid enough to swear in their names lightly.

His eyes darkened again, but this time the expression seemed sad rather than angry. "I can't make that vow, Marissa."

I tensed, preparing to leap to my feet. Liana didn't even bother trying to hold me back.

He rushed on. "Not because I was directly involved by any means. I can vow that here and now. But I'm afraid that former—business partners of mine *could* be responsible. And, by drawing their attention to her, I may have played an indirect role in her disappearance."

I counted to five, trying to get a handle on the Rage skimming beneath my surface emotions. "What do you mean, you drew their attention to her?"

Dre licked his lips. "Ahhh, well, I confess I handled the breakup rather poorly. My therapist claims that confession is good for the soul, so I can admit that now." Narcissus had nothing on any Orpheus. Dre Carrington especially.

"I may have—traded—some information about Vanessa and her Fury duties to an associate of mine, who may in turn have passed that on to others down the line. Because soon after our discussion, she vanished."

My legs twitched with the need to leap off the sofa, but I fought it down. "You *may* have. They *may* have. I don't have time for *may have*s and *shoulda, coulda, woulda*s. Is there concrete information you can offer me? Because, after the shitty day I've had, busting through you *and* your guard dogs to take Amaya back is starting to sound more like fun than work."

Liana's lips parted, but this time I was the one to grab her hand and squeeze. She remained silent.

He laughed, the musical sound very similar to the elevator's chime. "Never one to quibble, are you? Very well. I knew you'd never believe I hadn't done harm to Vanessa three years ago, so I took out a little insurance to keep myself safe." He nodded toward Liana. "Amaya is unharmed and happy enough, I can assure you. She could return to the family fold today if you promise me one thing, Marissa."

Liana leaned forward, eyes intense.

"And what promise is that, Dre?"

"To do no harm to me or mine from this day forward, and to make sure no other Furies do harm to me or mine for any wrongdoings we may have committed."

My mouth dropped open, and even Liana looked surprised. "Are you completely insane? I can't make that promise." What was he playing at? Why was he coming to me with this now, after he'd had Amaya captive for at least two years?

He shrugged. "Then Amaya remains a guest of mine indefinitely. And I won't give you the information I recently acquired. Pity. I think you would have found it quite intriguing. And useful."

This time, I counted to ten. And then added an extra five for good measure. "What information?"

He shook his head. "Nuh-uh-uh, Marissa. No promise, no information."

I blew out a breath. "How do I know the information is worth the price you ask?"

"Come now, isn't the freedom of your lover's sister alone worth that promise?"

"Ex-lover," I corrected automatically. After the past three years I'd spent loathing Dre, I couldn't believe I was seriously considering making that vow. Then again, now that I knew there were much more sinister forces than Dre behind Vanessa's abduction, it didn't seem like such a large price to pay. Especially in light of the fact that I couldn't see Dre going to all the trouble of blackmailing the Murphys into protecting him from me and then making them bring me here if he wasn't damned sure of himself.

Tiny beads of sweat broke out on his brow the longer my silence continued. That almost cheered me up enough to smile. Instead, I let out a huge sigh and rolled my eyes. "Fine. I can vow to do no harm to you or yours from this day forward as it relates to Vanessa's disappearance, and to make sure no other Furies do harm to you or yours for any wrongdoings committed regarding the same incident. That's the best I can manage."

"Done." He agreed so quickly, I knew that was what he'd hoped for all along. And I'd made it a cakewalk for him.

I gritted my teeth. "Now, the information."

"First, the vow."

Jeez, this guy was relentless. And smart enough to know I wouldn't break such a promise, once made.

"I, Marissa Holloway, Fury of the Sisterhood, do vow before all the gods and goddesses to do no harm to Andre Carrington, Orpheus, or any of his brethren or followers, for any of the wrongdoings they may have committed regarding the disappearance of Vanessa Turner, sister

Fury. I also vow to ensure that my sister Furies maintain the same vow, from now hereafter, as regards the same incident. This vow is conditional upon the full and immediate release of Amaya Murphy, along with the information Andre Carrington claims to have regarding Vanessa Turner's disappearance."

The moment I choked the last few words out, I dropped Dre's hand and stepped away. "The information?"

He moved to an old rolltop desk across the room, drawing something out and approaching me. I frowned but accepted it without complaint. An ultramodern PDA.

"What do I need a BlueBerry for?"

"BlackBerry."

"Whatever. How's *this* going to help?"

"It's a specially spelled BlackBerry with a magical GPS. It's keyed to Vanessa." His eyes softened when he said her name. "I had it made back before—before the breakup. Her duties as a Fury were so dangerous, and I just wanted . . ." His voice trailed away. He cleared his throat. "Anyway, that will lead you straight to her once activated."

My vision grew hazy. "And you just *now* thought to give this to me?"

He took several quick steps backward. "It has a limited range or I would have contacted you sooner. You have to be within five miles of the spell's target. I've kept a close watch on it for three years now, and it's never indicated she's been near enough to locate. Not since the night she disappeared."

Sheesh, he'd been even more of a stalker than I suspected. "So, what's changed?"

"The investigators I hired to find her, or at least some trace of what happened to her, have finally turned up a solid lead. The lead ties her to those former associates of mine I mentioned. It's not much, but it does give you a solid area to start searching."

Something stirred in the back of my mind. A memory of the conversation with the Sidheborn spirit. "Let me guess. It's in Western Mass."

He nodded, surprise flickering. "How'd you know?"

"Let's just say, a little birdie told me something earlier today, but I never guessed it was a clue to Vanessa's actual whereabouts. Hell, up until recently, I believed she was dead."

His eyes fluttered. "And that I'd killed her."

The matter-of-fact tone oddly embarrassed me. "Well, yeah."

He stalked across to me and met my gaze unflinchingly. "I, Andre Carrington, Orpheus, do vow before all the gods and goddesses that I did not kill Vanessa Turner, Fury of the Sisterhood, and further that I did not abduct her or cause her to be abducted, and still further that I have never physically harmed Vanessa Turner or caused her to be harmed."

The passion in his voice, along with the unasked-for vow, took me completely by surprise. *Oh, hell. The bastard's actually telling the truth.* Further proof I'd royally screwed things up.

Rather than acknowledging either of those things, I simply waved the BlueBerry—BlackBerry—back and forth. "How does this thing work?"

His fingers tapped over the tiny machine's even tinier buttons, showing me how to activate the tracking spell, and also showing me how to retrieve several documents containing all the information his private investigators had come up with. Granted, it wasn't much, but it was more than I currently had to work with.

Once satisfied I could work the magically enhanced machine on my own, I shoved it into a pocket. "Now, then, that brings us to Amaya."

His vulnerability disappeared so completely, I wondered

if I had imagined it. The cocky smirk was back full throttle. For once, though, I didn't have to fight back the urge to rearrange his facial features. He touched an intercom on the wall. "Amaya, sweetie, come see your mother."

I glanced at Liana, mouthing *Sweetie?*, but she appeared none the wiser than myself. We waited in front of the sofa, she fidgeting more than me, until the door whisked open and someone I'd never seen before ent—

Wait. That's not—that can't be Amaya.

An ebony-skinned woman with caramel-streaked black hair and striking silver eyes sashayed into the room, her tall, lithe form garbed in uber-feminine clothes that hugged her curves, of which there were many. Her face had been expertly made up with every form of cosmetics known to mankind, so much it should have appeared clownish, but didn't. This woman was absolutely, amazingly glamorous. The Amaya Murphy I remembered had been a tomboy in the extreme. Pretty, but nothing spectacular.

She moved first to Dre, wrapping her arms around him and giving him a very friendly peck on the cheek. *Too* friendly.

Liana thought so, too. "Amaya?"

She gave her mother a puzzled look. "Oh, hello there. Do I know you?"

Liana staggered as if she'd been struck. I narrowed my eyes and took a step forward. "Dre, what have you—"

The warning in my voice came across loud and clear. He placed his arm around Amaya's waist possessively. "It's not as bad as it looks."

"I think you have no idea just how bad it looks. Are you or are you not sleeping with her?"

Liana may have discussed her son's love life with few qualms, but that question had her amber eyes flaring and her teeth bared. Dre finally picked up on just how precarious his situation was.

"That came later, long after her recovery."

"*What* recovery?" My voice came out in a good approximation of a Warhound's growl.

"I never snatched Amaya, any more than I did Vanessa. She showed up on my doorstep, half-starved and out of her mind, just days before I hired the other Murphys as extra security. At first, I had no clue who she was, only that she intrigued me and was almost as beautiful as me."

I rolled my eyes, but he ignored my derision.

"I hired the best doctors and nurses to bring her back to health, along with investigators to figure out who she was and what had happened to her. Even with the best care money could buy, she has never been exactly the same. At least, not the same as how others have described her previous personality."

Liana recovered enough to approach her daughter. "Amaya? It's me. Your mother."

Amaya tilted her head, resembling her mother to a heartbreaking degree, which only seemed more tragic since her eyes didn't hold any hint of recognition. "My mother?"

Liana's maternal instincts might have gone into overdrive, but my screaming Fury's intuition would have blown them out of the water. "So, when you identified Amaya as the misplaced Murphy heir, you decided to take advantage of the situation."

He inclined his head without the slightest hint of shame. "What did it matter to Amaya? She had only vague knowledge of her past. And by then, she and I had developed . . . feelings . . . for each other." He squeezed her hand, and she smiled adoringly into his eyes.

I wanted to puke. "Did your sorceress ever offer any theories as to how her memories came to be altered?"

His expression grew thoughtful. "No, at least none that made any sense. She mentioned something about her physical coloring seeming not quite right based on earlier pictures of Amaya, but that didn't make any sense."

My heart thundered in my ears. "Her—coloring—wasn't quite right?"

He nodded. "She said her eyes are darker than in the pictures, but that could be poor photography. The streaks in her hair are much lighter, her skin a deeper shade of black."

Liana frowned, regarding Amaya with a hawklike stare. "My God, he's right. I just assumed her hair had been colored . . ."

Oh hell. I grabbed Liana by the arms and pulled her back a few steps. "Liana, I hate to break this to you."

She tried to brush me off, but Fury strength outweighed Warhound any day. "Break what to me?"

"That's not your daughter. She's a Sidhe trapped inside her own glamourie."

CHAPTER EIGHT

LIANA RECOILED INSTINCTIVELY. DRE'S EYES widened, and he regarded Amaya—Fake Amaya—as if she'd sprouted a second head. Interestingly enough, however, he didn't drop his arm from her waist.

"B-but, Sidhe are extinct. They have been for decades."

I hugged Liana, offering what little comfort I could. "I recently learned that isn't entirely true."

She frowned. "And how did you learn that?"

Dre's attention focused on me as intently as hers. "Yes, how *did* you learn that?"

I considered pulling rank and saying it was Fury business, but I figured they both had the right to hear at least part of the story. However, I didn't want to have to go over the same damn thing later, so I nudged Liana to a sitting position before facing Dre again.

"I'll tell you both everything, but first I want to call Scott and have him bring the rest of his family here. Or we can take—ah, pseudo Amaya—over there, if you'd prefer?"

Dre's eyes darkened, and he tightened his hands. "No, she's not leaving here until I find out what the hell is going on."

I'd suspected as much. Lover boy had it bad. "Then may I?"

He showed me to a phone, and I jabbed in Scott's familiar cell number, knowing he hadn't changed it. Only the fact that I had an audience kept me from alternately chewing him out for not telling me about Amaya and apologizing for all the awful things I'd said to him when we broke up. I settled for giving him the short version of how I'd come to be inside Dre Carrington's home—including the fact that his sister wasn't really his sister—and he agreed to bring over the available Murphys right away.

He made good on his word. Minutes after hanging up, Scott, his father, two of his sisters, three of his brothers (thankfully *not* including Sean), Elliana, and Mac tromped into the music room. Morgan moved immediately to Liana's side and took her into his arms. The fierce look of love he gave her sent regret spinning through my heart. God, I'd been such a fool to let their son go. Once, *he'd* looked at *me* like that . . . Liana murmured something to her husband, and his head whirled as he zeroed in on Fake Amaya. He narrowed his eyes and bared his teeth in an expression that would have done the Hound members of his family proud.

Scott touched me on the arm, raising a brow. I leaned against his hand. His warmth felt good against my arm, but I allowed myself the pleasure for only a moment.

"So," he drawled when I moved away. "Tell me again why we shouldn't kill this bastard and bury him where no one will ever find him before we go find out who the hell really took my sister."

Dre shifted slightly but managed to keep his expression cocky as ever. "Because Marissa vowed to do no harm to me or mine."

I couldn't help myself. "Yeah, but that vow only binds Furies. Not Warhounds."

A grin spread across Scott's face. He cracked his knuckles loudly.

Dre's confidence faded a notch, but he didn't back down, merely nodded at me. I humored him, launching into the story of how we'd come across the Sidheborn spirit earlier that day, and why I believed Amaya wasn't really Amaya. Then I explained how I planned to verify that fact.

Everyone rushed into action, arranging cushions on the floor, grabbing candles from elegant candelabras and placing them according to my specifications, gathering around the pentagram I inscribed on the expensive hardwood floor with very cheap chalk that was a bitch to clean off. (Dre might not have killed Nessa, but he was still an asshole.)

Fake Amaya complied with my request to sit at the eastern point of the pentagram easily enough. That right there made me suspect that whoever was locked inside Amaya's form, she truly had lost most of her memories, or had them wiped away. Had she been an actual operative like the feds who'd attacked us outside Cori's school, she'd have already gone into escape—or suicide—mode.

I adjusted the items I'd placed in the center of the pentagram. The Sidheborn spirit's hair, flesh, and blood. Three of the body's most vital essences, three of the strongest components to use when working magic. Someone dimmed the room's lights. Candlelight flickered from each corner of the pentagram, casting Fake Amaya's face in an eerie glow. The more I looked into her eyes, the more I realized just how "off" she was. She never would have fooled the members of Scott's family for long, but Dre hadn't known the *real* Amaya.

It took longer for the Sidheborn spirit to answer my call this time. She'd have a more difficult, arduous task in following the trail from her body to the pentagram holding these small bits of her physical remains. Harder to be sure, but my call was something she couldn't deny.

A half hour passed before she made her appearance. One moment, Fake Amaya and I were bathed in soft candle glow. The next, bright white light flashed in the center of the pentagram, illuminating us as brightly as sunlight until it dissipated somewhat. Several of the room's occupants gasped, especially those old enough to recognize the telltale marks of a full-blooded Sidhe. I don't think most of them had believed I'd known what I was talking about. But now, faced with the exotic creature floating before them, they could no longer deny the truth.

The spirit's eyes focused on me immediately. "So, you summon me once more, Fury. Have you rescued my brethren so soon, then?"

"No. And I'm not sure I should bother."

She advanced on me, anger making her eyes snap with unnatural light. Those eyes widened when she reached the circle of salt I'd sketched out at the heart of the pentagram. One of the most effective barriers against summoned spirits. And that pissed her off even more than my words.

"Explain yourself."

Her haughty tone of voice brought a smirk to my lips. "In case you've forgotten, sugar, *I* order you around. Not vice versa. So why don't *you* explain *yourself*?"

"I know naught of what you speak."

My expression grew cold. "Why didn't you mention the fact that your captors had some of your brethren willingly working for them?"

She sagged, running a hand through her ectoplasmic hair. "How could I be sure you would deign to help the others if you knew about the turncoats?"

"Yeah, well, your stupid decision to hold out nearly got me killed. How the hell am I supposed to free your brethren if I'm dead?"

Her expression grew solemn. "Aye, right you are, Fury. Please accept my humblest apologies."

I snorted. Sidhe didn't know the meaning of the word *humble*.

"You can make it up to me by answering more questions."

"As you wish."

I gestured behind her, to where Fake Amaya sat with legs crossed and hands folded in her lap. "Do you know her?"

She spun in the air. "Ohhh, poor Mya." Obviously Sidhe could see through the glamourie of other Sidhe without any special effort. Her voice sounded surprisingly tender when she glanced at me from over her shoulder. "She is one of the earlier products of the mortals' unMagic. Somewhat touched in the head, if you take my meaning. Sweet and innocent and unable to conduct herself as a true Sidhe." Which meant she didn't have it in her to cheat, mislead, and backstab up a storm like "true" Sidhe. Good to know.

"All right. Why would they dress her up in this form and send her to Dre Carrington?"

Her eyes widened in recognition. "That name strikes me as familiar. Some of our captors spoke of him from time to time."

I threw a dangerous look his way. He met my glance unflinchingly. Easy for him to do, now that I'd made that damnable vow.

"And what exactly did they speak of?"

"That he was a source of information allowing them to more easily find specimens for their experiments."

Nausea pooled in my stomach. Oh hell. "Specimens? What kind of experiments?"

Surprise flickered. "Have you not yet realized the truth?" She shook her head. "Of course not, or you wouldn't ask. The Sidhe are not the only arcanes upon which my captors work their unMagic. They hope to unlock the secrets of our immortality and glamourie, 'tis true. But they also seek to build their own magical army. They strive to clone other arcanes to accomplish this goal."

Dre's gaze locked with mine from across the circle. "Then the reason they sent Mya disguised as Amaya . . ."

The spirit's voice sounded much calmer than mine. "Was to prevent her family from realizing she had been taken for their experiments. They learned from their mistake with your sister Fury when you wouldn't leave the case alone. The bastards didn't mind sacrificing poor Mya to their cause, and they arranged for her to be found by Dre instead of her family to decrease the chance that their switch would be discovered."

My pulse skittered from being so close to having my dearest hope confirmed. "Then the Fury whose form they forced you to take *is* still alive."

She nodded. "Or was, last I saw her. Alive because they are using her, attempting to clone their own pet Fury."

"Over my dead body," I growled, jumping to my feet. Rage pulsed, but I used it to my advantage, formulating and discarding a dozen different plans in the space of seconds. "Now then. Just so there is no misunderstanding, I'm making this a command. Tell me everything you know about your captors, the place they held you, and this unMagic they are working on their 'specimens.' And I *do* mean everything."

BY THE TIME WE RETURNED TO HOUNDS OF Anubis, it was far too late to set out for Western Mass. A few Warhounds and one Fury against who knew how many secret government agents and a potential army of cloned arcanes? I don't think so.

The past couple of hours had been chaotic but productive. The Murphys wasted no time in telling Dre to take his job and shove it (couldn't blame them for not giving two weeks' notice), though they'd also relinquished any claim over Fake Amaya, which seemed to be all Dre had hoped for by that point. He knew how lucky he was none of Amaya's brothers took the opportunity for a little payback. Mostly because they were now completely focused on helping me track down their sister's true whereabouts.

No sooner did we set foot back in Command Central than Kiara swept Scott off to take care of some minor emergency. I fought back the sudden twinge of disappointment and took the chance to slip into the back office.

After checking in with David and Cori via telephone, I logged on to the Internet to search the headlines for news of Trinity's condition. The *Herald*'s front-page headline proclaimed, *Cop Hero in Stable Condition, Chief MI Still Missing.* I sent another prayer for Trinity's health winging skyward. I just didn't think I could stomach losing one more person I loved.

Next, I turned my attention to the Sisterhood. The Elders might have forbidden Stacia from helping me without hard evidence of a mortal conspiracy, but I had an ace up my sleeve now. Testimony from the dead was just as valid as living testimony in the Sisterhood's eyes. More so, since spirits cannot lie to us.

My lips curved in a tight smile as a scene played out in my mind. Me, sweeping into the Palladium and immediately presented to the Conclave—the Greater Consensus, of course. A little flash and dazzle and voilà! Cue *the* revelation of the past fifty years—that Sidhe were not in fact extinct, and some splinter group of mortals was cloning a secret army of arcanes—and the Elders would soon accede to my every wish . . .

"Yeah right." I couldn't even *think* that with a straight face.

I shook my head and turned back to the computer. My fingers tapped slowly but surely at the keyboard. The machine loaded the graphics-intensive website that usually took eons to show up on my POS back in the PD. A frown creased my face at that thought, so I forced my attention back to the sleek piece of machinery purring in front of me. I couldn't hold back a whistle of appreciation. Mac had more than outdone himself.

The typical rigmarole of logging in both electronically and magically zipped by in a flash, and I got lucky bigtime. I had to wait only a few minutes for Stacia's face to appear onscreen.

Concern marred her normally pristine features. "Marissa, are you well?"

I blinked. The spell linking my little spot in the mortal world to her pocket of the Otherrealms worked just like a mundane webcam. She shouldn't have been able to see the bandage on my knee. "Couldn't be better. Why do you ask?"

"It's well past midnight. I hadn't expected to hear from you so soon."

"Oh. What can I say? I work fast."

Her turn to blink. "You've—found something already?" Her voice didn't sound quite as enthusiastic as I'd expected. Then again, it *was* after midnight.

"More than I expected. I know what's going on now."

Surprise flickered. "That was certainly fast."

I couldn't help a smirk. "I aim to please." She tossed an amused look my way before ordering me to spill the beans.

Stacia's lips settled into a narrow line at the news that Vanessa was most likely alive and being used as a lab rat by mortals. The double whammy that the arcanes who were supposed to be extinct actually weren't seemed anti-climactic in comparison.

"This supposed Sidheborn spirit. What exactly did she tell you about her captors?"

I didn't miss her stressing the word *supposed* but tried to hide my impatience with her obvious suspicion. Elders took the word *skeptical* to a whole 'nother level. "Not a whole lot of specifics, unfortunately. Just that they were mostly mortal, although the mortals have quite a few brain-washed Sidheborn clones who do their bidding."

"She couldn't tell you anything of their leaders? Or where they're holding Vanessa?"

"Nothing on their leaders. As for location, she believes the arcanes are being held in Western Massachusetts." I rolled my eyes. "Her original words were, 'somewhere to the west.'"

Stacia snorted. "Damn Sidhe."

"My sentiments exactly. Still, there's no denying that's what she is. Was."

"What makes you so sure?"

"No mistaking a Sidhe's Candy Land coloring, or the fact that she was damned near a dead ringer for Vanessa— other than the slightly off-color tats and the spirit that most clearly did *not* match its outward shell."

She nodded, lips pursed in thought. "True, there is that."

"So, when should I expect you?"

"I'm sorry?"

I narrowed my eyes. "When should I expect you to get down here to help me? I got the proof you wanted." Her wince was *so* not the reaction I wanted. "Don't tell me you're not coming!"

"Okay, I won't."

"Dammit, Stacia. What, do you want me to steal the frigging corpse from the morgue and drag it through the subway tunnel?"

"While I might very well pay to see that sight, Marissa, I don't think that's necessary. All the altered corpse proves, even if you summon the spirit in front of the entire Conclave, is that the Sidhe are not dead and at least some mortals are involved. It doesn't prove that their government knows or, more important, condones the experimentation on arcanes. I need more."

I pushed back from the desk and let out an explosive breath. Sometimes her obsessive-compulsive quest for perfection drove me absolutely batty. Even if she probably was just erring on the side of caution when it came to persuading the tight-assed Circle of Elders to get off said asses and *do* something constructive. "Fine. But when I bring you that *more*, I damned well expect you to get the hell down here."

She nodded, eyes gleaming. "Don't worry. I may just pop by when you least expect it."

"Promises, promises," I muttered before ending the chat session with a sharp stab at the keyboard.

If I'd been acting in my regular capacity as Chief MI, I'd have had the strength of the department behind me, and I'd have gone in, guns blazing. But I was stripped of those powers. All right, fine. So I needed to find something that definitively linked the mortals-turned-modern-day-Frankensteins to the feds who just wouldn't take no for an answer. I could do that. Somehow.

The office door squeaked open just then, and my eyes shot to the doorway expectantly but were met by the sight of the wrong Murphy brother. *Speaking of people not taking no for an answer . . .*

That uncharitable thought had me pushing to my feet

and forcing a smile. *Give the poor kid a break, Riss. It's just a harmless little crush.* And not like it would be the first time I'd been on the receiving—or giving, come to think of it—end of puppy love.

Sean's smile was crooked, and endearingly sweet, as he nudged the door closed with one leg and leaned against it with the other. Once again my gaze zeroed in on the oh-so-fine sight of his tight shirt clinging to the chiseled length of his chest and abs. Mmm, yummy six-pack abs that just made me want to . . .

Jesus, would you cut that out! He's Scott's brother. His baby *brother!*

My voice was decidedly high-pitched when I managed to speak. "Uh, hey, Sean. Sorry, I'm finished here if you need the computer."

The smile that had seemed sweet seconds earlier suddenly became smoldering. Either that or someone had cranked the heat up a dozen notches. "Nope. I just came to enjoy the scenery." His eyes grew distinctly heated as he gave me a long, slow once-over. "The amazing scenery."

Oh gods. I was *so* going to hell for the way my eyes kept wandering from his chest to his abs—and even lower. I jerked my gaze up to his face and tried to think of a graceful way to exit. Easier said than done, seeing as how he lounged against the room's only escape route and seemed in no hurry to move.

Or so I thought. But he must have sensed my desire to flee, because suddenly he was across the room in two ground-eating strides, and then his arms locked around me and his lips pressed down on mine—hard. Time slowed to a crawl, my skin grew flushed, and desire speared where his hands now roamed along my arms, skimming across the crimson expanse of my tattoos. I pushed him off, wiping my mouth with the back of my trembling hand.

Holy shit. I'd made out with Scott not even five hours earlier and now, here I was letting his baby brother play tonsil hockey with me. Triumph glowed in his whiskey-colored eyes, making him look far older than his tender years. *Yeah, just focus on that little fact. He's more than ten years younger than you. A baby.* Well, now anyway. Once we were both past our forties, it wouldn't seem like such an age gap for immortals, but right now—ouch!

"Ah, uh, gotta go." And with those eloquent words, I fled the room as quickly as I could, thanking all the gods that the main room was empty. Guilt and frustration flooded through my veins. Guilt because I hadn't pushed Sean away sooner, and frustration that he'd gotten my body all revved up again. I considered saying to hell with it and hotfooting it out of there, but since when had I ever cut and run when that was the smartest thing to do?

No way I would crawl back to Scott so soon, though, so I settled for a short walk around the block to cool off. My feet had barely touched the building's front stoop when the door slammed open and shut behind me. I stiffened and turned, ready to chew out Scott or Sean. Instead, I found myself facing someone unexpected: Mac.

He arched a red-gold eyebrow and joined me on the stoop. Again, I had the strangest sensation I'd seen him before, though I knew that I hadn't. But the shape of his wide-set green eyes, the way his long, thick eyelashes (wasted on yet another man) made his eyes look even greener, the way he folded his arms over his chest as he twisted his lips and looked down at me—something about it screamed out *Remember me?*

But I didn't. Come to think of it, I wasn't even 100 percent clear whether he was mortal or immortal, and that had me frowning. I couldn't remember the last time I hadn't immediately cataloged someone's status as arcane or mundane based on the way they moved and the unique magical scent coloring the air around them. Mac, however, seemed an enigma in more ways than one.

My inability to pinpoint just *what* he was had me scowling. "What do *you* want?"

He blinked, making me envy his long, red-gold lashes again. "Going somewhere?" At my silence, he added, "Alone?"

"Did Scott send you to babysit or something? If he did, you can just get the hell back inside. I'm a big girl now."

Amusement had his lips twitching, but he managed not to smile. "Scott didn't send me. Elle did."

This time I was the one to blink. "Ellie sent you?"

He laughed at the bafflement in my voice. "Yes. As Scott's second, she takes the duty we owe to you quite seriously. It wouldn't look at all good for us if you were kidnapped or killed on our own front porch."

Gods. Showed how pissed-off and confused I'd been, to go charging away from sanctuary without thinking about the consequences. Plenty of arcanes (and mortals, for that matter) knew of my past ties to Scott and his family— making this a logical place to look for me when I failed to turn up elsewhere. What good did it do me to hire backup if I was just going to take off on my own at the first hint of emotional turmoil?

"I need a walk. Too much Rage," I grudgingly admitted.

Recognition lit his eyes and he nodded, motioning me to precede him. My respect for him rose a couple notches. He obviously knew more about Furies than the average Joe Schmoe, because he didn't ask any questions.

All remained silent on the city streets around us, except the sound of an occasional car passing by. Most of the buildings on the other side of the street (since the Murphy compound took up the entire block on the near side) housed a mixture of residential buildings and storefronts that, like Hounds of Anubis, had already closed up shop for the night. Other areas of the Belly would be nowhere near so quiet.

Mac allowed me to set the pace, for both the walking and the talking. Silence went only so far toward soothing the Rage inside a Fury. At some point, she had to actually talk herself the rest of the way down from that intense ledge, or engage in physical activity much more strenuous than a walk around the block.

"So, how'd you hook up with Ellie, anyway?"

He showed no surprise when the question popped out of my mouth a good five minutes after we started walking. "We met when her family hired me to handle all the electronic security for her ah, formerly pending nuptials."

I shot him a sideways glance. "Wait. Her family hired you to keep her safe on her wedding day, and you ended up stealing her for yourself?" Talk about irony.

"Well, actually, it was pretty much the other way round." He ran a hand through his spiky hair. "See, Elle got it in her head that she wanted one final fling before she committed herself to the stuck-up Hound her parents had arranged for her to marry—pretty much from the cradle. *After* she found out he'd had a fling of his own the night of his bachelor party."

I winced. Even Ellie didn't deserve *that*.

"Only problem for her was, none of the men she had access to were stupid enough to mess with an engaged Banoub, especially not considering how rich and powerful her fiancé was. Lucky for her, I had just moved to town so pretty much knew zilch about Boston's branch of the Cabal, and well . . . Let's just say Elle can be damned persuasive when she wants to be."

I bet. He didn't comment on my eye roll, just kept talking as we walked.

"The thing was, neither of them felt the slightest bit of love, or even lust, for each other. Still, Elle planned to honor her parents' wishes once she felt she'd evened the score. But then she found out that to *really* even the score between them, she'd have to take out a nationwide ad to recruit a whole hell of a lot more clueless me's."

"You mean, he'd been cheating on her the whole time?"

He nodded. "Oh yeah. Been cheating on her the whole time they were engaged, and planned to go right on cheating afterward. But he was seriously old-school, and did *not* buy into the what's-good-for-the-goose-is-good-for-the-gander routine. When he found out that she'd retaliated sexually, he went a little crazy. Tried to beat her into telling him who her lover was—his first mistake. Elle was trained from infancy how to defend herself, seeing how volatile Cabal politics are. His second mistake was ambushing me in a dark alleyway after he realized I had entered the scene just before Elle threw her affair in his face."

"You survived an ambush from a *Warhound*?"

His green eyes were suddenly illuminated by the glare of a nearby streetlight. For a second, they seemed to flare with emerald fire, almost like—Nah. Couldn't be.

"Not only survived, but persuaded Elle's ex it would be far better for his health—physical and financial—if he stayed far away from both of us." Something fierce crossed his face, something I couldn't quite name but recognized on a visceral level.

"So, new to the area. From Scotland, right?"

He grinned. "What, lassie, does my wee accent give me away, then?"

I laughed as he deepened his normally light brogue until I could barely understand him. "Just a little."

"Turnabout's fair play then, lass. How did you 'hook up' with Elle's favorite cousin?"

Huh. Last time I'd been in the picture, Scott and Ellie

hated each other with a passion. Wonder what had changed all that.

"Pretty much your typical 'Hound meets Fury, Hound pisses off Fury, Fury dumps Hound' kinda deal."

He nudged me slightly. "Now, now. Don't think I'll be letting you get away with that load of bollocks. How did the two of you meet?"

I sighed, eyes going slightly unfocused as I thought back. "Well, I'd just been promoted to Chief Magical Investigator not too long before we met, and was having a bitch of a time getting the cooperation I needed from the mundanes. Most of them were too chickenshit to follow me into the Belly when I needed backup. Half the time I had no choice but to hire mercs I trusted to help with particularly dangerous investigations, especially the apprehensions. Unfortunately, the merc I preferred to work with the most—a tough-as-nails but trustworthy Giant named Charlie—was out of the country on a job when I needed help taking out a den of Bhuta who'd been terrorizing the Belly for months before I finally figured out just what the hell was doing it." Thinking of Charlie brought a pang, since rumors pegged him as having died in a firefight a few months earlier.

He tilted his head. "Bhuta?"

I would have liked to claim that was a hint he had to be mortal, but truth was, few arcanes but Furies knew as much about other immortals as we do. "Yeah, they're from the Hindu pantheon and are like a mix between ghosts, zombies, and vampires. Only worse."

"But zombies and vampires—"

"Don't exist," I finished for him, grinning at how much his voice reminded me of Trinity's when I admitted the existence of demons. "There are more things in heaven and earth, Horatio . . ."

"Than are dreamt of in your philosophy." He finished before I could, earning an approving nod.

"Exactly. But you're partly right. Zombies and vampires as the Western world views them do *not* exist. But certain sorcerers and spirits can reanimate corpses for brief periods of time, which would technically be termed *zombies*, though nothing like the horror flicks you've seen. And the creatures mortals might choose to term *vampires* do *not* feed on blood to survive. Far more worse, they feed on the life force of others. Lucky for the mundanes, though, only the essence of arcanes will do."

Mac actually shivered, which made me lean again toward categorizing him as arcane. "And the Bhuta?"

"Bhuta can only act at night and, also like vampires of legend, cast no shadow or reflection in the mirror. Disgustingly enough, they can actually reanimate corpses for their own purposes, the closest they come to having true physical form. In rare cases, Bhuta can grow strong enough through feeding on arcane essences to actually possess a living, breathing person—which most often results in death for the host. Not to mention whoever the Bhuta crosses paths with in that form."

He regarded me with serious eyes. "How did you kill them?"

"That's just it. How do you kill something that's already dead, especially without taking out the innocent host?" I thought back to that harrowing night and shivered myself. "Charlie recommended a merc agency he trusted, one he'd freelanced for previously."

"The Shadowhounds."

I nodded. "Lucky for me he did, too. Warhounds are one of the few types of arcanes that can be neither fed on by Bhutakind or possessed when in human form. Their ties to Anubis grant them a certain immunity from most undead." Made sense, seeing as how Anubis was the Egyptian lord of the underworld. "Anyway, to make a very long story short, Morgan, Scott, and Amaya took the job of keeping my ass alive while I tracked down the den, which turned out to be an abandoned building deep in the heart of the most dangerous section of the Belly."

Mac's lips twisted in a smile. "Imagine that."

I rolled my eyes. "My sentiments exactly. It was their immunity to the undead along with their super sense of smell that let us find the Bhuta so quickly. They were also able to keep the spirits corralled while I took them out, one by one."

"So how *did* you kill them?" he asked again.

Remembered Rage danced along my spine, easy to fight down since it held the ghostly touch of memory rather than new emotion. "Whereas Hounds are immune to possession by the undead, Furies can actually force spirits to enter their bodies, and then channel the Rage into the foreign spirit to exterminate it."

Mac's mouth dropped open, and the horror in his eyes mirrored that in my own. "And by channeling the Rage into the Bhuta, you felt every bit of agony the spirit felt until you banished it to the underworld. And risked losing control of the Rage and going Harpy, or giving the Bhuta enough control to consume your own life force. Leaving it full access to your body while you'd be gone forever."

I just nodded, narrowing my eyes and searching his face for some sort of answer to the question still puzzling me. What *was* he, that he knew more about Furies than any non-Fury I'd ever met?

He didn't hear my unspoken question, just stared down at the uneven cobblestones beneath our feet. Silence stretched out for what should have been an uncomfortable length, but wasn't. Something about being with him seemed right. Companionable. An odd feeling for me when with some-one I'd known such a short time. Finally, he looked up and met my gaze.

"So you risked your life, your immortality, and your

soul to save the Belly, while the mortal police just sat back and watched. And yet you still work for them now."

He kept his tone neutral, but I sensed the emotion lurking beneath the surface. Downright bafflement. And he wasn't the first to react that way to the work I did for the mortals, especially considering the predicament they'd placed me in that night. Then again, it's hard for other arcanes to understand a Fury's natural tendency to try to keep the peace between mundane and immortalkind. None of them start out 100 percent mortal—and thus completely vulnerable—the way we do. Probably one reason that adrenaline became as addictive as crack for Furies. We felt the rush of fear and excitement so much more than other arcanes could.

"You ever heard that old mortal phrase, 'Two wrongs don't make a right'?" At his nod, I started walking again, and he kept pace easily enough. "Hokey as it sounds, it's true. Just because the mortals weren't willing to go out of their way to help arcanes that night doesn't mean I shouldn't do my damnedest to help them whenever I can. First of all, it's my job, no matter what they do or don't do. And second of all, the only way things are going to improve between mortals and immortals is if those of us who know better hold ourselves to a higher standard."

"So, you think sustained peace between the two is actually possible?"

His voice was carefully neutral again, but I got the feeling he had a lot more invested in my answer than he showed. "Not only possible, but inevitable. The only question is whether that peace will come at the price of another war neither side can afford."

We wound up back at the front stoop to Hounds of Anubis, each staring up at the gilt storefront and pondering our own thoughts. Just when I started toward the doorway,

Mac's soft voice gave me pause. "We go to gain a little patch of ground, that hath in it no profit but the name."

Goose bumps pricked my flesh at his words. Whether he quoted from *Hamlet* again as an echo of the past war, or as a prediction of another, I don't know. And, right then, I was just glad my abilities didn't include precognition. Although, for all I knew, Mac's abilities *did* . . .

MAC HEADED HOME TO THE LITTLE WOMAN after dropping me off outside Liana and Morgan's apartment. My plan was to find out what my sleeping arrangements were going to be for the next little while. Of course, once Scott's not-so-sweet mother opened the door and told me, I forgot all about my happy-happy, joy-joy thoughts of spreading peace between mortals and arcanekind.

Liana smiled serenely as I crossed arms over chest and narrowed my eyes. "What do you mean, there's no extra space anywhere but Scott's apartment?"

Her smile merely widened as she leaned against the doorway of the penthouse suite she and Morgan shared. "He said to tell you the door's unlocked and to make yourself at home."

My expression soured. I just bet he had. Whatever tiny amount of guilt I had felt for disturbing her so late evaporated in the face of her obvious smugness. Fortunately for us both, though, she had the good sense not to laugh in my face as I stomped back to the elevator for the ride to Scott's floor. One added benefit to my annoyance at being manipulated was the fact that the bizarre incident with Sean and the frustration of trying to figure out what Mac was had pretty much fled my mind.

Repeated jamming of the elevator button did not, big shocker, make the car arrive any faster. By the time the doors dinged open, my boot heel had all but worn a hole in the carpeted floor and steam no doubt spewed forth from my ears. I tried a calming technique Stacia had taught me once, with mixed results. Anger did not morph into Rage, but neither did I feel very Zen. When the doors swung open seconds later, I marched down the—this time tiled—floor, taking vicious pleasure in making much more noise than necessary. I imagined leaving a swath of enemies in my wake, which of course didn't help with the whole calming technique. Scott's door loomed up before me, and I twisted the doorknob, jerked the door open, and prepared to kick Scott's ass for thinking he could just push me into doing whatever it was he want—

"Oh." I could barely breathe past the sudden lump in my throat. Scott lounged on his sofa, modestly garbed in sweats and a tee, and with sheets, pillow, and blanket making it clear where he planned to sleep. Which meant he wasn't using this as a thinly veiled attempt to get me into bed again, since his apartment had only one.

I didn't know whether to laugh or cry.

So I decided to snarl instead. "Why the hell did you force your mother to lie to me?"

He narrowed his eyes, and even though he wasn't in Hound form I could sense his hackles rising. "Excuse me?"

I crossed my arms over my chest and glared. "You know exactly what I'm talking about. Or do you expect me to believe that you're the only family member who has a sofa that guests can crash on?"

"Did it ever occur to you that maybe nobody else in the family *wanted* you to sleep on their sofa?"

My mouth opened and shut a few times as my eyes started stinging suspiciously. Oh hell no, I refused to cry in front of him. Even if it felt like he'd stabbed me with a hundred needles. "I should be used to Murphys not wanting me around by now."

He scowled. "What do you mean by that?"

"Oh yeah, like you don't know. Have you forgotten our last morning together, when you gave me a giant ol' kiss-off?"

"Oh for the love of Anubis. Are you rewriting history now, too? *You* were the one who walked out on *me*."

"Yeah, after you screwed me literally one minute and then screwed me figuratively the next. Do you have any fucking idea how much you broke my heart when you told me your family was basically choosing fame and fortune over me, not to mention protecting the same bastard we all thought kidnapped Nessa?"

He shook his head emphatically, yellow eyes darkening to a deep shade of amber. "Oh gods, no wonder you got so pissed when I told you about Da taking Dre on and me taking over the Shadowhounds. You thought I was choosing them over you."

My nails dug into my palms as memories of that last day swept through my mind. I'd tried too hard not to think about what happened, what he'd done and what I'd said. Tried and failed and kept right on failing for two hellishly long years. "How could I think otherwise? When you told me you were kissing off all our plans for the future to help your father protect Dre's ignorant ass . . . You never even told me about Amaya, for gods' sake."

"Shit, Riss, I couldn't. Dre made us submit to a loyalty spell that prevented us from going into details with anyone outside the family. But we planned all along to have a family member spying on Dre twenty-four/seven. We figured someday he'd drop his guard, and we could break Nessa's case wide open."

I threw my hands in the air when he reminded me of

another thing that drove me insane. Men (like my father and brother) who thought they could wrap their "little women" up in lace, ribbons, and bubble wrap, when a Fury was about as likely to put up with that as to go to a Harpy slumber party. "Did you forget that it was my job to do that? My job to find the truth, to break the case, to spy on Andre Carrington day in and day out if need be."

"You're very good at your job, Riss. I've never doubted that. But not even you are completely infallible. He got to one Fury—or so we all thought; he could have gotten to you, too. Maybe better, since you were so consumed with bringing her killer to justice back then, you might have done something—"

My eyes narrowed. "Stupid?"

"No, never that. Reckless."

"Well, it would have been my right to be reckless."

"Yes, but don't you see? I could have lost you just as easily as you lost Nessa. And I couldn't bear that. Couldn't stand the thought of waking up one day and you not being there and me never knowing what happened to you or why. Just suspecting, day in and day out, and never being able to do anything. I wanted—no, I needed—to protect you."

My breath hitched and my pulse picked up speed. "And why's that, Scott?"

"Because I—I cared about you so damned much."

"You cared about me, past tense," I stated flatly. "Right now all you give a damn about is the Sisterhood's money. Isn't that the only reason you agreed to help me?"

He ground his teeth together for several seconds, a large vein in his forehead throbbing in visible anger. "I'll help you out of this shithole you've dug us both in for old times' sake. And somebody with a shred of self-control has to make sure my sister gets rescued. But once she's safe, we're done. The past is the past."

"Oh, I couldn't agree more, puppy dog." I was the one

with no self-control? Who had been the one to shove his tongue down my throat? It took a few seconds for my words to penetrate his brain. By then, I was most of the way to his bedroom door.

"Have fun dreaming about what could have been with *my* assets, lover boy. 'Cause that's sure as hell the closest you're ever going to get to them again!" His bedroom door made a satisfyingly loud thump as it slammed behind me. The only sweeter sounds were the muffled curse Scott ground out seconds later followed by the sound of the bathroom shower cranking on—for his sake, I hoped what they said about ice-cold showers was actually true.

DESPITE THE FACT THAT I'D BEEN AVERAGing only four hours of sleep a night lately, not to mention all the grief and emotional stress I'd gone through the day before, my internal clock woke me up before dawn the next morning. No use fighting it. Once my eyes opened, I was up for the day. I mumbled under my breath and shifted on the silken sheets, sighing at the way they caressed my skin ever so softly. Scott's sheets, and Scott's bed. I closed my eyes and inhaled the sharp, masculine tang clinging to the fabric and considered rolling all around until that heavenly scent clung to me as well.

Not that I'd need to with all the Hounds and their superhuman powers of smell crawling all over the building. That thought led me back to the reason I was here, deep in the heart of Murphy territory. Nessa.

I only had to think her name for the Mandate to make itself felt. Pressure nudged at my head, threatening to burgeon to full-blown pain if I didn't get my rear in gear.

Guilt crept into my heart, and I slipped out of the bed to focus on tracking down Vanessa and her captors. First things first, though—washing off Scott's scent. In the living room, Scott sprawled uncomfortably across his sofa and I couldn't hold back a smirk. His body was *way* too long for that thing, but after last night's little spat, I didn't feel particularly guilty. I *did* make the concession of padding quietly to the apartment's single bathroom down the hall, doing my best not to wake him. Scott had always been pure night owl.

The marble tiles of the bathroom floor were cold against my feet. I cranked up the hot water in the shower, hopped in once the mirror above the sink started steaming, and closed my eyes. Scalding water beat against my back in a soothing staccato. I arched my back, sighing in pleasure. Nothing like a white-hot shower for a red-hot Fur—

The sound of the shower door banging open was the only warning. My airway cut off as someone wrapped a viselike grip around my neck. I snapped my eyes open but couldn't see my attacker. They jerked me back against their body, increasing the pressure against my throat. Panic flared, but I fought it back, hands scrabbling at my attacker's hands. The steely grip only tightened. My lungs burned with the need for air. Confusion set in. Why couldn't I break my attacker's grip? I should be stronger than whoever it was. And then the stink of sulfur hit my nostrils, and my heart sank.

No way I could take out a Harpy without being fully Fury. I used the last of my strength to shift into full Fury form. Nemesis and Nike burst into life. The moment they sensed our enemy, they struck. Her arms dropped as she grappled with the serpents seeking a weak spot. Not that there were many on her kind.

I spun, nearly slipping on the wet tiles, seeing my suspicions confirmed. The Harpy hissed, talons flashing as she swiped at Nemesis and Nike. Straggly, dirty white hair surrounded an ugly pale face straight from mortal nightmares. Her body was athletic but whipcord thin, birdlike, especially when coupled with the talons and her unfurled wings. No wonder the ancient Greeks had likened Harpies to bird-women.

She managed to get her hands around my serpents, shaking them in the air several times before throwing them against the hard tile walls of the shower. Eerie yellow-green eyes that mockingly echoed a Fury's pupil-less orbs lit in triumph, and she cackled.

That pissed me off. "Big mistake."

I pounced, passing through the shower doorway and taking her to the floor. The impact jarred us both, but we brushed it off and wrestled for the upper position. We must have made enough noise to disturb Scott, because I heard him stirring in the other room.

Pain flared when the Harpy got a good swipe in. I winced as blood welled. No telling how much filth the bitch had under her talons. My momentary daze was enough for her to flip me onto my back and bash my head against the tiled floor. Stars flashed and I forgot all about the wound on my arm. She cracked my head again, and I screamed.

The bathroom door flung open, and a very naked Scott barreled inside. He took in the sight of the Harpy knocking me senseless. A concussion of magic beat the air. Scott's mortal form slipped away, to be replaced by pure War-hound. Purely pissed-off Warhound.

Mottled gray fur bristled along his Hound's body that now rivaled a small pony in size. His wolflike face bared wicked sharp canines that would rend as effectively as the Harpy's talons—and he had a lot more of those than she did of hers. Glowing amber eyes met mine, and he nodded.

I kept my body plastered as closely to the floor as possible, and he leapt. He knocked the Harpy back into the shower stall. She shrieked, head smacking against the wall with even more force than she'd hit me with. Nemesis and Nike took advantage of the situation, striking her unprotected arms and legs as they flailed uselessly. Scott, not to be outdone, tore into her throat, making a bloody mess of flesh, gristle, and bone.

Magic concussed again, and Scott crouched over me in mortal form. In very naked, very appealing mortal form. I giggled.

He frowned. "You all right, Riss?" His hands probed my body for broken bones. When they neared my head, I winced, and he paused. "Just how hard did she crack your head?"

I giggled again, unable to help myself. "Pretty hard." The laughter only increased the pain, but the whole situation struck me as incredibly funny. My laughter worried Scott. I could see that even through my chortles and chuckles. I wanted to tell him not to worry, but I couldn't. Fiery warmth stabbed through my veins, spreading from my arm all along my body. Spreading from my *wounded* arm.

Fear stirred but was drowned out by the laughter racking my body. Scott's eyes zeroed in on the narrow cut on my arm, and he cursed. "Fucking poison."

Now *that* wasn't funny at all, but I laughed anyway. He reached into the shower, grabbing Nemesis and Nike, who tolerated his touch because they could sense something horribly wrong. He settled them against my skin, and they zoomed straight for the wound on my arm, then hissed in sudden fury.

Magical poison, then, my remaining sane neurons diagnosed.

Magic stirred the air again as my girls began working, crippled by the fact that I was in no condition to aid them. They were much stronger acting as magical catalyst for me than on their own. Still, they had to try, or all three of us would soon be dead.

"Hang on. I'm gonna get Kiara."

Scott ran into the bedroom, returning a moment later

with his cell phone and barking orders into it. When finished, he dropped the phone and leaned down next to me. His fingers threaded through those on my unwounded arm. His eyes glistened with unshed tears. That warmed my heart for some reason.

Oh yeah. Means he does still care. Guess Mommie Dearest was right, then.

Laughter burbled past my lips, but much more weakly this time. The fiery warmth didn't seem so warm anymore. Frozen numbness spread where heat had once stabbed. Nemesis and Nike hissed, sending magical energy pouring into me, counteracting the freezing pain just barely enough to keep me from going completely under. I didn't think I could hold on much longer.

"You have to, baby. Don't die on me, dammit!"

I'd spoken aloud without thinking again. That had a grin spreading across my lips, but no laughter escaped. Guess I'd laughed myself out. Now, all that was left was dying.

"Stupid bitch," I managed to mumble.

"Now, now, there's no call for that. I'm here to help." Kiara's voice drawled from the open doorway. Despite the attempt at humor, I could hear her concern. That should have worried me, seeing as how she was still so pissed over what I'd done to . . . Hadn't I done something bad to her brother?

My eyes fluttered, and I didn't have the energy to open them again. A hand snapped against my cheeks, hard. A tiny surge of adrenaline flared, and I managed to blink open uncooperative eyes. They widened when I realized Scott had been the one to strike me. Not Kiara.

"B'sstrd," I slurred.

Other voices stirred in the bedroom, signaling the arrival of more Murphys. Damned Murphys. Never there when you needed them, always in the way when you didn't . . .

Oh fuck, Riss. You need them bad. You're dying.

I scowled, not liking the sane part of my subconscious one little bit. Voices murmured above me, but they sounded distant and unintelligible. Nemesis and Nike, gods bless their little hearts, had done their best, but the slow freeze outdid their efforts to warm me. My eyes fluttered closed again. This time, I knew they wouldn't reopen.

Hands brushed against my knee. I didn't have the energy to wonder why. I was too damned busy dying. But then white-hot agony stabbed, and it was more than enough to break through my lassitude. When my furious gaze turned onto my knee, I realized why blinding pain now flashed through my leg. They'd removed the magical bandage.

"Stupid bitch," I mumbled again, this time drawing relieved grins from both Scott and his sister.

Kiara prodded at the wound on my arm, poking several foul-smelling powders and creams inside. Agony burned through my veins, ripping straight through the freezing cold and bringing my blood to a boil. That, coupled with the lightning blazing through my knee, finally did me in. I sank into blissful darkness, no longer caring whether I lived or died . . .

CHAPTER NINE

SOMETHING SOFT TICKLED MY NOSE, ELICIT-
ing a sneeze that rocked me from head to toe. I stirred but
kept my eyes screwed tightly shut. *Just a little more sleep.*
A large, warm body pressed against mine, and fur caressed
my bare right arm. *Fur?* I drew a deep breath and smelled
hound. Warhound.

My eyes snapped open and met a soulful, amber-eyed
gaze. Scott, in Hound form. But why?

Images flooded my mind in quick succession. The
Harpy slashing my arm with poisoned talons. Scott bursting into the room, shifting to the form he now inhabited
and ripping out the Harpy's throat. Dying on the cold marble floor, only to be brought back by the stubborn ministrations of Kiara and Scott.

He whined, breath snuffling against my face. Fortunately,

Hound breath didn't smell nearly as bad as that of normal doggies. I patted him absently, but my gaze sharpened when I realized the tiny wound that had nearly killed me had vanished without a trace. Furies healed surface wounds wicked fast naturally. Complex internal injuries like my knee, not to mention magical poison, were another story entirely.

"Damn, Kiara's potions rock. I've *got* to get her recipes."

Humor lit in Scott's canine eyes. He nuzzled my arm again, then leapt down from the strange bed. Instead of Scott's king-sized, rumpled satin sheets, I lay wrapped in scratchy cotton. Clean, but still scratchy.

I frowned. "Where—"

Magic snapped through the air. Scott stretched his naked, now-human form and settled on the edge of the bed. "In one of our safe houses. One only Da and I know about."

"Why—" I rolled my eyes at my own dimwittedness, pushing myself to a sitting position. "That building was locked down tight as Fort Knox. Magically warded out the wazoo."

"Exactly."

"Which means . . ."

"Someone betrayed us."

I winced. If that was true, then he was related to the traitor. Only Murphy relatives dwelled in that building. Mostly Scott's siblings, with a few cousins and in-laws tossed in. Surely it was one of the less savory in-laws. None of the blood relatives would ever even *think* about betrayal. Murphys stuck together through thick and thin. Kinda like cockroaches.

My body tensed when I thought about my own family. "Cori and her parents?"

"Are in another safe house with Elle and Mac. I know you don't like her, but she'll keep them safe. She's become one of the best mercs we have."

And, someday, I *really* wanted to hear how *that* came about. I forced my body to relax, releasing the breath I'd been holding. If Elliana were a part of the plot against me, she'd had plenty opportunity to betray me at the morgue. Besides, someone as cool as Mac would never have married a *complete* bitch. Figuratively and literally speaking. "So, what do you think our next step should be?"

He did a double take. "Whoa, wait. *You're* asking *me* what step to take next? Maybe that poison did more damage than we thought."

I lobbed a pillow at him. "Hardy-har, funny man. Don't suppose we're near a Starbucks?"

"As it just so happens, there's a Starbucks right across the street."

Which meant the safe house wasn't in the Belly. Mortal chains had not yet gotten the courage to move into the arcane zones of big cities. Eventually, though, their love of profit would outweigh their fear of the big bad magical types.

"Clothes?"

He jerked a hand toward an empty doorway. "Kiara packed you some stuff she thought would fit."

I wiggled off the bed, feeling his eyes on me. I knew, without looking, that his eyes watched my every move. Lusting. Just as it should be, since my skin tingled just about any time I caught sight of his naked body.

I sauntered into the small, attached bathroom and closed the door with a thump. *The better to make him wonder, my dear.* Once the door snicked shut behind me, I leaned back against the door and exhaled with the force of pent-up emotion. Longing so fierce it made my hands clench. The worst part of *that*, though, was that I didn't even know exactly what I longed for. Not to go back and rewrite history. Even if Furies had that ability (which we didn't), Scott and I were both different people now. And I liked myself just fine, thank you very much. Thorns and barbed wire and all.

Though gods knew I was sick and tired of feeling so damned lonely all the time. Sure, Scott had never told me he loved me back then, but things had been good between us—both in and out of bed. Other than the whole putting-family-ahead-of-everything-else thing.

I shook my head and crossed the clean but uninspiring room to find whatever clothes Kiara had managed to scrounge up for me. Time enough to figure out what the hell—if anything—was bubbling up between Scott and me later. Right now, I had things to do and asses to kick. A large duffel bag sat on top of a battered hamper. I opened it, shuffling to put together an outfit. Though I *could* shift form and wear the magical uniform that came with the whole Fury gig, that would make me stick out like a sore thumb, seeing as how half of Boston had to be looking out for the city's missing Chief MI. Besides, one gets tired of tight red leather after a while. Great for hiding bloodstains and looking badass, not so practical for everyday wear.

I set my selections on the chipped tile counter. I looked haggard in the fluorescent glow of the ugly seventies light fixture. Exhausted. I made a face, turning away from the not-so-pleasing sight.

The narrow, half-rusted shower stall beckoned, but I hesitated after cranking up the hot water. *Come* on. *It's not like a Harpy's gonna bust in again. Not with Scott keeping watch in the next room.* I gritted my teeth and stepped inside, closing the clear door behind me, keeping my back to the shower wall and my eyes wide open.

Ten minutes later I entered the small apartment's even smaller kitchen, feeling slightly ridiculous in the hot-pink, too-tight T-shirt with the phrase *Hot Stuff* scrawled across my chest. At least the jeans were modest enough, just a touch too loose in the waist and flaring slightly at the legs.

Scott glanced up from the table, pausing in the act of sharpening a long, wicked sharp blade. "Nice shirt."

I rolled my eyes. "You should see the socks. At least everything fits. Mostly."

He flicked his wrist, and the blade disappeared somewhere inside the long trench he'd donned while I dressed. Amazing how many of those things he could hide all over his body. Though I suspected Warhound magic had something to do with it.

"So, I was thinking . . ."

I waved my hand. "Coffee first, thinking second."

He grinned. "That was part of what I was thinking. We can shoot you up with caffeine on the way to see a friend of mine. One I think can help."

I channeled Fury magic, modifying my features enough so others wouldn't recognize me, but vanity refused to let me go so far as to become the mousy brown-haired woman I usually became. This time I opted for reddish-blond hair, light green eyes, and increasing my bust a full cup size. Just to see if he noticed. "Tell me about this friend *after* we get coffee."

Laughter followed me into the dingy living room and out the apartment. Magic brushed against my skin when I crossed the threshold. Good, tight wards that had obviously been done by a pro. The Murphys may have chintzed on the luxury factor of this safe house, but no dime had been spared in magically securing it.

Scott wisely waited until I'd sucked down my first double shot of caffeine pick-me-up before resuming his earlier train of thought. The way his eyes kept wandering downward clued me in to the fact that he most definitely *had* noticed. "I know someone in the Bureau."

My fingers clenched on the untouched coffee cup while I tossed the other in a corner trash can. "As in the *Federal* Bureau? As in the same feds who could be trying to kill me?"

"Chill. Harper's straight as can be. Trust me. Besides, I doubt the FBI is involved with whatever secret agency is running the illegal cloning program. No way they could keep that under wraps very long. Plus, Harp's not an actual agent. She's a consultant specializing in arcane gangs. Her list of contacts is impressive. If anyone can help us narrow down where in Western Mass to start looking, it's her." Something in his voice sounded odd, but I let it pass. Probably my overcaffeinated imagination.

"She meeting us somewhere other than Fed Central?"

"Yeah, outside Faneuil Hall."

"You already called?"

"Yeah, while you showered." He nudged me toward a subway station, the preferred mode of transportation for most people in Boston, whether arcane or mundane. *Much* cheaper than maintaining a car in the city. Parking cost a freaking arm and a leg. The T also came in handy for slipping around the city anonymously, a damned handy thing during investigations since Furies tended to stand out big-time in the daylight skyline. "Don't freak out, Riss. Harp owes me majorly, and I *know* she can be trusted. Besides, if you'd said no, I would have just called her back."

I grunted and took another swig of coffee. "Fine, fine." We just barely made it onto a train heading northbound before the doors closed. "So, what's this not-a-special-agent like? I assume she's arcane?"

He nodded. Made sense, seeing as how the FBI—like most federal law enforcement agencies—had yet to name a single arcane to an official position in their mortal bureaucracy. "Harper's just—fantastic really." His eyes went a little unfocused. "Your typical strong-as-nails, don't-mess-with-me Puerto Rican who doesn't take shit from anyone. Gives as good as she gets. Really turns heads, too. Brown hair and eyes, tall, with legs that just won't quit."

Silence reigned for several seconds as his words sank in. His eyes remained hazy, and a small smile turned his lips upward. And just like that, I knew. "You *slept* with her."

He started, his eyes losing their glassy tinge and focusing on my face. "What?"

"Let me guess. Damsel in distress, hires you as a bodyguard, you save her life, screw like rabbits, and now you have her undying gratitude."

A scowl—which appeared distinctly guilty, if you asked me—spread across his face. "This is ridiculous. You have no reason to thi—"

"Oh *please*. It's written in your voice. Just admit it."

He fixed stubborn eyes on the floor. I jiggled my foot. Loudly. Finally, he gave in. "Fine. We slept together. Once."

"I *knew* it!" Funny how, for once, being right didn't fire its usual satisfied glow. Another few minutes passed in silence. I tried to pretend I didn't care, tried to pretend that jealousy tinged with Rage wasn't eating a hole inside me. And of course, failed miserably. "Did you screw her before or after we broke up?"

He shot me a *Go to hell* look. "You may not be a Hound, but you sure are a bitch."

The train screeched to a stop at the Park Street Station and I floundered for an answer. Before I managed to come up with one, Scott stormed off the train, coattails nearly catching when the doors slammed shut. One stop early.

A lump settled in my throat. He'd actually left me alone. Knowing that Harpies were out to kill me, not to mention psycho Sidhe who were supposed to be extinct. That bastard left me.

No shit he left you. You as good as called him a liar and a cheat. You are *a bitch.*

Part of me wanted to deny that, to rant and rave and call Scott nasty names and curse his antecedents. But I couldn't.

"Fuck." I earned a dirty look from the elderly woman across from me. Visions of my grandmother danced in my head. "Sorry." She harrumphed and went back to her knitting. Yeah, add some wings and a set of Fury tats and she'd be the spitting image of Grandma. Other than the fact that slumbering Grandma was probably twice this woman's age, yet didn't look much older than me.

The train squealed into Government Center minutes later. I jumped off and scurried up a flight of stairs, searching the crowd for Scott's familiar face. No such luck.

My fists clenched. For a moment I'd been sure he would be waiting out here for me. My lips trembled, and anxiety I hadn't felt since I'd been a flimsy mortal clawed at my insides. Coffee burned the back of my throat as the urge to gag hit. I managed to hold on to the contents of my stomach—barely. This time I'd gotten so far in over my head, no way I could do this without him. I forced myself to take in slow, even breaths as my heartbeat accelerated.

Wait. Faneuil Hall. Even if he's pissed at you, he won't stand up this Harper chick.

That calmed my skittering pulse and had me trotting down the huge-ass staircase that led to State Street. I crossed against the light, earning several dirty looks and even dirtier gestures from passing motorists, but I made it safely across the street and to the busy plaza surrounding my destination. Faneuil Hall.

I jammed my hands in my pockets and stalked the crowds of manic tourists mixed with harried businesspeople on the way to work. Too bad Scott hadn't been a bit more specific than "Faneuil Hall." The historic shopping center was always packed, even this early in the morning. The scents of gourmet coffee and fat-laden pastries warred with the less tantalizing odor of unwashed bodies and the occasional whiff of sewer. I kept my eyes peeled for a brown-haired, brown-eyed Latin American woman with legs that "wouldn't quit," face glued into a scowl every time I thought of the distracted way Scott had described her. *I wonder if his eyes would go all fuzzy like that if he described* me *to another woman*. My fingers jerked at that thought, and I stared down at my newly shifted Fury claws in surprise, since I hadn't consciously unsheathed them.

A brunette dressed in a snazzy skirt and tailored blouse drew my attention. She wore three-inch stilettos and I grudgingly had to admit she had some killer legs. She tapped her stilettos on the cobblestones and frowned down at her watch, glancing back over her shoulder to a nearby alleyway from time to time, making it obvious she expected someone to appear from that direction soon.

My body froze when a familiar figure trotted out of that alley and straight up to the woman. "Hey, Harp." She flashed a megawatt smile showing off dazzling white teeth. Hounds really went in for that. The woman—Harper—wrapped her arms around Scott and the two kissed. The way their lips locked and their bodies writhed was in no way platonic.

Coffee bubbled in my stomach again, but I shoved it down and took off in the opposite direction. Tears stung, but I forced them away, too. Scott had made his choice. I'd shoved him into it two years ago.

"There you are. I've been looking everywhere for you. Riss, I'm sorry."

Hands reached out to steady me. My thoughts slowed to a crawl as I tried to reconcile the Scott standing before me with the one playing tonsil hockey several dozen yards away.

Scott's hands tightened on my wrists. "You look like you've seen a ghost."

"More like the Angel of Death."

"What?"

"Shit." I tugged one arm free and pulled him along behind me with the other. "They're gonna grab Harper."

He didn't waste time arguing, just fell in step as I put on a burst of speed. I held off shifting form, not wanting to draw attention too soon. We rounded the last corner just in time to see the brunette disappearing toward the alley with Scott's evil twin.

"What the—" Scott double-timed it past me, and I let him. Jogging the last few steps into the alleyway, I reached for the Power beneath my feet, and shifted.

The surge of magic caught Fake Scott's attention. He snarled, grabbed Harper's arms, and slammed her into a brick wall with sickening strength. So much for snatching her. She cried out as her head smacked into the wall, body crumpling to the ground. And that set the real Scott right off.

His double scrambled backward as several hundred pounds of angry Hound confronted him with a muzzle full of wicked sharp teeth. Nemesis and Nike stretched their heads toward our adversary, but I tried to calm them down. Scott had things under control. The least I could do was check on his . . . friend.

I knelt next to her inert form and cursed. She was so still and pale, she *had* to be dead. I reached out to feel for a pulse, but just then her body twitched.

I scrabbled back several steps when the twitching turned to outright convulsions. Magic flared. The woman's neck, bent at an impossible angle, popped back into place and the bruises along the right side of her body faded one by one. Her eyes flashed open. Jade-green eyes bearing the narrow slits of a cat's pupils. Her back arched when she saw me, and she hissed.

I glanced from her to Scott, then back again. Holy shit. Just wait till Scott's mother found out. His little friend Harper, the one he'd slept with, was a Cat. Ninety-nine lives and all.

"Whoa, settle down, girl. I didn't kill you. *He* did."

She turned her gaze onto the Hound battling it out with his double. Magic stirred and I jumped back just in time. Her mortal form wavered, then fell away completely, replaced with red-black fur, nasty claws, and a slender, powerfully built body bred to be a killing machine. I could totally see why Scott's mortal ancestors had worshipped them as gods.

Harper's feline nostrils flared as she sniffed the air and then launched herself toward the Sidhe bastard who'd killed her, soaring over Scott's body and knocking his double to the ground. Scott backed off as the Cat raked claws along the Sidhe's torso and abdomen, drawing both blood and screams. The mortal authorities would not be far behind.

She toyed with the Sidhe, no longer such easy prey. But the Sidhe wasn't either, as Scott and I had learned when spiriting Cori away from her school. He got in a solid blow to her head, sending her skittering while he jumped to his feet. She shook her head, snarling and spitting and bunching her body for another leap.

A flash of metal and a soft click from a dozen feet away caught my attention. Fuck. No time to warn Scott. I leapt into the air, beating both wings to gain the momentum I needed, slamming into his body and knocking us both to the concrete. Bullets whizzed past where our bodies had just been, but they made very little noise. Someone was using silencers. Not to mention magical immortal-killing ammo, I was sure.

"Harper, stop!" Scott rolled toward the Cat, cuffing her on the head to distract her from the Sidhe who'd in fact been the one toying with her. Toying with us all, keeping our attention long enough for his partners to begin picking us off with more mundane means. And we'd nearly let them.

Sirens wailed in the distance. The Sidhe cursed and took off down the alley, not sparing us a second glance. The soft ping of bullets disappeared as well. Even so, I kept my body low as I worked my way over to Scott and the Cat. She followed my lead when I shifted form, looking none the worse for wear in her business clothes and heels. As if I hadn't felt bad enough in the loose jeans and ridiculous T-shirt.

"Scott, we have *got* to go. I can't afford to be taken in for questioning until we figure out which feds are involved in this mess."

Harper stiffened, now-mortal brown eyes narrowing. "What do you mean, feds are involved? And what the hell are you doing with the city's missing Chief Magical Investigator, anyway?"

No big surprise she recognized me after all. Kinda hard not to the way I Furied out back there. Scott touched her shoulder. "Way too long of a story, Harp. You trust me, right?"

Her sharp but pretty features softened. "Of course I do, Mutt."

I fought back a sneer. Mutt? Was that some twisted term of endearment or something?

"Then we need to get somewhere safe pronto."

She nodded, pushing to her feet briskly and motioning for us to follow. I debated taking off in the other direction but knew that was just wishful thinking. What was that saying about safety in numbers?

Harper led us around the back end of the marketplace at a quick clip, careful to avoid the worst of the crowds and even more careful to avoid the uniformed officers bursting onto the scene. She took us to a nondescript parking garage, where we piled into an even more nondescript four-door sedan, and then she started driving in random patterns meant to lose any would-be tails. She didn't do a half-bad job, actually.

"Okay, Scott, spill it," Harper demanded.

He glanced over his shoulder to where I lounged in the backseat. I just nodded.

"All right. You noticed my doppelgänger back there?"

I saw her lips twist in the rearview mirror. "Kind of hard to miss, considering he kissed me almost as good as you and then busted my head open on a brick wall."

Scott winced. "Yeah, sorry about that. Did you get any impressions back there?"

"Other than the one from my head hitting the bricks?" She pondered, making a sudden right that cut off the car behind her, earning as many glares and rude gestures as my earlier jaunt across the street. "Well, when I saw you in Hound form, I realized he must have been a shifter of some sort. Course, I knew something was up the minute he grabbed me. No offense, sugar, but you're neither that fast nor that strong."

I snickered. She shot me a considering glance in the mirror. "So, just what kind of shifter was he? Most of us can only assume one or two forms. Besides Furies, of course."

The challenging note in her voice had me bristling. "We Furies only assume other shapes when pursuing investigations, or to protect our asses when psycho federal agents are trying to kill us for no good reason."

She rolled her eyes. "If they were trying to kill you, I'm sure they had a perfectly good reason. To them."

"Hush." Scott gave us each a *Grow up* glare. "Mind letting me finish?" When neither of us responded, he went on. "That guy back there wasn't a shifter, not in the strictest sense of the word. He was Sidhe."

The car jerked to a stop as Harper slammed on the brakes and turned on Scott. "Have you gone out of your ever-loving mind? The Sidhe are extinct."

I bit back a smirk, though I couldn't quite keep it out of my voice. "And you didn't notice the difference when Mr. Double back there jammed his tongue down your throat?"

Brown eyes flashed with fire. Good thing she was seat-belted in. "I already said he kissed *just* about as good as . . ." Her eyes widened. "He mesmerized me."

"Yeah. One of them got me yesterday. For about thirty seconds. Then he tried to convince me to kill Scott, which was ludicrous. If I decide to do that, it'll be all on my own."

Scott grinned. "Nice to know you care, Riss." He turned back to Harper. "Suffice it to say we have reliable proof that the Sidhe aren't quite as extinct as we were led to believe. A secret branch of the mundane government has been holding the surviving members of the species since the War ended. What's worse, they've been breeding them in captivity, and they've succeeded in either brainwashing or bribing some of the Sidhe to work for them. And now they're trying to kill us."

Harper slid back into traffic, teeth nibbling at her lower lip. "Why would they want to do that?"

"Because I didn't fall for the little ruse they arranged the other day. Came across a body in the normal course of my duties, supposedly that of another Fury, except it wasn't. It was a Sidhe in full-blown glamourie, shifted into the form of my sister Fury. My best friend, who disappeared several years ago."

Her face took on a pitying cast, one I tried to ignore. "Why would they go to all that trouble? I mean, why risk someone finding out the truth? Why not just dispose of the Sidhe's body somewhere no one would ever find it?"

"Good question. Best I can figure is the fact that I've never given up on finding Vanessa. Add to that the fact that her ex-boyfriend Dre Carrington's investigators turned up a fresh lead recently—I'm betting they tried this as a last-ditch effort to get us both off the case. Still, dumping the Sidhe's body in my own jurisdiction was probably not the brightest thing they could have done. Another Fury might not have been as quick to notice the difference. And if her body had been dressed up for her funeral, I would never have noticed either."

"Huh. So, what do you two need from me exactly?"

Scott's shoulders relaxed. "Information. You've got the best network of arcane contacts in the state, not to mention the mundane contacts you can access through the FBI. We have reliable information that the Sidhe are being held in Western Massachusetts, but we'd like to narrow our search area down."

Harper pursed her lips. "And why should I risk getting involved in this, Mutt? I mean, sucks for the Sidhe and all, but they gave as good as they got before they were wiped out. Shit, they killed good friends of mine in the last couple of skirmishes. Friendly fire, my ass."

He touched her hand on the steering wheel. "Because they have my sister, Harp."

"Oh, hell, Mutt. I thought Andre Carrington had Amaya." It stung that Harper had known the truth Scott hadn't trusted me with. A lot.

"We thought the same thing, until Riss pointed out the now-obvious. The woman Dre has is *not* my sister."

"Let me guess. Sidhe?"

Scott's voice sounded weary. "Yeah."

Harper's hands clenched. "All right. Fine. I should be able to make some inquiries without raising any eyebrows at the Bureau. I'll stick to my arcane contacts for now, to make it easier. I assume you don't want the fact that Sidhe are involved to become common knowledge?"

I rolled my eyes. "That'd be just what we need. Every mortal-hating arcane with a grudge declaring war against all mundanes and tearing the commonwealth apart to find the nut jobs responsible. Yeah, if you could keep that little tidbit out, I'd appreciate it."

Her eyes glinted with humor. "I'll do my best. So we're looking for compounds big enough to hold an unknown quantity of arcane captives. And it has to be pretty secluded. I assume you'll take care of narrowing down the field once I give you a list?" At my nod, she asked, "Is it just the Sidhe and your sister being held captive?"

My fingers tightened on the PDA. "No. They have my sister Fury, too. At least, I hope they do."

"Oh, right. She'd have to be alive for the Sidhe to have copied her."

"At some point recently, yeah. And I'm sure you're aware of the unusual number of arcanes who have disappeared recently. Including at least two Cats that I'm aware of."

"I knew about the two missing Cats thanks to the family grapevine, though I'll admit I've been working on a major magical counterfeiting case for the Bureau so hadn't really paid much attention to anything else." She fluffed her deep-brown hair. "However, now that you mention it, I will take great pleasure in tracking the bastards down. Nobody holds a Cat against their will."

I grinned. Maybe Harper wasn't so bad after all.

CHAPTER TEN

I STARED DOWN AT THE LIST OF POSSIBLE locations Harper e-mailed the next morning and snarled. "If this is the best Harper can do, I'd hate to see her worst. Eight different places spread out all across the state? This will take *forever* to narrow down!"

Scott finished unfurling a map of Massachusetts on the kitchen table, ignoring my tirade as he placed a utensil at each corner of the map. He began sticking pins in the eight spots Harper had e-mailed to us minutes earlier.

"Hmm. That's not *too* bad. Most of them are within a few hundred miles of each other, and the locator works within a five-mile radius."

I crossed my arms over my chest and seethed. "That's still a lot of ground to cover. Especially for just the two of us."

"It *won't* be the two of us. No way I'm busting into a secret installation with just you and me."

"I figured we'd find the place, do a little recon, and send for backup."

He patted me on the head. "Yeah right, Riss. I know you. The second you saw a prisoner, Rage would hit and you'd try to kill every guard in sight, raising an immediate alarm and getting our asses caught."

My lips twitched. Okay, so maybe he had a point. "Who we taking, then?"

His fingers tapped the map idly. "Well, we can have Kiara and Sean take over guarding your family, which gives us Mac and Elle for sure."

I nodded slowly, doing my best to pretend the bizarre scene with Sean had never taken place. I figured what Scott didn't know—and I didn't acknowledge—couldn't hurt him. "Yeah. Those two seem competent enough."

Scott bit back a grin. "Whoa. You calling Elle competent? That's a miracle."

"Don't push your luck, Murphy."

"Yes, ma'am. Okay. I'm sure Harper would love to get in on the action, especially considering they used up one of her ninety-nine lives and some of her people could well be captives. With Amaya involved in this, our trouble with the family will be *limiting* the number of volunteers we get. I'd rather not risk too many family members on this, just in case . . ."

His voice trailed away, and I shivered. In case we fucked up and died, or were taken prisoner ourselves. To be experimented on like animals with no free will of our own. That more than anything pissed me off.

My stomach rumbled insistently, distracting me from burgeoning Rage. "You planning to feed me anytime soon?"

He rolled his eyes. "I swear, you eat more than any *two* Hounds."

I stuck my nose in the air and strolled toward the front door. "You're just jealous of my wicked awesome metabolism and girlish good figure," I tossed over my shoulder. The liquid heat in his eyes had me faltering a step. I covered my misstep by donning my new and improved busty disguise.

Scott rolled his eyes and led me on a roundabout course to a far-off diner so we could enjoy a nice, grease-filled breakfast. After we finished cleaning our plates—thank the gods for wicked awesome metabolisms, or squeezing my ass into my red leathers would take much more than a wing and a prayer—Scott handed me a fresh disposable cell phone and leaned back in the old-fashioned vinyl booth, a mysterious smile playing on his way-too-sexy lips.

"Here. I thought you'd like to check on your partner's status."

I blinked, cradling the phone and looking at him with widened eyes. He had kept close enough tabs on me not only to know about Trinity, but to know that I considered her my partner even though she wasn't, officially. His eyes met mine unflinchingly, though their amber depths didn't clue me in to what their owner was thinking. My fingers trembled slightly as I dialed Trinity's cell phone number. I held my breath as the line rang once, twice, and then a third time . . . And then what I'd been praying for. "Hello?" Her voice sounded more subdued than usual. I could tell she hadn't been sleeping well, which meant she was still in the hospital.

I struggled to keep my voice light and easy. "Hey, wuss. You *still* in the hospital? It's been what? Two days now?"

"Hey—bro. Good to hear from you finally. Mom's been going crazy trying to get a hold of you."

My fingers tightened on the phone. "Feds in the room?"

"Yeah, true that."

Scott sensed the tension in my body and quirked an eyebrow, mouthing *Trouble?* I held the other hand up in a *Wait a minute* gesture.

"Are you okay, Trin?"

"The docs got the bullet out, no problem, but I had a reaction to the pain meds. They kept me another night for observation, but I'm breaking out in a few hours."

I let my body relax. "Thank the gods. Trin—I'm sorry. It's my fault you got shot."

"Now, bro, don't go being stupid. Of course you don't need to fly a thousand miles just to hold my hand. No, I don't blame you at all."

Tears pricked at my eyes. Her words meant more than I'd expected. Then again, she *was* the closest thing I had to a best friend these days—well, barring me finding Vanessa alive and raring to go out and paint the town red, white, and Flaming Blue. I cleared my throat, turning from Scott just enough to wipe the tears without him seeing. "Damn, I'm glad to hear you're okay. That you're getting out soon. Sitting still so long must have driven you insane."

She laughed. "You think?"

Her slow, Southern drawl had me grinning. "I know. Okay. I'll try and make this quick. I hooked up with old friends of mine and we're working some solid leads. I'd tell you more, but someone could be listening in on your end. Just don't worry about me, get yourself healed. I'll call you again when I can." Scott jotted a number down on a napkin and slid it across to me. I nodded my thanks. "Oh wait, here's a number where you can reach me if you need to." I rattled it off, knowing that Trin's excellent memory for numbers meant I wouldn't have to repeat it.

"Okay, that makes sense. I'll be good as new soon, so if there's anything I can do to help you and the little wifey out, just let me know."

"Will do." Gods, I was beyond relieved she was now

out of the line of fire. My enemies would not hesitate to take her out in an effort to get to me—as they'd already demonstrated. Still, if I didn't give her *something* to do, she might come up with something much more dangerous on her own. "Hey, maybe there *is* something you can do for me. I'd like you to keep an eye out when you get back to the PD. See if anyone acts strangely, or seems more interested in me than they should be. Especially the asshole." I didn't have to specify which.

"Sounds good. And don't worry, everything will be just fine."

My voice sounded a little husky when I replied. "Thanks, Trin. Good-bye. And take care of yourself."

"Bye, bro. Love you."

Scott eased the phone out of my hands once I'd pressed End. He dropped it on the floor and smashed it to itty-bitty pieces. A few other diners gave him odd looks but remained silent. He smiled with feigned innocence and slid yet another disposable cell across the table. Hopefully the number I'd given to Trinity went along with *this* one and not the cell scattered all over the floor.

I rolled my eyes. "Dramatic, much?"

He winked. "Just playing it safe."

My hands began fiddling with a paper napkin as I went over the conversation with Trinity. I wondered whether I should have told her more, but then decided the less she knew, the better. I'd always made a habit of telling her as little about the arcane world as she needed to know to help me get the job done. No sense making her a bigger target than absolutely necessary.

I forced my thoughts back on target and my gaze on Scott. "Gods, I am not looking forward to driving all over Western Mass. Wish Dre had coughed up the dough to get a bigger radius on his Vanessa-seeking GPS. You sure I can't just fly solo to locate the secret base and then come back and get you?" My eyelashes batted with every ounce of innocence I could dredge up. Which, okay, wasn't all that much.

Scott obviously agreed. He shot me a *You wish* look and otherwise ignored that suggestion. "We might not have to drive *all* over Western Mass. Da has this old military friend, Red, who may be able to help us narrow things down. At the least, he knows a shitload about mortal intel and should be able to fill in some blanks for us. Da always raves about what a kick-ass soldier he was."

"Just why would a *mortal* soldier be willing to give *arcanes* the 411 on military intel?"

"Because he still owes my dad for saving his ass during the War—several times."

Ah, now tit for tat I could understand. Morgan had served in the mortal military during the Time of Troubles—okay, the War—and only converted to "our" side later, when he met and fell in love with Scott's mother. "Red's a little—quirky—these days, though. Made a lot of enemies over the years, and he'll most likely want to meet us somewhere public."

"That's fine. Probably best to keep moving around, anyway." Especially if the Murphys *did* have a leak to plug up somewhere. Less chance for him or her to figure out where our safe house was and arrange for another little ambush.

When our waitress stopped by to refill our coffees, Scott turned his sexy smile and roguish charm her way. "Hey, darlin'. Would you mind bringing a broom and dustpan? Had a bit of an accident with my phone."

She crossed her arms under her chest and shifted slightly. The better to show off her—quite impressive—girls. "Aw, now, that's a shame. Hope it wasn't one of those expensive buggers."

They flirted for another minute or two, pointedly ignoring me, until she wandered off for the broom. Scott threw down enough cash to cover the check and a good chunk of the woman's rent besides.

Scott noticed my sardonic expression and cupped a hand along my back, guiding me toward the door. "The better tip you leave, the less helpful the wait staff will be should nasty thugs show up asking questions about you."

"Yeah, sure, that's all that was back there."

"Riss, if we're going to work together, you've really got to get over that."

We made it outside and started toward the nearest T stop. "Over what?"

"The jealousy thing."

My back stiffened and I tinged my voice with frost. "Excuse me?"

"Yes, the jealousy. That Fury fire inside you made me fall crazy in love with you, but it also pushed me away whenever the whole jealous-shrew routine kicked in."

I didn't know whether to cuss him out for the "jealous shrew" comment or to marvel over the fact that he'd *finally* said he loved me—past tense. That made it easier to avoid fawning and focus on cussing. "And how the hell would I ever have guessed you loved me? It's not like you ever said it."

His eyes narrowed. "What the hell? When we were together, I told you how I felt with my every touch, my every move, my every breath. Was I not speaking loudly enough?"

My heart melted ever so slightly. Gods, the man really *did* have a way with words sometimes. But that thought reminded me of the three little words he'd never quite managed to say. The only words that could unfreeze my heart completely, no matter how many other pretty ones he strung together. "That's just it, Scott. You've never spoken it out loud at all. Not to me."

"You must be tripping, Riss. When we were together I told you I loved you a hundred times. Maybe a thousand."

I nearly weakened at the vulnerability leeching through his voice. But keeping things bottled up until I exploded hadn't worked too well for me in any of the relationships I'd been in. Including this one.

"You may have thought it a hundred times, felt it a thousand, but you never said it."

He shoved both hands in his pockets. A signal of frustration. With me or himself? I couldn't tell.

"I—well, shit. Could have sworn I . . ." His words trailed away and he shook his head, shaggy hair flapping much like his Hound's ears would have. "I never meant to hurt you, Riss. And I sure as hell didn't mean for you to think I didn't love you."

My heartbeat picked up speed, fluttering so quickly I thought it might burst right out of my chest. "Are you saying what I think you're saying??" I held my breath.

"Yes, Riss, dammit. I *loved* you." He stalked forward and slammed my body against his. "Was that loud enough for you? I loved you, you reckless, relentless bitch."

I sighed, closing my eyes and leaning against his chest, listening to his pulse race as quickly as my own. And felt the last few icicles crusting my heart crackle and then explode into a million tiny pieces. Maybe, if he really *had* loved me once, we *could* have a chance in hell when this madness was all over . . .

CHAPTER ELEVEN

"OH, GODS, SOMEBODY PUT ME *OUT* OF MY misery."

Scott bobbed his head to the beat of the twang-filled music, hair swishing with each motion. His hand tapped the booth behind my head, and a smile played about his lips when he spotted the sour look on my face. "What's wrong, Riss? Don't like the club?"

"Club?" I gestured to the animal heads on the walls and the denim-clad two-steppers on the dance floor. "This place hardly qualifies as a club." Even if it *was* located on the top floor of a brand-new building that housed multithemed clubs owned by the same person. Apparently the owner loved country more than rock, hip hop, top forty, alternative, or the metal death we could have been moshing to on another floor. Noooo, we got stuck with Morgan's military friend who was apparently as musically challenged as the owner of this building was.

His eyes glinted in the neon light washing over the room. "Just because you don't care for the music doesn't mean it's not a club."

"I absolutely hate country music, and you damned well know that. Why are we—"

"Now that's a crying shame, darlin'," an unfamiliar voice drawled behind me. "A pretty little thing like you hating God's own music?"

My head whirled and a bear of a man grinned down at me. His solid girth was encased in snug denim on bottom and black cotton on top. A silver steer's head gleamed from his belt buckle, and snakeskin boots and a battered cowboy hat capped off the ensemble. Good lord. Did every person in the joint except Scott and me shop at Rednecks "R" Us?

I turned my back in a pointed brush-off, but Grizzly Adams didn't get the message. His hand touched my shoulder. I stiffened. *Calm down, Riss. He's a mundane. Keep it under control.*

"Mind getting your hand off me, buddy?"

The jerk actually guffawed, slapping a beefy hand against his blue jeans. "Feisty little filly you've got here, Scott."

Feisty? Filly? Was this joker for real? His last word registered and my heart sank. He'd used Scott's name, which meant he was the guy we'd come to see. I shot my companion a dirty glare. *This* was the ex-military friend of Scott's father who was supposed to lend us his ear and whatever intelligence he could? Ha. This clown probably couldn't even spell the word.

"Hey there, Red." Scott motioned to the seat across from us. "Want a beer?"

The nickname seemed ironic, considering his pasty

white skin and muddy brown hair. He plopped down on the other booth, setting the whole thing shaking and the vinyl squeaking. "Now, son, when have you ever known me to turn down a beer?"

The men exchanged chuckles, and Scott flagged a server down. I sized up the man across from us while we waited, trying to pick out the uber-soldier Morgan had praised to Scott in the overly large, overly loud wannabe cowboy twirling a glass ashtray at the end of a gnarled finger. I just didn't see it. He was too brash, too obnoxious, too . . . He flipped the fortunately empty object into the air, twisted in his seat, and caught it behind his back without looking or even moving very much. His eyes followed my own as they tracked the ashtray's movement, then met his gaze. He winked, and then I knew. The Grizzly Adams routine was just that. An act.

And a damned good one.

The server dropped off Red's beer and scurried away before he could pinch her ass. If I hadn't seen the wink just now, I might have punched him on her behalf.

"Don't overdo it," I muttered.

He chuckled again, then dropped the good-ol'-boy persona and turned alert eyes on the two of us. "Your father tells me you have a problem. What can I do to help you out?"

Scott leaned forward. I shoved away the empty feeling when he dropped his arm.

"I know you're privy to a lot of military intel. Do you know anything about an installation in Western Mass? One concerned with avoiding public scrutiny—especially from arcane surveillance."

Red swigged from the longneck bottle, chugging half its contents in one swoop. "Whether I do or not, that's classified information. Could be worth more than just my pension to tell you anything."

My mouth opened to retort, but Scott's hand on my knee stopped me. "We're trying to avoid another war here, Red."

The other man's brow furrowed and he tapped the bottle idly. "Like the Gulf Wars, son?"

"No, more like the Great W—Time of Troubles, I guess you call it. Only worse."

Red snorted. "How could it get worse than that undeclared disaster? Thousands of mortals dead, not to mention hundreds of your people, the complete destruction of the Sidhe . . ." His voice trailed away when he noticed something in either our postures or expressions. He flattened both palms on the scarred wooden table. "You know."

"Know what?" Scott's hand squeezed, but I kept my question short and sweet.

"About the breeding program."

My boots (no way was I going to wear sneakers to a club, even a honky-tonk joint) slammed against the floor and I was halfway to shifting before Scott's arm crushed me to his body and he whispered, "Not here!" in an urgent voice. My breath whooshed out as I forced myself to back away from the edge separating mortal form from immortal.

He turned his attention back to Cowboy Curtis. "I think the more interesting thing here is that *you* know. How did your government expect to get away with this bullshit?"

Red waved a hand in the air. "Don't misunderstand, Scott. When I say you know, I assume you found proof of something most of us in the military only suspect. That a branch of the Forces experimented on arcane prisoners of war some time back."

I couldn't hold back my anger this time. "Is that what they call snatching arcane citizens off the streets these days? Taking prisoners of *war*?"

His bottle clinked to the table so hard it almost shattered. "Now hold on here. The program I'm talking about was launched halfway through the Troubles and disbanded once the Accord was reached. They never had much success anyway. Are you suggesting someone's still running it?"

"I'm more than suggesting it, cowboy. They abducted a sister Fury of mine as well as a literal sister of Scott's. Not to mention the Sidhe they're holding captive."

"Fuck me."

"No thanks," I responded without thinking, then flushed when both men glanced at me. "Sorry. Habit."

Scott patted my hand. "Spending too much time at the PD, Riss." His expression grew more serious. "She's right, Red. They have Amaya, and we've already confirmed they have at least one Fury and an unknown number of Sidhe. And their program isn't just breeding them."

Red's fingers clenched around his bottle.

"They're cloning them."

"Jesus." His voice shook. "That's wrong on so many levels I can't even begin to count them."

"Not to mention illegal," I added dryly.

"That, too. All right, I'll help however I can. If word of this gets out . . ."

"Exactly what we're trying to avoid." *For now,* I added under my breath. No telling how long we'd be able to keep the truth buried once we rescued our sisters and the Sidhe.

Scott asked him a few questions, and he launched into a discussion about the potential man-and-firepower we could face if coming up against a rogue group of mortal militants. I listened as raptly as Scott—I had never really gone up against mortal combatants en masse before. My skin tingled as adrenaline washed through me. The challenge of this could actually be fun . . .

Then I remembered just what was at stake, and my eagerness dampened. People were going to die, no doubt about that. Mortal and immortal alike. Possibly Scott, possibly me, possibly the very ones we were rushing in to save. Best for everyone if I remembered that and kept a tight grip on my Rage.

Scott excused himself to hit the men's room. A song more my style—as much rock 'n' roll as country—began blaring from nearby speakers. Red noticed my body bopping to the beat and grinned. He maneuvered himself out of the booth and held out a hand. "C'mon and dance with me, little darlin'."

Something reckless flared inside, and I found myself grinning back. No sense wasting the night's first halfway decent song, especially since it was way too late to start searching for secret mortal military installations. "All right."

He wrapped his powerful arms around me and whirled us onto the wooden dance floor. Other couples danced in complicated footwork I couldn't have duplicated without a handbook, but Red started me off with something simpler. After a half minute of paying careful attention to his instructions, I was soon two-stepping well enough to avoid making a fool of myself. And I had to admit, it was actually kind of fun.

"So, you're the one that got away."

I blinked. "Ah, sorry?"

He nodded toward the restrooms. "The one who broke my godson's heart."

I missed a step, but he made up for it and we didn't careen into any of the other couples. Crap. I hadn't realized Red and Scott were so close. "I'm not sure what he told you—"

"Oh, don't worry, I'm not gonna bite your head off or anything. It takes two to tango—ha—and I'm sure you had good reasons for what you did. I just wanted to make sure you weren't planning any repeat performances."

It became easier to move my feet and legs to the beat of

the music without conscious thought, so I was able to really think about his words. "I'm not planning to, no. But I can't guarantee you a happy ending, either."

His lips spread in a genuine smile. "Nobody can do that, darlin'. And long as you're not playing with my boy over there, that's just fine with me. 'Sides, I'm starting to like you, and it'd be a shame to have to kill you."

I faltered again, but then he winked and my pulse slowed. "You're a very brave man, Red."

He arched a brow, revealing where Scott had learned the fine art of brow-raising. "And why is that?"

"Not too many mortals would joke about something like that with a Fury."

"Who says I'm joking?"

My eyes widened and my mouth opened to speak, but a hand tapped my shoulder insistently. I turned my head and saw a man even taller and burlier than Red, garbed in similar cowboy gear and wearing a smirk every bit as obnoxious as Zalawski's.

"Take a seat, old man."

My mouth gaped even farther. Had I walked right into a country song cliché? Still, I wasn't worried. Red would tell the punk to move on and then we'd—

"All right. My arthritis is acting up anyway."

Red spun me into the stranger's arms before I could react. I threw a glare over my shoulder, staring at his receding back and trying to figure out what the hell kind of game he was playing. And then I saw Scott approaching from the restroom, and I had to bite back a grin. *Sneaky, sneaky man*. He *wanted* the night to take a spin toward cliché. Earlier recklessness flared anew, and I let the redneck twirl me around the dance floor. He wasn't nearly as graceful as Red and managed to smash both my feet several times beneath his steel-toed boots. I hadn't even realized cowboys wore steel-toed boo . . .

Something about that seemed odd. I sneaked a peek at the goon's feet, and sure enough. He wasn't wearing cowboy boots like every other man in the place. His feet were clad in combat boots. Military-issue combat boots. I threw a glance over my shoulder again and caught sight of Red pointing the now-frowning Scott in our direction. And that's when I noticed the seven men and women wearing combat boots closing in on them. *Shit!* We'd been found.

The fact that they were willing to attack us in a crowded mortal bar spoke of their desperation. And if they were that desperate, people were going to start dying a lot earlier than I'd thought. My mind raced as I sought a course of action that would lead to the least amount of bloodshed.

Since there was only one goon on me, he was obviously intended to serve as a distraction while the bulk of his colleagues took out Red and Scott. I had to act fast.

We spun close to the ladies' room, and I stumbled. "Oh, no, I think I'm gonna puke." I pulled myself from his greasy grasp, and his eyes widened at my display of strength. He'd allowed himself to think I was just another ordinary woman. Idiot.

His eyes followed me like a hawk, but I caught him glancing at his partners before the restroom door swung shut behind me. He let his body relax, no doubt thinking this was even better than him spinning me around the room. Less danger of me catching sight of what they were doing from inside the restroom.

The ladies' room was fortunately empty. I shifted the moment the door thudded shut, reveling in the play of magic across my skin, smiling when Nemesis and Nike burst into life and wrapped around my arms.

"Ready to dance, ladies?" They hissed in agreement. "First we need to clear the place out."

A smoke alarm rested in the ceiling just above the middle stall. I called to the magic lying far below, gathered it

above my extended palm, and manipulated it into the form
I needed it to take: fire. I stretched onto tiptoe, reaching my
arm as far as it would go. Not quite far enough. I siphoned
magic through the girls and increased the amount of flame.
It burned dangerously hot above my hand, but I ignored the
pain. *Come* on. *This* has *to work!*

One more burst of power, and thick smoke billowed
toward the alarm. A few seconds later and the alarm began
blaring angrily. Another few seconds, and the club's out-
dated sprinkler system kicked into effect.

I couldn't help a squeal as cold water soaked me immediately. Nemesis and Nike were none too pleased, but they
didn't protest vocally. Screams echoed outside the restroom and I heard the pounding of feet as people stampeded
toward the exit. Good. Ass-kicking time.

I fought down the thrill of fear that always preceded my
rushing into battle (hey, I'm a Fury, not a moron), allowing Rage to wash it away. A healthy dose of fear might be
a good thing in most situations, but too much of it would
kill you.

The odor of wet wood and fabric met my nostrils when
I burst out of the ladies' room. I wrinkled my nose, eyes
zeroing in on Red and Scott. They circled, back to back,
at the center of the dance floor, all seven of their opponents darting back and forth, swiping at them with wicked-
looking knives. That took care of one worry: no guns.
They'd been planning to slit our throats and slip out in the
confusion.

My dance partner spun seconds after I emerged, expression darkening when he saw me in Fury form. His hand
flicked toward his waistband but my foot lashed out, connecting against his hand with a loud crunch. He grasped
his injured hand with the other and fell to his knees, grunting in pain. Leaving him to writhe wasn't an option. The
moment I passed him to get to the others, he'd be on my

back and bringing me down. I channeled a trickle more Rage to do what was necessary. These people were neither innocent nor civilians. They were soldiers.

After breaking his neck cleanly, I jogged toward the dance floor, slipping and sliding but managing to keep my feet. Scott saw me coming, so he went into berserker mode to keep his opponents distracted. Unfortunately, he was way too successful. All seven goons advanced on him, blades flashing. No way I was gonna get there in—

Red dropped to his feet and rolled, taking out four of them like bowling pins. Scott closed in with the others, blades whirring and silver flashing as they moved in an intricately deadly dance. His savior was in trouble, however. All four of Red's attackers were kicking him while he was down. Literally. Red curled his body in a fetal position, hands protecting his face, but he wouldn't last long.

My heart thudded painfully when two of Scott's remaining opponents managed to get hold of him and the third, a wild-eyed woman, began beating the shit out of him. I could help either Red or Scott, but not both. Rage grabbed me in a chokehold at the choice forced upon me. Either I could save the man I loved and let the mortal who had tried to rescue him die, or I could save the mortal and watch my ex-lover be killed. Unless . . .

No more Ms. Nice Fury. I channeled the Rage churning beneath the surface rather than suppressing it as usual. Nemesis and Nike hissed in pleasure. They raised their heads into the air, hoods flared and tongues flickering, and bathed in the hot flood of chaotic magic I let loose.

The spell was an ancient one, a terrible one, one we Furies rarely unleashed. A visible line of black energy spread out from my raised arms toward the seven men and women in front of me. They sensed it coming for them and tried to run, but it was too late. They'd sealed their dooms the moment they'd accepted a contract on a Fury.

We called this spell Raging Justice because it was born of both. It spread out from a Fury in a large radius but acted in an extremely specific manner. The only people it would touch were those who had violence on their minds, violence toward a Fury. And it would do to them exactly as they planned to do to her. An eye for an eye.

Invisible blows ripped through their flesh, raining death from the black line of magic that separated them from me. They collapsed, instantly dead, fortunate that the magical death Raging Justice spread was much more merciful than they had any right to expect. Even torturers were spared the agony they inflicted on their victims, because nothing could be gained by visiting onto them what they brought onto their victims. But, oh, sometimes it was tempting . . .

Of course, one major downside to the spell (other than the inevitable guilt it brought, later if not sooner) was that it not only took an insane amount of magic, but also borrowed from the Fury's own life essence. If a Fury cast it a second time too close to the first, she would die as surely as those she unleashed it against. It also required active membership in the Sisterhood.

I shook my head to clear it, preparing myself to find seven magic-fried corpses on the ground. Only to find six dead enemies and one all-too-alive, crazy-ass woman running my way.

Shit. Never would have guessed she didn't have murdering me on her brain. And *that* was the other major downside to the spell, easy to forget because most Furies rarely cast this nasty little deathtrap. Intention was everything with Raging Justice, and, like the Golden Rule, would only do unto them what they planned to do unto you.

My lips twisted in a sudden feral grin. I'd never been one to turn away from a knock-down, drag-out fight. My new opponent danced around me on graceful feet, feinting a jab here, a kick there. Feeling me out. Her eyes remained fixed on mine, never once wavering. She felt absolutely no fear, and that told me a lot right there. The other soldiers had all been human, of that I was sure. This one might look the same, but the way she moved, the complete lack of fear, no way she was mortal.

She struck so quickly I barely had time to throw up a block. Her fist met my head in a surge of strength that sent me spinning. No time to lose my balance because she followed, raining blows and kicks as my body spun. I grunted with each blow, shocked at the pain, but I'd picked up a new move from watching Red. I dropped straight to the floor.

She skittered against the damp wood but was too late to stop. I rammed against her legs, bringing her down alongside me. Nemesis and Nike hissed as I rolled onto her body and pinned her to the floor by straddling her chest. They slid off my back and slithered along her legs, threatening but not actually striking. I barely managed to hold them in check.

Heat sloughed off her body and onto mine, but I paid it little heed. Her eyes met mine, still devoid of fear. She struggled, but I was sucking in as much magical power as possible, adding it to my already considerable strength. No more taking chances.

"Who sent you?"

She merely smiled.

I smashed my fist into her right cheek, but it barely fazed her. "What are you?"

"Wouldn't you like to know, Fury?"

My other fist slammed into her left cheek. Pain flared in her eyes, yet she remained silent.

"How did you find me?"

Scorn tinged her laugh. "Mere child's play with the company you keep."

She was looking over my shoulder, so I risked a quick

glance. Scott stood several feet away, helping Red back to his feet.

I rammed my arm against her neck and pushed. "No way he'd betray me. You're just fucking with my mind." My arm began to tingle where her bare neck touched it. She felt even hotter now than she had a few moments before. I frowned. What the hell?

Both her breath and voice grew ragged. "Suit yourself, Fury. It's your life to lose."

Nemesis and Nike wound themselves along my waist, complaining bitterly about the sudden heat. "Why are you so—" The satisfaction in her eyes triggered a realization. I knew exactly what she was—and why Raging Justice had not killed her.

I coldcocked her, sending her straight to unconsciousness, but that wouldn't matter. She'd already tripped the trap.

Scott's eyes widened when I grabbed him by the arm and took off running, yanking Red along with us as we passed him by.

"What in tarnati—"

Red's protest halted as a concussion of heat swept over our backs. He and Scott looked over their shoulders at the woman's body and gasped before picking up speed. I didn't look, but I knew what they saw. Her body gone up in flame, flares of magic and bursts of fire shooting wildly in every direction.

"Shit," Scott panted. "This place is gonna blow before we make it to the door."

"No it's not." I smiled grimly. "Hold on." I swept them both into my arms, cradling them against my body as if they were children. Nemesis and Nike wrapped themselves around the two men at my urging, granting them both a measure of magical immunity to the fire going haywire around us. I channeled one of the wild streaks of energy, shoving it straight toward the wall ahead of us. Bricks burst outward and a huge hole gaped in front of us. We were several stories up, but it didn't matter. I ran straight for the hole, panting with the exertion of carrying two full-grown men without magical augmentation (Fury strength went only so far), and then magic shrieked behind us as the creature's body hit critical mass and exploded.

My wings unfurled with a snap and I launched us out of the hole I'd created. We plunged toward the ground several dozen feet below, my wings flapping furiously to slow our descent. I couldn't redirect the energy used to keep us from going up in flames to deal with Scott and Red's extra weight, and the ground was hurtling toward us at an alarming rate.

"Brace yourselves," I grated out. "This is going to hurt."

I flipped around at the last minute, wrapping my wings around them so I could take the brunt of the impact. Scott would have been able to handle it, but not Red. We hit seconds later, just in time to watch a firestorm roar out of the hole we'd vacated and spread downward, eating up each floor of the building in no time flat.

"Fucking Phoenixes," I mumbled, then gave in to the darkness sucking me under.

•

CHAPTER TWELVE

MY KNEE WAS ON FIRE, PAIN RADIATING OUT-
ward, touching each and every part of my body. I groaned
and fled toward blessed oblivion once more. Tried to flee,
but failed.

"Hold on, Riss. Baby, I'm here."

Hands squeezed mine, setting off another round of pain.
Tears slipped down my cheeks. I struggled to remember
why I hurt so damned bad, and then memory hit. The Phoenix going kamikaze, incinerating the bandage protecting
my injured knee, and then flying/falling several stories and
slamming into concrete. No wonder it hurt so much.

I forced my eyes open, jerking as the glare of light
flooded them. "S-Scott?"

He squeezed my hands again but dropped them at my
wince. "Sorry, Riss. Where does it hurt?"

My throat felt clogged with dirt. I coughed, cleared it, and croaked, "Everywhere."

Voices murmured behind him, and then a figure I didn't recognize stepped forward. "The Oracle will be here shortly."

I stiffened. "I don't need any damned Oracle screwing with me. Where's Kiara?"

Scott smoothed my hair. "Protecting your family, remember? And yeah, you do need a damned Oracle. Nemesis and Nike are killing themselves keeping you alive, and only an Oracle has a snowball's chance in hell of healing all three of you."

Nausea flooded my stomach. I shoved the sheet covering me to the side and gasped at my ravaged body. Then I caught sight of the worn-out husks coiled around each of my legs and gasps turned to sobs.

"They're dead!" I fell back against the sea of pillows cushioning me. "Oh gods, I killed them!"

Scott took my hands gently in his. "Calm down, Riss. They're not dead. Not yet. Which is why you need the Oracle. Too much internal damage added to the external for them to handle alone."

I remembered the last time I'd allowed an Oracle to get near me and scowled. Nobody healed better than an Oracle—or screwed with your mind more. They just loved tossing out unwanted and unasked-for predictions that might or might not actually occur (prophecy sucked like that), speaking in riddles that hid truth inside enigmas. The Oracle who had been brought in to heal my deadly wounds after my first nearly botched Mandate had rambled on about dead people that weren't actually dead holding the key to great treasure, and that only through healing broken hearts could ancient magic be restored . . .

Wait. Dead people that weren't actually dead could

mean *a* dead people—the Sidhe. Great treasure could mean their immortality and magic, or Vanessa and the missing arcanes—or even all of the above. Healing broken hearts—well, that could mean mine for one, Scott's for two, not to mention all the arcane families whose loved ones had been disappearing for the past couple of years . . .

My eyes widened. "That Oracle wasn't a nut job after all."

"She's not here yet, Riss. Maybe you should go back to sleep until—"

"Not her, *him*. The one who saved me last time. He predicted everything, Scott. Vanessa's abduction, the Sidhe, you and me . . ."

"Did he tell you anything useful like where to find them or how to save them?"

I shook my head. "Of course not. That would have been too easy."

A lightly accented voice that would have sounded far more at home under the Tuscan sun echoed from the doorway. "I swear, arcanes are every bit as bad as mortals. You want a quick fix. Somebody else who can solve all your problems for you."

An unfamiliar, olive-skinned woman came into view. She looked like a runway model: tall, leggy, wearing an ultrahip short dress that bared a lot of cleavage and several pieces of flashy jewelry. My lips pursed. She had to be the Oracle, but she looked far more put together than any of them I'd ever seen.

As if she'd heard me, she stepped across the room, shaking her head with each step. "Come now. Don't tell me you buy into the stereotype."

Scott patted my hand. Whether to comfort him or me, I couldn't tell. "Stereotype?"

"Yes. That all Oracles are sloppy loons with crazy eyes who mumble all the time. That we walk around foretelling doom and gloom twenty-four/seven. Honestly, other arcanes really *should* know better."

He relaxed. "So you *are* the Oracle?"

Her lips curved. "Yes. Though I had a fine time convincing your guard dogs out there of that fact. You can call me Gianna."

She perched on the edge of the bed opposite Scott, eyes roving along my damaged body and the two serpents wasting away on my legs. Her face tightened. "What did you do to them?"

The accusation in her voice had my back stiffening. Which hurt like hell, of course. I tried not to let her see. "How about, what did the *bad guys* do to them?"

Her hand waved in the air. "You failed to protect them. Therefore, you are as guilty as the one who caused the hurts."

I shoved myself to a sitting position, ignoring the agony pounding through me, and shot her the dirtiest look I could muster. "Listen, toots, if you think you could have protected another arcane, a mundane, two Amphisbaena, and yourself while fleeing a kamikaze Phoenix and jumping off a ten-story building only to slam into concrete better, you're free to try and prove it. Otherwise, put up or shut up."

Gianna blinked impossibly dark eyes. "You escaped a dying Phoenix?"

"Damned straight I did. And kept all five"—I quirked a brow at Scott and he nodded—"of us alive." My eyes fell on the girls again, and my voice hitched. "Can you help us or not?"

Her hands moved toward the nearest serpent. Nemesis. They settled on patchy, flaking snakeskin. Within minutes, a soft green glow spread from hands to serpent. A low humming filled the room, soon followed by the scent of growing things. Of jasmine and magnolia, of pine and honeysuckle, of a dozen other flower and tree perfumes. Warmth spread through the air as well, a warmth that had me settling back against the pillows and closing my eyes. Damn, it felt so good.

Scott's hand fell away, only to be replaced by Gianna's once she finished with both serpents. I felt earth magic flowing from both her and the girls. My eyes shot open and tears welled once more when I saw them winding their way toward my chest, restored to their former hissing glory.

The gentle warmth generated from their healing flared to outright heat that danced between pleasure and pain. The Oracle pressed my body down on the mattress. Fire flashed from chest downward, searing every inch of flesh and bone yet also beginning to knit them together in proper order. I wondered for the twentieth time why something meant to save your life had to hurt even worse than the injuries threatening it to begin with, and then it was done, and pain faded away—except for my knee.

She furrowed her brow, hands moving downward and probing. Her breath hissed, sounding just like Nemesis and Nike, and she jerked her hands away as if scalded. "How did you do this? I should be able to heal *all* your injuries."

I tried to ignore the flare of agony her prodding and poking had set off. "That didn't come from the fall. It happened earlier."

"And why didn't you tend it when first it happened?"

"Didn't have time."

Her cheeks flushed, and her skin turned nearly purple. "You didn't—have time . . ." For a moment I thought she was having a heart attack. "I've wasted my time and power on an idiot, apparently. Do you have any idea what you've done?"

I narrowed my eyes and crossed my arms over my chest. "Yeah. I saved his life and my own—not to mention my innocent niece's—by using magic to ignore the injury long enough to take down the S—sons of bitches who were pounding on us."

Gianna shuddered, veins bulging in her forehead. Not so elegantly put together at the moment. "You've butchered your knee beyond repairing. Nothing I can do—and I am one of the best Healers in either the mundane or arcane worlds—can fix it. Nothing *you* do can fix it. How did you manage to flee that Phoenix carrying two grown men without falling on your ass?"

I jerked a hand toward Scott. "His sister is a wiz with magical remedies. She patched up my boo-boo so I could function."

Her lips thinned into small lines of disapproval. "Well, I suggest you stock up on her remedies to block the pain, Fury. You'll be needing them to function for the rest of your life. That knee will never heal fully, not after what you've put it through. Even then, you may well become a cripple."

My hands fisted. No *way* I would become crippled. No freaking way. She had to be wrong, had to be lying to scare me. I'd used magic to ignore pain and injury before, and things had turned out just fine. Granted, never such a serious injury, and definitely never something so screwed up internally. Usually they had been surface wounds . . .

"Look. Don't think I don't appreciate what you did for the girls and me, because I do. But for someone so concerned with living down the stereotype, you're preaching enough doom and gloom for a dozen Oracles."

Gianna sniffed, pushing to her feet and heading for the exit, addressing her final words to Scott over her shoulder. "You will want to get more of the remedies from your sister, or the Fury there will be useless to you. Mark my words well. That knee will never heal."

And with those words of hope and inspiration, she disappeared.

DENIAL, SUCH A WONDERFUL THING. I WAL-lowed in it like a pig in mud, refusing to discuss the Ora-cle's prediction with Scott, shutting him up by pretending to sleep. Only when one of his mercs showed up with a care package from Kiara—along with a brief, hearts-and-flowers-covered note from Cori updating me on the family's prog-ress researching—did I actually bother to sit up in bed again. Despite his obvious annoyance with me, he tended my knee with gentle hands. Tears welled despite his great care. It hurt so damned bad I almost had to confront the truth head-on. But then the bandage slipped into place, and blessed relief stilled the raging inferno that was my knee.

I blew my breath out in an explosive rush. *Thank the gods!* Scott held out a hand and helped me to my feet. I walked toward the door, placing as little weight on my left leg as possible. Absolutely nothing. No pain, not even the slightest twinge. Ha! The Oracle had obviously exagger-ated. Crippled, my ass. I hadn't so much as broken a leg since high school, and the thought of my indestructible Fury nature failing me just when I needed it most had my stomach twisting in knots all over again. So, naturally, I completely and totally ignored it.

"Hmm, remind me to give Kiara a big fat kiss next time I see her."

Scott grinned when I turned toward him. "I'll be sure and do that, if only to see her beat you down when you do. You know you're not butch enough for her tastes."

I sneered. "As if she could." My eyes glanced down at the plain white tee I was wearing. Warmth suffused my cheeks when I realized it must be his. "Ah, got anything else I can wear?"

He arched a brow. "Going somewhere?"

My arms folded across my chest. "Uh, yeah. We've got a case to crack, remember? Places to go, people to kill. I mean save."

Scott tapped his watch. "Not tonight, princess."

"What, I only slept a couple hours? Feels like longer."

"It *was* longer. Like thirty hours longer."

"That's—that's impossible." Shock gave way to suspicion. "You let me lie there killing the girls for thirty hours before you sent for the Oracle?"

"You weren't killing the girls at first. They seemed to have things under control most of last night and this morning. It only became obvious then that they weren't really making much progress. That's when they started dying themselves."

"What time is it now?"

"Just after eight P.M."

"And it took another what? Ten, twelve hours to call in an Oracle?"

He hesitated, arms falling to his side and eyes roving around the room as if he didn't want to meet my eyes.

"Murphy. Answer me."

"We started trying to get an Oracle in early this morning."

"What do you mean, trying?"

"Exactly that, Riss." He sighed, crossing to me and pulling me to his chest. At first, the open display of affection took me by surprise. It felt good, though. Damned good. "You've got a bit of a—reputation—among the Oracles. It took us hours just to find one willing to come and take a look at you. And that only because of her cousin."

It took him *hours* just to find someone willing to keep me alive? I fought back the sting of rejection and focused on his last statement. "What the hell would her cousin have to do with this?" He tilted his head in a *Go on, guess* gesture. "Oh fuck. Are you telling me they got an *Oracle*, too?"

He nodded, and Rage welled up stronger than ever. No matter my personal opinions of the soothsayers, Oracles were inviolate, one of the few groups of arcanes who usually held themselves neutral during magical disputes. Other arcanes ignored their sacrosanct nature at great peril. Rather than fighting the Rage, I channeled it, stalking to the bathroom and rifling through the duffel bag Kiara had packed for me—what was it now? Two days ago?

Scott came up behind me. Rather than arguing, he simply leaned against the doorway. "It's awful late to be starting anything."

I shoved on a sweatshirt, words muffled by the thick cotton. "Which is why I'm finishing something instead."

"And that would be?"

"Getting ready to take our people back. Tomorrow."

His hands pushed mine away from the sweatshirt, and he stretched the material enough to fit my head through. "No way can we be ready to strike by tomorrow."

My grin was predatory as I slipped into another pair of slightly loose jeans, followed by a comfy pair of sneakers. "Watch us."

"Riss, you know how much I want to get Amaya—and Nessa—back, but I don't think—"

"Stop thinking, Scott, and *help me*. One way or another, I want this finished. The sooner the better."

"You were dying just a few minutes ago."

"And now I'm perfectly fine." I jumped up and down, waving my arms wildly. "See?"

He shook his head. "Gods, you are a stubborn bitch."

My lips quirked. "Just the way you like 'em."

A matching grin spread across his face. "Maybe."

I stretched to my full height and wiggled slightly. "Definitely."

He made a visible effort not to watch my jiggling body parts, focusing on a spot just over my head instead. "Fine, then. Let me change into something more practical. Though I'm still not sure what that devious little mind of yours has planned."

I wrapped my arms around myself, taking pleasure in the fact that he trusted me enough to follow where I led. "Where else would a woman want to go after a near-death experience? Shopping!"

GRANTED, MY IDEA OF THE PERFECT SHOP-ping trip was a bit different from the average woman's. Instead of searching for a bitching outfit or pair of shoes, I went hunting for commando gear and weapons. The arcane version.

Scott needn't have worried about it being too late. In fact, the place we needed to go was open twenty-four/seven nearly every day of the year. Gunmetal Alley, where every-one went when they wanted the best of mundane weapons blended with the finest of arcane spells. Normally, I didn't mess with hybrid weps, but there was an occasion for everything. Busting into a military outpost definitely qual-ified as one.

Ellie and Mac tagged along with us, eyes searching the dimly lit alley for any hint of trouble. I still hadn't figured out exactly what Ellie's Scottish hunk of a husband was. An absolute magician when it came to mundane technol-ogy, he nevertheless walked with the grace and assurance of an arcane being. But the number of arcanes who truly excelled when it came to using mundane technology with-out magical modifications was exceedingly small. The only thing I could be sure of was that he wasn't Sidhe.

"Why are you staring at Mac?" Scott's voice tickled my ear.

I shivered and huddled deeper into my sweatshirt. "Just trying to figure out what he is."

"What do you mean, what he is?"

My mouth opened to respond, but I closed it when we reached the outskirts of Gunmetal Alley. Two bouncers stood to each side of the makeshift entrance, arms folded across their massive chests and night-dark sunglasses obscuring their eyes. Those shades gave them both night vision and the ability to pick out anyone trying to sneak past them via magical means.

The bouncer to the right stepped into our path and raised a meaty hand. "Now, now, now, you know I can't let you in here, sweetheart."

I amped up my vision magically, squinting up at the eight-foot-tall man grinning down at me like a maniac. "Holy—Charlie, is that you? Oh my gods, I thought you were dead." A major reason I'd gone crawling back to Scott for help.

The Giant—literally—gathered me up in a bear hug, nearly taking my breath away. I caught Scott frowning out of the corner of my eye and couldn't help a small smirk. Nice to know I wasn't the only one hit by the green-eyed monster.

"Nah, just laying low for a while. I'd heard the same thing about you lately, sweetheart, and I'm glad to see those rumors were *also* wrong."

Charlie set me back on my feet. Hard. I managed not to trip, planting my feet in an aggressive stance and tilting my head. "And what do you mean, you can't let me in?"

The other bouncer coughed, but remained silent. Charlie's grin grew even bigger, splitting the huge but handsome features of his face in half. "You're a full member of the Boston PD, Riss. And the Alley's proprietors don't want any trouble with the mundane authorities."

Translation: Some of the stuff in here isn't exactly legal, and they didn't want me turning them in.

"Well then, there shouldn't be a problem since I'm

currently on suspension." My voice hardened. "And I need our kind of firepower to finish handling the case that got me suspended."

He hesitated. "What case?"

If he'd been anyone but Charlie, I would have told him to mind his own freaking business. But Charlie and I went way back, and we'd saved each other's lives a few times. I trusted him, probably as much as I trusted Scott. Maybe more, since *he'd* never broken my heart. Then again, to him I *was* the size of a small child.

"Arcanes have been vanishing lately. I've figured out the who, what, and why; now I just have to track down where. And when I do, I'm going to need as much firepower as I can come up with."

He exchanged a glance with the other bouncer. Their expressions had grown somber, more somber than my words deserved. Which meant . . .

"Oh hell. They got one of you, too?"

"Two. Husband and wife." Charlie's eyes flashed with anger. Though his kind were nowhere near as slow and stupid as mortal folklore portrayed them, they could be every bit as vicious when their anger was aroused. "Just last night."

The other bouncer's fingers tightened. "If you need more backup, Fury, you have but to ask. Several of us would welcome the chance to take back our brethren."

My pulse picked up speed as I considered the possibilities. Four or five Giants would even the score considerably. Each Giant warrior was worth several times their smaller counterparts when it came to taking out enemies. "We could use four of you. Five tops." Would be hard to be stealthy with too many more than that.

His lips curved into a hungry smile. "Done."

Charlie nodded in satisfaction. "Fighting alongside you again will be an honor."

My cheeks reddened slightly. Fortunately, the dim light concealed that fact. "The honor will be mine. Now, about those weapons?"

Charlie gestured to the entrance. "Just make sure you keep a low profile. If anyone tries to give you trouble, send them to us. Oh, and make sure you stop by on your way out so we can coordinate."

This time I was the one to nod. "Done."

We passed them by, stepping straight into the heart of Gunmetal Alley. Ramshackle lean-tos lined each side of the alley, butting directly against buildings that housed slightly more reputable establishments like taverns, inns, and pawnshops. Yeah, even arcanes got desperate enough to put beloved possessions in hock to stave off starvation another day. Or keep all kneecaps intact.

This portion of the Alley was better lit than the part we'd left behind, thanks in no small part to the hybrid security system the Alley's proprietors employed. Only slightly better lit, however, because most of their clientele required anonymity to conduct their business. This wasn't—exactly—a black market, but it marched right up to the line dividing gray from black, as evidenced by the fact that they had initially barred me entrance.

Ellie put hands on hips and broke the silence. "So, just *what* are you looking for?"

"Exactly what I told Charlie. Firepower, and lots of it. You can be sure the mundanes will have enough for a small army, and we'd best have the same. Magic will only get us so far. Hell, they may have blocked off access to most of the underground reservoirs, so we may only be able to call on our own inner reserves." I swept an arm toward the rickety storefronts. "Hybrid weps will pack the biggest bang for our buck since they come equipped with their own magical reserves."

She blinked. Something like admiration flickered across

her expression, gone so quickly I must have imagined it. "They're also hella expensive."

My lips twitched, but I held back the smile. "Don't worry. It's all on the Sisterhood tonight."

Avarice gleamed in her eyes. "In that case, I know the perfect weps for Mac and me . . ." She tugged her husband along in her wake, scurrying across the Alley and into a nearby store.

"Should I be worried?" I mused aloud.

Scott patted me on the shoulder. "Worried?"

"Yeah. She looked way too greedy just now. The Elders *do* have their limits, after all."

He laughed. "Trust me, when you successfully rescue your missing sister along with my missing sister and the other arcanes, not to mention reveal the existence of the captive Sidhe, they're not going to argue the cost."

I perked up. "True. Especially since they can then spread the bill out among the other arcanes when they get their people back."

"Exactly."

"Come on, then. We've got a lot to do and not a whole lot of time in which to do it." I tugged the hood of my sweatshirt up, doing my best to follow Charlie's advice to keep a low profile. Scott shadowed me, his eyes darting around the dimly lit alley for the slightest hint of trouble. A goofy smile split my face when I noticed. I couldn't believe he still cared about me. Dared I hope for more? Despite the accusations we'd hurled back and forth, all the reasons it would be monumentally stupid to start things back up between us, working together again just felt right—*being* together felt right. If I closed my eyes, I could pretend we had already spoken everything out loud, that we were on the road to getting back together and headed straight for our own happily ever after. That, quite honestly, scared the bejeebus out of me, and I was too scared to say anything to him. Too scared to hope I was right, too scared that speaking the words out loud would break the spell and this would all turn out to be a pipe dream.

Inwardly I cursed my own weakness and forced my thoughts back to the task at hand. We made it to the first store without incident. Magic caressed my skin as I stepped across its threshold, but the store proprietor barely glanced up at the chime signaling that a dangerous arcane had entered the building. Pretty much par for the course here.

The wizened old man finished tinkering with whatever he was working on, wiped his hands on a grubby towel, and hobbled toward us. It was only when he got close to the nearest light that his skin took on an odd, greenish glow and it became apparent his wrinkles were not so much due to age as to heredity. Half Goblin.

"Whaddyawant?" His voice grated against my ears with the consistency of gravel, his scowl growing with each syllable.

I threw back the hood so he could see my face. Beady black eyes widened and he stumbled back a step. "You!"

"Yeah, me, Allazzar. Did you think you wouldn't see me again after your little double cross?" Scott growled next to me, but I patted his arm to keep him quiet.

Allazzar straightened to his full height of four and a half feet and narrowed his eyes. "Me, double-cross a customer?"

"That wep you sold me three months ago was a dud, Allazzar. It misfired and nearly got me killed."

His Adam's apple bobbed as he took a nervous swallow. "Er, whaddyamean it misfired? My weps *never* misfire."

"Lucky for you I know that. Which is why I'm giving you a chance to make it up to me—*without* involving the Elders."

His greenish skin had taken on a distinctly white pallor. Messing with a pissed-off Fury was bad enough. Offending an Elder, on the other hand, was a hundred times worse. They had powers that made mine look like child's play.

"I swear, Fury, I didn't know your wep was a dud. Modified it myself, I did. Perhaps your enemies interfered with . . ." His voice trailed away as I crossed my arms over my chest. "Yes, well. You have my humblest apologies and of course you can select a replacement at no extra charge."

My hand reached out and caressed the length of a crossbow hanging nearby. Some arcanes still preferred the old ways—amped up with magic, of course. "I have a better idea, Al. You can outfit my friend and me here, and give us enough firepower to outfit several other companions of mine, at your cost. Then we'll be square, and I *won't* have you shut down."

His mouth trembled as mutiny flashed across his face. Not even self-preservation could interfere with his greedy Goblin ways. "Preposterous. You and your friend I could outfit at cost, and that would equal the one wep you dest—er, that misfired. Several others? At cost?! Are you trying to drive me out of business, Fury?"

I glanced at Scott and saw his lips twitching with the effort to hold back laughter. I winked and turned back to Allazzar.

"Now, Al, if I were a less trusting sort, I'd believe that someone bribed you to give me a nonfunctioning wep." Several drops of sweat broke out on his forehead. "But I'm going to give you the benefit of the doubt since I ordered it off the Net and anyone could have screwed with it in transit." Hell, it'd been recently enough that it could have had something to do with the current case. Doubtful, but possible. "That means you need to work with me. None of this gold-gouging Goblin crap. I'll give you ten percent over cost for everything we get tonight, plus another ten percent bonus once we complete our mission and provided that all the weps—*all* of them—work properly."

He spit into his hand and held it out. Before he decided he could wrangle more out of me, I spit into my palm and placed it around his own. We shook hands. Magic shot from the ground to where our essences mingled, flaring with brilliant green sparks that sealed our deal—and meant he couldn't try to cheap out on me like he'd done with the Internet deal. My own fault for trying to beat the system.

The bartering done, Scott and I walked up and down the narrow aisles, occasionally testing the feel and weight of various knives, swords, and guns, trying to decide which would work best for us and which might work for those we had in mind to use them. Not surprisingly, I kept gravitating toward Al's hyped-up Sig Sauer P229s, the same model Mr. Asshole had confiscated from me, though I splurged and upgraded to the Elite Stainless. The Sisterhood *was* buying, after all, even if they didn't know it yet.

Al seemed much more enthusiastic when he saw the sheer amount of weapons we laid on his counter. Even just ten percent above cost of everything we had selected would be a very nice night's profit for him. The extra ten percent made it even sweeter.

And, of course, made it less likely he would try anything sneaky.

We made arrangements for him to deliver everything except our own personal weps to Hounds of Anubis later that evening, since we sure as hell couldn't trust anyone else with the location of the safe house. Especially not Goblins. They'd sell their mother's darkest secrets if it brought enough (make that any) profit.

After meeting up with Ellie and Mac, we stopped to make arrangements with Charlie and his fellow Giant, then headed back into the Belly and toward Hounds of Anubis, figuring it would be safe enough for the few hours it would take our purchases to be delivered. Halfway there, however, I wasn't so sure.

The others gave me questioning looks the third time I paused in the middle of the sidewalk for seemingly no reason. Sure enough, the footsteps that had been trailing us since we left Gunmetal Alley stopped milliseconds after we did. I started walking again, continuing the thread of conversation we'd been engaged in, then muttered into the pause, "We're being followed."

The two Hounds seemed disgruntled that I'd heard something they hadn't, but I didn't bother explaining that I'd had my senses magically augmented the entire time we'd been back in the Belly. We kept up the ebb and flow of conversation, hissing and discarding several plans of action until we finally agreed on the most straightforward. Mac and I continued onward, letting the two Hounds dart into the shadows and trail around until we had our pursuer trapped between us. A minute or so later, howls split the air and Mac and I whirled, running back the way we'd come. Mac shocked me when he kept up pace for pace. I really *had* to figure out what he was.

I shifted as we ran, reveling in the wash of magic pounding through my body, soothing Nemesis and Nike mentally and preparing for a good ass-kicking. We broke out into the middle of an abandoned street and my body tensed. Scott and Ellie were herding a cloaked and shadowed figure our way. I pounced, landing and ripping the cloak away so we could see our pursuer. Wide, frightened eyes stared back at me from a familiar, achingly beautiful face. Amaya.

Or, more accurately, Fake Amaya.

Adrenaline morphed to disappointment, and then suspicion flared. "Why the hell are you following us?"

She blinked, confusion marring the crisp perfection of her face. "I—I don't know."

Scott and Ellie exchanged looks mirroring my own doubts perfectly. Mac just stood there, lips pursed thoughtfully.

"What do you mean, you don't know?"

Rage dripped from my lips, and she cowered back a step. "P-please. I truly don't know. I only remember leaving the apartment for an appointment, and the next thing I know I'm being chased by—by them." She gestured to Scott and Ellie as if they were complete strangers. Which, come to think of it, they were.

I bit back the retort raring to burst from my lips. Who said Furies couldn't exercise tact when the situation called for it? Taking a deep breath, I shifted to mortal form and held out a hand. "Come on, then. We'd best see you safely home."

She eyed my hand warily. "Home?"

"Yeah, to Dre's place. That *is* your home now, isn't it?"

Her hand settled into mine a moment later. "Yes, it is."

Ellie raised her brows when I tugged Fake Amaya in the direction of Hounds—and Dre's penthouse suite. I mouthed the word *Later* and draped a hand along the back of Fake Amaya's shoulders. She walked along meekly, not commenting on the fact that I was acting so buddy-buddy to her even though we barely knew each other. For once, I didn't find her easy compliance spooky.

I sent tendrils of magic curling around her, probing to see whether someone had recently tampered with her by magical means. At first, I didn't detect anything unusual. But then I struck pay dirt in the form of a tight knot of magical energy located at the base of her skull. Someone had compelled her within the past few hours.

We walked in silence for the first few blocks. My mind whirled, trying to figure out who stood to gain the most from sending Fake Amaya out to do their dirty work. I just kept coming back to the obvious conclusion—whoever was the traitor among the Murphy family—but something about that didn't quite ring true. How would they have the opportunity to work such a complex spell on the fey creature who Dre kept practically under lock and key?

My mouth dropped open as we crossed the threshold of Dre's building. The doorman escorted us to the elevator while I chewed on the realization that had struck. I watched the digital numbers inscribed above the gilded elevator doors ticked downward. Twenty . . . nineteen . . . eighteen . . .

Sudden urgency tugged at me. "Amaya—Mya—whoever you are—does Dre always let you leave the building for appointments alone?"

The number above the doors continued ticking downward. Eight . . . seven . . . six . . . five . . .

"Oh, I wasn't alone. My bodyguard was with me."

A chime rang out as the elevator doors swooshed open. We piled inside the vehicle, empty except for the uniformed sorceress-cum-operator. The elevator zoomed quickly upward.

Excitement surged. Finally we were getting somewhere. "And who was that?"

Mya chuckled, gesturing a graceful hand toward the sorceress who was smiling at us widely. Too widely by far. "Doreen, of course. She always escorts me when I leave the apartment."

Oh fuck.

Magic, a hell of a lot, stirred beneath our feet. I knocked Mya back and herded the others into the corner behind me. Only Mya protested; the others had done the math and come up with the same conclusion I had. That bitch had set us all—

The elevator ground to a halt, brakes squealing so loudly my ears rang. Doreen's lips were moving in a silent chant and the energy beneath our feet was rising to her call.

Shit. Oh, shit.

I shifted—or tried to anyway. Something blocked me off from the inner pools of magic I used to change from mortal to Fury. Panic flared. How the hell was I supposed to fight a badass sorceress (for Dre would hire none other) without magic?

Scott's equally panicked voice sounded softly in my ear. "I can't shift."

"Me, neither," Ellie muttered.

We were *so* toast right now. I braced myself to make a noble, futile flying leap onto the sorceress, but then I froze. My lips curved when I remembered where we'd just come from.

Magic churned between the sorceress and us. I may not have been able to touch it, but I sure as hell could feel it. She had brewed a nasty piece of work, undoubtedly fatal. No sooner had that thought crossed my mind than she began to aim the magic in our direction.

"Drop!" I screamed, grabbing Mya's arm and jerking her down with me. The five of us barely made it to the floor in time. A burning hot flood of energy rushed overhead, passing so close I swore I smelled singed hair. It reminded me of the fuckup with the Phoenix, and that just pissed me off.

Doreen was gearing up for another go, and this time it wouldn't take her nearly as long to build up the magic. I waited until she was committed to the spell. "Stupid bitch!" Her expression tightened at my words and she began siphoning magic at greater speed.

I worked my hand beneath my sweatshirt while she was distracted, flesh meeting the cold, hard length of steel marking manmade sidearm. Clicking off the safety, I leaned over so the ground wouldn't impede my reach. Once the sorceress could no longer safely withdraw from her spell, I drew.

Her eyes widened when I pointed the wep. Then she

did the very thing I'd assumed she would never be psycho enough to do. Released the unfinished spell.

Magic sizzled and burned into a deadly maelstrom. A completely uncontrolled, uncontrollable maelstrom rampaging through the tiny confines of the elevator.

Ah, hell. Now we're all *gonna die.*

Instinct had me firing off a half dozen rounds, but they simply passed harmlessly into the thick wall of energy whirling between predator and prey. On the plus side, her act of insanity had one benefit. It disrupted whatever magical block she'd placed on us.

I shifted into partial Fury form, leaving off the wings. Nemesis and Nike took one look at the whipping inferno of magic headed straight our way, and their hoods immediately flared. "Brace yourselves!" I shouted over my shoulder, then raised the girls up high and sucked magic through them in a violent rush. I began building a bubble of protection around the five of us, creating it as quickly as I could, adding layer after layer of buffering energy meant to work off as much of the raging torrent as it—

The maelstrom exploded before I had even a half dozen layers fully in place. I saw Doreen go up in eerily beautiful sparks and flames, crazy green eyes blazing with triumph since she was sure we would soon follow her into death. And she might have been right.

The unleashed, half-formed spell devoured layer after layer of protection, but slightly more slowly than I'd anticipated. My breath hitched at this realization.

I manipulated magical energy more quickly than I'd ever before dared, creating additional layers of magical buffer. Stacia would have had kittens if she'd seen the shoddy work I made of it, but these individual shields didn't have to be perfect. They just had to slow down—and destroy part of—the maelstrom eating through the outer layers. If only I could create more than the spell had teeth for . . .

A half minute, and then a minute passed. I stayed four layers ahead of the maelstrom, and then three. As one minute passed to two, my lead narrowed to two thin layers of magic separating us from certain death. And the spell seemed to have way too many teeth.

Voices muttered behind me, but I paid them no heed. Any waver of my attention now and we would crash and burn for sure. I barely noticed when the elevator shook once, twice, and then began moving upward. The spell continued burning itself out on my makeshift shield, but there was still more spell left than bubbles of protection. Despair tickled my throat.

It had me changing from the tack of protecting all of us to searching for a way to sacrifice myself to save the four crouched behind me. Maybe if I—

Chimes rang out and viselike hands gripped my arms. I barely got out a choked protest before they yanked me back and to the side. My last layer of protection sizzled and popped as the spell ate through it and then exploded into the air where we'd just been. I covered my head with my arms and braced for a death that never came.

Magical fireworks burst, creating a light show that would have been lovely if not so very lethal. I finally had the presence of mind to register that we'd somehow reached the penthouse suite. Scott's arms loosened when I squirmed. I sat up and searched anxiously, relaxing only when I'd counted three other bodies nearby, all alive and well.

Wait, make that four other bodies. Dre Carrington, minus the blond hair that was his pride and joy, had plastered his body over Mya's and was now checking her for the slightest hint of injury. That bumped him up several notches in my esteem, even though I didn't want it to.

"Well," I drawled when his eyes met mine. "Looks like they bought themselves another traitor."

He tensed, but then nodded and drew Mya up, wrapping

his arms around her protectively. "And I owe you yet again, it seems, for saving the one most precious to me."

The wheels in my head started spinning, and then my eyes lit up. "Well, now that you mention it, there *is* a little something you can do for me . . ."

CHAPTER THIRTEEN

DRE HAD SOME ANSWERS FOR US LESS THAN an hour later, but none of them gave me what I'd been looking for: the name of the traitor living in the Murphy family's midst.

"So Doreen only went rogue tonight, then?"

Denton, Dre's secretary—excuse me, *personal* assistant—nodded. "It appears so. A very large sum of money was wired to her checking account just three hours ago."

I gestured to the elevator. "She worked a very big spell in a very small amount of time. I'd be impressed if she hadn't been trying to kill us."

Dre's eyes flashed. "You must accept my apologies. I've never had an employee betray me like this. She came with the highest recommendations—"

I waved his apology off. "Happens to the best of us, Dre." I left the *and you're hardly the best of us* unspoken.

Going soft in my old age. "That makes sense that they only now bought her off, seeing how she was the one to point out Mya's odd coloring."

His hands tightened around her shoulders. He looked in no rush to let her out of his reach. Not that I could blame him.

I turned toward Scott. "Think Mac could work some of his technical mumbo jumbo and trace down whoever wired her the money?" Seeing as how I couldn't exactly request that the PD run the trace through more legal channels.

Scott nodded. "Piece of cake for him. We should get back to Hounds so we can supervise the delivery and ask Mac to do his thing."

My eyes blurred with weariness, but I merely rubbed the moisture away. "That's right. The delivery should arrive any moment."

Dre arched a brow but didn't pry. Two points for him.

I returned my gaze to Denton. "Think you can get the truck by tomorrow afternoon?"

His lips curved into an almost-smirk. "Of course. It will be at the Murphy loading dock at precisely two P.M. tomorrow."

My breath whooshed out as I nodded. One less thing to worry about. "All righty, then. Dre, keep a better eye on your girlfriend, will you?"

He tensed, raring for a fight, until he realized I'd been joking. Mostly. Rather than joining in the banter, however, he became uncharacteristically solemn. "And you find out what they did to *her*. Save her if you can."

We shared a long, measuring look that spoke volumes more than we could ever say out loud. I held out a hand and we shook. Scott touched my back again, so I turned and followed him out of the penthouse. This time we took the freight elevator, since the fancy-schmancy one would be out of commission for a while.

Dre sent an armed escort with us, same as he'd done for Mac and Ellie when they went back home, ostensibly to check on the Murphys.

Despite the fact that I'd been eager to have Mac trace down the source of Doreen's recent financial windfall, suspicion settled into the pit of my stomach. *Someone* was feeding the mortals info from the inside. I drew in a deep breath before breaking the peace. "Scott, do you think it the wisest thing to go back to Hounds right now?"

"We need to organize the artillery before tomorrow, don't we?"

I braced myself for a fight. "Yes, but we've only found one traitor tonight. Which leaves at least one more out there."

"We don't even know for sure—"

I made my voice gentle, yet unyielding. "Yes, we do."

We walked in near silence for a moment, the scuff of boots the only sound in our immediate vicinity. Finally, he relented. "Fine. We can just return to the safe house."

I pressed my eyes tightly before taking the plunge. "When exactly *did* Ellie give up her family ties and turn merc for you all?"

He stopped. Our temporary bodyguards drew several feet away, giving us a measure of privacy while still watching the nearby streets for danger. Right now, the pissed-off Hound next to me was the biggest danger of all. Especially to my tender heart.

"What the hell kind of question is that?"

"One that has to be asked. Why would a pampered princess like Elliana Banoub renounce her heritage to play around as a merc? Why would she—"

"—throw over the high and mighty Banoub clan in order to slum it up with us Murphys?"

I reached a hand out to touch him, but he took a step back. "Scott, I didn't mean it like that."

"No, then how did you mean it, Marissa?"

The silky soft ice in his voice cut me a hundred times less than his reverting to *Marissa*. I jammed my hands in my pockets and took off so quickly I nearly passed the two guards in front of us.

Scott cursed and then jogged to catch up. "Riss, I'm sorry. It's just—"

"Forget it." I'd been stupid to ever think I could mean as much to him as his family. He'd proven time and time again that I would never measure up to them. Not even Elliana, and once she'd been his least favorite relative of all. What did that say about any chance of a future for us?

"I didn't—"

"I said, *forget* it. I'd like to sleep sometime tonight. Two—three—whatever number of near-death experiences in one day is enough for me."

Something rumbled softly in my pocket. I nearly let out a scream before I realized it was the surviving disposable cell phone on vibration mode.

I flipped the phone open and tapped it on with more force than strictly necessary. "Yeah?"

"Riss?"

My face softened into a smile. "Trin. Good to hear your voice again. How you feeling?"

"Fine. Look, I need to speak to you."

"Aren't we speaking now?"

"No. Face to face."

"Not sure that's really possible tonight."

Her voice became slightly exasperated. I could just imagine her overdramatic eye roll. "I'd rather not discuss this where not-so-little ears can hear. And trust me, you want to hear what I have to say."

I let out a breath at the suggestion that her phone was tapped. Hell, I'd suggested it myself when she was still in the hospital, but hearing her say that reminded me how much danger she could still be in if they believed she could lead them to me. Which, of course, she could.

"Where and when do you want to meet?"

"Our favorite little place to eat. The one that gives you heartburn. Give me three hours."

Okay, guess we *weren't* going to get much sleep tonight.

"Great. See you then. And, Trin . . . be careful."

Her voice sounded tired, way too tired, when she replied. "Yeah. You, too."

Scott had caught up to me while I'd been distracted. He didn't touch me, but his eyes looked concerned when I met his glance. "Trouble?"

"Could be. Trin wants to meet me in Chinatown in three hours." I glanced at the digital numbers backlit on my cell. "It's not too far from here, so we should have enough time to check on the delivery before I head over."

His lips tightened. "Before *we* head over, you mean."

"I thought . . ."

He rolled his eyes. "You thought that just because we got pissed at each other I'd leave you high and dry? Jesus, Riss. Give me more credit than that."

My body relaxed. I hadn't even realized it needed to. "That's not what I—oh, hell. Let's just go."

THE DELIVERY ARRIVED AND WAS PLACED under lock and key in the freight area of Hounds of Anubis. Scott's Uncle Ian agreed to keep watch over it overnight, and Scott and Ellie took charge of sorting everything out while Mac and I headed to their apartment so he could hack into Doreen's financial records. I still wasn't 100 percent convinced Ellie wasn't the traitor, but rationality reminded me she'd had ample opportunity to kill me a dozen times already. Especially in the elevator. Then again—if she'd interrupted my shield-building, her ass would have gone up in flames, too.

A yawn cracked my jaws wide open as Mac ushered me into the one-and-a-half-bedroom apartment he and his little woman called home. The half bedroom consisted of a closetless room too small to be considered a true bedroom, more like a closet itself. Mac muttered something about me being free to make myself at home and scurried into the "closet."

I went off in search of the elixir that could cure the exhaustion that ailed me.

"Ahhh, coffee!" My mouth curved in a satisfied grin, which only widened when I recognized the gourmet bag nestled next to their fancy coffeemaker. Ten minutes later I carried two Snoopy mugs (either Ellie had a bigger sense of humor than expected, or Mac enjoyed tweaking her nose) into the tiny office set up as Mac's electronic wonderland.

No fewer than five flat-screen monitors sat atop a wooden credenza that had been converted into a desk. A virtual smorgasbord of hard drives sat beneath, wires running every which way in barely contained chaos. Several laptops sat on a newer glass-and-chrome desk that ran perpendicular to the credenza. Two humongous plasma TVs were mounted to the wall above the flat-screen monitors, and Mac had his gaze plastered on the one to the right. His hands flew along a keyboard hooked up to one of the hard drives—which, in turn, must have been attached to the plasma TV—and he made little sounds of satisfaction from time to time.

The gibberish scrolling across the screen was all Greek to me, but apparently it meant something to Mr. Techno Wiz. He merely grunted when I crossed the three feet of open space in his closet of an office and read over his shoulder. That lasted precisely twenty seconds before my eyes started to blur.

"And *this* is what you do for a living? Gods, I'd slit my wrists in an hour."

"Hmm?" He threw an exasperated look my way, the glint of his green eyes clearly saying, *Can't you see I'm busy here?* When he saw the mugs of steaming coffee in my hands, however, he perked right up. A man after my own heart. Too bad he was already married. Oh, and that I was kind of, sort of, still hung up on Scott.

"That for me?"

I nodded. Mac accepted one of the Snoopy mugs and sipped as I leaned over him to tap the monitor. "Does any of this bizarre foreign language tell you who paid off our pal Doreen?"

Annoyance and humor warred across his face, with the humor winning out. "If you call someone who tries to kill you a pal, I'd hate to meet up with someone you consider an enemy."

I snorted. He cleared his throat and gestured to the text dancing across the plasma screen. "In a nutshell, I traced the source of the funds wired to Doreen's account around the world and back again. It was shuffled across a few ghost accounts belonging to fictitious corporations, bounced here and there and everywhere. Whoever did it is an expert at covering electronic tracks."

"Yeah, well, I thought *you* were an expert at this electronic crap."

His eyes rolled, and he hit a few keys before pointing again. "I didn't say they were better than *me*." His lips curved arrogantly. "I take great pride in being the best at what I do." Those words had my hands clenching around the coffee mug, since they echoed a sentiment my mother had often expressed. I pushed aside the sudden pang of longing and focused on him. "After weeding out the ghost accounts and fake corporations, I tracked down one that seems real enough."

"Seems?"

A tight smile flashed across his face. "It's an officially registered company located here in Boston, and I can find online traces of it actually conducting business, but the address is phony."

I leaned against the only empty stretch of wall and pursed my lips. "The name of this seemingly real company?"

His smile faded and his expression grew troubled. He hesitated before striking a few more keys. The window on the plasma screen switched to a web browser, and a webpage popped up. My mouth dropped open and the mug of coffee nearly slipped from my fingers when the glossy corporate logo splashed across the page. Erinye Unlimited.

Erinye, the Greek version of the Roman mythological creatures nearest and dearest to my heart—Furies.

Rage exploded, pushing me away from the wall and as close to the plasma screen as I could get. "You have *got* to be kidding me!" I scowled up at the ugly winged woman smirking down at me—one that resembled a Harpy much more than any Fury I'd ever come across. "That's some sort of sick joke, right?"

Mac coughed before replying. "I can't say for sure, Riss. But either someone's messing with you, or there's yet another traitor waiting in the wings."

I planted hands on hips and arched a brow. "What makes you say that, other than the whole name thing?"

"Because. The funds that Erinye Unlimited ultimately wired into Doreen's account did *not* originate from their own checking account. They were rerouted from another corporation's account." His eyes met mine unflinchingly. "The Sisterhood of Furies."

WE SPENT ANOTHER HOUR TRYING TO CRACK the corporate façade known as Erinye Unlimited, but even

Mac's genius hacking skills were no match for whatever electronic miracle they'd woven to protect themselves from detection. Which meant I was going to have to tap into official resources after all, starting with Scott's feline friend Harper. And maybe Grizzly Adams, to boot.

A check of the time showed that Scott and I had less than fifteen minutes to make our rendezvous with Trinity. We left Mac and Ellie to crash for a few hours in their apartment and headed for Chinatown. Paranoia reigned, and I cloaked myself in the plain-Jane disguise before working a complicated, power-eating spell on Scott. It blurred him to the sight of mundane and arcane alike, enough so that most people would walk right past him without even noticing. It was also a bitch to maintain, but I figured that the extra bit of exhaustion would be a small price to pay.

Trinity was waiting for us in our favorite twenty-four-hour Chinese restaurant when we strolled in minutes later. She sipped a glass of soda, eyes weary and expression ragged. She looked like she'd run a marathon and then conquered an obstacle course.

Her eyes narrowed when we approached. She started to give us the brush-off, but then relaxed her body. "Riss?"

I nodded, maintaining the blurring routine on Scott. We didn't want to risk anyone putting two and two—and us—together. I motioned for him to slip into the booth, but he shook his head stubbornly and insisted I take the inner seat. In no mood for a major argument—another major argument—I slid into place.

"You okay, Trin? You don't look so hot. Even for a gunshot victim."

"Gee, thanks." Her voice was dry as her hands fiddled with a laminated menu. "Never mind me. I'm worried about *you*. The precinct's going crazy looking for you. We've gotten word at least twice that you were dead."

"Well, as you can see, those rumors were greatly

exaggerated." I counted my blessings she hadn't seen me either of the times I'd been near death's door that day. "Isn't it a little early for you to be back at work? I didn't think Cappy would let you anywhere near the place."

"He didn't want to, but I strong-armed him into it."

My brows arched. She didn't look like she was in any shape to strong-arm a can opener, much less a fellow police officer.

"I got him to agree to desk duty. Told him I'd go crazier at home than the precinct. Which is true."

Completely true, knowing her. "Desk duty. Thus the rumors you picked up on."

She nodded, tapping the plastic edge of the menu on the table before finally meeting my eyes straight on. "The feds came back—well, one of them did. He had a couple new bozos with him."

Yeah, seeing as how we'd killed the others. "Oh yeah?"

"Yeah. They're claiming you went rogue and killed a couple agents. That true?"

Scott's hand fell on my knee and squeezed. "Not exactly."

Trinity bit at her already-ravaged lip. "What do you mean, not exactly? I need the straight story, Riss. None of your Fury bullshit."

I placed my palms flat down on the chipped Formica. "I didn't kill any true federal agents, Trin. They were immortals disguised as mortals."

Her lips turned downward and she furrowed her brows. "Disguised as mortals? But only Furies can disguise themselves so fully. And none of you would—"

My breath whooshed out. I'd hoped to avoid the total truth with her, thinking the less she knew, the better off she'd be. But the decision had been taken from my hands. I couldn't let her think I'd gone rogue.

"They weren't Furies, Trin. They were Sidhe."

Her jaw worked silently, opening and closing as her fingers clenched on the table. "Wh-what do you mean, Sidhe? That's—"

"Impossible?" I suggested dryly. "Yeah, that's what I thought, until I came across several of them. The first of which was disguised as my dead best friend."

Trinity's eyes widened, and realization washed across her face. "Vanessa's corpse. You said it had been altered magically, that it wasn't a Fury. She—it—was a Sidhe?"

"Yeah. I communicated with the body's true spirit a couple times since we found the corpse."

Her lips twitched. "Yeah, I heard someone broke into the morgue and tore out a chunk of flesh. Everyone assumed it was just some Ghoul."

Scott and I shared a grin before I got back to being serious. "Listen, Trin, I hate to be the bearer of bad news, but those feds strutting around the PD aren't real feds. They're Sidhe in disguise, working, I think, for some secret arm of the mortal government."

"Oh, hell."

"Yeah. But it gets worse."

She took a long, slow drink of soda, slopping some over the edge when she slammed the glass back down. "Okay, spill it."

"This group is responsible for spreading it about that the Sidhe were extinct, but all the while they've been breeding them in captivity. Even then, their numbers were so small they may actually have gone the way of the dinosaur, except . . ."

"Except what?"

I took another deep breath. "Except that the mortals finally unlocked the key to their flagging fertility." She leaned forward, eyes focused on me. "By cloning them."

Her look of intensity changed to one of revulsion. Most mortals considered cloning sentient beings completely immoral, as evidenced by the fact that it was illegal in just about every mundane nation. "You're shitting me."

My lips twisted as I flashed back to the last time she'd accused me of that. Right before I got shot in the chest. "I would never shit you about something so serious."

Her eyes fell to the dingy Formica. She barely noticed when an overly chipper waitress scurried up to offer me a drink. I ordered coffee while the gears in Trinity's brain kept on whirring. Finally, she glanced up to meet my gaze.

"I—I think they've gotten to Cappy."

My mouth dropped open, since that'd been just about the last thing I'd expected her to say. "Gotten to Cappy?" I repeated like a doped-up parrot.

She nodded. "That was the real reason I wanted to meet you tonight. I had to be sure you weren't—that you hadn't . . ."

I picked up where her voice trailed away. "Gone Harpy?"

Her breath rushed out explosively. "Yeah. That you'd gone Harpy, or rogue, or whatever they're accusing you of."

My heart hammered against my chest. "Cappy—Cappy's accusing me of going rogue?"

She nodded. "Yeah, but, Riss, I don't think it's him."

"Oh shit. You mean . . ."

Another nod, this one absolutely miserable. "They either compelled him to do whatever they say or switched him entirely so they could better use the precinct's resources. And it's working out pretty good for them, Riss. It's a damned good thing you're traveling around in that disguise." Her tone grew chastising. "Especially since you're alone."

Scott squeezed my knee again. I patted his hand as surreptitiously as possible, then zeroed in back on Trinity. "Do you have someplace safe to go, Trin?"

She frowned. "What do you mean?"

I gestured to her haggard face. "I don't think the gunshot wound alone is responsible for you looking like hell. I think someone's been messing with you, trying to get to me."

"You mean magically?"

I nodded. "Yeah. I'd like you to call in tomorrow, take some of the sick time I know you have coming to you. Just tell them going back so soon was as bad an idea as Cappy said it was."

"I don't really know where I'd go, other than home."

I glanced at Scott. He nodded. "Then you're coming with us."

She smirked. "Using the royal *we* again, Riss?"

My lips twitched. "Let's just say I'm not quite as alone as you thought I was."

"Well, hallelujah. Nice to know you're smarter than you look."

I rolled my eyes. "Yeah, yeah. Now let's hit the road. We've got a long ride ahead of us."

Which would give me plenty of time between here and there to make sure that Trinity was, in fact, Trinity, and to remove any tracking devices they might have planted on her. Not that I didn't trust Trinity implicitly, but one could never be too sure when dealing with the Sidhe. And clones.

Attack of the Evil Faerie Clones. Sounded like a very bad science fiction movie.

Or just another day in my life . . .

CHAPTER FOURTEEN

SCOTT CALLED SEAN AND KIARA TO CHECK IN midway through the T ride. Once they'd assured him there had been no major catastrophes (lucky them), he handed me the phone.

Fortunately, Sean didn't try to ambush me over the phone line. Instead, Cori's voice bubbled into my ear first thing. "Aunt Riss? You okay?"

"Er, yeah. Why wouldn't I be?"

Trinity smirked at my forced innocence. We'd gone ahead and filled her in on all the attacks in the belief that ignorance *could* get you killed.

"Gee, I don't know. Maybe because of the Harpies?"

My feet slapped to the floor. "What Harpies?"

"The ones who accepted the hit on you. Sheesh, Aunt Riss, you're good at ticking people off, aren't you?"

Out of the mouths of babes. "And just *who* have you been talking to, niece of mine?"

"You asked us to search for anything that could help you on the Net, remember?"

My thudding heart slowed fractionally. The last thing I needed now was to worry about Cori sneaking out to try some investigating of her own.

"Yeah, I remember. But how did Harpies enter into the equation?"

"Well, you wanted to know about unusual arcane disappearances or murders. There have been a lot over the past few years. A *lot*. Apparently spread out in different places, though, so the police haven't connected the dots yet."

"And that led to Harpies how?" My gods, had she been searching on the same forums Scott had?

Her voice grew more reluctant. Obviously she'd been hoping to throw me off the scent. "Well, one thing kind of lead to another and I ended up on this really cool website where arcanes post problems they want taken care of and people respond to the ads. Like on Craigslist."

I rolled my eyes. "Cori, sweetie, people don't advertise for hit men on Craigslist."

"Not obviously, no. You gotta be sneakier than that."

"Sometimes you scare me, angel. You really do."

Her grin came across loud and clear through the phone. "You sound like my mom." I decided to ignore that one for now. "Listen, Aunt Riss, I came across something even more interesting on a different website. I think it had to do with the Harpies. Something about a misplaced package and needing to track it down ASAP and I was thinking—"

I frowned. Her words tickled something in the back of my mind, but I couldn't quite suss it out. I lost the thread of conversation.

"—you think that's a good idea?"

"Ah, sure. Hey, can you put Kiara back on the phone?"

Her voice sounded decidedly chipper. "Yeah. Take care of yourself, Aunt Riss."

"You, too, angel."

Kiara agreed to keep an eye on Cori and make sure she didn't sneak out of the safe house. I tried to hint that Kiara should watch out for any signs of arcane abilities appearing in her charge, and I think I got it across to her without having to spell it out directly. Knowing the gods' excessive sense of irony, they might very well choose *now* to blast Cori's Fury gifts wide open. Assuming she'd inherited them. The odds that she had were hellaciously high—better than my odds of someone trying to kill me again—and those were pretty damned good.

We made it to the safe house without incident, thanks no doubt to Scott's insistence that we get off several stops after our normal one and circle back in random loops before he was sure no one was trailing us. I'd long since made sure Trinity was not an Evil Faerie Clone and wasn't carrying any bugs or tracking devices.

Trinity let me bundle her into a pair of Kiara's cast-off sweats and steer her toward the apartment's surprisingly comfortable sofa. Scott, perceptive as always, sensed our need for some alone time and headed straight for the shower. She curled up on the sofa and huddled under the gaudy plaid comforter I pulled from the hall closet. The pale tinge to her normally dark skin along with the deep circles under her eyes had me worried.

I tried not to jostle her when I settled on the edge of the sofa, but her wince signaled my failure. My eyes narrowed at the reminder that she'd been shot all too recently. "I'm not sure they should have let you out of the hospital, much less back on duty."

She perked up enough to throw a scowl my way. "Well gee, *some* of us don't have super-uber-magical healing powers. Doesn't make us fragile little dolls."

All righty then. Someone needed to get a little mad on. "Never said you were, girlfriend. But have you looked in the mirror lately?"

Her lips tightened into a mutinous line, though they didn't stay that way long. She jerked the ugly blanket up to her chin and glanced pointedly toward the hall. "Guess the frail and useless mortal should just get to sleep before she keels over, then."

My eyes blinked rapidly while my brain tried to put two and two together. Hadn't gotten much sleep lately myself. "Uh, Trin . . . Did I do something to offend you?"

The apologetic tone of my voice placated her. Slightly. She let the blanket drop back to her waist, though her scowl didn't fade completely. "Tell me something, Marissa." Ouch. "Do you trust me?"

"I—wha—huh?" Of all the things I'd expected her to ask, that wasn't one of them.

"You heard me. Do you trust me. Really, truly, trust me?"

My frown made her own look pathetic. "What the hell kind of question is that? You're the only mortal I trust to watch my back, aren't you?"

She crossed her arms over her chest and shot me a *Drop dead* look. Kiara could have taken a few lessons from her, actually. "That's the trouble right there. I'm always going to be just another mortal to you, aren't I?"

My feet slammed to the floor, and I felt only a teensy measure of guilt when her body stiffened slightly. "I would *never* call you just another anything, Trinity." Two could play at the full-name game. "What the hell bug crawled up your ass, anyway?"

"The kind that's sick of being left out in the cold when it comes to certain parts of these damned arcane investigations. Especially this one. I feel like I'm a day late and a million dollars short. I'm a fucking lieutenant detective in the Boston PD, a senior member of the Arcane Task Force, and your partner even if the stinking bureaucrats haven't made that official. Yet you're constantly hemming and hawing and only telling me what *you* deem necessary, like I'm on some need-to-know-only basis. And then, half the time you're trying to protect me by leaving me out of certain shit like I'm some snot-nosed rookie who can't protect herself and I'm sick and tire—"

Pressure built up behind my eyeballs the more she ranted. And not just because of her rising tone. A niggling voice in the back of my brain whispered that she was right. I *had* been doing just that. A habit started with protecting David and Cori (and, to a lesser extent, Nessa) at all costs, but while Trin may not have been arcane, she also wasn't a civilian. And she damned well deserved better.

"You're right," I said softly.

"—d of being treated like a chil . . . wait. Say what?"

My turn to thrust my arms across my chest. Why did people always react like that when I agreed with them? You'd think I never admitted when I was wrong or something. "I *said*, you're right. You *are* my partner, no matter what those pencil pushers say. And you deserve to be treated as such." I ran a hand through my majorly disheveled hair and then focused on her bewildered face. "Hit me with your million-dollar questions."

Her hands began plucking at the frayed edges of the comforter. "Well, for starters, it'd be nice to get more than the whitewashed, pansy-ass version of events behind the end of the Troubles—'scuse me, the War of Mortal Aggression."

I didn't know whether to be impressed that she'd actually referred to the Time of Troubles as an all-out war, or annoyed that she'd used the condescending name antimortal arcanes used. Which was ironic, considering which of us was the actual mortal.

"So, what? You want the arcane version of how the War went down?" I rolled my eyes. "I don't think either one of us could stay awake for that."

Amusement lightened her expression momentarily. "I said the *end* of the War, not a dissertation on the whole damned thing."

I pursed my lips, trying to figure out why she'd decided this conversation had to take place *now*, of all times. Surely it wasn't just to test how much I trusted her. "You have a theory."

She adjusted the blanket primly and then leveled a no-nonsense look my way. "Spill it, Holloway."

"I . . . well, shit, Trin. Care to narrow down what you're looking for slightly? Or we really *could* end up here all night."

"I want to hear things from your viewpoint, unbiased by any of my thoughts or opinions. Specifically, I want to hear the major events that led up to the signing of the Accord. And not the gung-ho *mortals rock* bullshit they teach in the police academy."

My lips curved into an unconscious smile of approval. That was my girl, and one of the reasons she and I got along so well. She was truly a proponent of the "there's always more than one side to a story" school of philosophy.

"All right. Sheesh, you're gonna make my brain hurt dredging up all this history crap." But I couldn't completely hide the pleasure in my voice. "Well, you know how the Sidhe managed to piss off mortal and arcane alike in the last few battles of the War. The Sidhe always believed they should have inherited the earth—literally—by virtue of being the 'Supreme Race.'" We both snorted at that. "Toward the War's end, they weren't particularly careful with their kamikaze tactics and ended up taking out nearly as many arcanes as mortals with a few suicide attacks. Killed more than their fair share of civilians of both persuasions, which lead to arcane and mortal alike turning on them at the Second Battle of Bunker Hill." We shared a moment of silence for the thousands of lives lost that day—and the supposed extermination of an arcane species whose overweening pride had brought that doom upon itself.

"Now, here's the bitch of it. Though the arcane species who had suffered losses at the hands of the Sidhe had damned well wanted revenge, they sure as hell hadn't intended to assist the mortals in completely eradicating another arcane race. And that, more than anything, finally woke them up to the harsh reality that the mortals were a major power in their own right. Gone were the days that arcanes could perform a little hocus-pocus and be worshipped as gods. And, if they truly wanted to immigrate here from the dying Otherrealms without risking further extinction, they were going to have to actually negotiate with mortals as equals. Not as triumphant conquerors."

Her expression was thoughtful as she listened, but I shifted uncomfortably, feeling like a smug professor lording it over a classroom full of bored students. Then again, she *had* asked for it. "Of course, the academy really pushes the belief that the mortals kicked major Sidhe ass all on their own and terrified the arcanes into submission. At any rate, that battle was what really helped allow the Furies to finally accomplish what they'd been fighting so hard for during the five years of the War that—according to the mortals—wasn't actually a war. Get both sides to the negotiating table."

She nodded as if I'd confirmed something. I arched a brow. "Care to clue me in now?"

"Well . . . this whole thing just strikes me as too pat."

"Meaning?"

"Remember when you suggested that it might not have been an arcane who altered the Sidhe's corpse into looking like Vanessa's?"

"Yeah . . . so?"

"Well, that does appear to be the case. But what if, just like at Bunker Hill, it's not mortals alone who are involved. What if we're just supposed to think that's the case? Some arcanes consider mortals beneath them. Inferior. What if someone wants the chance to reclaim their shot at glory? To be hailed as the conquering heroes?"

Queasiness settled in the pit of my stomach as her suggestion set wheels skittering through my brain. Especially when the logo of a certain slick website forced itself to the forefront. The website of a corporate front that had successfully funneled money from the Sisterhood of Furies—an organization ostensibly dedicated to policing the arcane society—*and* to fostering harmony between that society they became part of upon manifesting their magical abilities and the mortal world they started out in by virtue of having no such powers until later adolescence.

Okay, okay, hold on a damned minute. Maybe arcanes are involved in this sick plot. But nothing says a Fury's involved. Anyone could have hacked into that account. And would a Fury—an Elder, since only Elders have access to that account—really be stupid enough to use something so obvious as Erinye as a name for a fictitious company?

That partially mollified the Rage lingering beneath outward exhaustion. A yawn escaped before I could hold it back. Trinity's turn to tell me I looked like hell warmed over and to chivy me to bed. I let her, more for her sake than mine. And also because I wanted to sort through her theory before discussing it any further. Though she felt frisky enough to shoot me a knowing smirk when I disappeared down the hallway to join Scott in the apartment's only bedroom. Too damned bad I wasn't going to get as lucky as she thought I was—Scott had already told me grudgingly that we were sharing the bed only because Trin needed the sofa.

Course, I was too damned tired to really mind. Exhaustion tugged at me with every step I took. Scott had left the bathroom light on and the bedroom door cracked, but I still stumbled over the threshold. Rather than vanishing them magically, I shucked off my red leather boots and kicked them onto the bathroom floor. They'd still be there in the morning. After washing my face with scalding-hot water and brushing my teeth with ice-cold, I slipped into bed next to Scott. Still pretty pissed-off about the scene on the streets of the Belly, I scooted as far away from him as I could, determined to stick to my guns . . .

OF COURSE, I MIGHT AS WELL NOT HAVE BOTHered. A warm, solid length pressed against my back and rear as wakefulness stirred. I sighed, burrowing closer to it. Consciousness beckoned, and I finally let it rush over me. My body tensed when I realized Scott and I were spooned together, but I forced it to relax. Last night's disagreement seemed so petty in the light of day. What had even started it?

Scott mumbled something and pulled me against him more tightly. His morning arousal pressed against my rear, sending waves of desire pulsing through my body. But the paper-thin walls provided a painfully flimsy barrier between us and our new housemate, and one thing I'd never been was a sexual exhibitionist. Guess I wasn't getting any action anytime soon. Probably for the best, with things still so unresolved between us. Sex just made things messy—in more ways than one.

I wriggled away from my sleepy-eyed Hound, padded to the bathroom, and took a very hot shower. A cold one might have done my frustrated desire more good, but considering what we were about to go into . . . If this ended up being my last shower, it sure as hell wasn't going to be a cold one. Tired of wearing only castaway clothing, I paired my sexy-as-hell Fury boots with my red leather pants and a simple but flattering black cotton shirt of Kiara's. Remember that vanity streak I mentioned earlier?

I slipped into the kitchen to brew a pot of coffee, then ducked onto the tiny balcony just off the kitchen to get my fix without waking Scott or Trinity. I leaned against the railing and breathed in the fresh tang of Folgers and smog. Ahhhh, nothing beat the scent of coffee—and Boston—in the morning.

Once again, no warning preceded the attack. One moment I leaned against the rickety balustrade sipping coffee, the next razor-sharp talons pierced my shoulders and hauled me through the air, hurtling me toward the broken concrete of the nearby alley at a dizzying speed. Instinct had me hurling hot coffee up toward my captors, but I got more of it on myself than them. Through the fading scent of coffee I managed to pick up the faint whiff of sulfur. Oh shit. Not again.

I looked up and, sure enough, two Harpies flapped wings furiously to slow our descent before depositing me on the ground amid more than a dozen of the wild-eyed creatures.

I'd used up my quota of Raging Justice on the Phoenix. No way I could cast it now—and survive. That didn't mean I'd go down without fighting. I shifted, leaving off my wings so the Harpies couldn't use them to incapacitate me, and leapt for the nearest Harpy. Fear flickered across her face, and she did something unexpected. Jumped away from me.

I landed on cracked concrete, talons extended, teeth bared, and Amphisbaena spitting. "What, are you girls too chickenshit to face me one on one? Had to bring your whole flock?"

Several of them snarled, but they stayed back, arranged

around me in a loose circle. I kept moving in circles of my own, unwilling to allow any of them to remain at my back for long. What the hell were they up to?

And then I turned to find an almost normal-looking Harpy, and I knew. They weren't here to kill me. They wanted to talk.

Her bone-white hair wasn't as tangled as that of her sister Harpies, and her strange, yellow-green eyes carried as much sanity as *insanity*. She was garbed in the finest clothing of all of them and on first glance might pass as a mortal. All of which pointed to a fact I wasn't sure meant something good or something really, really bad. I'd come face-to-face with Calaeno, the Harpy Queen.

"Calm yourself, Fury. We're not here to kill you." She gestured, and the Harpy nearest her extended a jagged stick bearing familiar green leaves. An olive branch, the arcane version of a white flag.

That only appeased me somewhat. Olive branch or no, these were Harpies, and there was a damned good reason my kind loathed them. Berserker anger and strength came in damned handy when confronting multiple arcane enemies. But it could—and would—eat Furies up if given half the chance.

Nemesis and Nike writhed along my arms, obviously unhappy I'd laid off the offensive. I did my best to soothe them without turning my attention from the Harpy Queen. "Why are you here, then? Forgive me if I don't curtsy."

The other Harpies hissed at the insult, but Calaeno merely smiled. A cruel, twisted smile, but better than the alternative. "We are here to discuss a matter that concerns us both. The contract that was taken out on your life."

Hearing her say that so matter-of-factly sent a shiver down my spine. Maybe the olive branch had been a ruse after all . . .

She must have seen my body tense, because she raised

a hand quickly. "We are not here to fulfill the contract. We are here to possibly rescind it."

My eyes narrowed. "Possibly?"

"Yes. Whether we do depends entirely on you."

"What the hell does that mean?"

"On whether you killed one of our sisters, or two."

I frowned, glancing from her to the olive branch and back again. Was this some sort of trick question? I started to speak, and then Cori's words flitted through my mind. "Listen, Aunt Riss, I came across something even more interesting on a different website. I think it had to do with the Harpies. Something about a misplaced package and needing to track it down ASAP . . ."

"You sent only one sister after me so far, but you're missing two."

Her teeth clenched, and every Harpy around her tensed their bodies in anticipation of her command to attack. A command that never came.

"Rinda was an acceptable loss. She died honorably in combat, attempting to fulfill the contract we accepted from the mortals. But Serise went missing yesterday and not at my request. She would never go after a mark alone without explicit orders, so that means something else befell her. And I do not believe in mere coincidences."

"The mortals," I breathed, stunned at their stupidity—or sheer audacity. To abduct a Harpy after you'd engaged their services to carry out an assassination . . .

"Just so. I do not know exactly what they are up to, but she went missing not too long after she was supposed to check in with a mortal representative. And then they tried to blame her disappearance on you."

I shook my head emphatically. "Only one of your sisters attacked me, and that was above Hounds of Anubis."

"As I expected. Well then, in light of the fact that the mortals have stolen one of our own, the contract between us has been rendered null and void. We will not help you in your current quest, Fury, but no more will we hinder you."

Her words must have been a signal to the others, because one by one they scurried back the way they came. Calaeno waited until the Harpy bearing the olive branch disappeared to speak again. "Find Serise, Fury. Return her to me dead *or* alive, and I will owe you a boon in kind. And that is no small thing."

My eyes widened, but she vanished before I could respond. The Queen of all Harpies owing me an unnamed boon? No small thing indeed.

CHAPTER FIFTEEN

SCOTT AND TRINITY POUNDED INTO THE ALLEY-way moments later, skidding to a stop as they attempted to catch their breath when they saw me safe and sound. Not that the silence lasted long.

He advanced on me first, fists clenched at each side and lips twitching with barely suppressed fury. "What the hell was *that*, Riss?"

Had he seen the Harpies? Surely he didn't think I was in cahoots with them. "Ah, what was what?"

Scott's hands locked on my arms, and he shook me. Not painfully, just enough to get my attention. "You ran off without leaving a fucking note. I was scared shitless when I couldn't find you."

The vehemence in his voice surprised me. "I didn't run off, Scott. The Harpies snatched me." I shifted back to mortal form and gestured to the bloody tears in my shirt.

His anger faded, and he tugged me into his arms and embraced me tightly. "You're going to get yourself killed if you don't learn how to call for help, Riss, and then how will you be able to protect anyone?"

Warmth pooled in my stomach. I allowed myself the luxury of nuzzling his cheek before pushing him away firmly. "You're right. I'm sorry."

"Don't argue with . . . What did you say?"

I bit back a snicker. "I said you're right, and I'm sorry."

Trinity gave an unladylike grunt. "Jeez, that's the second time in two days she's said that. The apocalypse can't be far behind." She and Scott shared a glance of commiseration. One I chose to ignore for what was most important. Filling them in on what had just gone down with the Harpies. Of course, that just reminded me that we still had a traitor in our midst. Possibly two—even if I *didn't* want to consider the possibility that a Fury might actually be involved.

"Scott, you can't bury your head in the sand anymore."

His expression turned wary. "Excuse me?"

"I'm sorry to keep harping on this, but you've got a mole. A very talkative mole."

His golden eyes took on a hard glint. "You think someone on the inside collaborated with Doreen."

"It's a distinct possibility. And we didn't exactly keep our little arsenal secret last night." I ran a hand through my hair in frustration. "Shit. We're gonna have to call the whole thing off."

Scott tensed. "Bullshit, Riss. They've got my sister." Ironic about-face, seeing how he'd tried so hard to persuade me to hold off our attack when I'd been fresh out of my deathbed.

"They've got mine, too, remember?" I stomped several feet away, trying to get a handle on the sudden flare of Rage. "Or does she not count because she's not blood of mine?"

Trinity glanced from Scott to me, eyes wide but wisely saying nothing.

He took a step in my direction. "That's not what I meant, and you know it. But I won't leave her—either of them—to be experimented on like lab rats."

"Scott, think with your head, not your heart. What do you think will happen if we rush in to rescue them when we know we have a traitor in our midst?"

He gritted his teeth and I winced. The grinding noise raised the hair on the back of my neck. "So what, you're just giving up?"

"Don't be stupid, Scott. When have you ever known *me* to give up on anything?"

"Even when it might be the smart thing to do," Trinity murmured under her breath. Not quietly enough to escape the acute hearing of either Hound or Fury. She shot us both an innocent smile when we glanced at her.

Scott let out a breath, frustration seeping away from his voice when he spoke again. "Fine, then. What did you have in mind?"

"Funny you should mention rodents," I said. "I think it's time we catch our own little rat . . ."

BEFORE WE COULD BAIT OUR TRAP WITH THE proverbial cheese, it was time to tie up another loose end. Scott arranged for a meeting with both Harper and Red—the better to pool their extensive networks of sneaky resources, since I couldn't exactly use my own. I only briefly considered suggesting that Trinity wait at another safe house before deciding I'd rather keep all my teeth intact. Besides, I had to get over that pesky instinct to protect her from all harm if our partnership was ever going to morph into something more solid.

And I *really* wanted to avoid the need for expensive dental surgery.

I tried not to curl my lip as we entered the smoky, out-of-the-way honky-tonk Red suggested as the rendezvous point. Guess he never got the memo that variety is the spice of life.

My eyes widened when we approached a semiprivate booth at the rear of the joint and saw an animated Harper sucking down a longneck beer and hanging on Red's every word. Funny, I'd never pictured her for a beer-guzzling country music fan, but there she was dressed in tight jeans, pretty red-and-white checked shirt, and expensive black cowboy boots. Her body swayed in time to the heavy twang peppering the air.

Red shot us a smug grin as we slid into the booth across from him and Harper. I rolled my eyes with a mock groan. "It's like déjà vu all over again. Don't expect me to save your ass if you start a barroom brawl again."

His full-throated laugh had his belly jiggling more enthusiastically than Harper. "Sugar, if you'll recall, those polecats were after *your* pretty little ass last time."

I mouthed *Polecats?* with an exaggerated look of disbelief, which only had him chuckling all the more. He sobered after a waitress brought another round of beer. "Seriously though, darlin', I'm glad to see you back in action. It was touch and go there for a while."

Scott's arm tightened along my shoulder, his only visible reaction to the reminder of how close we'd come to losing out on our potential second chance. Something stung my eyes, but I pretended not to notice.

"Thanks." I cleared my suspiciously husky voice. "Glad you could break away from the men in black for a brewsky, Harper."

Her eyes crinkled in amusement as she tossed back another slug of beer. "Glad the Sisterhood is buying."

My lips twitched but I forced them into a scowl. "Better be drinking the cheap crap, then."

Scott snickered. "Harper never buys cheap anything. One reason we never—" He cut off at the sudden glint in her eyes. "Ah, so, nice laptop."

She tilted her head, narrowed her eyes, and pursed her lips, but let his little dig go as she slid the laptop around so we could see the screen. A bunch of statistics marched along the monitor, but one line of text especially caught my eye.

"Oooh, that the dirt on Erinye Unlimited?" It *really* sucked that I couldn't currently access my databases to dig up my *own* dirt. Made me feel handicapped in a big way.

Harper nodded. "Yeah, everything Red and I could track down on them. I've already sent the encrypted file to Mac's secure e-mail address as requested, and I brought a CD as backup. Erinye first registered with the Department of Revenue about a year after the War ended. They've dabbled in a few different industries since them and seem to be mostly a holding company for other corporations. Recently, they've put just about all their liquid assets into one particular venture—which is possibly the reason they took the risk of funneling money from the Sisterhood in order to pay off the sorceress to take you guys out at the Carrington Building."

I couldn't even hear that without rolling my eyes. The Carrington Building. Never let it be said that Dre lacked a healthy ego.

Red cut in. "By the way, after our little incident the other day, I wanted to make damn sure and well the government I devoted my life to serving wasn't involved in this unholy mess. And you have my wholehearted assurances that the program I told you about *was* disbanded just after the Accord was struck. Whatever mortals are participating in this evil do *not* have the support of the United States government."

A weight I hadn't realized I'd been carrying was lifted from my shoulders. "I appreciate you telling me that, Red. It's nice to know I'm not working for the assholes trying to do me in."

That brought a much-needed moment of levity and had us all chuckling.

"So, back to the misappropriated funds, were they sending some sort of statement by robbing the Sisterhood to assassinate one of their own? Or . . ." My lips tightened and I couldn't bring myself to say it out loud. Scott patted my back while Trinity slapped another beer in my hand. I used that as an excuse to swig and avoid finishing my sentence.

Harper continued without missing a beat. "I have to say that, in my opinion, it's highly unlikely that a complete outsider siphoned those funds from the Sisterhood and into Erinye's coffers. As anyone with half a brain would guess, the Sisterhood's accounts are *very* well protected, both electronically and magically. No second-rate hacker living at home with Mom and Dad could even hope to pull something like this off. Or a first-rate one working for a shadow governmental organization, either."

"I have to concur with Kitten here." Red winked when I tossed him a sardonic look. My, hadn't they become friends awfully darned fast? "Much as it pains me to have to tell you that, little darlin'. You're looking for an insider here, and my money would be on someone placed up high. Real high."

Which could only mean an Elder. All signatories on Sisterhood accounts were required to be Elders—generally those with seats on the Lesser Consensus. Excitement thrummed in my veins at that realization. I'd just narrowed my list of suspects from the thousands in the Sisterhood, to the hundreds of active Elders, to the handful currently serving in the Lesser Consensus. So our traitor was most likely one of fifteen women.

My lips twisted as I thought back to my appearance before the Conclave just days earlier, and I went over the list of suspects in my mind, trying to figure out which sister might be most likely to have a motivation strong enough to betray not only the Sisterhood to which she'd sworn the strongest of vows, but all of arcanekind. Not surprisingly, one sister in particular shot straight to the top of my list—Ekaterina.

She's the coldest, most ambitious bitch of a sister I've ever seen. And she is currently the number one signatory on the accounts. She could do anything *without anyone else gainsaying her . . .*

Honesty forced me to admit that although that was true, she was also the Fury I most loathed, so mine was not exactly an unbiased opinion. I needed to run this by another sister, preferably an Elder, who would know her fellow Elders better than lower-ranking sisters like myself. And right now, I could only trust one Elder completely.

"Well. Looks like Stacia's going to have to get her ass down here whether she wants to or not." And now, I just had to figure out how to make that happen . . .

FOR ONCE, THE FATES DECIDED TO BE KIND and (as Trinity would have said) help a sister out. I didn't have to come up with some big, convoluted scheme to entice Stacia to the mortal realm. She ambushed me before we even left Red's honky-tonk du jour. Inside the ladies' room.

When her face appeared behind mine in the cracked mirror without any warning, I was fully shifted and halfway spun around before my mind registered friend rather than foe. The grim set of her lips relaxed enough to give a tight, approving smile, and then she reached behind me to lock the outer door.

"How did you—" I shook my head. Senior Elders had some sort of travel power the rest of us could only have wet dreams about. "What happened?"

"We have a traitor, Marissa. A gods-bedamned traitor in the bloody Sisterhood."

"Well, hell. And here I planned to tell *you* that. Shoulda known you'd beat me to the punch somehow."

She blinked in surprise. "How do you know about the traitor? I only just found out." Her eyes narrowed. "And why didn't you inform me immediately?"

"I only just discovered proof, and filling you in was the next box on my to-do list." I went over what Mac, Harper, and Red had uncovered, which had her alternating between curses and nods.

"The minute I heard about the sorceress attacking you on that elevator, I realized we could very well have a leak somewhere feeding the mortals information. How else have they managed to repeatedly track you down so quickly when you have been bouncing around the whole bloody city? So I launched a detailed search myself and found that a very large sum of money had been wired from our account to another."

"Erinye Unlimited."

"Exactly." Her fists clenched at her side, and she looked like she wanted to finish destroying the already-damaged mirror barely hanging on the wall. "I tracked you down immediately because I wanted to warn you to keep all communication strictly between you and me until we find out who has betrayed us. Trust no one in the Sisterhood— not even the members of the Conclave."

"You mean *especially* not the members of the Conclave. Only one of them could have transferred those funds."

Her expression grew even grimmer. "Indeed. And only fifteen sisters currently have signatory powers on the Sisterhood's bank accounts."

I tilted my head. "Are countersignatures generally required on these accounts?"

She nodded, and her eyes narrowed suddenly. "Except in certain narrow situations. There is one sister who can authorize fund transfers without a countersignature."

Excitement tingled my skin and I knew exactly what she was going to say next.

"The currently acting Moerae, Ekaterina."

"Which makes her our most likely suspect." Something that had my body relaxing and my lips curving ever so slightly. Gods knew I had never wanted to believe that the Sisterhood had a traitor stalking its number . . . *But I never liked that fox-faced bitch. And apparently, for good reason.*

This time her hands twitched with the effort to hold them back. She shook them, and then the fingers of her right hand began tapping against her left thigh in that unconscious habit of hers. Finally, she nodded and pressed what felt like a business card into my hand.

I stared at the unfamiliar ten-digit number it bore. "What's this?"

"A disposable cell phone I just purchased. Use only that to contact me until I tell you otherwise. And stay away from all other Furies, Marissa. Especially the Moerae. I can't afford to lose you."

The uncharacteristic passion coloring her voice touched me. I reached out to pat her arm, and she actually drew me into one of her rare embraces. "Be careful, Marissa. You mean more to me than the Sisterhood and the mortal realm combined."

I pushed back, tucked the card into my pocket, and

dredged up a reassuring smile. "Don't worry, Stacia. You taught me well."

Her lips curved in an answering smile. "Go make me proud, Tisiphone."

So I turned away to do just that.

BEFORE WE COULD TACKLE THE LARGER TASK of figuring out which Fury had betrayed the Sisterhood, we needed to find out who—or what—at Hounds of Anubis was leaking like a sieve. Add the fact that a Harpy had attacked me inside the Murphy stronghold to all the overly convenient ambushes at locations where only limited people knew our whereabouts, and it seemed pretty clear the Murphys had a mole. I filled Scott and Trinity in on my plan to accomplish that goal on our way back to the Belly. Scott hated the idea of using me as bait to draw out the traitor—big surprise—but Trinity and I managed to tag-team him into agreement. It wasn't like we had a whole lot of choice. One of those damned-if-we-did, damned-if-we-didn't situations.

Still, he reached out and squeezed my hand just before we stepped into the back room of Hounds of Anubis, communicating his concern for my safety without using any words. I squeezed back, then dropped his hand and stepped across the threshold. The wards whispered against my skin, settling down when they recognized me as a Fury. The scents of cigars, whiskey, and sweat warred in the air. Though none of them were my particular favorite things to smell, somehow they made me feel comforted. At home.

Trinity and Scott followed me closely. The current on-call gang of mercs looked up at our entrance. A couple of Scott's cousins, several aunts and uncles from his father's side, and as according to our plan, his mother.

She kicked into immediate action. "Scott! Your brother and sister just called. They need us there now."

Scott frowned, glancing from them to me. "Did they say what's wrong?"

Liana shook her head. "They weren't sure the phone line was clear on their end."

Time to play my part. I clenched my fists to each side. "We've got to get over there. Now."

Scott rounded on me with a scowl. "*We've* got to do no such thing. You'll go on up to my apartment, same as we planned before. *I'll* head over to the safe house with Mom."

I narrowed my eyes, advancing on him with threat etched on my every feature. "That's *my* family they're guarding!"

"Which is why you're going to stay put, princess. They'd be in more danger with you there."

"That's ridiculo—"

He tapped me in the shoulder. Hard. "Just shut up, Riss. Why the fuck are you arguing, anyway? After what happened last night, you *know* that's true."

I wrapped my arms around myself, shifting my scowl from his face to the floor. "You're playing dirty, Scott."

"Whatever it takes to see you safe, Riss. And your family. That's what you're paying me for, after all."

Rage tickled the back of my throat. I forgot we were acting for a moment. Rage nearly won out over reality, but then I shoved the berserker anger aside and backed down just in time to avoid bloodshed. Barely.

"Fine, then. But you should take more than just your mother with you."

This time his eyes were the ones to narrow. "Are you telling me how to run my own business, Fury?"

"No, I'm telling you not to underestimate our enemy. Again."

He gritted his teeth, the sound grating on my nerves in the extreme. Finally, he nodded. "All right." He turned toward his father's oldest brother, Ian Murphy. "Can you escort Riss and Trinity upstairs, Uncle? And assign guards to both the hallway and fire escape."

Ian, a burly redhead with a short temper but an equally sharp sense of humor, nodded, eyes moving from nephew to me. He smiled grimly. "Don't worry, nephew. You can count on me to keep the lassies in line. Especially the Fury."

I muttered under my breath and stalked toward the heavy door separating store from residential hallway. "You better keep *them* safe, Murphy, or you'll wish your uncle failed in the task you lay before him."

The two men exchanged knowing looks before heading off in separate directions: Scott to slip outside with his mother, Ian herding Trinity and two of his sons after me. Of course, Scott and Liana had no intention of going far. The plan was for them to drive far enough away to fool any watchers and then circle back to slip in the rear of the building. They should be back in plenty of time to be there if—no, *when*—our traitor realized that I was all by my lonesome with only a mortal for company. Once he or she figured out how to get around the arcane guards waiting in the wings.

Ian checked Scott's apartment himself, leaving his sons behind in the hallway. He stuck his head out the door several minutes later to give the all-clear.

"Now, then, don't you lassies go causing trouble for us. Stay put until Scott gets back. He'll sort things out quick as can be."

I stalked across to the couch and threw myself down. "I know that, Ian. You're acting like I don't trust him or something."

He snorted. "Where was all your high-and-mighty trust in my nephew two years ago?"

The coward didn't wait for my response, however, just slammed the door behind him and turned the key in the door. Voices muttered on the other side, but I couldn't quite make them out clearly. Still, I knew the gist of the conversation. Ian, instructing both sons to stand guard in the hallway until someone was sent to relieve them.

Trinity grew bored within ten seconds flat and flipped the TV on to some forensics show. I managed to make it five minutes before the thousand tons of stress pushing down on me, added to the inane goings-on splashed across the TV screen, did me in.

"How can you watch this shit? Don't you get enough blood and guts during the day?" Trin's mouth opened wide, and then she tried to speak. I cut her off. "I need to change my clothes." I stalked into Scott's room and slammed the door behind me. Guilt nudged until I shoved it aside as ruthlessly as the door. Maybe it wasn't Trinity's fault that I didn't have any control over what was going on, but she'd do as a target in the meantime. Truth was, I just needed a moment to myself. I didn't even have any clean clothes here—we'd vacated the no-longer-safe house without grabbing those Kiara had packed for me. I settled on the edge of the bed and wondered how the hell life had spun so far out of my control in just a few short days. The dual uncertainties of whether I'd be able to save Vanessa or where things stood with me and Scott had stretched my already-fraying patience to just about the breaking point. I wasn't sure how much more I could—

The front door opened and closed, and voices murmured in the living room. My body tensed, but I forced it to relax when I registered no sounds of forced entry. Curiosity flared when the voices continued in the other room. I wondered if Ian's sons had decided to keep watch from the inside. I thrust my shoes back on and went to investigate.

Or at least, I tried to. Magic pulsed the moment I stepped

through the door. Trinity took me to the ground before my mind registered the fact that she was attacking. She lashed out, snaking my arms behind my back and securing them with something plastic that bit into my skin. The shock of her betrayal warred with the incongruity that she had managed to subdue me so easily. She was a mortal . . .

"What the fuck, Trin?"

She ignored me, eyes glazed and lips pressed into a tight, emotionless line. That look seemed so familiar. I tried to place it . . .

"Don't get mad at Trin, darlin'. She's not acting of her own free will, I'm afraid."

Somehow, the sound of that faint Scottish brogue hurt almost as much as thinking Trinity had betrayed me. Elliana I could have expected this from, but not him. I'd truly *liked* him, dammit.

"Mac," I said, as much to acknowledge him as to drive it home to my breaking heart that he was the traitor in our midst—that he had been all along. Even worse, I'd finally figured out what he was. Only one group of arcanes could bewitch others so effortlessly. "You're Sidhe."

He stared down at me, expression inscrutable. "Partly," he admitted after a long, tense moment.

That made sense. I'd written him off as a Sidhe earlier because he didn't "match" the magical signature of any of the Sidheborn clones I'd run into thus far.

"But not part mortal," I mused aloud. "Else you wouldn't be able to compel Trinity to betray me so easily."

"Also true."

"What else are you, then?"

He shook his head. "Time for that later, darlin'."

I narrowed my eyes. "What else are you?"

His lips tightened and he crouched down next to me. "Be silent, Marissa. Else I'll—"

I took advantage of the fact that he didn't immediately wish me harm to bind him with a small but effective spell. "What else are you?"

Had he been a full-blooded Sidhe, or even just expecting it, he might have had a chance to resist the Rule of Three—an ancient spell that works only on those with the slightest drop of Sidhe blood. One of the few advantages non-Sidhe arcanes had when dealing with them—and one reason they typically made their sucktastic bargains with mundanes, who had no such protection. He struggled against the magic coursing from my body to his, lips clenched and every muscle trembling. But he lost.

Rather than answering verbally, however, he did something unexpected: shoved up the sleeves of his long-sleeved sweater and revealed something I never saw coming. Two rainbow-hued serpents wrapped around his arm from elbow to shoulder, shimmering with the blended shades of blue, green, and red.

"Y-you're—" I couldn't even stutter the last out.

So he did it for me, reaching a hand down to stroke my hair as he did so. "I'm a Fury." Where his skin touched mine, magic flared again, this time of like calling to like. The shock of what he was worked to his favor, weakening my resistance to the point where he had no trouble overpowering me. As darkness swept from his hand to my mind, I realized just how screwed I was.

FIRE LICKED ALONG MY LEG, RADIATING FROM my knee downward. I bit back a scream as consciousness returned, reaching down to adjust Kiara's bandage, but my fingers felt nothing beneath the stiff denim of my jeans except bare skin. I gave in to the groan hovering on my lips. Where the hell was the bandage?

"They took it," Trinity murmured from beside me. Her arm wrapped around my shoulder and she hoisted me to a sitting position. Bedsprings squeaked beneath us. I fought back both pain and near-hysteria long enough to take in my surroundings. Soothing sage-green walls, multicolored bedspread, and matching curtains that swayed in the early morning breeze.

I frowned. "This doesn't look like a lab."

Trin hugged me. Whether to reassure me or keep me immobilized, I couldn't tell. "That's because it's not."

Either the pain faded or I was getting better at ignoring it, because I managed to focus enough attention on her to realize something crucial. Her eyes were clear and bright, completely free of any compulsion whatsoever.

"Good. Easier to escape then."

"Riss, you may want to wait on that one."

I wriggled away from her slightly, eyes roaming over her face, seeking any hints I might have missed seconds earlier. "You don't look like you're under his control anymore . . ."

"That's because I'm not." She pulled me to her side again and patted my arm. "Riss, do you trust me?"

Befuddlement wrapped around my brain as I tried to figure out what the hell she was talking about. Trinity had been a cop longer than me, and she'd obviously been awake longer. She wasn't bound by the same disability I was, and the movement of the curtains suggested a possible route to freedom. Why weren't we already halfway back to the Belly?

"Didn't we already have this conversation?"

Door hinges creaked, cutting off whatever she'd been about to say. My head swung in the direction of the sound. I expected to see Mac, brainwashed Sidhe clones, or even mortal scientists come to experiment on the captive Fury.

What I most certainly did *not* expect to see was another familiar face. One more dear to me than any other save perhaps Scott's . . .

That of my long-lost, presumed-to-be-dead mother.

CHAPTER SIXTEEN

LOOKING INTO HER FACE WAS LIKE STARING into a mirror. More than two decades had passed since I'd last seen her, decades in which my features had aged while hers gained the smooth agelessness of an Elder Fury. We could have passed for sisters, if not twins.

"M-Mom?" My voice trembled even more than my shaking hands, which I now realized were held out toward her beseechingly.

She closed her eyes briefly, stepping forward and shutting the door behind her before opening them and meeting my own. "Marissa." Rather than reassuring me, the calm acknowledgment edged me toward hurt and anger. She hadn't seen me since I'd hit puberty, and all she could say was my name?

"Wh-what's going on? We thought—we thought you were dead."

I left the rest unspoken for the moment. That Dad had drunk himself into an early grave, leaving David the downer task of raising his teenaged sister. How *he'd* become so fearful of losing me that he'd nearly succeeded in turning me away from my path as a Fury. All because of her.

"Your knee pains you, does it not?"

Her cool tone of voice and noncommittal expression drove me further toward the edge. I managed to fight Rage back only by promising to unleash it later. Hopefully I'd have a proper target for it then, because I didn't want to celebrate my mother's miraculous emergence from death by sending her there myself.

It was a struggle, but I kept my voice as calm as hers. "Yeah."

She crossed the room, removing something from a bag dangling at her elbow. Trinity pressed me more tightly, keeping me pinioned in place, and—for the moment—I let her. The sight of the missing bandage in my mother's hands was a welcome one. She wrapped it swiftly around my aching knee, reminding me of the dozens if not hundreds of times she had patched up lesser wounds with the certain magic of Scooby-Doo Band-Aids. Physical pain dissipated, but emotional agony welled up to take its place.

"What. The. *Hell*. Is going on?"

Her eyes fluttered closed and open like a butterfly's wings. I'd known all her expressions well as a child, but the chasm of two decades made me more uncertain than I'd ever been. Was that regret? Guilt? Frustration? Or all of the above?

"Marissa, I know what a shock this must be for you."

I broke free of Trinity's grasp, leaping from the bed and stalking to the half-open window. The scent of freshly mown grass and wildflowers in bloom helped ground me, providing enough physical distraction that I managed to keep a leash on the Rage throbbing deep inside.

Anger helped me ignore the slight twinges of pain pulsing through my knee. The bandage just needed time to reach full potency again. That was all.

"I very seriously doubt you know anything about how I feel right now. Mother."

She blanched at the icy contempt in my voice. I'd never once spoken to her in that tone, or called her *Mother* for that matter. Always Mommy or Mom.

"Please, Marissa. Allow me to explain."

I whirled, my eyes spitting fire and my hands clenched to each side. "How the hell does anyone *explain* allowing their children to believe they were dead for twenty years? You can't just drop back in and say, 'Oh, hello there, darling. Kiss kiss.' Why should I listen to anything you say?"

"Because." She held a hand out to me, mirroring my earlier gesture, her fingers and voice trembling and tears threatening to spill. The same tears I wouldn't let appear in my own eyes. "Vanessa wasn't the first Fury those bastards snatched, Marissa. I was."

Wind seemed to whoosh in my ears with the violence of a jet plane. It took a moment for me to realize it was just blood rushing to my ears. My mother had been the first Fury taken captive for genetic experimentation? That changed everything.

And suddenly I realized why Mac had always seemed so damned familiar to me. His accent was straight from the shores of Scotland, true enough, but his patterns of speech, mannerisms, and bone structure were all hers. Which made Mac . . .

"But that's impossible!"

"Believe me, baby. It's the only thing that would have kept me away from you."

She made to stand, but I waved her back. "That's not what I meant. I was talking about Mac."

Her eyes grew wary. "What do you mean?"

"He's yours, isn't he?"

Trinity made an odd noise. I glanced at her wide, frozen eyes and knew she was as shocked as I was. She hadn't been party to this, as I'd momentarily feared.

Mom nodded. "He is."

"But the age isn't right. He's my age, or at least not much younger. You've only been gone twenty years. He can't possibly be that—unless you cheated on Dad?"

This time she *did* jump up, lips pressed into a tight line and eyes narrowed. "I most certainly did no such thing, Marissa Eurydice Holloway. I gave birth to Mac just over eighteen years ago."

"Impossible!" I repeated."

"Perhaps not for mortals—which includes potential Furies—but for Sidhe, that's another matter entirely. You know how fast they mature, until they 'freeze' at their adult age. Think, too, how fast someone with Sidhe blood who has been genetically and magically manipulated would age."

My fingernails dug into my palms, drawing blood, but I ignored the pain. I'd known that, somewhere inside, but wanted to ignore it. Somehow it seemed a hundred times more disgusting to think of those things being done to my mother.

"I think you'd better tell me everything. From square one."

She nodded. "Of course. You deserve nothing but the truth." Her eyes moved from me to Trinity, and I read the hesitation in her body language.

"Anything you can say to me, you can say to Trin. She's my partner as well as my friend."

Trinity sent me a reassuring smile, scooting forward on the bed and turning an interested ear my mother's way. I perched beside her, not yet ready to sit beside my mother, but no longer so angry I might kill her accidentally. Or not so accidentally.

Mom took a deep breath, twisted her hands in her lap, and then launched into her story. "Twenty years ago I was called before the Conclave to accept what I believed to be a routine scouting mission. Rumors had come to us of a group of mortal scientists who seemed to know more about arcane physiology than they had any right to. More than most arcanes themselves knew." Her lips curved into a humorless smile. "Ironically, I was actually the second sister considered for the job. Too damned bad she suffered a serious injury and they had to send me in to replace her."

Unease stirred, and I shifted forward. "Who was the first candidate?"

She made a sour face. "That fox-faced bitch, Ekaterina."

The amusement at hearing her use my exact words to describe the current Moerae quickly gave way to the first stirring of Rage. Wasn't it an amazing coincidence that Ekaterina just *happened* to get injured on that particular mission, and the Fury she hated the most just *happened* to get chosen to serve in her place? Too bad I didn't believe in mere coincidences.

Mom didn't notice the tension tightening my body and continued with her story. "I was supposed to get in, find out what they knew, and get out. But there was one problem with that little plan. They knew I was coming."

I pressed my feet tightly into the carpet, watching the pale beige strands of fiber giving way beneath me. "They were ready for someone to break in?"

"No, darling. They knew that a Fury—they knew that *this specific* Fury—was coming. They let me get halfway to my target—the bunker where their main laboratory was hidden—before springing their trap. I didn't even have time to shift before their Sidheborn watchdogs were on me."

She crossed her legs, sighing at the memory. "Gods, I felt so stupid and pathetic when I woke, chained to a wall with spell-worked steel and unable to shift enough to send my Amphisbaena for help. And all I could think about the whole time was how the three of you would never know what happened to me, or how I died."

Gods, I was going to take great pleasure in tearing that fox-faced bitch apart limb from limb once I got my hands on her. After I found the proof that would justify her execution. "But you didn't die."

"No. Though over the next eighteen months I wished I had, many times over. It would have been better by far to die cleanly than go through what they did to me." She shuddered, skin growing pale. "Rape after rape while they try unsuccessfully to impregnate you naturally. Then they try artificial insemination. After several miscarriages, they finally admit defeat and move on to artificial insemination crossed with both genetic and magical manipulation of the fetus. And finally, finally they succeed. This time you don't miscarry in the first month, and you know you're screwed."

I don't think she noticed the tears that spilled down her cheeks or the hollowness of her voice as she began speaking of herself in the second person. Rage stirred inside again, this time on her behalf. Those pieces of shit . . . I'd been pissed enough when hearing what they were doing to other arcanes, but even thinking that they were experimenting on Vanessa hadn't cut me to the bone quite this badly. This was my *mother* those bastards had repeatedly violated. Oh yeah, they were going to pay.

I threw myself to my knees and crawled to her, wrapping my arms around her legs and placing my head in her lap as I'd done so many times growing up. She clutched my shoulders, fingernails cutting into my skin even more painfully than my own had, but I didn't protest. She needed this as much as I did. Maybe even more.

"But I suppose I should thank them for that," she said, bitterness tinged with wonder coloring her tone. "After all, it was the knowledge I had more than my own life to worry about that gave me the courage and motivation to stop wallowing in self-pity and start thinking about survival for both of us."

"You—and Mac?"

She nodded, accepting the tissue that Trinity thoughtfully provided from the bathroom. "Yes. Though when I first realized that this latest pregnancy was actually going to stick, of course I assumed *he* was going to be a *she*. I knew they were trying to breed their own"—her lip curled—"pet Fury."

I tried to lighten the moment slightly. "Bet you got one hell of a surprise when your new bundle of joy actually arrived."

"Never in a million years did I suspect they'd successfully created what had never been born in millennia of the Sisterhood."

Trinity hazarded the guess that we two Furies knew for fact. "The first male Fury?"

"Exactly. Perhaps the babe was forced upon me, perhaps he was conceived in unnatural ways, but that didn't change the fact that he *was* my child, every bit as much as the two I'd chosen to carry. Of course, that's what the bastards used against me. My love for him. They threatened to kill him if I didn't comply with their wishes. Later, by the time I realized he was far too valuable for them to kill, they changed their threats to include David and your father, instead."

Suddenly it made perfect sense why she'd never managed to escape, why she'd left Dad to muddle along on his own, eventually giving in to the addiction that only Mom had been able to keep him away from. She'd had no other choice. The weight of bitterness borne of twenty long years lifted from my shoulders as I was finally able to defeat my deepest, darkest fear. My mother hadn't abandoned us willingly.

My brow furrowed. "But—how *did* you escape? And why did Mac go through all the subterfuge? Why couldn't he just tell me who and what he was when we first met? I've been going crazy trying to figure out why the hell he always seemed so damned familiar."

She hesitated until the sound of a car door slamming echoed through the open window. "Why don't we finish this story outside? It's not only mine to tell, and there's someone down there who has been waiting a very long time to meet you, brother to sister."

Hearing her say that brought a warmth to my heart that I hadn't expected. I was used to being the baby of the family, but I'd often wished my parents had given me a younger sibling. Generally, I'd imagined that sibling to be a girl. A sister Fury in both blood and magic. But, in one way, that wish had been granted. Mac was, at least partly, a Fury.

My *brother* Fury.

CHAPTER SEVENTEEN

MAC'S LONG, LEAN FRAME DRAPED AGAINST the hood of a nondescript SUV. The screen door slammed behind me. I stumbled slightly, having expected Mom and Trinity to come out. Guess they were giving us a little heart-to-heart time. I covered up the misstep by crossing my arms and asserting my usual 'tude. "So you couldn't just drag me onto *Jerry Springer* like any other self-respecting, genetically created long-lost brother would do. You had to knock me out and kidnap me instead."

He pushed away from the car, taking the dozen steps that separated driveway from front porch in ground-eating strides. "Sorry, love. You all were hell-bent on catching a traitor, and I wasn't really in the mood to die trying to convince you it wasn't me." I noticed that despite his use of the endearment *love*, he had completely lost the whole Scottish-brogue routine. Close up, I also had the surprise of realizing his green eyes were now the exact same shade of blue as Mom's. And mine. Guess he'd decided to drop the entire charade.

My left foot tapped a staccato on the uneven floorboards. "Excuses, excuses. How like a man."

He quirked his lips. "So you see me as a man, despite knowing the truth?"

"That you're actually my eighteen-year-old brother in the body of a thirty-year-old? Don't suppose you've seen that Tom Hanks movie?"

"Please. *Big* was a road map for my childhood. Along with *Jack*."

The grin teasing my lips faded. "You're not—"

He shook his head emphatically. "No, no. The mad scientists wanted to breed their own Miracle-Gro army, not a bunch of decrepit old men."

I let out a deep breath. "So you're not going to waste away anytime soon?"

"Nope. Might get my ass killed taking those bastards out, but I'm not going to die of old age anytime soon."

I couldn't resist tweaking his nose. "Such language, young man!"

He leapt up the steps and bear-hugged me. "Don't 'young man' me. I'm bigger *and* smarter than you. Got you here for Mom, didn't I?"

The screen door creaked open behind us. "He's been watching over you for some time now, Marissa, though you have made that just about impossible the last little while."

I turned as Mom and Trinity stepped onto the porch. Mac settled his arm along my shoulder. It felt good to stand there next to my baby brother.

Until he drawled, "That's for damned sure. Every time I manage to misdirect the mad scientists, you do something else to gain their attention. Has anyone mentioned you're just a tad bit reckless?"

Scott, like ten thousand times before. But who was counting? "So, Mom, care to finish your story now?"

She herded the three of us to the oversized wicker chairs on the far side of the porch. "Well, it started three years ago with Vanessa's disappearance." My hands clenched in my lap. She settled hers atop them. "I always loved that girl, and when she vanished I knew it wasn't her ex that took her. I feared you might be next, and knew I could wait no longer."

Mac picked up the thread. "The scientists raised me to know and love Mom, but they used our love for each other against us. They trained me to spy for them and forced me to seek out arcanes they could later abduct to use for their own purposes." He stared at his feet. "I'm not proud of it now, but at the time . . ."

Mom broke in. "They brainwashed him, Marissa. Brainwashed him from birth to believe he was helping both mortals and arcanes move toward peace. And *she* brainwashed him most of all."

The bitterness in her voice had me blinking. *"She?"*

"The bitch Fury who betrayed me, who betrayed the entire Sisterhood, and was in cahoots with the mortals all along. Though I still haven't figured out why."

I leaned forward eagerly. "Who?"

Mac put a comforting hand on Mom's shoulder. "Unfortunately, neither of us know her true identity. She always wore a disguise when she appeared to us. Even though she treated me as her own son most of the time, she never trusted me with that knowledge. I only know her as Erinye."

My eyes narrowed. Fit right in with the holding company siphoning money from the Sisterhood. And was it too much of a stretch that both *Erinye* and *Ekaterina* started with an *E*? I didn't think so.

"So what finally prompted you to bust Mom out of prison? I assume that's what happened?"

They both nodded, though she let him respond. "I was

given the task to infiltrate the Murphy clan in whatever way possible, something that was considered pretty sodding hard to do. Finally, when Elle's wedding to the Houndling was announced, we thought that might be my only way to gain entry to their family circle."

I smirked. "Ahh, so you *did* set out to seduce her!"

He flushed. "Ah, no. That was completely unplanned, like I told you. I figured if I got in good with her, she'd get me in good with the Murphys."

"Only you got in with her in more ways than one."

Mom shot me one of *those* looks. "We don't need to hear *all* of the details, thank you very much."

Mac coughed to cover embarrassment, then forged on. "Long story short: Elle and I fell in love, I grew to truly care about the Murphys, and when I realized who and what you were to me . . . I found ways to talk to Mom without being spied on, something I'd never done before. And the more she and I talked, the more I realized just how wrong I'd been. That Erinye and the scientists were the bad guys, and I had been working for the wrong side all along. So a few weeks ago, I secretly helped Mom break out of the ranch in the Southwest where they were holding her. That location was shut down almost immediately, and they launched a hellacious manhunt for us. Took a lot longer to smuggle her back here than I expected. And then we had to make sure that . . ." His voice trailed off and he looked embarrassed.

Mom took pity on him. "We didn't come to you right away, sweetheart, because we had to be sure you were you. That they hadn't gotten to you trying to get to me."

Okay, that made way too much sense. Though it didn't really explain why they'd had to go to such extremes to come clean to me. "So what prompted the whole shanghai-Marissa routine? And"—I scowled at another thought—"is Scott in on this?"

Mac shook his head. "No, but he and Elle should be

here any minute. And I brought you here to kill you." This time the other brow arched. "Well, that's what my superiors think, anyway. As of last night, you are officially dead."

I pushed myself upright. "Now, that could come in handy."

A smug smile curved his lips. "I know."

Mom coughed slightly. "And whose idea was that, son of mine?"

He leaned across the glass table to pat her hand. "Our brilliant mother's, of course."

She nodded once, satisfaction gleaming in her eyes. "Just so." Her gaze met mine. "Bringing you here had two purposes. One: to throw Mac's superiors off your trail long enough to put your plans in action. And two: to flush out the true traitor in your midst. Unfortunately, I think we've only succeeded in one of those aims."

I tilted my head. A car droned not too far off in the distance, but I tried to ignore it. "So nobody took the bait last night except Mac?"

His voice became rueful. "Nope. Which was surprising, seeing as how Trinity and I managed to sneak you out right under their very noses."

My toes began tapping on the warped floorboards. "Well, if the traitor's working for the mad scientists, and they thought you were taking me out, is that really a surprise? I doubt they'd want to lose both their agents if they could avoid it."

Mac pursed his lips. "I thought of that myself, but they haven't hesitated to throw everything they have against you every other time they've tried to take you out. You're a bloody Fury, Riss. And you've managed to survive every single assassination attempt they've made."

"True. Maybe we've been looking at this all wrong."

Mac and Mom focused their attention on me. Trinity seemed to be staring off into the distance.

"Maybe you *were* their only agent at Hounds. They could just have an extremely talented tail on me. Or," I added doubtfully, "maybe a tracking device of . . . some . . . sort." My heel clunked against the floor with a particularly loud thump, and my voice trailed away as I thought back to that instant of biting pain on the beach where we found the Sidhe's corpse. "My boots."

Mac shot me a look that clearly suggested I'd lost what few marbles I had. "Your—boots?"

I yanked the fabulous piece of leather off my left foot and eyed it regretfully. *This is going to hurt me more than it does you.* And then I ripped the heel off with one swift jerk.

"What did they ever do to you?" Mac drawled.

"Well, if my suspicions are correct, they've been leading those assholes to me all this time."

His expression grew intrigued. "They got a tracker on you without you noticing?"

My cheeks flushed slightly. "I was a little preoccupied by the fact that my best friend's body had just washed up in Boston Harbor. And I didn't really think much about the nail I stepped on at the time."

"Whoa. They planted a tracker on you through a nail next to the corpse they dumped? How the hell did they make sure you stepped on it?"

"I don't think it actually *was* a nail. I just chalked it up to that at the time. They must have used some device that implanted the tracker in the boot, and I felt it enough to think I'd stepped on something sharp. Gee, ain't technology grand?"

Mac grinned. "Damn straight it is." Hrmph. Damn man probably owned stock in Apple *and* Microsoft. Sort of like me and Starbucks.

Blocking out his voice, I sifted through the mess of leather and wood but came up empty. Not the tiniest sliver of out-of-place metal or plastic. I frowned, and then felt a whole lot of stupid. *The pain came from your* other *left,* I thought sourly.

Trinity scooted closer. "What's up?"

I growled, dumping the now-ruined boot and jerking the other off even more violently. "Wrong foot." All three of them bit back smiles and purposely avoided looking at each other. Jerks.

A triumphant smirk replaced my scowl when a small circle of plastic and metal gleamed up at me. "Aha! Gotcha."

My fingers were less than an inch away from plucking the manmade hitchhiker from my boot when the purring engine suddenly became an all-out roar. I froze, eyes widening when I realized the awful truth. I'd found the tracker too late.

I snatched the bug, smashed it beneath my good boot, and then shifted into full Fury form, repairing the damaged boot with a smidge of magic. I vaulted from a sitting position clear over the porch railing, landing on bare earth and trampling several early spring flowers in the process. Fury magic pulsed at my back. The familiar rush of warmth pleased me absurdly. I hadn't worked with a sister—or brother—Fury in too long. Not since Vanessa.

Footsteps pounded into the house, no doubt Trinity in pursuit of a conventional weapon. An unfamiliar car squealed into view just down the driveway. My muscles bunched and I *leapt*, wings flapping to gather momentum. I aimed for the hood of the car, intending to smash as much as I could in one swoop.

Mac's screamed "Stop!" reached my ears at precisely the moment I recognized the wild-eyed driver. Scott.

"Shit!" I backwinged to slow my fall and tried to redirect my landing. Disaster loomed—no way was I going to miss the several-ton bullet speeding toward me—but Hound reflexes kicked in at the same time as Fury. Scott jerked the steering wheel and stepped on the gas, hard. We missed by barely a foot, and the ground slammed up to meet me in a dizzying blur.

I had the presence of mind to twist just before I hit, body instinctively going limp. Most of the impact spread through my lower back and rear. Much preferable to hitting legs or knees first.

Still, my vision grew dark for a moment and I blinked back stars. Somehow I found the energy to shift back to mortal form. Car doors slammed open and shut, and gravel crunched as someone ran toward me. Voices rose and fell in heated exchanges, but then hands closed around me and I knew everything was all right.

"Took you long enough." I settled into Scott's arms when he swung me up in one powerful lurch. His eyes ran up and down my body, and I moved arms and legs slightly just to show I could.

"Sorry, baby." Hearing him call me *baby* again sent shivers down my spine. He threw a scowl over his shoulder. "My *cousin*"—he injected more venom into that word than Nemesis and Nike could manage on a good day—"is fucking lucky I didn't rip her apart when she let me in on her dirty little secret."

He swept me toward the still-running car, and three people I hadn't expected jumped out of the backseat: Cori, Jessica, and David. *Oh, this has all the makings of a happy family reunion.* All three—even Jessica—hurried over, fussing and assuring themselves I was uninjured, a fact that seemed somewhat doubtful since Scott flat-out refused to let me down.

Gravel crunched again and I stiffened at Elliana's voice, followed by Mac's and then my mother's, all of whom spoke too quietly for the mortals to really hear. But then they drew close enough to spit on. For a moment, I thought

Scott was going to do just that to Mac, but David's eyes zeroed in on our mother, and he cried out.

He shoved both wife and daughter behind him, backing them toward the car. "It's another one of *them*!" When neither Scott nor I reacted, truth dawned across his face with agonizing quickness. "No, it's *you*."

Mom reached a hand out, but David stumbled back another step. His face flushed red, then paled, then grew red again as conflicting emotions warred through him. I knew exactly how he felt, having gone through the same thing not that long ago, though at least he didn't have immortal Rage to contend with.

"Son of a . . . you're dead."

Not wanting to see him put her through the same hell I had—especially now that I knew everything she had already gone through—I squirmed until Scott had no choice but to let me go or drop me. "They held her captive, David. Just like Vanessa."

Some of the tension left his body. He glanced, briefly, from Mom to Mac, but then his eyes zeroed in on her once more as he drank in the sight of her. I counted, silently, one . . . two . . . three . . . and then he did the double take I expected, neck twisting from Mom to Mac, then back again. And he finally saw the resemblance to our mother neither of us had noticed when seeing Mac alone. Or with green eyes instead of brilliant blue.

"What in the hell is going—"

Jessica grabbed his arm. "David," she whispered. "Isn't that your—"

Cori's eyes widened as she finally fit the pieces together, recognizing Mom from all the pictures we'd shown her over the years. "Grandma?" Her voice trembled and tears pricked at her eyes. Her lips twisted in determination, and she flung herself forward. "It *is* you, Grandma!"

Tears flooded down my mother's cheeks as she clutched Cori to her as if someone might snatch her away. "Oh, my baby." She looked over Cori's shoulder to David and me. "All my babies with me at last."

David's glance flickered back to Mac, unease furrowing his brows. "Is there something I should know?"

"It's not what you think, David." I cleared my throat. "Well, it's not *exactly* what you think. Remember how we always wanted a little brother? Mom came through for us eighteen years ago."

Mac's lips twisted, but he kept silent, eyes trained on David as if on a wild animal that might suddenly attack. Kind of funny, considering which one of them was mortal.

"Riss." David shot a pained glance my way. "Did he hit you on the head when he abducted you?"

"Actually, no. But, if you will recall, we've been investigating a group of mad scientists who use both genetic and magical manipulation to create arcane test-tube babies. Like our little brother here."

Cori pushed back and regarded Mac with great interest. "Wouldn't that make him my uncle?" I nodded. "Wow. And you're only two years older than me? Does that mean I don't have to listen to you like I do Aunt Riss?"

"Cori!" Jessica's cheeks turned bright red.

Mac's rich voice rang out in a full-bellied guffaw. He tugged on the end of Cori's ponytail. "I'm bigger and smarter than you, so I outrank you no matter what."

I snickered. "He tried that on me earlier, Cori. Don't let him get away with it."

Jessica shot me an exasperated look. "Don't give her any ideas, Marissa."

Cori batted her eyelashes. "Yeah, don't give me any ideas, Marissa."

She ducked a cuff from her mother and took off toward

the front porch. "I don't know about anyone else, but *I'm* hungry." Trinity appeared at the screen door armed with a butcher knife. Cori didn't even blink; she just waved, chattering like a magpie, and had a bemused Trinity halfway to the kitchen before *she* could blink.

Jessica made a vexed noise. "Teenagers. Act like you never feed them." She and David hurried after their daughter.

Scott turned to Mac and Ellie, lips set in a grim line. "Let me know when the others arrive. Other than that, or dire emergencies involving someone being dead, I don't want to be interrupted. Let's see if you two can get back into the habit of actually following orders."

They both winced, then nodded without saying anything. Scott pointed toward the house. "After you, ladies. We have some catching up to do."

Mom led the two of us back to the bedroom where I'd earlier awakened. She and I took turns telling the long, sordid story to Scott, who alternately paced, frowned, and asked for further clarification. At the end of the tale, his face relaxed slightly. "Well, that explains a whole hell of a lot."

My body released the tension I hadn't realized it'd been holding in. "Yeah. That's pretty much what I said."

He stepped over to my mother, holding out his hand. "It's a pleasure to meet Riss's mother, Mrs.—Ms.—"

"Call me Allegra, dear."

"Allegra, then. I'm glad to see you reunited with your family. Especially your daughter."

The tone of his voice was possessive in the extreme. It almost sounded like a warning. I blinked, glancing from him to my mother, then back again. Was he actually "marking" his territory by getting into a pissing contest with my mother, of all people? Then again, my father had died before Scott and I even met. Maybe he was making up for lost time.

Mom just smiled. "I'm glad, too. And I apologize for the way Mac handled things. He wasn't sure how you all would react if he revealed the truth to you back at your headquarters. Being vastly outnumbered and all."

My lips trembled with the sudden urge to grin. Her words were no less a warning than Scott's. *Even think about harming my son for what he did, and suffer the consequences.* Seeing the two facing each other down made me realize something. No *wonder* I'd fallen head over heels in love with Scott. Only someone as tough— and slightly crazy—as him could ever match a Fury. My father had been like that once, although as a mortal he'd been more susceptible to the doubts and uncertainties that loving a Fury could instill. And once he'd embraced the bottle to drink away my mother's memory, all toughness had quickly drowned in a sea of Scotch.

I opened my mouth to make a snappy comment, but an engine rumbled noisily outside and the sound of brakes squealing pierced the afternoon air. My body tensed as I prepared for possible battle, until my brain put together the pieces of the puzzle: Scott's comment about the others along with what sounded like a semi pulling up outside.

My lips twisted into the smile I'd been holding back. "Well, what do you know. Dre came through for me after all."

CHAPTER EIGHTEEN

AND INDEED HE HAD. A SLEEK BLACK 18-wheeler sat in the driveway behind the car Scott and company had arrived in a bare hour earlier, and several SUVs were parked behind it. Assorted arcanes poured out of both semi and SUVs, taking in their surroundings with sharp-eyed gazes before heading straight to Scott and me. Mac and Ellie faded into the background, more than willing to let us take the lead.

Charlie was the first one to step up, not really a surprise considering the hellaciously long stride on the Giant. Two male and two female Giants trailed behind him, one of whom I recognized from Gunmetal Alley.

"Charlie!" I pelted forward and engulfed him in a hug. Or tried to, at least. My arms would only fit halfway around his waist.

He had no such trouble, arms easily encircling me and

patting my back with a little too much force. I winced but
didn't complain. "I see your Hound caught up with you
after all. Did you decide to stop running finally?"

Anyone else I might have slugged, but Charlie knew
more of the story from my point of view than anyone else.
Except maybe Trinity. I took advantage of his bear hug to
whisper into his ear, "Now, now, behave yourself. We're
here to work, not play."

He snickered, setting me back on my feet and motioning
to his fellow Giants. By the time he made a quick round
of introductions, our other allies—including Sean and
Kiara—had arranged themselves in a semicircle around
the porch, eyes and ears focused on not Scott, but me.
Gianna, the Oracle who had saved my life and then pro-
nounced me a lifelong cripple, nodded at me from a bevy
of apprentices, the only other Oracles she could pledge to
our cause. Because Oracles were always strict pacifists
(except in cases of self-defense), they couldn't give direct
help in the rescue. Instead, they were going to run an infirmary from the back of Dre's semi.

Butterflies tickled my stomach as my gaze wandered
from arcane to arcane to arcane to . . . I sucked in my
breath and battled the nausea welling up in my stomach.
For a second I thought I'd come down with a sudden case
of the stomach flu, but then reality intruded. I was nervous. Scared-out-of-my-brain nervous. I was responsible
for them all. The weight of that suddenly seemed to settle
in my stomach like a ton of rocks.

Scott's hand squeezed my shoulder. He met my eyes
unflinchingly, and the faith in them steeled my resolve. I
noticed the rest of my family gathered behind us, including Trinity. And all of them looked just as sure of me as
Scott. My heart picked up speed. I could do this. I *had* to
do this.

I took a deep breath and then let the words pour from my heart. "First, I'd like to thank you all for answering the call to arms. I'm not going to lie to you: The odds are stacked against us. The renegade mortals have an unknown number of Sidheborn clones on their side, not to mention superior numbers and technology. But we have the might of right on our side. No one, neither arcane nor mundane, has the right to steal our loved ones, our family and friends, from us. No one, neither arcane nor mundane, has the right to experiment on them like they have no minds or souls of their own. No one, neither arcane nor mundane, has the right to breed other sentient beings like animals. Make no mistake, we *will* take back our people."

A round of applause and wild cheers broke out, quieting quickly when they saw I had more to say. Their enthusiasm fired me up even more. I reached behind me to pull Trinity forward. Her mouth and eyes widened, and she looked like a rabbit caught in a hunter's sights. "Second, I want to make sure all of you understand one thing. We are not at war with the mortals. This mortal is a beloved friend of mine, and she has dedicated herself heart and soul to helping right the wrongs wrought against us. I trust her as I trust myself. The renegades who have taken our loved ones do not represent the mundane world as a whole. They are just that—renegades—and their government has disavowed any part in this whole sordid mess. If any of you intend to use this night as an opportunity to kill mortals for vengeance's sake—you need to leave now. I speak as a Fury with a gods-blessed Mandate. Any arcanes found to take the lives of innocent mundanes, or to use more extreme force than necessary to carry out our mission, will be judged as harshly as those renegades who took our loved ones to begin with."

A few mutters broke out, but they lasted less than

a minute. But none of the arcanes left, and not a few of them sent supportive smiles and glances Trinity's way. She pulled from my grasp and stepped back, no longer looking scared but neither looking particularly pleased with me. She hated being put on the spot. Or in the *spotlight*.

Tough, I thought with an inner smile. If I had to take one for the team, so could she.

"Finally, as far as strategy goes, I'm going to choose several of you to serve as lieutenants for this mission. We'll then assign each of you to a team who will report to one of those lieutenants. At that point the blood-oath will be administered and you will be tied as completely to this as I am tied by Mandate. If anyone wishes to back out, now's the time."

Not a single person even appeared to consider backing out. Good thing, too, because I would have had to waste precious time and energy in doing a brain drain so they couldn't give the rest of us away.

"All right. Once the lieutenants are selected and the blood-oath taken, the rest of you can prepare for battle while we plan the mission. Again, thank you all for coming here tonight. Your bravery and honor will not be forgotten."

Once the blood-oath took root, Scott and I led the lieutenants into a study in the rear of the old farmhouse and got down to business. While the rest of us formulated a basic strategy, Scott made some phone calls. First to his father, to check on things back home. Then to Red, who'd bugged all his old military contacts but hadn't managed to narrow the lab's location any further. Scott had just hunkered down next to me when his phone started barking *Who Let the Dogs Out?* After murmuring an apology, he checked the Caller ID and then flipped the phone open, a look of concern on his face.

"What's up, Harp?"

My body tensed. Scott's look of concern changed to

outright alarm. And that reignited the nervousness that hadn't completely faded from my stomach.

"Understood." He glanced at his watch. "See you in twenty. Be careful."

He slammed the phone shut and looked straight at me. Several tragic scenarios played out in my head in the seconds it took him to speak, but, as usual, reality was even worse than imagination.

"Harper finally got the location pinned down for us." A big relief, since Plan B—driving all around Western Massachusetts hoping to get a hit on Dre's way-too-limited GPS—pretty much sucked. Excitement rippled through the room, but I kept my gaze locked on Scott, waiting for the other shoe to drop. "But that's because it's being evacuated. They know we're coming."

"OH GODS, WE'RE TOO LATE."

My hands shook as I stared down at the valley below us. Hollowed-out shells littered the ground, embers glowing in the early twilight and smoke curling toward the sky. It took me a moment to realize they marked where buildings had once stood—until the bastards learned we were coming for them and decided to torch everything rather than risk evidence falling into the wrong hands. Tears pricked my eyes. We'd been so close to getting them back. *Oh, Nessa, I'm so sorry . . .*

Scott's voice murmured in my ear. "Hey, look at that."

"What?"

He pointed to the BlackBerry in my hand that I'd drawn from my pocket and activated moments earlier. "It's glowing."

I raised the tiny machine to eye level and blinked. He was right. Pale blue light spilled out from its display screen. Mystic symbols flashed across too fast for me to pick out any individual emblem. A soft beeping sound began to chime at the same time words appeared in the center of the screen. *Target acquired.* The words faded away, replaced by a map of the surrounding area and a blinking red dot less than a half mile away. The first time we'd gotten close enough for Dre's damned GPS to actually work.

Scott's eyes met my own when I jerked my gaze upward. "She's still here!"

We scurried down the hill to meet the rest of the scouting party we'd put together. My mother and Mac, who knew what we were up against better than anyone else. Ellie, since she'd refused to let Mac go without her, and Charlie and his fellow Giants because they were too damned valuable in a fight not to bring along.

I scowled when I remembered Ellie's refusal to escort my family back to the relative safety of the Belly, but forced my annoyance back down. How could I blame her for wanting to stay by her husband's side? Besides, Sean and Kiara were perfectly capable of driving them back to Boston. He might have been young (not to mention acting strange lately) and she might have been more Healer than warrior, but a Hound was still a Hound. Loyal, and viciously good at defending those under their protection.

Mom glanced up sharply when we skidded to a stop next to the two SUVs. Her eyes looked sad when they met my own. "Anything left?"

I bit my lips, then shook my head. "Not much. One or two buildings are only half-burned instead of fully destroyed."

Sarcasm tinged her tone. "They must have left in a hurry."

I shook the BlackBerry, excitement ripping through my body again. "She's still close. Either they didn't take her too far, or she made a run for it." I didn't need to say who *she* was.

A smile spread across her face. "If she did, that's our girl."

I let a matching grin touch my lips and turned to the others. "Mom, Scott, and I will track down Nessa. I'd like the rest of you to search the buildings to see if you can find any clues or evidence. Or other survivors." With the carnage spread along the valley, I doubted that last, but we still had to try. "Charlie, you're in charge down there. If you see the slightest hint of a trap, pull out immediately. Give the signal, and we'll meet you back at the rendezvous point. Don't wait for us. Mom and I can get Scott and Nessa out ourselves."

The brawny Giant nodded, then began barking orders to the others. Ellie's lips tightened mutinously for a moment, but then she fell into step like a good girl. Harper nodded, a hint of what might be approval in her eyes, and then jogged after Charlie and his Giants.

Mom and I shifted into full Fury form, serpents hissing and wing feathers fluttering in the evening breeze. Scott followed suit, assuming his large canine form and growling softly. I ruffled the fur on his head, then nodded. "Let's find her."

The terrain surrounding the valley was mostly forested hills, although parts were rocky and tough to navigate. Or would have been, had we been in mortal form. Scott had an easy time bounding over any rough patches, while Mom and I had only to use our wings to do the same. I glanced at the glowing BlackBerry from time to time, making sure we were headed in the right direction. Nervousness settled in my stomach again the closer we drew. Why wasn't the blinking dot moving at all? She should have put as much distance between her and the burning valley as she could. That she'd gotten only a half mile away bothered me. A lot.

We topped a particularly steep rise, and I checked the

GPS once more. "She should be on the other side of those trees." I frowned. "Strange. I don't sense her yet."

Scott's amber eyes glittered as he sniffed the air. Because he couldn't speak in Hound form, he nodded toward the group of trees I'd pointed out. Which likely meant he smelled someone.

I fought back the nerves battering my insides and slipped through the trees, Mom and Scott fanning out to flank me. The wind whistled along the leaves, muffling the soft sounds of our passage. Pale white moonlight spilled down through the branches, lighting up patches of ground here and there. Goose bumps pricked my flesh, caused as much by the eeriness of the night as the cool breeze. Maybe more so.

Rounding the trunk of a particularly large oak towering overhead, I noticed the ground dipping downward just slightly, culminating in a craggy mound of stone that spread out both east and west. The mouth of a cave slashed through the middle of the rock. Masking the glow of the GPS with my hand, I consulted it. The blinking red light indicated our target was straight ahead. Inside the cave.

The wind momentarily shifted, bringing with it a sharp, metallic odor. Blood. My body tensed. I dropped low to the ground and skulked forward, nose sniffing and eyes peering along the uneven earth. I sharpened my Fury senses and soon saw what I sought. Drops of sticky red liquid splattered every few feet on the ground. The patterns of blood grew steadily larger as they approached the cave.

"Well," Mom murmured into my ear, nearly startling me into a shout. Which spoke volumes about how shaken up I was. "At least she found somewhere to hole up and heal her wounds."

My breath exploded forcefully, tension spilling out along with it as her words hit home. She was right. That Nessa had found shelter while wounded was a *good* thing. I rose from my crouch and started forward, but then another scent hit my nose, this one even more disturbing than the first. The tinge of sulfur that marked Harpy.

Mom let out a low growl that sounded decidedly Houndlike. Her muscles bunched as she prepared to bound forward, Fury instincts screaming that the ancient enemy must be slain at all costs. My own instincts urged the same action, but I knew something she didn't.

I grabbed Mom's arm in a viselike grip. "Settle down," I whispered. "The Harpies lost one of their own to the mad scientists."

She let her body go slack, but her eyes looked pissed when they turned to mine. "And your point?"

"Ah, well, Calaeno and I have sort of an understanding."

"You made a deal with our most hated enemy?" Yeah, *pissed* was an understatement.

"I return her missing Harpy, and she owes me a boon."

Mom's eyes widened. "You got Calaeno to promise an unspecified favor?"

Smugness laced my voice. "Yeah, I did. And I know just how to cash that chip in. But you've got to get hold of the Rage and let me handle things in there."

Her lips tightened, but she nodded.

A low growl sounded nearby. Scott telling us to hurry the hell up. I took the lead again, creeping toward the cavern entrance as quietly as the rocky ground allowed. Rustling fabric was my only warning before a shadowy shape barreled toward me. I threw myself backward, smacking into Mom and sending us both to the ground. The figure launched toward me, but Scott's canine body knocked it away with audible force. The stench of sulfur rose into the air again, and my dazed mind finally caught up.

"Serise?"

The Harpy pushed away from the snarling Hound, head

swiveling toward the sound of my voice and body maintaining an aggressive stance. "Who sent you?"

"I'm here to retrieve one of my missing sisters, but your Queen *did* ask me to keep an eye out for you."

She stepped into the moonlight, yellow-green eyes flaring briefly. Her whipcord-thin body still held most of its earlier tension, but at least she lowered her razor-sharp talons. "Your sister?" She sniffed the air and then nodded. "Fury, then."

"*Furies*, actually." I gestured to my mother, just in case the Harpy was tempted to give in to her own instincts. My voice took on a harsher edge than I intended. "My sister?"

Serise nodded behind her. "With the midwife. I smelled you Furies coming a mile away." Her teeth bared in a feral grin. "Though the Hound's odor masked your own stench."

"Midwife?" My pulse kicked into speed. "Why does she—"

Mom pushed past me. "Which midwife?" Urgency laced her voice.

Serise's eyes narrowed slightly. "Eugenia Flowers. And you would be wise to remember she saved your sister's life." She flexed her fingers, drawing attention to the mini daggers that capped them off. I flashed back to her sister Harpy's attack and the poison-smeared claws that had nearly ended my life, and goose bumps pricked my flesh.

Recognition flashed in Mom's eyes, which seemed suspiciously wet all of a sudden. "Of *course* she saved Nessa's life. Genie's the only damned mortal in the entire compound that treated us as more than cattle to be experimented on. There's a reason I named her Mac's godmother."

The Harpy's head tilted, hand settling across her belly as she regarded my mother silently. The way she held her hand, as if cradling something precious, seemed familiar. My eyes widened.

"You're pregnant." She stiffened again and raised her hands threateningly. "Oh hell—and so's Vanessa."

Sadness, something I couldn't ever remember seeing on a Harpy, flickered across her face. "She *was*."

My turn to stalk forward and growl. "What do you mean, she *was*?"

Serise beckoned toward the cave. "Come and see. And make it fast, Fury. There's not much time." And with those dire words, she ducked back into the shadows.

Mom hurried after, and I made to follow. Magic played across my skin, and Scott rose from a crouching position, now garbed in mortal guise. "I'll wait out here, just in case . . ." He didn't have to finish the sentence. I nodded, grabbed his hand and squeezed painfully hard, then scurried into the gaping mouth of the rocky beast.

CHAPTER NINETEEN

DARKNESS WRAPPED AROUND ME IN A CHILLY embrace, bringing to mind my earlier visit to the morgue. *Now* there's *a cheerful thought*. I struggled to concentrate on my surroundings. A narrow tunnel led steeply downward for a dozen paces, and the temperature grew a degree cooler with each step I took. Tons of suffocating rock seemed to close in on me, and just when panic began to demand I turn around *now*, the tunnel opened out into a cavern actually deserving the name.

The stink of death slammed into me with physical force. I stumbled on the uneven floor, barely managing not to slam to my knees. Mom and Serise heard my feet scramble for purchase and turned to check on me. The awful stench emanated from just past them, though neither was the source. That left either the pale-faced mortal seated on the floor behind them—or Vanessa.

I rushed forward and threw myself down next to her. "Nessa?" I swallowed the lump of fear welling up in my throat. No wonder she smelled so sharply of death. Tears streaked from eyes glazed with confusion and pain. Drab gray sweats covered her from neck to ankle, dirt and blood caking the ugly gray cotton. My eyes were drawn to the pool of blood collecting beneath her, and the lump came back in full force. So this was what the Harpy meant by saying she *had been* pregnant. She'd either had or lost the baby, recently by the look of it, and now . . . now she was just dying.

Tears slipped down my cheeks. "Oh, Nessa, no."

Mom's hand settled on top of my head like a heavy weight. "I don't think she can hear you, Marissa."

The mortal gripping Vanessa's hand choked out, "Allegra? Is that you?"

Mom knelt down next to me, gaze locking on the middle-aged woman staring at her in shock. "Hello, Genie. Miss me?"

The mortal—Genie Flowers—fell back on her rear, hand falling away from Vanessa's. "Oh, God. I thought they killed you when you tried to escape! That's what they told us, anyway." Her eyes widened. "Did Mac help you break out?" Mom arched a brow, and Genie flushed. "Well. I guess it's better if I don't know anything about that, anyway. Just in case . . ." In case she had only helped Vanessa and Serise escape in order to find and recapture my mother. I could tell where Mac had learned to imitate a Scottish brogue so accurately. Genie's voice was thick with it.

Vanessa let out an agonized moan, and my heart skipped a beat. I glared at Mom and Genie as a sudden rush of Rage swept over me. "Save the reunion for later. Vanessa's fucking dying here!"

Mom sucked in a breath, redness tingeing her cheeks. I focused all my attention on the Fury bleeding out her life force in front of me. Something didn't seem right about the way her twisted body lay on the rocky cavern floor, broken and alone. My eyes narrowed in sudden realization. "Why aren't her serpents healing her?"

Serise crouched next to me. She reached down, causing me to tense my body, but I forced it to relax when she simply raised one of Vanessa's sleeves. Shock slammed into me with sickening force. Her tattoos were gone!

"They have to be here somewhere!" My eyes searched the surrounding floor for the sign of emerald splashes of color. And found nothing but bare rock.

The Harpy eyed me with another uncharacteristic expression. Pity. "They *were* healing her, Fury. Until an hour or so ago, when they just—disappeared." Her voice echoed with the remembered loss of her own Amphisbaena—at her Rage-crazed hands when she'd Turned.

Genie moaned, head nodding up and down rapidly. "It was horrible. One minute they were there, doing their best to heal her, and then they let out the most godawful shrieks and they—turned to dust." Her fingers shook as she pointed to a spot between her and the bleeding Fury. Sure enough, a large pile of what I'd taken for crushed rock littered the ground. And that's when I had to admit the unthinkable. Vanessa wasn't going to come back from this.

Anguish clogged my throat, tasting bitter in the extreme. I dropped down on all fours and let my head lie across Vanessa's chest. "Oh, Nessa," I said again, tears spilling out in a sudden flood. "How could I find you only to lose you again?"

Something whispered against my hair. It took me several seconds to realize it couldn't have been the night breeze, seeing as how we were in the cave. Which could only mean . . .

My head jerked back and Vanessa's eyes met my own, momentarily lucid. Her hand reached out and I grabbed it out of reflex. It felt cold, painfully so, but still, it was so damned good to have her there with me, actually aware of who I was, and most definitely not a Sidheborn clone, that I almost started bawling like a baby.

She licked her lips before speaking again, no doubt repeating whatever I hadn't quite heard the first time. "Riss. I knew you'd come for me."

I bit the inside of my mouth so hard the salty tang of blood ran over my tongue. "Of course I came, Nessa. You're my best friend. My sister."

Her lips curved into a smile. "Sisters forever, isn't that right?"

"You know it." My voice grew husky, and I cleared my throat. "I'm so sorry I let you down. Should have been here sooner."

She shook her head, wincing in sudden pain. "Not your fault, Riss. They're the ones who . . . forced me into labor at the start of their evacuation. It was awful . . ." Her voice trailed away as a fit of coughing overtook her body.

Genie picked up the thread of conversation. "The bastards could have waited until they got her moved and done a C-section, but for some sick reason they put her through agony instead. And the evacuation messed up the plans for escape Serise and I had already made. We had to improvise. I helped Vanessa through the labor as best I could, but it didn't take long to realize something was wrong. Very wrong."

I frowned. "Was the baby breech?"

Genie's voice faltered. "N-no. Worse."

Vanessa's eyes bore into my own as I tried to figure out what could have been so horribly wrong. "My baby is half-Fury, Riss, but only one-quarter Sidhe. The other quarter is Warhound."

Realization zipped across my body like a lightning bolt. One-quarter Warhound. Mother Hounds always gave birth in their canine form—to very large, not-at-all-human-shaped pups, though once born the pups shift to human form. And Furies cannot risk shifting shape during the physical and magical onslaught of childbirth. Oh gods. That certainly explained all the blood. She saw the horror in my eyes and nodded. "By the time they realized the baby wasn't in human form, it was too late to turn back." Her lips suddenly trembled. "The worst part was, they didn't even let me see my daughter before they took her away."

My gaze softened momentarily. "Her?"

A small smile brightened the pain on her face. "Yes. My little girl."

"What—" My voice came out too husky to understand, so I cleared my throat and tried again. "What's her name?"

Vanessa's eyes fluttered open and closed like butterfly wings. "Olivia."

Tears pricked my eyes at the mention of her mother's name. The mother who had died giving birth to her because she'd been out of reach of both medical and magical intervention. One big reason Vanessa had spent so much time around my family growing up—and another reason her disappearance had so devastated Jessica. Her big sister had been more like a mother to her than a sibling.

How morbidly apropos that Vanessa chose that same name to give to her own little girl, the one she would never set eyes on the way her mother had never lived to see her. The gods-bedamned circle of life.

Her eyes flew open and she clutched my hand in a suddenly strong grip. "You have to save her, Riss. Get her away from those bastards for me. Please!"

I forced steel into my voice. "Of course I will, Nessa. I'll get her back, and I'll make them pay for what they've done to you." I glanced at Serise, whose eyes glittered with unshed tears. "What they've done to you all."

The strength in her grip faded away as abruptly as it came. Her breathing grew more labored. The stench of death became so sharply acrid I nearly threw up. Vanessa sighed, sagging back against the floor in a boneless pile. "Olivia belongs to you now, Riss. Keep her safe for me. I love you both, so much."

My vision grew blurry and I leaned my head on her chest again. "I love you, too, Nessa. Gods speed you home, little sister."

She let out a breath that sounded more like a sigh, and her eyes fluttered shut once more. This time, they didn't snap back open.

THE STINK OF DEATH FADED. AT FIRST IT WAS a relief, but then I had to face the reality of what it meant. Vanessa was gone. This time forever.

Grief flared into Rage in a heartbeat. I let it wash over me and took shelter in it, finding its red-hot edge preferable by far to the choking despair on its other side. Vanessa, childhood friend and adolescent confidante, was gone. And the ones who stole her from me had gotten away.

I leapt to my feet and howled, a harsh, inhuman sound that reverberated in the oversized cavern. Anger burned, hot and heavy, increasing in leaps and bounds rather than the typical dribs and drabs. And I let it. Soon I could barely breathe from the sheer brunt of it beating against my every sense. A cold, clinical part of me realized how desperately close to the edge separating Fury from Harpy I had drawn, but I didn't care.

Fortunately, those around me did. Mom's hand cracked against my cheek with sickening force. I rocked back a step, tasting blood in my mouth and seeing stars flash across my vision. Even so, it was barely enough to distract me from blazing Rage.

"Snap out of it, Fury!" Serise advanced on me with claws raised high. "How are you going to save her daughter if you can't control yourself?" The words hit harder than my mother's physical blow. But her next words were the ones to talk me down off the ledge. "I'm going to need your help to track her down."

Shoving aside the superhuman fury took every ounce of self-control I possessed. My fingers dug furrows into my palms while I took long, slow breaths, focusing on the Harpy's last few words, repeating them over and over in my mind. *Track her down, track her down . . . Have to help track her down!* At last, the twin distractions of pain and being needed allowed me to step away from the edge. My voice even sounded sane when I looked up and spoke again. "You can track her?"

The others' sighs of relief were audible to my over-heightened Fury senses. Serise motioned to the blood staining the ground. "Mother and daughter are bound by their shared blood ties. I can use that of the one to magically track the other—with your help to control the Rage long enough."

My mouth widened. The first I'd heard that a Fury could help a Harpy control her unpredictable Rage. Then again, the only Furies willing to help a Harpy would have to be magically coerced or tortured into doing it.

I glanced away from the blood and met Mom's sympathetic eyes. "We'll have to leave her here for now. Olivia's what matters most." I nodded, lips thinning to a tight line. She squeezed my hand. "We can seal the mouth of the cavern to make sure nothing disturbs her before we lay her to rest." My breath blew out explosively, and I let my body relax before nodding again.

It became too much for me. I whirled, fleeing up the tunnel and stumbling out of the cave's entrance as if demons were pursuing me. Scott's clenched hands and tense body

caught my attention immediately. He'd heard my cry of
Rage but had remained at his self-assigned post. His unspoken faith bolstered me in a way nothing else could have.

He wrapped his arms around me when I threw myself
against him, murmuring soothing words that held little
meaning other than the fact that he cared enough to speak
them. Deep, painful sobs wracked my body. I somehow
managed to spill out the story, and he even more mirac-
ulously understood my blubbering. Moments passed,
moments in which I managed to regain control over my
grief and despair, and then footsteps heralded the arrival of
the others. I pushed away from Scott and watched as Serise
and Genie stepped over to join us. Mom, however, turned
to face the mouth of the cave. She raised both hands, honey-
blond hair glowing in the soft moonlight and flapping in
the evening breeze as she began sucking in huge amounts
of magic. She looked like a Celtic witch or a pagan god-
dess, both of which I numbered among my friends, and the
Power surged around us as she called it to her as surely as
if she were both. The ground rumbled as she channeled
that massive amount of energy into the earth. The terrain
surged beneath our feet, churning once, twice, and then the
rocky wall surrounding the entrance buckled in on itself,
until nothing remained but a smooth, unrelieved mass of
stone.

Mom's body trembled as she approached. I hurried over
and wrapped my arm around her, taking half her weight
against me and helping her along the rocky ground. Her
face looked haggard, and well it should. What she'd just
done had taken a tremendous amount of strength. I know
I could never have managed it. Working with earth forces
like that had never been my strongest suit. I was more a
fire-and-air sort of girl, myself.

Scott was the one to break the heavy silence. "Now
what?"

Serise gestured with her hands, drawing attention to the blood-soaked gray cotton she gripped tightly. I blanched. "I can use this to track the girl-child, but not without food and rest. We'll also need backup, and a lot of it."

I wanted to rail against the delay, but knew that only fools rushed in. And Harpies might have been tougher than nails, but even they had their limits. She'd been held captive for days and tortured, then fought her way to freedom. Not to mention the fact that she'd done her best to protect Vanessa. I would never forget that. And, to top it all off, she was pregnant.

"Don't worry, we have plenty of backup. And a safe place to regroup. We'll rendezvous with the others at the farmhouse and plan our next step. Besides, they'll probably expect us to rush right in, magic and guns blazing. I'd hate to be so boringly predictable." A small, smug smile brushed my lips as I glanced from her to my mother. "Not to mention, I have a chip to cash in."

THE CHIP IN QUESTION WAS WAITING FOR US by the time we made it back to the farm. Serise had no problem flying Genie out, but I had to support an exhausted Mom in addition to carrying Scott, and that slowed us down considerably. I had to give Calaeno props. She'd responded to my cell phone call quickly and efficiently (more than I could say for Stacia, who did not answer my repeated calls—I might have worried if I'd had the time), and a good dozen Harpies—probably the ones she'd had with her in the alleyway outside our safe house—poured out of the barn the moment they sensed their sister land. Or it could have been the scent of two of their most ancient enemies that had them hustling so quickly.

I found myself glad Calaeno showed the sense of

keeping her "girls" in the barn, rather than joining the others inside the house. Furies weren't the only ones who disliked Harpies, not by a long shot. And seeing as how we were all going to have to work together—and trust each other—in the coming hours, I would definitely prefer to avoid any little "accidents" that might make that prospect impossible.

Calaeno smiled the moment Serise's feet touched the ground. The wiped-out Harpy rushed to her Queen and bowed deeply. Her legs trembled from the effort, and she let out a surprised noise as they collapsed beneath her and she fell toward the ground. The Harpy next to Calaeno—the Queen had introduced her earlier as her second, Penelope—grabbed Serise by the arms just in time. She seemed somehow familiar, though probably because I'd seen her in the alleyway the day before. The three of them murmured words too low for me to make out, since I was more focused on helping my mother cross the yard at the moment.

Scott's eyes met mine, and I nodded toward the house. "Get her to bed, please. I'll handle things out here."

Mom mumbled a protest, but Scott handled her with ease, taking my place at her side and browbeating her across the yard, much as I would have done. I couldn't hold back a grin. Damn, I loved that man.

That thought nearly had me stumbling worse than Mom. Oh gods. I really did still love him. And probably always would . . .

But then thoughts of Vanessa intruded, and I felt guilty for feeling even a moment's happiness when her daughter was still in so much danger. I shoved both emotions aside and went to deal with the devil.

Serise fell silent midsentence at my approach, falling into line between Calaeno and the Harpy who had saved her from falling on her ass. *Oh, so that's how it's gonna be.* I felt foolish for feeling a pang of betrayal. After all, her kind and mine had been enemies for countless centuries. Millennia, even.

Calaeno stepped forward, hands outstretched. Surprised, I let her take hold of mine. She kissed me on one cheek, and then the other. Odd. I hadn't known Harpies could be this civilized. Then again, normally we were too busy trying to kill each other to socialize much.

"We are grateful for the return of our missing sister, and we will take great pleasure in fulfilling the bargain we made with you. We thirteen shall stand with you as you rescue the captive arcanes. All enmities will be forgotten in the time it takes to accomplish this. For that period of time, we will be as one in spirit and purpose."

Her words sounded friendly and sincere. Still, taking them for face value would make me nothing less than a moron. "Your words warm my heart, and I agree that all enmities shall be forgotten while we engage in this common cause. Still, I assume you will not mind taking the same blood-oath that all of us have taken?"

She curved her lips in a wolfish smile, the Harpy gazing out from her face with hungry eyes. I fought back a shiver. "Of course. Providing all of you are willing to affirm your peaceful intents toward me and mine with another blood-oath."

Crafty bitch. I was kind of hoping she wouldn't think of that. It might have come in handy later on. "Of course," I echoed. "I assume binding just the lieutenants to the new vow and having them bind their people in turn will suffice?"

The Harpy Queen merely nodded.

"Excellent. I would be honored if you would serve as lieutenant over your sisters. I'd rather not split any of the other groups up since the blood-oath has already settled."

"A wise idea."

I gestured to the house behind me. "I regret that I cannot offer any bedrooms for your use."

She pointed to the barn. "This building is more than adequate for our purposes."

"I'm glad to hear that. If you and Serise would accompany me inside, we can see the additional blood-oaths taken and plan our next course of action."

Calaeno's eyes narrowed. "What is your interest in Serise?" Her voice dripped with thinly veiled menace. Whoa! Apparently I'd struck a nerve.

"Only the fact that she can offer the most recent, most accurate information on those we must soon face in battle. And her offer to track them down."

Serise flushed when her Queen turned an arched brow in her direction. "You neglected to mention this offer, sister."

"I meant to, Majesty. But—"

Calaeno waved a talon-tipped hand. "Never mind. Come along." She murmured orders to the rest of her entourage before herding Serise toward the farmhouse. "The sooner we find those we seek, the sooner we can discharge our duties and be on our way."

That sounded like a damned good plan to me.

CHAPTER TWENTY

WITH LIMITED PLACES TO SLEEP, IT SEEMED stupid to insist on separate bedrooms when we could draw comfort—even if not sexual—from each other. Several hours later, I lay in bed next to Scott listening to him snore softly, staring up at the ceiling and trying to figure out what was bugging me. Well, other than the fact that I'd watched my best friend die in front of me.

I was glad that Calaeno had so readily agreed to assist in our assault on the new lab. After she'd earlier stated that the Harpies wouldn't be helping with that little endeavor, I'd figured it would take some wrangling to get her to let me claim that as my boon. Sure, she seemed impatient to get it over with—that whole "The sooner we find those we seek, the sooner we can discharge our duties and be on our way" comment.

A frown crossed my face as something about that

statement niggled at the back of my brain. Slipping out of bed, I paced to the half-open window and peered across the yard to the old-fashioned, red-slatted barn crouched in the darkness. More than a dozen of Furykind's staunchest enemies were currently holed up in that building. But that wasn't what was bugging me.

An owl took flight, hooting as it soared from the top of the barn toward the nearby woods. My eyes tracked its path as it flew, and I began running everything Calaeno had said the day before through my mind. She'd asked how many Harpies I'd killed, and seemed unsurprised when I'd said only one. The loss of her first sister, Rinda, hadn't bothered her much, since Rinda had died "honorably" while trying to carry out a mission. Serise, on the other hand, had vanished after a meeting with one of their clien . . .

My hands clenched on the windowsill. Wait a minute. If Serise had disappeared only two days ago, how the hell could she possibly know she was pregnant already? She'd cradled her belly—her very flat, taut belly—exactly the way a pregnant woman would—or one who'd only recently given birth.

I spun from the window and crept out of the bedroom, making my way past the sentries at the front porch and stalking across the yard. The Harpies sensed me coming, of course, and Calaeno met me just outside the door. She looked too alert to have been sleeping. Then again, I wasn't even sure Harpies actually *had* to sleep.

The Harpy Queen's voice sounded cooler than the night air when she spoke. "Can I help you with something, Fury?"

I pasted a saccharine smile on my lips. "I believe you can, Your Majesty." *Nice. You actually managed to say that with a straight face.* "I thought we might discuss the terms of the boon you promised me."

She stiffened, yellow-green eyes glowing with sudden

wariness. "Have I not pledged my sisters to aid you in your cause?"

"You have, for which I am most grateful. But that hardly counts as a boon, considering you were planning to do that anyway once your sister was out of harm's way."

"What makes you think that?"

"Oh, I don't know." My smile grew feline as I played my hunch. "The fact that Serise voluntarily bore a child for your former clients, who then reneged on their agreement to hand the child over to you. And then, to make matters worse, they abducted Serise to impregnate her again. This time against her will."

Shock tinged her features, telling me I'd hit the nail right on the head. "How did you—did Serise tell you this?"

She looked even more pissed-off than my mother had when I first told her about my deal with the devil—I mean the Harpies. "She didn't have to. What I want to know is, why?"

Calaeno sagged, eyes closing momentarily. When they flickered open, she seemed resigned. "I would think our reasons fairly self-evident."

The words had hardly left her lips when realization snapped through my mind. "You want to create Harpies biologically."

She merely nodded. Harpies were the only arcane species that did not actually procreate. They weren't born to Harpy mothers; they were made when Furies succumbed to Rage.

"So, what? They were supposed to create one Harpy baby for you as a gesture of good faith?"

Her facial muscles tightened. "Indeed. They were to prove they actually *could* create a viable Harpy child by artificially inseminating Serise with the donor of our choice. But Serise realized something was wrong the moment her daughter was born. The baby had her mother's eyes, but her hair was purple."

Purple. Only one race of arcanes numbered *that* particular shade among their possible hair colors. "They crossed her DNA with that of a Sidhe."

"Indeed. They tried to cover that fact up by claiming the baby died soon after her birth. Serise pretended to believe this, and they returned her to us as agreed. After she had sufficiently recovered from giving birth, I allowed her to resume her duties as liaison with the understanding that she would use the opportunity to find out where her daughter was being held. She must have given herself away, because she vanished after the very first meeting."

"How old *is* Serise's daughter?"

"She was born six weeks ago."

Serise's voice sounded from just behind her Queen. "But she looks like she was born six *months* ago."

Calaeno cast a sharp gaze Serise's way. A battle of wills played out, neither saying a word but communicating all the same. It showed in the set of their lips, the narrowing of their eyes, the stance of their legs. Surprisingly, the Queen was the one to back down. She motioned for Serise to join us, stepping to the side to make room.

My eyes zeroed in on Serise's. "They let you see her?"

Excitement radiated from every feature when she nodded. "They drugged me and returned me to the lab. I wounded two of my guards and nearly killed another, so they figured I might be more cooperative if they let me have supervised visits with Rinda."

Awww, how sweet. She'd named her baby after the Harpy who tried to kill me.

I crossed my arms over my chest and turned my attention back to Calaeno. "You know, a less charitable person might think you deliberately kept this information from her so you wouldn't have to give up something of actual value to repay your debt." Her hands clenched to each side, and she took a half step forward. "But it's your lucky day. I am the very soul of generosity, so we'll just assume it slipped your mind."

She gritted her teeth, the relatively quiet sound grating on my ears worse than nails on a chalkboard. "I trust you have a boon in mind that will satisfactorily conclude our bargain?"

My smile turned more wolfish, à la Scott. "Why, now that you mention it, I believe I do. And this time, Your Majesty, we'll seal the deal with blood so as to avoid any little misunderstandings. Here's what I want you to do . . ."

SCOTT AMBUSHED ME THE SECOND I CREPT back into our darkened bedroom. "What the hell is going on between you and the Harpies?"

I jumped about a foot into the air. Once my pulse slowed to a dull roar, I focused on his shadow stalking across the room. No *How you holding up, baby?* No *Gee, I'm sorry you watched your best friend being murdered right in front of your very gorgeous but equally helpless eyes.*

My turn to play dumb. "What do you mean?"

He put up with my bullshit just as well as I put up with his. "Don't give me that shit. You sneak out of our bed after midnight when you think I'm sound asleep"—he ignored my attempt to interrupt—"and don't return for damned near three hours. I know you, Marissa. You've got something planned, something you don't want me to know. Now out with it."

Damn, he looked so freaking sexy with a fist clenched at each side, chest rising and falling with the intensity of his emotions, amber eyes snapping, and shaggy hair bouncing with each forceful gesture he made. "Gods, I love you."

The widening of his eyes was my first clue I had actually said that out loud. I sure as hell hadn't meant to, though as distractions went, that one had to rate right up there. Thoughts of the Harpies flew right out of his head.

"You—what did you say?"

I folded my arms across my chest and thinned my lips stubbornly. "Oh no you don't. I'm done being the only one to say that."

He stepped forward, his expression so intense I took a step backward, but his arms flashed out and stopped me. "If that's the only thing holding you back, baby, then I'll gladly say I love you, too." He shook me ever so slightly. "Now say it again!"

Lord, I couldn't resist him when he got all forceful. "I love you."

He pushed me back against the wall and nuzzled my forehead. "I thought I'd never hear you say that again. Thought I ruined everything with my stupidity."

"You thought *you* ruined everything? I was the idiot who dumped you."

"But I'm the shithead who never even told you how he felt about you. And I should have tried harder to let you know about Dre. I just love you so damned much, baby. I couldn't stand the thought of losing you. I know Furies can take care of themselves, but you're *my* Fury, dammit. I need you."

My skin tingled as heat washed over me. I had to have him, now. This might be my last chance, considering what I was planning to do in all too short a time. He opened his mouth, no doubt wanting to keep talking, but I had other things in mind. Like fisting my hands through his hair and flicking my tongue against his. He tried to resist, hands twisting to lock around my arms with painful strength. Rather than deterring me, however, it merely made me all the hotter. One of the reasons we'd *never* had problems in the bedroom. Animal instinct drove us both more often than not.

I had just enough presence of mind left to wrap magic around us in a soundproof bubble. Arcanes liked it loud—especially Hounds and Furies. I wrapped my leg around his and jerked, knocking him off balance. We fell together, collapsing on the floor, limbs meshed together and breath panting. He grunted when we hit, tried once more to break away, but then my lips crashed down on his and he was lost.

His head nuzzled between my breasts, and he wrapped his arms around me crushingly. I gasped, thrilling in his aggression, and thrust my fingers into his hair. Something good to be said for the longer 'do. Made it much easier to grab on to.

His teeth nibbled at the apex of skin between my bra, moist breath fanning out and raising a hundred shivers. My moan made him more frantic, and he ripped the fabric off with one hand. I barely noticed the tearing sound, not that it mattered much, since it was Kiara's. Then his mouth found my bare breast, and I could no longer spare the energy for idle thoughts. My hands jerked in his hair when he bit down on a nipple, hard. He alternated suckles and bites, moving from one breast to the other until I had trouble breathing, much less thinking.

Once he'd had his fill, his hands wandered lower, skipping over the waistband of my jeans and caressing the juncture of my thighs. I pressed myself against his fingers, seeking the friction my body so desperately craved. He rubbed, harder and harder, a lazy grin playing about his face when I groaned in frustration. It felt good, but it wasn't enough. Not nearly enough.

After what seemed an eternity, he took pity on me and yanked the jeans all the way off—along with my panties. My whole body shuddered. Oh gods, I'd missed this rough, wild heat so damned much. How could I have ever given it up?

His fingers found my most sensitive spot and began stroking, moving in and out with expert precision. He knew my body so well, knew exactly what drove me crazy. And for now, I was more than happy to let him have his way.

Seconds later I came, breath hitching in a drawn-out sob, arms wrapping around Scott and pulling his mouth to mine for one desperate kiss. When starburst after starburst went off behind my closed eyes, I let out a choked scream, which he muffled by claiming my lips in another fierce kiss.

When the last pinprick of light faded, my eyes snapped open. He wore such a look of pleased arrogance, I took it as an immediate challenge.

"My turn," I drawled, calling on arcane strength and whirling us both until it was *his* back pressed against the wall, *my* hands roaming along his body. His T-shirt ripped as easily as my bra. Excitement flared in his gorgeous amber eyes, and he grabbed my hair and tugged just as I had.

His flesh felt hot and hard beneath my fingers. Heavy breathing turned to quick, tiny pants as I worked my way lower. His jeans clung to his body perfectly, meaning I had to actually take the time to unfasten them before tugging them down. I just used the extra seconds to make him want me even more. His eyes closed and he yanked my hair one last time before moving his hands to steady himself against the wall.

His jeans pooled into a puddle on the floor with a loud swishing sound. I left them there, hands moving to the black silk boxers concealing my prize. Then I gave as good as I'd gotten, playing with the obvious symbol of his arousal, rubbing slowly at first, then fisting my hand around his erection and tugging, then releasing, tugging, then releasing again. His growl had me laughing softly. But then his eyes flashed open and told me playtime was over.

He waited for me to push his boxers to the floor, then struck. He had me flat on my back against the carpet, before I could do anything but gasp in anticipation of what was to come.

I nearly screamed when he plunged inside me, the heavy friction exactly what I'd been begging for just minutes before. He pressed another wet, hot kiss against my lips, and I thrust my tongue inside his mouth, tasting the male essence that was uniquely his before mischievousness made me bite down on his lips. Hard. He growled and then shoved my shoulders back against the floor and began pounding inside me so fast and furious that conscious thought fled. All I could do was feel, and damn, did it feel good.

My hips worked in tandem with his reckless speed, and we found a frenzied, familiar rhythm that had us both panting in seconds flat. His hands kept me pinned to the floor, but that only turned me on even more.

I could tell he was holding himself back, just slightly, wanting me to find my release before giving in to his own. He'd always done that, except for the few times I'd managed to turn the tables on him and bring him to pleasure first. I wondered again how I could have ever lived without this. Without him.

And then an orgasm hit, rocking my body from head to toe, and this time I couldn't hold back the cry. Scott's body moved against mine another few moments, and then he shuddered and his muffled grunt told me everything I needed to know . . .

We gathered our scattered clothing once the glow had faded and showered together, letting the lukewarm water sluice our sweat away, soaping each other and touching as much as possible. Each time his warm skin met mine, my ice-cold heart thawed a little bit more. It really sucked that only now, when I might have to give my life to save others, we had finally admitted we still loved each other.

And that was the awful truth I wanted to distract him from. I'd made Calaeno promise to carry the clone-children—most especially Olivia—to safety the moment we'd freed them, no matter what happened to me. I was going to take down the mortals—and arcanes—who'd abducted magical beings to use as their very own lab rats. Even if it meant sacrificing myself.

"DO YOU REALLY HAVE TO *DRINK* THE BLOOD?"

Serise paused in the act of tipping back the small glass vial filled with my best friend's blood, shooting me a look that could have sprayed my *own* blood on the walls had it been translated to physical strength. Or if we'd actually been *inside* walls. "Yes." She ground the word out as if talking to a very small, very slow-witted child.

"But Furies don't drink the blood, and our tracker spells work just fine." Of course, our magic didn't allow us to track others using the blood of relatives. We had to have the blood of the person in question, or no dice.

Serise yanked a handful of coarse white hair with her free hand and jerked. "Do I *look* like a Fury to you?"

I suddenly *felt* like a very small, very slow-witted child. "No."

"Well then. Shut the hell up so I can get this right the first time."

My cheeks flamingo pink, I scooched backward and fell in line with Mom and Scott, both of whom studiously avoided looking me in the face. Jerks. Calaeno, too, seemed to have better things to look at. Namely, the Harpy getting ready to make like a vampire. And with *Vanessa's* blood. My stomach suddenly heaved with the urge to vomit. *Stop thinking about it.* Of course, predictably enough, that only made my damned subconscious want to think about it even more.

Dark-red blood spilled along the glass and plunged inside Serise's mouth. I wanted to look away, but couldn't. Magic, the sickly green shade I'd come to associate with Harpies, sparked immediately to life, emanating from Serise's mouth and seeming to shoot from her eyes like twin beacons of flame. Her voice sounded hollow when she spoke. "I sense her. The girl-child is not too far northwest of here. Perhaps an hour's flight."

I rubbed my hands together. "Hot damn. That's even better than I hoped for. We can be there in no time."

Calaeno shot me a quelling glance. "That's one hour for Harpies. Not Furies."

My neck hunched up as I bristled. "What do you mean, not Furies? I can fly with the best of them!"

"Harpies *are* 'the best of them' as far as flying is concerned. My slowest sister could easily outpace your swiftest."

"If I'm such a slow-ass flyer, how am I supposed to help Mommie Dearest over there channel her Rage while tracking Olivia?"

Calaeno's second in command, and Serise's earlier savior, Penelope, stepped forward with a smirk. "Don't worry, little Fury." Something about the way she stood, the tone of her voice seemed familiar. I wondered if I'd known her when she'd been a Fury. Generally, the transformation was so complete it was difficult to tell, a very good thing indeed—made it easier to kill the psycho Harpy when visions of the Fury she'd once been weren't dancing in your head. "We'll take turns sharing our superior speed with you."

I narrowed my eyes. That better not have meant what

I thought it meant . . . "And how do you propose to do that?"

She tapped her fingers against her thigh, smirk only growing bigger. I felt like wiping the smirk off her face, but there was the little matter of the truce we'd sworn. "By carrying you, of course."

Oh hell. It *did* mean what I'd been afraid it did. "Absolutely no—"

Calaeno shot me an impatient look that would have outshone any Elder. Succeeded in shutting me up, too. Damned if I wasn't starting to respect her, against my better judgment. "Do you want to find your sister's child or not?" I nodded silently. "And is time not of the essence?" I nodded again. She stared pointedly at my serpent tats. "Sharing a magical bond with you will hurt Serise more than you can imagine, and yet she is willing to do it. Will you do any less?"

I felt about twelve inches tall. "No," I answered softly.

"Very well, then. Let us continue."

Mom and Scott pulled me off to the side, speaking in low urgent tones that informed me in no uncertain terms what they thought of me flitting off with my former assassins. Finally, I blew off my excess frustration on them, since I couldn't vent it on the Harpies. "Do you have wings, Murphy?" He glared. "Nope? And you," I turned to Mom. "Been flying around in captivity much lately? In peak condition then? You just heard them say they're going to cart me around in the air. Doing that for two Furies would take more resources than thirteen Harpies would be able to come up with." She scowled, but remained silent.

I sighed. "Look, I don't like this any better than you two. But the sooner we track down Olivia, the sooner you all can join us at the new compound."

Calaeno succeeded where I hadn't, stalking over to chase

them off, snapping at them that we would damned well call when we found the compound and they could make themselves useful by getting everyone on the road and heading northwest. Then she dragged me over to Serise so we could perform the spell that would—temporarily—bind the two of us together in some sort of Harpy-Fury magical hybrid.

Something about that image was so wrong it made me want to throw up in my mouth, but I managed to fight back the gag reflex.

Serise watched me approach with a expression nearly as serene as her Queen's. She held the vial of blood out toward me, and I recoiled. "Oh hell no. Nobody said *I'd* have to drink that. I'm not a damned vampi—" The gesture Calaeno made had me snatching the vial from Serise's hand and tossing back the smidgen of Vanessa's blood remaining. The salty tang rolled over my tongue and down my throat as I forced myself to swallow.

Dizziness struck, bringing a much more physical urge to vomit. Penelope and an unnamed Harpy jerked my arms to keep me from falling as sickly green threads of magic spread from Serise to me. She chanted something in low, guttural Latin, but I couldn't concentrate enough to pick up her exact words. Her magic thrust its way inside my body, a sickening violation worse than any I could remember, and she opened some sort of channel between us that sent Rage bouncing from her to me, and then she somehow *pulled* sapphire strands of Fury magic from my body to hers, using it to filter the Rage before it passed on to me, slowing the violent flood into a much more bearable trickle. I don't know *how* she did it, and I sure as hell could never duplicate the spell, but damn. I was impressed.

At some signal I didn't recognize, the flock of Harpies took to the air in a rush of wings, dragging me along for the ride. The bond between Serise and me hit me a hell of a lot harder than it hit her, and I could see another benefit to the Harpies carting me along like dead weight. Because, basically, that's what I was.

The ground grew dizzyingly small beneath us, and I could do little but stare down at it in a daze. Minutes passed by, with Penelope maintaining her tight grip on my right arm and the other Harpies (except Serise and Queenie Girl, big surprise) taking turns supporting my left. The fact that Penelope never needed to be relieved spoke volumes for her strength and endurance, and I made a mental note to try *not* to deliberately piss her off in the future. Would hate to face her in a fight.

Serise continually drew on our bond for the next half hour, using Fury magic to filter the dizzying amounts of Rage Harpies had to deal with constantly. My sympathy for our former sisters went up several notches, because damned if I didn't find myself wishing for someone to knock my ass out after maybe five minutes of the hellish flight. How the hell they handled this day after day was way beyond my understanding.

Another agonizing half hour slipped by, no doubt much more slowly for me than them, but finally—finally Serise drew less and less on my magic, and more and more on her own. And then we were descending, with the ground rising up to meet us at a pace that made me yet again feel like tossing my cookies.

Penelope's talons loosened just a moment before my feet touched the ground, making me slam down with much more force than I expected. "Oops!" she said with fake apology in her voice. The other Harpy snickered and released her grip as well. I was way too fucking tired to say anything, much less exact a little revenge.

Serise and Calaeno strode over to us, and abruptly, the bond between Harpy and Fury dissolved in an instant. Shockingly, so did the fog of exhaustion that had made me a virtual zombie for the past hour. I flexed my own wings suddenly, "accidentally" smacking Penelope in the process. "Oops!" She growled low in her throat, but one warning glance from Calaeno had her backing down. Ha. Who said revenge was a dish best served cold?

I glanced from Serise to Calaeno, to the unending line of dense forest land surrounding us. "So, where's this compound we came to find?"

Serise nodded. "Beneath us."

"Uh . . ." I looked down at the patch of scraggly grass just visible in the darkness. "Color me crazy, but shouldn't there be like, you know, buildings and shit like that if this is a former mortal military base?"

Penelope rolled her eyes in an amazingly mortal-like gesture. "Slow in more ways than one. Ever heard of underground bunkers, Fury?"

I bit back the retort itching to roll off my tongue and then blinked. "Hmm, underground bunker . . . Wait. This could actually work to our advantage." The more I considered that new tidbit of information, the more I smiled. The Harpies remained silent while I pulled out my cell phone and dialed Scott's familiar number. He answered on the first ring, sounding relieved to hear my voice, though he didn't verbalize that relief.

"Hey. We tracked down the new base. Can you put Charlie on the line? I have a little gardening project for him . . ."

CHAPTER TWENTY-ONE

CHARLIE PEERED DOWN AT THE BLUEPRINT spread out on the SUV's lowered tailgate, oversized fingers running along the heavy paper while he considered. Harper stood just to his left, lips curved into a smug smile. She deserved to be smug. Damned if she hadn't managed to give Mac enough information to hack into a military database and "borrow" an accurate schematic for the underground base Serise and I had uncovered. Okay, figuratively uncovered. Now we needed the Giants in order to make with the literal uncovering.

Impatience bubbled up inside me, spilling over when Charlie's silence seemed to drag on and on. "Can it be done or not?"

He glanced up, lips pursed, seemingly unaffected by my outburst. "Of course it *can* be done. The only question is whether the five of us can pull it off fast enough."

I frowned. "What do you mean? I've seen you dig before, and it was plenty fast."

Charlie's partner from the Belly, I think his name was Michael, snorted. "You probably saw him digging through dirt, sweetheart. Even a slowpoke like Charlie can make that look fast."

Confusion tugged my brows downward. I glanced from the blueprint to the hillside several feet away. "Call me crazy, but isn't that brown stuff over there dirt?"

Michael guffawed, slapping his knee with a loud, meaty sound. "Sure, on the topmost level. And then there's rock, more dirt, more rock, and finally, concrete and steel. This *is* a military installation, sweetheart."

My eyes narrowed. Charlie calling me *sweetheart* was one thing. He'd earned the right to such familiarity. But this bozo was really starting to irk me. I put hands on hips and took an aggressive step forward. Charlie must have recognized the look in my eyes, because he rushed to intervene. "I think we can do it, Riss, but once we get through to the concrete and steel, we're going to need a distraction elsewhere. Their alarms are going to go haywire once we bust through."

"Hmm, that's not a bad idea anyway. Coming at them from two fronts. But I don't see how we'd get in . . ." My voice trailed away as I swung toward the Harpies grouped off to the side. Calaeno arched her brow when our glances met, but mine slid past hers to lock on Serise. The haggard-looking Harpy needed no words to catch on to my plan. She nodded.

I spun, hand slapping down on the opposite side of the underground installation from where Charlie and company had already decided to tunnel through. The base's front entrance. "They still think Mac works for them, so we'll use that to our advantage. He, Ellie, Mom and I will 'capture' Serise and Calaeno and escort them inside. When you guys give the signal, our 'captives' will make a break for it. The ensuing chaos should let us cull down their numbers and give you a big enough distraction to break inside."

Scott leveled a pissed-off stare my way. "I don't think so."

My brow arched. "Excuse me?"

His right index finger jabbed at the base's front entrance depicted on the map; his left slammed down on the location of the proposed tunnel. "There'd be more than a mile of space between the tunneling group and yours. You'd be effectively cut off from any sort of backup."

A snarky smile curved my lips. "I'm pretty damned sure that one Warhound, her badass husband, two Furies, and two Harpies are more than capable of handling themselves until we can meet up." I leaned down and tapped an area near the center of the map. "Here. It's near the block of cells that are the most likely place for them to keep the captives."

His lips set in a mutinous line. Suddenly, I knew exactly what was bugging him. Not that we'd be effectively cut off from backup, but that he wouldn't be there with us.

I touched his shoulder. "Mac can get Ellie in under the pretense she's chosen her husband over her blood. Mom and I can assume the forms of mercs Mac hired for the extra firepower. There's no way they'd buy you turned against your family, Scott. And we can't sneak you in as our guard dog, either."

My attempted humor fell flat, and he didn't crack a smile. But at least he finally nodded. "You're right." His hands jerked away from the blueprint. "What sort of signal did you have in mind?"

I shot a saucy grin toward Charlie. "I was thinking you guys could shake things up right before you break through the walls."

He threw his head back and laughed, the sound booming

overly loud in the evening air. "You're nothing if not ambitious, Riss. You want us to dig through a half mile of dirt and rock, cook up an earthquake, and *then* tunnel through a dozen feet of concrete and steel?"

I tossed my hair back with a smirk. "What, like that's hard?"

Michael and the other Giants exchanged looks that bounced from amused to annoyed and back again, but they didn't bother speaking. Charlie was their appointed leader, and they'd abide by whatever he decided. Sometimes I wished other arcanes could be so practical.

My eyes zoomed in on Scott. Then again, life would be a whole hell of a lot more boring without a good fight now and then. *Mmm, and makeup sex. Nothing beats makeup sex.*

Charlie sketched a surprisingly elegant bow. "Your wish is our command, milady Fury. We'll call up an earthquake—a very minor earthquake—before we start on the walls. That'll be your cue to stir up a shit storm."

"Excellent." I stepped back, withdrew my cell phone from my pocket, and noted the time. "All right. We'll let you guys get most of the way through the dirt and rock before we approach with the 'prisoners.' Let us know when you think you're about a half hour away from the walls, and we'll head out."

Charlie nodded, folded up the blueprint, and shoved it into his back pocket. The other Giants fell into step behind him as he headed to the nearby hillside. I watched for a moment, skin tingling as the five of them spread out, leaned against the grass-covered mound, and called on the magic that was the purview of their kind. They stretched their arms out, clasping hands, and channeled that magic into the dirt before them. The evening air began to hum, setting my teeth on edge, as the Giants commanded the very earth to move out of their way—and it did, melting away

like ice, rearranging itself to extend the hill farther outward while creating a tunnel the width of the five Giants
joined together.

"Jeez, that's freaky," Trinity murmured in my ear.

I spun to face her, concern for her well-being in the
upcoming battle warring with pride that she'd chosen to
stand beside us and fight. I wouldn't give voice to that concern, not after the heart-to-heart we'd had. She deserved
better than that. "You know, you really should come up
with a few more adjectives, 'cause that one's more tired
than your love life."

Trinity looked disgusted. "Look at you. Finally get laid
again and suddenly *my* love life's tired?" She ducked my
halfhearted punch, her expression abruptly sobering. "You
be careful in there, *chica*. I don't want to have to come and
bail your ass out of trouble again."

Emotion swelled in my throat. I had to fight to swallow
it down. "I'll take as much care as I ever do."

She rolled her eyes. "That's what I'm afraid of."

"Listen, I've got something I want you to have."

Her brows rose in suspicion. "This isn't one of those 'I
think I'm going to die so I want to give you something to
remember me by' moments, is it?"

Her words cut way too close for comfort, so I forced a
smirk. "Yeah, because I always go into fights planning to
lose." She snickered while I reached under my leather vest and
drew out the hybrid wep that had saved my life only the day
before. Her eyes were immediately drawn to my hands and
grew round when I caressed the sleek stainless steel slide.

"Oooh, pretty shiny!" Pure lust radiated from her body,
and she held out her hand imperiously. I slipped the wep
into her hand, watching as she stroked it far more enthusiastically than I had. "Go ahead and make my day," she
drawled. "Tell me there's more to this gun than meets the
eye?"

Laughter bubbled from my lips, inspired by her child-like glee as she examined the weapon this way and that. "Damned right there's more to that than meets the eye. Which means I never gave it to you, you never used it, and you can't take it home with you." She pretended to pout. "This Sig has been modified so it only uses magical ammo created from its own energy reserves. Shoot a target once and it will stun them for a couple of hours. Shoot them twice, and they won't be waking up. Ever."

"Oh. My. God. Why aren't these standard police issue?"

I grinned. "One, because they're not entirely legal. Two, because they're hellaciously expensive. Three, because only arcanes can recharge the wep's magical reserves." I tapped the Sig's barrel. "This one's at full strength, so you should get at least three hundred nonlethal shots off. But remember, every lethal shot uses up the same energy as two nonlethal, so if you shoot a target twice, it's as if you shot it three times."

She crinkled up her nose and shuddered. "That's too much like doing math. No wonder they don't hand these puppies out on the force." Her fingers trailed along the rosewood grip. "Still, not having to worry about reloading will freaking rock."

"No doubt. The nifty bonus feature of this little baby is the magically improved aim. Focus on your target completely when you're aiming, and you're pretty much guaranteed to hit it. Just make sure you know for sure whether you want the target to stay down or not before you get all trigger happy."

A frown creased her face. "Wait. I can't take this. What are you going to use?"

I rolled my eyes, refusing to hold my hand out when she tried to return the gun. "I can't take that with me. No way the merc I'll be impersonating could afford one of those, and I very seriously doubt the gate guards are going to let us take weapons in with us. That's why I want you to have it." *Besides,* I added mentally, *you're the only mortal on our side, and you'll damned well need that more than I will.*

She looked torn. "Well, only if you're sure you don't need it . . ."

"I'm sure. Just don't get too attached, Trin. I *will* want it back." She made an ugly face. I leaned forward and gave her a sudden, fierce hug. She'd suspect something was up if I told her good-bye, so I settled for, "Keep an eye on Scott for me, okay?"

"Sure thing, Riss. See you soon."

I wasn't 100 percent sure she actually would, so I merely nodded before walking away. Time to do all I could to make sure I *wouldn't* have to make the ultimate sacrifice. I'd go down fighting, if nothing else. The Fury in me would make sure of that.

Calaeno seemed preoccupied when I approached. Serise and several other Harpies were deep in discussion with Mac, Ellie, and Mom, so I took advantage of that fact to pull Calaeno off a little ways. "What's wrong?"

The Harpy Queen pursed her lips and motioned toward her sisters. "Notice anything odd?"

I glanced over, smiling slightly at the animation in my mother's face as she described the firepower we could expect to come up against, and then forced myself to focus. Hmm. Mac and Ellie stood to each side of Mom, listening as raptly as the Harpies. All twelve of them fidgeted with nervous energy, expressions showing a whirlwind of emotions as their kind was so wont to do. And—

My body tensed. "One of them's missing."

Calaeno's breath exploded forcefully. "Indeed."

I couldn't hold back a gasp when I realized which one. "Penelope?"

Her voice let out a single, clipped syllable. "Yes."

The significance of that was not lost on me. She'd been with her sister Harpies after they'd finished their scouting expedition and directed us to this secluded side of the immense hill housing the underground compound. That she wasn't now could only mean one of two things. Either she'd met with some sort of foul play—or she'd turned traitor. In which case, they might very well know we were coming.

Maybe she'd slipped off to meet with Ekaterina . . . That thought had Rage stirring, but I fought it back and considered the situation as logically as possible. "We can't postpone this any longer, or it *will* come to war."

She nodded. Once, I would have assumed the Queen of the Harpies would welcome the chance to spread dissension and strife throughout the world. But I was starting to realize Calaeno wasn't the typical Harpy, and she wanted more for them than the simple surrender to their base emotions that was the typical status quo. For that, I admired her.

"We'll just have to keep our eyes peeled. If they don't buy our ruse, we'll have to fight our way inside and keep them occupied long enough for the Giants to breach the walls."

"Agreed."

We joined the others, not participating in the discussion of favored fighting tactics, just doing our best to exude the confidence that would bolster the courage of those around us. Even if victory no longer seemed quite so certain . . .

MOM AND I TROOPED ALONG BEHIND MAC AND Elliana, wearing the guise of half-Giant mercs Scott knew were currently out of the country and had the reputation for taking any job for the right price. Unfortunately, they

were also male. I *hated* wearing male forms. Besides the
obvious fact that the equipment was completely different from my own, there were a dozen things to remember
when impersonating a male. Men walked differently than
women, talked differently than women, hell, they even
breathed differently.

I shifted Calaeno from one shoulder to the other, trying
to be as gentle as I could, but her huffy grunt indicated I
hadn't been too successful. Resisting the urge to pat her on
the ass took an awful lot of willpower.

Two guards, not surprisingly armed with automatic
weapons, peeled away from four others and stopped us
twenty feet short of the reinforced steel doors that separated the underground bunker from the outside world. I did
my best to act like the big, tough, slightly slow merc I was
supposed to be, keeping a blank, disinterested expression
on my face. His face.

"Macgregor." The false surname by which the mad scientists knew Mac. "Heard you took out that Fury that had
everyone up in arms."

Mac gave a cold smile that seemed completely unlike
him. I shivered at the menace in his eyes. "You heard right.
Though it really pissed off her friends and family."

The guard chuckled and then nodded at us. "So what's
all this?"

Mac turned slightly and did what I hadn't—smacked
Calaeno square on the ass. Her body tensed but she stayed
silent. I bit back a grin as he drawled, "We tracked down and
captured the little Harpy who managed to escape from the
old HQ. And we got a nice bonus, too. The Harpy Queen."

The second guard widened his eyes and took a step
back, fear pouring from him like a physical scent. Mac shot
him a contemptuous look. "Don't wet your pants. They're
both drugged, bound with magical rope, and being held
by half Giants. They're no threat to anyone. Had a bitch

of a time tracking this place down. Neither of my handlers answered my calls, and this was *not* on the list of evacuation sites."

The first guard shoved the other with his elbow, turning back toward the door. "A lot of shit went down. People fired, arcanes with their panties in a bunch, and a battle royale for the upper hand. Right now, some arcane bitch none of us even know seems to have the upper hand." I had *my* money on a certain fox-faced Fury. "Pretty much all of us mortals left are strictly low-level. Anyway, we'll buzz you inside. They'll check your clearance and confirm the identity of your prisoners."

Mac frowned slightly. "Have they changed protocol again?"

The guard shrugged. "Yeah. Happened when we evacuated the first base." He turned narrowed eyes on Mac. "But you shouldn't have anything to worry about, right, Macgregor?"

"Less than you do, seeing as how my clearance is higher than yours."

That put a grin on the guard's face. He said something to the other guards, who stepped aside. One of them swiped a key card through a sensor, another pressed his finger atop a scanner, a third man typed something into a laptop, and the first guard spoke into a microphone hooked up to the same computer. The steel doors swished open, leading straight into what looked like a freight elevator.

Mom and I exchanged glances. Jeez, they really *had* beefed up security. Good thing we hadn't decided on a frontal assault.

The first guard waved us into the elevator, waited for us to pile inside, and then sent the car plunging downward. My shoulder began to ache. Sheesh, Calaeno weighed a ton. I turned to Mac. "Did they—"

"Shut up." He glared at me, nodding surreptitiously

upward. "I told you, as long as you do what you're told and keep your lips zipped, you'll get your money."

Which meant they had the elevator under surveillance. Not exactly a huge surprise, but I should have picked up on that myself. I called myself various nasty names, trying to distract myself from the fact that we were descending farther and farther into the earth. I'd never been a huge fan of spending extended periods underground, but lately I seemed to be tripping over a cave, tunnel, or subterranean military base every time I turned around.

The elevator car jerked to a stop and the doors slid open. I tensed, but when nobody ran toward us with guns blazing, I figured that was a good sign. Mac led the way off the elevator, down a narrow hall, and through the only available doorway, where more guards checked Mac's security badge, fingerprints, and voice identification, then double-checked that Serise was indeed the Harpy who had escaped during the evacuation. We were loaded onto another elevator along with an escort of six guards and deposited, at last, on the main floor of the compound. Good thing, too, because it was the floor where the Giants were supposed to tunnel to.

I held my breath and sent magical senses questing outward. The forced evacuation along with the mortal and arcane conspirators battling for the upper hand meant they hadn't had time to block off the surrounding reservoirs of magical energy. The exhilarating rush spelling untapped pools of magic nearby had my indrawn breath exploding out in an excited rush. *Jackpot!*

The best part was, since their new "secret" laboratory was underground, accessing the earthbound reservoirs would be far easier than usual. *So far, so good . . .*

The corridor leading away from the second elevator was much wider and better lit than the previous one. Dozens of doors lined each side of the hallway. Uniformed guards, mortals in lab coats, and even the occasional Sidhe (the brainwashed ones) bustled to and fro, barely giving the six of us a second glance. A digital clock on one of the walls caught my eye, and I frowned. Almost an hour had passed since we left the others behind, and Charlie had estimated it would take them no more than forty-five minutes to breach the walls. A dozen horrible scenarios flashed through my mind, from the Giants accidentally burying themselves beneath a ton of rock, to Penelope turning traitor and leading a troop of soldiers to murder everyone still outside.

My concentration slipped, and I nearly lost control over my assumed form. Color flooded my cheeks. I hadn't blown my cover in years. The stakes were *way* too high for me to regress to adolescent angst for even a second.

I glanced around and found one of the guards staring at me suspiciously. My hands tensed around Calaeno's inert form, and it looked like we were going to have to start the distraction ahead of schedule. But Charlie, bless his heart, showed impeccable timing. The ground began to tremble ever-so-slightly beneath our feet. Adrenaline pumped through my body, heightening my senses to a razor-sharp point. The tremors grew in strength and I had trouble staying on my feet, especially with the added burden of the Harpy on my shoulder.

Mac threw a questioning look over his shoulder, and I nodded. "Oh, goody," I drawled, setting Calaeno on her feet just before the ground stopped shuddering. "It's showtime."

Mom lowered Serise and we shifted in unison. The Harpies raised their bound arms, stretching as far as the material allowed, and Mom and I slashed with well-placed swipes of our talons. Mac and Ellie were already occupied with two of our guards. The other four had barely managed to lift their weapons when we fell upon them. I disarmed my opponent easily, knocking his head against the wall and watching as he crumpled to the floor.

We subdued all six guards in less than a minute, but it didn't matter. A group of technicians on the far side of the room saw us and fled in the opposite direction—after one of them tripped the nearest alarm. Sirens blared and red lights flashed overhead. Normally, I might have freaked out, but the technicians had played right into our hands. We *wanted* all eyes focused on the six of us.

Mac gestured ahead to where a corridor intersected our own. "So where to now, big sister?"

I yanked out Dre's magical BlackBerry and pulled up the electronic version of the map now stuffed into Charlie's back pocket. It only took a moment to scroll to the area displaying the three choices spread out before us, but it was a moment too long.

The softest of sounds caught my attention. "Down!" I screamed, throwing myself at the person between the cocking gun and myself, careful to cradle the BlackBerry in one hand while striking with the other. Elliana barely had time to get her hands underneath before I sent us both crashing to the ground. Even so, her chin whacked the cement floor with an audible crack—just before bullets roared directly overhead.

"There!" I pointed to the bisecting hallway, where the barrel of a gun poked out from around the corner. Its wielder heard me and promptly darted out to send further gunfire blazing our way. Ellie and I rolled toward opposite walls while Mac and Mom ducked into an open doorway for cover. Calaeno and Serise, on the other hand, launched into the air, hurtling at the gunman at speeds my eyes couldn't keep up with. *Damn, those girls* are *fast.*

They hit the man hard, one from each side, claws and blood flying through the air. Harpies channeled Rage far differently than Furies, since they lived just past its razor-sharp edge at all times, plunging deep into its depths whenever locked in combat. Also unlike Furies, they nearly always went for the killing blow. This time was no different.

I averted my gaze when the rest of us caught up to the Harpies standing over the bloodstained corpse. Too many lives were at stake for me to get squeamish.

Calaeno's yellow-green eyes bled to red at the edges, a sure sign of the bloodlust she'd just unleashed. Her voice sounded amazingly calm when she spoke. "Which way?"

I consulted the map and pointed down the left side corridor. "That's the direction the others will be coming from." I jerked my hand toward the right. "But that's the most likely place for them to keep—"

Something slammed into my side, throwing me several feet back the way I'd just come. A hammer slammed into my exposed abdomen, once, twice, three times, before I managed to get my hands into a protective pose. Shouts rang out, only some of them voices I recognized. My glance flew upward and I saw an unfriendly face I *did* recognize. The Sidheborn prick who'd mesmerized me at the softball field, then scurried away.

He still wore the same mortal guise as before, along with an absolute look of hatred. He raised his steel-toed boot to ram it against my stomach again, but this time I was ready. I grabbed on to the boot and twisted, throwing every ounce of my superhuman strength into the motion, using the momentum created by swinging him away to leap to my feet. He hit the wall with a thud but didn't fall to the floor as I'd hoped.

"Ready to die, little Fury? I'm going to rip your throat out like you did my brother's."

His brother? Oops. No wonder he looked so pissed-off.

I spared a millisecond to check on the others. Voices

rose and fell in threats, grunts of pain, and plain old cursing. Several more Sidheborn clones pressed their attack
on my companions, and it looked like they had the upper
hand.

Movement flashed at the corner of my eye. I spun just
in time, raising my arms to take the brunt of the Sidhe's
attack. Pain stabbed through both forearms as his boots
snapped against them with sickening force. The bones
remained intact, but just barely.

I shifted Nemesis and Nike from tattoos to spitting, hissing serpents. They blunted the pain shooting down my arms
and turned their attention toward our opponent. Their sudden
surge of anger indicated they'd also recognized the prick.

"The only throat that's going to get ripped here is yours,
traitor."

He wove around me in a graceful dance, poised on the
balls of his feet and hands raised in a martial pose. "No
traitors here, Fury."

I ducked one of his feints, twisting my body to keep
his in front of me. Nemesis and Nike wound themselves
around my waist, leaving my arms free to swing. "Sure you
are. You're actually helping the bastards who imprisoned
your parents, raped and tortured them, and are doing the
same thing to other arcanes. Sounds like a traitor to me."

His eyes lit with insane fervor. "Those Sidhe freaks
got no less than they deserved. Full-blooded arcanes are
a plague upon the earth, sowing bloodshed and violence
wherever they go. And since you won't willingly go back
to the realms where you belong, you must be made to with
whatever weapons it takes."

"Weapons like you?"

"Yes, living, breathing weapons like me. And once we
crush your kind completely, our mortal brethren will eradi-
cate all signs of arcane genes from our body, purifying us
and allowing us to live in harmony with . . ."

He rattled on a little more, but I shut his psychobabble out and tracked his every movement, tuning my body into the rhythm of his. When I saw a break, I leapt forward in a blur, jabbing talons toward his throat. And missed.

The prick both outfoxed and outmoved me, whipping his body around and behind mine and seizing me with an iron-hard grip. He slammed my body into his, hands digging into my upper arms painfully. Nemesis and Nike surged toward him, but he ignored them. Hot, sickly-sweet breath fanned along my bare neck, tickling my ears and fanning toward my nostrils. "Didn't anybody ever warn you not to let a Sidhe get hold of you twice, little girl? You're mine, now."

And I was. Horror flooded through my brain when I tried to push away from him—and couldn't. Nemesis and Nike reached my arms and spat venom in the one and only warning shot he was going to get. But he didn't need the warning. They did.

His tongue flicked against my ear, raising competing shivers of pleasure and revulsion. "Banish the Amphis-baena." I shuddered, but did as he asked, returning Nem-esis and Nike to tat form. His words had become music to my ears. I wanted only to please him.

And yet, that seemed somehow wrong. The sounds of feet slapping the ground, flesh hitting flesh, and cries of pain coming from the crossroads drew my gaze. I wanted to give a cry of my own, wanted to warn them I was in trouble, but couldn't.

He turned me to face him, and this time I did whimper. He dropped the veil of mortality, flashing a smile filled with razor-sharp teeth that glinted in the harsh fluorescent glare. Silvery-white skin, glittering copper eyes, and darker copper-colored hair that had never graced mortalkind paid proof to his Sidhe heritage, but his rows of sharklike teeth made me wonder exactly *what* creature Sidhe DNA had been blended with to create him. Then he snapped those teeth and I decided I did *not* want to know.

"I said I'd rip your throat out, Fury. And Sidhe always keep their promises."

Terror battled my sudden intense need to please him. He'd lessened the trance just enough to let me know what was coming. Bastard. Tears slipped down my cheeks as he lowered his head, a cruel smile playing about his lips. Funny, I'd never imagined it ending like this, and I'd been close to death a hundred times or more. I closed my eyes and prepared to die, waiting for those horrible teeth to close around my throat.

"And a Warhound always defends his mate."

My eyes snapped open just in time to see silver burst through the Sidhe's chest and slash downward. Blood spurted, coating my vest and pants thickly. The Sidhe gave a single, startled sound and then crumpled to the floor, revealing a very pissed-off Scott. He yanked a wicked-looking blade from the Sidhe's back. It sizzled, glowing with unnatural silver light, and the blood dissolved in an instant. One of the weps we'd picked up from Al.

He sheathed the blade and took two quick steps forward, jerking me into his arms and planting a bruising kiss on my lips. His hands moved to my cheeks, brushing my tears away with tenderness in direct opposition to the punishing kiss. Gentle and rough, darkness and light. No wonder I loved him so much.

A dozen things to say buzzed through my mind. "Did you mean it?" I blinked because that had been the last thing I'd expected to pass my lips.

He pushed me away slightly so he could see my face. "What?"

"When you called me your mate. Did you mean it?"

His eyes seared mine hotter than the Phoenix's flash and burn. "I'm a man of my word, baby. You know that."

My lips trembled and I was dangerously close to a crying jag. And the middle of the mess we were in was hardly the place for that. I broke away from him, struggling to get back into the ass-kicking frame of mind. Suddenly, the incongruity of what had just happened hit me. "Hey, how the hell did you get here from that direction? The Giants were supposed to tunnel in through the other corridor."

"They did. Once they broke through, I assumed doggie form and circled around to provide cover. Good thing I did, too."

This time, *I* jerked *him* close for one hard kiss.

Gunfire punctuated the sounds of fighting that were still going on behind us. We nodded at each other, turned, and ran straight into the fray, he with sword swinging and I with talons—and restored Amphisbaena—at hand. And damned if I didn't have the biggest, scariest grin on my face. As The Thing would have said, it was clobbering time.

CHAPTER TWENTY-TWO

MADNESS HAD BROKEN OUT IN THE CROSS-roads. A dozen more Sidheborn clones and mortals, along with some welcome reinforcements from our own group, had waded into the battle. Charlie towered in front of Trin, providing a bulletproof shelter from which she darted out to take well-aimed shots with the Sig. She was a damned good shot, too; miles better than I'd ever been. I was an up-close-and-personal kind of gal.

Which was my way of saying that, other than up close, my aim sucked.

My eyes ran over our allies, anxiously searching for the ones I loved most. Mac looked bruised but mostly intact, dividing his attention—and his wep—between a mortal guard on his left and a female Sidhe to his right. Elliana was in Hound form, darting in and out to take chunks of enemy flesh from legs that came too close to her canines.

Mom had taken a page from the Harpies' earlier tactic, leaping into the air, swooping down, and raking claws across any exposed backs she could reach.

Speaking of the Harpies, Calaeno was currently guarding Serise's back while she took off down the right-hand branch of the intersecting hallway. Serise's eyes flashed and her nostrils flared as she sniffed the air. That immediately caught my attention.

I turned to Scott. "I think she has Olivia's trail again."

He nodded. "Then you have to go."

My glance flew back to my friends and allies scattered about the left side branch. I bit my lip. Part of me wanted nothing more than to leap into the fight, rending and ripping those who dared raise hands and weapons against them. But the rest of me—the rest of me remembered the deathbed vow made to the dearest friend I'd ever had.

Scott smacked me on the ass. "Get while the getting's good, idiot! We'll give you as much time as we can."

I planted a kiss on his lips and ran after the Harpies. Calaeno gave me an approving nod as I jogged up. "Serise says the girl is very close."

"Good. The others are going to buy us enough time to track them down. But we have to hurry."

"Of course." We fell in step with Serise, eyes roaming the hall and the branching hallways we came across, seeking any signs of trouble that Serise, in full-on hunting mode, would miss. She led us in an unerring path down the corridor, straying from her arrow-straight path only once to lead us down a narrow, dimly lit hallway that raised the hairs along my neck and arms. Nemesis and Nike writhed along my arms, radiating unease. Something was definitely giving us all the heebie-jeebies. Even Calaeno the unflappable seemed to feel it. She stepped in front of Serise when the hall dead-ended at a reinforced steel door.

The other Harpy tilted her head as if listening to some

voice we couldn't hear. She raised her hand and pointed at the door. "There," she said in a singsong voice straight from one of those evil-children horror movies that scared the bejeebus out of me. "They're both in there."

A grim smile split my lips. "Excellent. We'll kill two birds with one stone. And however many assholes get in our way."

Calaeno spared a smile of her own. "I like your thinking, Fury. Now, let's go." She stepped forward, digging her talons into each side of the door. Sickly green light pulsed along her hands. A low humming sound throbbed rhythmically, setting my teeth on edge as it echoed through the air. It reached a fever pitch, and then her talons slid *inside* the door. Her back muscles strained as she bent slightly, grunted in effort, and ripped the door completely off its perfectly solid, made-from-steel hinges.

My eyes widened and I whispered, "Holy shit." I don't think I could have done what she did, not even souped up on super-good drugs and armed to the teeth with every ounce of magic I could muster. Calaeno gestured me forward. "Remind me to never piss you off," I murmured as I brushed past her.

The edge of her irises bled to red as she shot me a completely *un*reassuring smile. "I hope you never do."

I shivered, suddenly feeling completely outclassed in a way my very healthy ego usually prevented. Maybe her position as Queen of the Harpies set her apart in ways beyond merely seeming more sane than the rest of them.

The room beyond the door was set up like a schoolroom. Old-fashioned green chalkboards graced three of the walls, including both halves of the wall we entered from. Twenty or so wooden desks I was sure would crush beneath my weight were lined up in four neat rows of five apiece. A halfhearted attempt had been made to brighten the room with alphabet wallpaper and cheerful posters, but they couldn't disguise the utilitarian floor, ceiling, or light fixtures overhead.

Another heavy-duty door lay on the opposite side of the room. Calaeno looked ready to attack it the same as the first, but I laid a hand on her shoulder. "Let's see if it's locked first, okay?" She gave a grudging nod, and waited for me to ease the doorknob to the right. When it slid silently in response to my turn, she backed up a few steps, body assuming an aggressive stance. Serise followed suit. They waved me onward.

I shoved the door open and it smacked against the inner wall with a bang. Several men opened fire immediately, but I was already rolling along the floor. Calaeno and Serise leapt into the air, wings earsplittingly loud in the enclosed space, each landing on a gunman and setting to with vicious glee. I ended my roll by knocking a third man off his feet, then kicking the fourth in his knee from a crouch. When he screamed and dropped to the floor, my own knee twinged in sympathy, but I pretended the pain didn't exist. Kiara's magical cure was *not* losing its efficacy. It wasn't.

The man I'd sent sprawling lost his weapon in the fall but recovered quickly and jumped onto my back. He freaked out when Nemesis spat venom into one of his eyes. His piercing falsetto sounded distinctly girlish as he clawed at his eye, trying to dislodge the acidic liquid but only digging it in even further. Idiot.

I took the time to knock out both One-Eye and One-Knee, surprised when I glanced over and saw that the Harpies had incapacitated their two victims rather than killing them outright. *Aw, maybe I'm rubbing off on them.*

But then I heard the wailing cries coming from behind yet another door, and I realized that wasn't it at all. Their maternal instincts had just kicked in.

And who ever woulda thunk Harpies *could get the warm fuzzies?*

They were already through the door before I gained my feet. I rushed after them and stopped just over the threshold, finding myself inside a small but cozy nursery. Several cribs lined the far wall, but all were empty. Two nurses in cartoon-covered scrubs—oh yeah, like this was just your friendly neighborhood daycare center—cowered between the cribs, each one's arms wrapped around a precious baby girl.

Psycho Bitch's namesake was easy to pick out, what with the spiky purple hair and yellow-green eyes. She babbled happily around the two fingers stuffed in her mouth, little nonsense syllables that brought an unconscious grin to my face. Jesus, I'd never in a million years expected a Harpy baby—even one only *half* Harpy—to look so damned cute and cuddly.

My gaze zeroed in on the other infant, one with tufts of reddish-brown hair and big hazel eyes that stared directly into mine. As if she recognized me. My heartbeat picked up speed. Damn, she looked like a miniature copy of her mother, down to the little dimple in her chin.

She is *a copy of her mother.*

The Sidhe and Hound DNA lurked beneath the surface rather than shouting themselves to the world in physical characteristics. I wasn't sure if that made it better, or worse.

Serise crossed the room in ground-eating strides, eyes edged in red and hands stretched out. She didn't need to speak. Nurse Number One practically *threw* Rinda into her mother's arms, then rolled under the nearest crib and started crying.

Calaeno watched her sister with wide, happy eyes, but held back, allowing Serise to revel in the reunion with her daughter. And suddenly I couldn't hold myself back. I ran toward Nurse Number Two.

She had more backbone than the first woman, meeting

my gaze with narrowed eyes and tightening her arms around the delicate, swaddled bundle of joy. I hardened my expression. Fear shadowed her face, and her hands trembled when she offered me Olivia.

"Wise choice," I said sweetly, claiming the baby with no trace of the nervousness sweeping across my body. Hell, I hadn't held a baby since Cori had been itty-bitty, and *that* had been more years ago than I cared to think about. But Olivia cooed and gurgled, eyeing me with such a trusting expression that my heart melted immediately. Oh sweet gods, I held a little miracle in my hands.

Death blew into the room. The air thickened, feeling like mud as I turned in impossibly slow motion. Serise still cuddled Rinda close, both looking like they'd won the lottery and completely safe, so I kept spinning. And then I saw the one thing the three of us should have kept foremost in mind. Traitors walked among us.

Blood exploded from Calaeno's abdomen as magic-wrought steel punched through her body and then ripped toward her heart. She let out a soft sigh as she slid to the ground in a neat, crimson-splattered puddle. Death claimed her in an instant.

Penelope jerked the long, jagged dagger from her Queen's back with much the same force and expression Scott had used earlier. The obvious hatred mixed with self-satisfied smugness had Rage flaring in an instant. This bitch was *so* going down.

"Serise!" I barked. As if we'd rehearsed it, she shifted Rinda to one arm and held out the other. Having witnessed the quicksilver reflexes of Harpykind firsthand, I tossed my precious bundle toward her without qualm.

I pounced before Serise caught Olivia, channeling red-hot Rage and clearing half the distance to Penelope in milliseconds. Her eyes locked on mine and she smiled. The irises were edged in red, but strangely, returned to typical yellow-green when they settled on me. I growled. She might not be feeling bloodlust right at the moment, but I was.

She danced back a few steps, passing through the doorway and into the schoolroom. That suited me just fine. Calaeno had sworn a blood-oath to me, witnessed by Serise, who was now bound to keep the same vow: to protect Olivia with her life. I kicked the door closed behind me, and the lock slid home seconds later. I spared a brief moment to pray that Penelope did not have the same strength as her Queen, or Serise and the babies were in big-time trouble if I failed.

Easy solution, Riss. Just don't fail.

Eerie calmness settled over me, particularly strange because Rage still coursed through my veins. But for the first time ever, it wasn't like channeling a hurricane. More like steering a stubborn mule somewhere it didn't want to go.

"What, Fury, so eager to join Calaeno?" Penelope's smile struck a chord inside, seeming so damned familiar I paused to stare. She found my hesitation funny, throwing back her head in a full-throated laugh.

Her laughter choked off when I funneled magic and moved with the same superspeed I'd siphoned into Cori what seemed like eons ago. My fist rammed into her cheek with a crunching sound. She hissed and fell back, hand touching her face with obvious shock. A smile curved my lips. Nice to know she wasn't the only one with tricks up her sleeve.

"Come on, Traitor Girl. What, not as easy a kill as you thought? Funny how that works when you don't stab someone in the fucking back."

Rage swept over her features and she closed in, fists raining super-fast blows from every direction. It took every ounce of my skill and speed just to defend myself. For several moments we sparred in ceaseless motion, she pressing the attack while I did all I could just to avoid her punches and kicks. Had even one of them landed, I would have been in a world of pain.

It took another minute or two for me to figure out the truth. She was toying with me, holding herself back and letting me tire myself out. Something about the way she darted here and there, something about her entire tactic, screamed familiarity to me. But damned if I could figure out why.

I disengaged, skittering backward and putting an entire row of desks between us. She let me go, red-edged irises calming to yellow-green once more. At least she seemed as tired as me. Her sides heaved with the effort to draw in enough breath for oxygen-deprived lungs. And again it seemed I should know her.

Get her talking until you figure it out. "So, why'd you do it? Couldn't take the fact that Calaeno was ten times the Harpy you'll ever be? And where's Ekaterina?"

Her laughter bubbled up again, this time seeming halfway sane. That bugged the shit out of me. "Oh, Marissa, if only you knew the truth."

The tone of her voice and the way she said my full name stopped me cold. *No, it can't be . . .* Her left arm started to caress her right, then stopped as if something were missing, but her right fingers continued drumming against her thigh. It was a habit I was only too familiar with, since I'd seen it hundreds if not thousands of times.

Shock cut through my body so strongly it felt like a physical blow, and I voiced the impossible truth out loud. "Stacia."

The Harpy gave a half bow before drawling, "The one and only." And then she shifted.

BONE-WHITE HAIR FADED TO SHIMMERY BLACK; yellow-green eyes deepened to faceted emerald; whipcord thinness filled out to lush curves; harsh, barely familiar features became the pretty, youthful face I had spent years trying to emulate. A sickly green glow morphed into the electric-blue flare of Fury magic, killing the sudden wild hope that a Sidheborn clone was trying to pull one last sick trick on me. Nobody could emulate the magical signature of a Fury. Nobody.

Which meant the impossible had happened. A Fury of the Sisterhood had somehow gained the ability to shift to Harpy—without killing her Amphisbaena—and shift right back to Fury form. My mind didn't even know where to begin processing that impossible—should have been impossible—fact.

Stacia brushed at her red leather pants before crossing silver-tattooed arms over chest and smiling. "Sorry I'm late, Marissa. You would *not* imagine how hard it is to put down mortal uprisings. Those little worms were harder to kill than I expected. Guess they learned something from all our years of working together, after all."

"You bitch," I spat as Rage tried to gain a chokehold over me. "You hell-spawned bitch." This entire time she had been feeding my suspicion that Ekaterina was the Sisterhood's traitor, when all along *she'd* been pulling my strings like a puppet. She'd kidnapped my mother and essentially killed my best friend.

"Tut, tut, Marissa. Such language, to both an Elder and your mentor. I'm appalled."

"You're going to be *dead* in a minute." I circled the nearest desk and started walking up the aisle in single-minded determination.

Rather than closing in with me, she backed up at the exact same speed, turning the opposite way I did, always careful to keep a dozen paces between us. I snarled in frustration.

"Marissa, love, neither of us is going to die. That would

upset plans I made a very long time ago, plans that are finally coming to fruition."

I continued circling but didn't increase my pace. My eyes narrowed and my fists clenched. Nemesis and Nike radiated impatience. They wanted to strike our enemy *now*. But I couldn't help myself, I had to hear what reasons she thought were good enough to betray not just one people, but two. And how the hell she could walk among them both to begin with. Though that explained where she'd been disappearing to often enough lately that rumors of her retirement had started circulating.

I swallowed down Rage enough to snarl, "What plans?"

She plastered a megawatt smile on her face, one that almost always charmed the socks off anyone she turned it on. Now it just made me want to spit. "Why, the plans for you and me, of course, darling girl. You didn't think it coincidence that I took you under my wing just after your mother disappeared, did you? No, I had my eyes on you for quite some time. You had your mother's heart and spirit, and the double strength of bearing Fury blood on the paternal line as well as the maternal. I knew you were mine from the moment of your birth, notwithstanding which Fury actually gave you life."

Sweet gods. She sounded even crazier than I'd expected. Crazier than the craziest Harpy who'd ever tried to kill me, and that was pretty damned crazy. "What do you mean, I was yours?"

"Why, the one destined to be my heir, to rule beside me."

My brow arched. "Rule over what? Hello. The Sisterhood's a democracy."

A very large smile tugged her lips upward. "Not for long. Once I've solidified my position as Harpy Queen, once I've claimed control over all *my* lovely Sidheborn clones I've bankrolled from the moronic mortals who thought *they* were in charge all along, it will be time to claim my rightful place over the Sisterhood. As its Queen."

I couldn't hold back a bark of laughter, which caused the very faint lines around her eyes to tighten. "Not in a hundred years. Not in a *thousand* years will anyone convince the Conclave that it should cede its authority to a single sister."

"They will once war breaks out, you silly little girl, and they discover that the only way to survive is by joining forces with our once-fiercest enemies, the Harpies. And once they realize the only way to that alliance is through me."

The woman had gone way past the point of madness, bypassed the land of loons, and zoomed straight on to stark, raving, batshit crazy.

"Just how do you plan on keeping control over both groups at once? They'll turn on you in an instant."

"Now that, Marissa, is where you come in."

"No way will I ever help you. Besides, since you murdered Calaeno, that puts Serise in direct line for the throne."

"Not once I kill her and claim her child for my own. Without her to bear witness against me, it will seem they both gave their lives to save the babe. And *I* am Calaeno's chosen second. *I* will rule in her stead."

"Even if you manage to steal the Harpy throne, I will *not* help you rule over the Furies."

"Oh, darling, I don't intend you to help me rule over the Furies." She finally stopped backing away, closing the distance between us before I could do much more than blink. "You're going to become *Penelope's* second, and hold down the fort over the Harpies while I claim my rightful place as Queen of the Furies."

My mouth worked soundlessly until I managed to find my voice. "They'll never take orders from me, no matter how much Calaeno cooperated with me. No matter what boon she promised. I'm a Fury."

Again she purred in that very scary tone. "Not for long."

Well, hell. The proverbial lightbulb flashed on inside my head. She hadn't allowed the mortals to try to kill me or hire the Harpies because she'd wanted me dead. No, worse, much worse—she'd wanted them to drive me into Turning Harpy.

She fell on me with such speed and intensity that it confirmed my earlier sense that she had been holding back. She flickered from Fury to Harpy to Fury, kicking my ass up and down the room with frightening ease. Her fists and booted feet landed against my flesh and bone in near-debilitating force. I managed to block maybe half her blows. Blows that *hurt*. Her fighting style changed with every shift, each slightly familiar at its core, but different enough that I had trouble switching up my strategy for defense. Blood flowed from a dozen cuts, filled my tongue with its bitter taste, blocked my vision when it ran into my eyes. Rage stirred, growing exponentially with every painful strike. I struggled but finally managed to call on the earlier center of calm that had allowed me to claim control over the dark edge of inhuman anger. Which was when she started cutting me verbally.

"Haven't you realized the truth yet, little girl?"

She backed off slightly, so I took advantage of the chance to catch my breath. Sweat and blood ran down my face. I flicked them both away, eyes focused on her. "What truth? That you're my new choice for Psycho Bitch of the Year? No, make that Century."

Derision lit her eyes, currently yellow-green. Harpy eyes, when they had no right to that color. "Didn't your mother ever tell you I petitioned the Conclave to let me train you rather than her?"

My breath sucked out. "You what?"

"Petitioned for the right to train you instead of her. It was my right, as sole survivor of the wing of Furies I led in the War. I should have had first claim on any apprentice I wanted after what I suffered at the hands of those hell-spawned mortals."

Suddenly everything seemed just a tiny bit clearer. "So you're willing to sacrifice as many lives as it takes for nothing more than revenge?"

Her eyes shaded to bloodred on the edge. "This isn't about revenge, girl, it's about *justice*. Justice for centuries of their kind discriminating against ours. Justice for the War they brought about. Justice for the discrimination that even *still* runs rampant in the system they forced us to become complicit co-conspirators in. Do you know how many arcane judges there are in mortal courts? Four, maybe five? And how large a percentage of the population do we make up? Ten percent? Well over fifteen if you add in the half-breeds. Racial discrimination may have been outlawed decades ago, but interspecies discrimination is still alive and well, and it will continue on its same bloody course unless someone does something about it."

I pitched my tone to its most sarcastic. "And that someone would be *you*?"

"Who better? You know how I survived that ambush that took out my whole wing, Marissa? I didn't just fall over the edge of Rage, I fucking well owned it, jumped over it full barrels blazing, claimed the Rage for my own and made it do *my* bidding. Went Harpy and killed every last one of those mortal bastards before they even knew what hit them. And changed right back to Fury again. That takes a strength of self and force of will most people only dream of having. The exact strength of self and force of will you have, that I honed to the same point of perfection as my own."

"No!" This time my voice edged on hysteria. "I'm nothing like you!"

"Think not, little girl? I made you, took the child Allegra left and made you into the always-certain-she's-right woman you are today. But that iron-hard purpose deep inside you is all yours. You can't tell me you've never felt the Calm, Marissa."

My heartbeat became erratic and I couldn't do anything but stare at her, mouth wide open. The Calm. That sounded way too similar to the eerie calmness that had come over me just after Penelope—Stacia—slaughtered Calaeno. Something I had felt a handful of times over the past several years, now that I thought about it. But that couldn't . . . I wouldn't allow it to mean . . .

"You have it in you to become *exactly* like me, Marissa." Her voice become smooth, cajoling. "An incredibly special, amazingly powerful being. Someone who can shift from Fury to Harpy at will, and then back again. Someone who can command both types of magic; someone who can not only channel the Rage, but claim it as her very own. No longer will it rule over you—instead, *you* will rule over it."

A hundred emotions flooded through my heart, each warring the last for supremacy. Fear, denial, anger, hope, determination, frustration, terror, doubt, and, most of all, Rage. I fought that Rage down with every fiber of my being, refusing to let this bitch push me into the very monster she wanted to create.

"Never!" I screamed the words, pouring every one of those emotions into it. "I will *never* become what you want me to be!"

Regret seemed to flick across her face, but then she played her trump card, one I never saw coming, even though I should have. "Who do you think arranged for the idiot mortals to kidnap your mother? Arranged for her repeated rapes and forced impregnation? Arranged the same fate for Vanessa when you started distancing yourself from me? Who do you think arranged her *death*? I did."

The red-hot fury that overtook my body in that single instant of clarity nearly knocked me to my knees. I shuddered with its force, staggering back several steps and fighting to hold it in. Satisfaction rushed over Penelope's—Stacia's—face, and she focused all her attention on me. Which meant she missed the figure hurtling toward her until it was too late.

Mom wielded a hefty bar of metal like a baseball bat, winding it up and smashing it against Stacia's back hard enough that her body flew over an entire row of desks and crashed against one of the chalkboards before tumbling to the floor. Damn. Easy to see where Cori got her softball skills.

Mom looked like my very own avenging angel as she shook her makeshift bat at the unconscious Harpy/Fury. "I always knew you were an egocentric bitch, Stacia. Had no idea you were a psychotic traitor, too." She dropped her makeshift bat and turned to me.

Rage washed over me with more force than a hurricane, sweeping me up in a blinding vortex of anger I could no longer deny. "Oh, Mom," I sighed. "You're too late." I briefly considered seeking out the Calm Stacia had put name to, then forced that temptation down. No *way* was I giving in to her. I would rather die, would rather turn pure Harpy than fall in with her psycho plans.

A peaceful smile slowly spread across my face. I knew what to do.

Mom leapt, hands grabbing me and shaking. "Fight it, Riss, do you hear me, sweetheart? Fight it back! Don't let her win!"

Chaos broke out in the hallway just behind her, drawing ever nearer. From the sounds of it, the good guys weren't doing too well. We had never really stood a chance. Stacia had played us from the beginning, drawing us where she wanted so she could take out Calaeno and try to recruit me in the same fell swoop. Well, she'd half-succeeded. My gaze flew across the room at a sudden flash of motion. She might have gone down, but not for the count. Even now she was stumbling to her feet. Any moment she would regain control of her senses and launch herself at me—and the woman who stood between us as she always had. My mother.

Oh hell no. You're not killing her, and no more of my friends will die under your fucked-up little delusions of grandeur. This ends, here and now.

A voice shouted my name from the doorway, and I couldn't help looking over. Scott, battered and bloody but alive. And he was damned well going to *stay* that way.

Mom's eyes met mine, and hope flared. "Riss?"

"I'm sorry, Mom. There's only one way this can end well for us. For all of you."

In that instant she knew what I intended, and knew just as surely it would kill me. No Fury could do what I was about to do twice in so short a time. Not if she planned to survive. Good thing I had no such plans.

She would have taken my place if I let her. The look in her eyes told me that. But it was a risk I wasn't willing to take for two reasons. One, the Rage ripping through me was so freaking strong I didn't think I could keep from Turning Harpy anyway. And two, Mom had been out of active duty for so long, she might as well be retired. There were no guarantees she could cast the spell and survive any better than I could—especially considering the massive earth spell she had cast hours earlier to protect Vanessa's body from predators. David and Cori had gotten her back too recently to lose her again. No sense in them losing both of us.

I paused just long enough to say good-bye. "I love you, Mom."

Stacia rushed into the edge of my field of vision, taking my focus from Mom. I reached for the magical reservoirs of energy just beneath my feet but found that they had been blocked. Rage welled to towering heights I'd never before felt, and all that skittering emotion had to have *somewhere* to go. But without more energy, a whole hell of a lot more energy, I would never be able to safely funnel it away.

"Sweetheart, *I* love *you*, and hope you forgive me someday."

I blinked vacantly. "Forgive you for what?"

"For this." She kissed my forehead gently, leaned down, slashed her talons twice, and ripped Kiara's bandage away from my knee. Rage immediately faded, subsumed by the inferno of agony that tore through every inch of my body. Nemesis and Nike hissed as intensely as I screamed. We dropped to the ground in a pile of writhing bodies and limbs, watching helplessly as Mom turned and ran toward Stacia. Sapphire energy gushed from the floor and into her body, whipping her hair in a sudden magical frenzy. Stacia backed away, horror filling her eyes as she recognized the shape my mother twisted that torrent into. The very one I'd been planning to cast, the very one that might do to Mom what I'd been willing to let it do to me. Kill her.

Raging Justice.

Rage and pain drowned me in a sea of torment, both warring for supremacy, both burning uselessly against the other. I realized then that my mother had saved my life by causing me excruciating pain. Rage would cancel agony out long enough for the first to die down to bearable levels, and take just enough pain away for me to survive until someone could block it away again. She had saved my life, likely at the cost of her own.

"Oh, Mom, no." Tears blurred my vision more surely than pain. "I just got you back."

A hammer forged of crackling blue power smashed down from my mother's raised hands to the floor in front of her, sending out a maelstrom of black energy that sizzled outward and did to everyone what they had been planning to do to her. For those who meant her no harm, no harm was done. But for those who intended to kill her, it served as judge, jury—and executioner.

One horrifying memory speared through me as my mother made that ultimate sacrifice: the scene at the first honky-tonk when I had cast Raging Justice—and it failed to kill the suicidal Phoenix because she had not planned to kill me directly. She'd no doubt risen from the ashes of her own funeral pyre—I'd been too fucked up to go after her—which was one thing we didn't have to worry about Stacia doing. But my former mentor was smart, and far more devious than any of us had ever realized. She was plenty smart enough to *not* have death on her mind for the only two people around who could call down that age-old deathtrap spell.

That possibility gave me the strength needed to cling to consciousness. Dizziness had my vision blacking out momentarily, but when it returned I saw Stacia, now in Fury form, drop to the ground, soon followed by every other guard and Sidheborn clone with violence on their mind; saw my mother cry out and fall as well, wanted to help her, to make sure death wouldn't claim her as one of its own, but I couldn't. Someone had to focus on the double traitor in our midst.

My sense of hearing seemed to follow vision in going on the fritz. Scott's mouth screamed my name as he rushed toward me, but I couldn't hear his voice. He threw himself down next to me, and his gleaming, wicked sharp blade clattered to the ground as well, only I couldn't hear that either. Chaos ensued as all the clueless among us tried to figure out what the hell had taken out three-fourths of our enemies, and it became all too obvious nobody was paying attention to the biggest threat of all. Stacia.

I ignored Scott's attempts to get me to respond. His body partially blocked mine from her view, and that worked just fine for me. My hand reached out with one last spurt of energy. He had eyes only for me, so he missed what I saw all too clearly: Stacia struggling back to consciousness, proving that she'd only planned to knock Mom out to get to me. Her form flicked from Fury to Harpy and back again so quickly it made my already fuzzy head spin. She called up a surge of her own strength, leaping to her feet and hurtling toward Scott. I didn't know whether she planned to kill him or knock him out of the way in order to get to me—and I just plain ol' didn't care.

Nemesis and Nike responded to my request for just one tiny burst of magical energy, and it was me who shoved Scott halfway across the room. Stacia's rush of speed got her where she wanted to go faster than I could ever have moved—and it impaled her on the silver length of Scott's hybrid wep so forcefully that I only had to stand there. Sound broke through my daze at last. The blade sizzled as it greedily devoured the arcane blood now washing over it. Stacia's breath rushed out in a soft cry of surprised pain, and then the life went out of her eyes as she fell in a crumpled ball at my feet, this time locked in the shape that suited her insanity best—that of the Harpy traitor, Penelope.

The moment the last breath passed her lips, the sharp magical zing that heralded the fulfillment of a Mandate pulsed along my skin. And only then did I realize that the divine assignment I'd been handed had been for so much more than merely ferreting out the truth behind Vanessa's disappearance. The gods had chosen as their tool for divine retribution the Fury who had once been the traitor's apprentice. Poetic justice indeed.

My eyes fell on my mother's completely motionless body, and the overwhelming sense of purpose that had filled me evaporated. Rage faded, too, with pain roaring in to take its place, chasing me into the unwelcome but blissful realm of unconsciousness.

CHAPTER TWENTY-THREE

I CLAWED MY WAY OUT OF THE DARKNESS, gasping and shaking as the memory of unbearable pain chased me toward the light. My hands flew to my injured knee and felt comforting cotton tied tightly around my leg. A slight echo of pain still nagged, but *this* I could handle.

"Careful, baby." Scott's warm hands settled on my shoulder. I glanced over at him, my brain feverishly trying to make sense of what was going on. Things had seemed hopeless just moments before. I'd been on the point of sacrificing myself to save the others when . . . my mother had taken my place.

"Oh gods, Mom!"

His grip tightened and he nudged my head in the opposite direction. Mac and Ellie knelt alongside my mother's still body, both trying to rouse her to consciousness. Her

Amphisbaena seemed sluggish, but at least they moved. Which meant—

"She's still alive!" The Fates had decided to toss me another bone.

Scott relaxed his hold. "Yes, she's still alive. And now that you're back with us we'll get you both to the Oracle."

He made good his word, supporting me with the help of Trinity while Charlie swept my mother up with gentle hands as if she weighed nothing. Mac and Ellie stayed to convince Serise the coast was clear.

Walking back through the compound's echoing hallways was unpleasant indeed. Both friends and foes littered the floor, most covered with gruesome, fatal wounds, although here and there pitiful moans indicated the presence of survivors. I averted my gaze, knowing I was no help to anyone in my current state. Besides, several of our arcanes scurried through the corridors, helping ally and enemy alike. Considering that Mom had taken out the vast majority of the surviving guards when she worked her mojo, there weren't too many of the latter to deal with.

The next thing I knew we were stepping off the elevator into the cool evening air. Dre's semi sat only a dozen feet away from the front entrance.

Gianna appeared at the rear of the truck, her hands covered in blood and a harried expression on her face. She sized up Mom and me in a moment and chivied Charlie inside the infirmary. Scott and Trinity assisted me up the ramp. One of her apprentices bustled over and I spent the next few minutes being lectured on the fact that I had crippled myself for life, blah, blah, blah.

Once assured I was fine—as fine as possible, considering the circumstances—Scott and Trinity excused themselves to oversee the chaos sweeping through the compound. The Oracle scurried over when the first of the captive Sidhe

were brought in. I reached a hand out to stop her. She arched
a brow imperiously.

My throat was dry as I nodded toward the cot where
she'd laid my mother. "The other Fury?" I licked my lips.
"She's my mother."

Her expression softened minutely. "She is dehydrated
and disoriented, and her inner reserves are drained. But
she's going to be fine."

I let out the breath I'd been holding. "Th-thank you."

She nodded, glared at my bandage-wrapped knee as if
it offended her (which it probably did), and continued on
toward the new arrivals. The sudden bounce to her step
let me know she found the Sidhe much more interesting
patients. Then again, how could Furies stack up to a species that had been extinct for the past fifty years?

"Aunt Riss!"

At first I thought I was hallucinating, that I'd called up
Cori's voice from my mind. But seconds later her solid body
slammed into mine. I winced as my knee buckled slightly,
but I ignored the pain and hugged her close, eyes drinking in the sight of her father and mother over her shoulder.
Kiara stood a step behind them, cradling her right arm in
the crook of her left.

I met David's shell-shocked eyes and frowned. "What
happened? You guys are supposed to be in Boston."

Jessica clutched David's arm, shivering from what
looked more like fear than discomfort. "I—we—I don't
know."

David shook his head as if to clear it, then said slowly,
"Neither do I."

Cori hugged me harder. Her voice seemed much smaller
than usual when she spoke. "One minute we were on our
way to Boston, the next more of those Sidhe were shoving
us out of the car just down the road."

Kiara broke in, amber eyes wide and horror-stricken. "Oh gods, they took Sean. I don't remember *how* the hell we got from there to . . . here. Wherever here is."

I kept my voice soft and soothing. "Outside the underground bunker where they took the captive arcanes, who we managed to free." Kiara's sides heaved and she seemed close to hysteria.

Cori, bless her heart, slipped her hand into Kiara's and said, "Don't worry, they said they'd let him go unharmed once he drove them where they needed to go."

I blinked, eyes zeroing in on Cori. Interesting, that she was the only one out of the four of them to have a halfway decent memory of their close encounter of the Sidhe kind. Wonder if that meant . . . Nah, time enough to worry about that later.

"I know this is hard, Kiara, but try not to worry about Sean. Scott and I can head out to search for him as soon as we get things settled here. If they said outright they would let him go unharmed, they will." The one and only good thing about Sidhe was they always kept their word.

Speak of the devil, and he shall appear. "Are we late for the family reunion?" Scott drawled, coming up alongside David and Jessica. Several others, including Trinity, Charlie, and Harper, trailed behind him. Charlie's incredible strength had been put to good use again; he supported most of the weight of a battered-looking woman. I couldn't help but smile when I recognized who it was. Amaya. And, this time, *not* Fake Amaya. Scott could barely keep his eyes off his sister and looked like he'd bite the hand of anyone who tried to take her out of his sight.

Cori chose that moment to push me toward Scott. I went willingly, especially when I saw the squirming bundle in his hands. "Olivia!"

He thrust her into my arms and I held her even more tightly than Cori, drinking in the smell of baby powder and savoring the feel of her silky-soft skin against my cheek. I could have stayed like that for hours.

Jessica sounded more hesitant than I'd ever heard her when she spoke. "Is that—can I—"

My eyes met hers and recognized the helpless wonder written across her face. Part of me deeply resented her butting in, especially since she'd spent so long focusing on her grief at Nessa's loss while completely denying my own. But when push came to shove, I couldn't do that, not to someone who I knew loved Vanessa as much as I did.

"Of course. She's your niece, after all." Olivia stared up at her aunt raptly when I passed her over, hazel eyes wide and solemn for such a young infant. David and Cori crowded in, the three of them cooing and fussing over the baby so much they seemed more like mother, father, and sisters than . . .

Heartache stirred as realization stabbed sharply. I'd been entertaining the idea of raising Olivia as my own. I was her aunt by marriage, her mother's best friend, and a Fury. Surely that made me the perfect choice. But reality reared its ugly head. I worked shitty hours, put my life in constant danger, and lived alone. Taking Olivia away from the family now surrounding her would be selfish in the extreme. But oh, how admitting that hurt.

"You can visit her whenever you want, you know." Scott nuzzled my ear, pitching his voice so only I could hear.

I closed my eyes briefly. "Yeah, I know."

"And you can take her as your apprentice when she's old enough."

My eyes flashed open and a grin spread across my lips. The mentor-apprentice relationship among Furies was sacred, almost as special as the bond between mother and daughter—one reason Stacia's betrayal had cut so deeply. And *when*, not *if*, Olivia became my apprentice, that was something nobody could ever take away.

"Of course. Can't trust the first Fury-Sidhe-Warhound hybrid to just *anyone*, you know."

Scott tipped my chin upward so he could look into my eyes. "So you're going to tell the Conclave about Olivia?"

"I have to. The truth needs to come out. Besides, what's to stop mortals from trying this again? And we don't know how many of their brainwashed zombies escaped. What better to fight them with than others of their kind?"

His head nodded slowly as he glanced back at Olivia. Tenderness touched his features, making them even more achingly gorgeous than usual. He looked so wistful.

I had to take a deep breath and screw up my courage before voicing my next thought aloud. "You want one of your own, don't you?"

He smiled, tenderness shifting to amusement. "One? Riss, I'm a Hound."

"Oh gods. You want a *litter*?" My voice squeaked out the last two syllables. Thinking about having one child of my own was bizarre enough. Trying to wrap my brain around the concept of a dozen mini Scotts running around my town house like they ran rampant over Hounds of Anubis . . . I shuddered.

He leaned down and brushed his lips over mine. "Stop freaking out, Riss. We can take things slow. I know how much you like it that way." His voice tickled my ears suggestively as he nuzzled his way along my neck.

And he was right. Taking things slow was a damned good idea. We may both have confessed that we had loved each other during our first go-round, but nothing said we'd reach that same level now. And he might have called me his mate—might even have actually meant it—but nothing was set in stone until we took formal vows of commitment to each other. Once we did that, there'd be no turning back.

For now, I could cuddle close and savor the sights

and sounds of my loved ones celebrating, secure in the knowledge we'd pulled off the rescue of the century and prevented certain war. I'd tracked down Vanessa like I'd sworn I would, and saved her daughter from a lifetime of brainwashed slavery. The man I loved had forgiven me for breaking his heart and was, at least for the moment, all mine. So Kiara's bandages weren't working quite as well on my knee, and Scott's brother might have become a psychotic stalker. I had enough strength of self and force of will to continue kicking ass in a big, bad way.

After all, I *was* one red-hot Fury.

ACKNOWLEDGMENTS

First and foremost, thank you to my amazing husband, Shawn, for always supporting my writing (not to mention handling most of the cooking, cleaning, and laundry). I know how extremely lucky I am to have such a considerate husband (thanks, Mom-in-Law!), and I love you more each day. Second, hugs and kisses to my beautiful baby boy, Zack. (I *still* can't believe how fast you're growing!) You inspire me to try harder and do better every day. Also, you make me grin every time you see Mommy's book cover and squeal, "Your book!" Thanks also go to my little sis, Kelsey, and bros, Chris and Dustin, my baby niece, Bella Mia, for being so darned sweet, Nana, Pappy, Stepdad Larry, Uncle Bobby, Aunt Pat, Mom- and Dad-in-Law Linda and Yvon, Sis-in-Law Christine (and Beaker!), and any family members I'm forgetting. I love you guys.

Mega thanks to my rock-star agent, Ginger Clark, who fell in love with *Red Hot Fury* as much as I did, and found the perfect editor who shared that love, Jessica Wade. You both are so patient with all my questions, and I'll definitely have to send you on another joint spa retreat soon. Thanks to everyone else at Ace who helped bring this book to print. You guys seriously rock. Copy editor Amy J. Schneider: You did a fabulous job, and thanks so much for the character sheet and timeline.

Cover artist Judy York: OMG, it's like you peeked into my brain and channeled that when designing the cover art. You truly brought Riss to butt-kicking, name-taking life. Thank you! Sales, marketing, and publicity gurus: Thank you, too!

Thanks to my best friend, Julie, for always being there when I need you. Thanks to my "adopted mom," Ginny, and my "adopted sis," Jennifer. You were both there in the early stages of me pursuing my dream—look, I made it come true! I'm sorry Bill isn't here to see it, but I know he's smiling down on us. Thanks to my friends at AT, especially Sandy F., Joy M., Susan H., Pamela S., Melissa S., Susan B., the Public Finance & Real Estate Department, and the HR ladies. There are MANY others I could list, but just know that I enjoyed my time at the firm and think about you all often. Also, kudos to the Saint Louis Bread Co. restaurants in South County, where most of *Red Hot Fury* was written, and in Arnold, where most of *Red Hot Fury* was revised. LOVE your food, friendly faces, and free Wi-Fi. Hi, Suzy and Cecilia!

I have to acknowledge the online writing community as a whole. I am proud to be part of such a warm, welcoming, and supportive group of people. Paying it forward has always been one of my favorite concepts, and you all do an absolutely fantastic job living by that motto. I have to especially thank Holly Lisle for creating the Forward Motion writing community, which is where I got a lot of helpful information when I first got serious about publishing. To the FM chat crew, especially Zette, Albatross, Glassquill, Suelder, Dogma, Brenria, Indirectly, Wen Spencer, Tamara Siler Jones, Val Griswold-Ford, Nyxix, Andi, June, Koneko, Mooseythehut, and anyone I haven't listed by name but has become a good chat friend—thank you! You help me feel connected with the writing world in a more immediate way than forums, Twitter, and Facebook can do.

To my writing buds: Jill Myles (can you believe we're both finally published?!?), Chris Marie Green, Jackie Kessler,

Michelle Rowen, Heather Brewer, Jeri Smith-Ready, Stacia Kane, Kari Stewart, Rinda Elliott (hope you don't mind I named a murderous Harpy after you!), Cindy Pon (bootay shake!), and anyone I am leaving out—thanks for helping me keep my sanity on this crazy ride. You all rock! To my agent-mate, Gretchen McNeil: You make life a HECK of a lot more fun, and I'm so glad we share our rock star. Which brings me to last but not least: Team Purgatory at the Absolute Write Water Cooler. You are one crazy, wild, hellaciously talented bunch of people, and I am SOOOO glad to be a part of the mayhem. PORK CHOP!

Okay, I lied. One more extremely important group of folks to thank: the readers, including booksellers and librarians. Without your love for books and support, *none* of this would be possible. Thank you!

The "addicting"* Sookie Stackhouse books
by #1 *New York Times* bestselling author

Charlaine Harris

DEAD UNTIL DARK

LIVING DEAD IN DALLAS

CLUB DEAD

DEAD TO THE WORLD

DEAD AS A DOORNAIL

DEFINITELY DEAD

ALL TOGETHER DEAD

FROM DEAD TO WORSE

DEAD AND GONE

DEAD IN THE FAMILY

Also available:

THE SOOKIE STACKHOUSE BOXED SET

A TOUCH OF DEAD:
SOOKIE STACKHOUSE, THE COMPLETE SHORT STORIES

"Great heroine and great
supernatural adventures."
—**Jayne Ann Krentz**

"[A] delightful southern vampire
detective series."
—*The Denver Post*

***The New York Times**

penguin.com

M128AS0110

THE ULTIMATE IN FANTASY!

From magical tales of distant worlds to stories of those with abilities beyond the ordinary, Ace and Roc have everything you need to stretch your imagination to its limits.

Marion Zimmer Bradley/Diana L. Paxson

Guy Gavriel Kay

Dennis L. McKiernan

Patricia A. McKillip

Robin McKinley

Sharon Shinn

Katherine Kurtz

Barb and J. C. Hendee

Elizabeth Bear

T. A. Barron

Brian Jacques

Robert Asprin

"I loved it. Kasey Mackenzie is a brilliant new talent, and *Red Hot Fury* is fun, inventive, and has an awesome heroine."
—Karen Chance, *New York Times* bestselling author of
Death's Mistress

"A fantastic, wild ride of a debut. I couldn't put it down!"
—Nalini Singh, *New York Times* bestselling author of
Bonds of Justice

"If you're ready for a unique spin on all things paranormal—and you're ready to stay up a little too late reading—grab *Red Hot Fury*. Kasey Mackenzie's first Shades of Fury novel sets a new standard for urban fantasy."
—Chloe Neill, author of *Twice Bitten*

SWEET SURRENDER

"Time to hunt," I whispered, then leapt into action.

Magic responded to my call in an instant. I gathered arcane energy and thrust it inside my body, grunting as threads of magic temporarily reknit the fabric of my being. Although I couldn't manage true invisibility, this particular spell allowed me to redirect my normal shape-shifting abilities into a hyped-up form of camouflage. I dashed along the nearest wall, blending in with the natural play of light and shadow. Adrenaline flashed through my body, and I allowed it to amplify, dancing along the edge of full-blown Rage. And then I surrendered, allowing my mortal psyche to be subsumed by Fury.